I, GRACE NOTE

I, GRACE NOTE
A Novel

♪♪♪

J. SCHWARTZMAN

Aventura Books
an imprint of
GREAT MARSH PRESS

PUBLISHED BY AVENTURA BOOKS
AN IMPRINT OF
GREAT MARSH PRESS

ISBN 1-928863-03-5

Library of Congress Catalogue Number 99-90863

Manufactured in the United States of America

Aventura Books / Great Marsh Press
PO Box 2144 Lenox Hill Station
New York, NY 10021

http://www.greatmarshpress.com/

The book is set in Adobe Apollo, a face designed by Adrian
Frutiger in 1961 for the Monotype Corporation. Designed
and typeset in the foothills of the Adirondacks by the folks
at *Syllables*.

Cover design by
CRESCENT HILL GRAPHICS
Brooklyn, New York

ACKNOWLEDGMENTS

Thank you to my friends for sharing the details of their professions: Ann Hampton Callaway, Matthew Greenberg, Richard Morgan, and Marc Dannenhirsh (who answered endless questions about bands, modes, and music). I am grateful to each of them.

Thanks also to Thomas Zweifel, for sharing my commitment to excellence; Pam Barnard, universal reader; Bill Weintraub, Jay Harris, Madeline, Florence, Joseph, and Beverly Schwartzman, Sam Pincus, Gene Winick, Jackie Jones, Curt Akin, and Peter Cooper.

I

THE FIRST ACT OF THE EVENING was already on. Beneath a single spotlight, the artist known as Sheldon Bagg caressed a toy stuffed monkey and wept. The otherwise silent loft was pierced by the sound of his gentle sniffling. It was all very sad, and if I hadn't been concerned about my own act which was on next, I might have lost myself in Sheldon's convincing display of regret.

I took my eyes away just long enough to check the program. "Swan Venom," it said in capital letters only slightly larger than the words "Trois Glaces avec Crème Chocolat." This was the order of events tonight, my band, then dessert. When I looked up again, Sheldon Bagg had been joined on stage by his partner in the performance art team of Bagg and Rhombus. Harvey Rhombus drifted to Sheldon's side where he began to tear the cotton stuffing out of the toy monkey, accompanied by electronic music that sounded like a duet between a sitar and a clothes dryer.

Sheldon began a mournful dance, and the stage turned into a chaotic jumble of black turtlenecks and pale performance artists under a rain of cotton stuffing. I didn't know what it all meant and it might take time, maybe years, to figure it out. Perhaps they were making a statement about primates, or maybe they were using stuffing as a metaphor. Whatever it was all about, I only hoped they cleaned up the stage when they were done since it's hard to play guitar with fluff jamming your effects pedals.

By the time their piece ended, the monkey was no more than a shell with pompoms and a hat, and small piles of cotton drifted across the stage. There was a moment of puzzled silence before the audience realized it was time to applaud. Ray, our guitarist, couldn't stand it any more.

"God damn it, why do those guys always have to rip things up? What's their problem?"

"I don't know. They're exploring shredding, I guess."

"Screw shredding, how can we play now? I'm going to have all those particles floating around my rack system. "

"They'll clean it up."

"Can we vacuum?"

"No time," I replied, as we inspected the platform just vacated by Bagg and Rhombus.

"I'm never going on after them again, Grace, ever. Do you hear me?"

"Fine. We'll talk about it later," I said, for the lights had just come up and the mood changed instantly from enigmatic truth-telling to frenzied band set-up. In fifteen minutes we were on.

A whirl of activity blew across the stage where only a few minutes earlier, nothing happened. Amps rolled out, microphones and cables appeared, and Ray and I pulled our guitars from the coat check where we had stashed them.

This was not the first time we had crossed paths with Bagg and Rhombus at downtown events. We've both achieved the same degree of nominal fame and are often invited to perform at the same low-level benefits and events. This time it was a fund-raiser for the Dance Theater of Bangor.

But you're probably wondering, as I did, why the Dance Theater of Bangor was holding a benefit in Manhattan. As Winston, its director, says, "Who the hell in Bangor is going to give money to a dance theater?"

I've known Winston since his early days as a young dancer in New York City. The Maine winters have made him bitter, especially since he learned most people would rather hunt than watch modern dance. Winston still retained enough contacts in New York to fill the room they had rented for the occasion, a handsome loft whose claim to fame was its fancy radiators.

It was a hot July night. The air conditioning barely cooled the roomful of black draped bodies and high ceilings of the Soho loft. The strain of carrying my equipment didn't help; my amplifier felt like it weighed a thousand pounds. Sweaty, my crepe miniskirt sticking to my legs, I was checking the PA system when my gaze wandered to a man standing by a large, open window.

He stood against the background of dark Manhattan buildings, a thread of light illuminating his silhouette. Unlike most of the tuxedoed men in the room, he wore a dark blue suit, no tie. He seemed detached from the uproar in the ballroom around him. I noticed he was watching me. Every few moments he looked down and wrote something in a small pad. I wondered if he was a reporter. He saw me looking and smiled.

"Hi," I mouthed, adjusting the microphone stand.

He could not hear me from where he stood, but he mouthed back the word, "Hi."

"Having fun?" I said. The sound man turned on the equipment just then and my words boomed across the ballroom. A few guests turned around and nodded. The man by the window laughed, then said yes with his eyes.

But there was no time for gazing. Swan Venom was on.

After a short introduction by Winston, we launched into a rocking set, one we designed especially for patrons of the arts, with plenty of upbeat tunes so people feel good about giving away money. We finished up with our post-metal, neo-flamenco version of Dance of the Infidels, including a stick-breaking solo by Steve, our drummer, while Winston stood on the side waving at us like a scarecrow in a Danskin. He wanted us off before the crowd got too excited to sit through his troupe, who were on during dessert.

It wasn't until we were finished playing that I had time to think about luxuries like handsome strangers and by then I had more pressing problems. We had to move our equipment to the side in order to make room for Winston's dancers. The crowd wanted dessert and they weren't going to get it until Winston performed. We hurried. Finally, the stage was ready and Winston's troupe commenced a performance of their lengthy signature piece, Homage to the Carlton Drawbridge.

I stood in the back of the room by the buffet, glad to be finished with our part in the evening. Maybe Ray was right, I thought, this was a lot of aggravation just for carfare and a meal. On the other hand, I enjoy benefits. They let us bring our music to a whole new crowd. They create good will for the band. And I like hearing fans tell me they heard us play at a life-affirming event, like a benefit for a puppet theater, instead of a half-filled bar somewhere in New Jersey.

The dancer's music, all chimes and synthesizers, drifted from the stage and looped infinitely forward, as did the dancers. Dreamily, I noticed two men standing nearby. Each man was quite attractive in his own distinct way. One had dark curls, a slender nose, and stubble; the other, sandy-colored hair and delicate lips. Looking again in the brighter light of the cheese table, I could see that the sandy-haired man was the same man I had noticed earlier in the evening by the window. He smiled at me. I smiled back and before you could say, "Give them a five album deal with an option to renew," he was by my side with his hands in his pockets.

"I really enjoyed your music," he said. He seemed shy. I looked into his eyes and said "Thanks." His friend remained a few steps away by the hors d'oeuvres. He asked if I ever listened to Jack Weed, or the band, Toast. I said, of course, can't you tell? We laughed.

"Are you a musician?" I asked.

"I work on Wall Street," he answered. He introduced himself and shook my hand. "Roger Woodryder," he said between waterfall sounds.

"Grace Note," I said.

"What?" he said.

"Grace Note, that's my name."

"Oh, I see, I'm sorry," he stammered. I could see he was nervous, and he hadn't even heard of me. I tried to make him feel at ease, but this was difficult since I know nothing about stocks, business, or money. I pick my checkbook designs annually, but other than that I have little experience in financial matters. It's a question of opportunity; being a musician, I rarely have the occasion to worry about sums that contain more than three figures, or five figures if you include cents.

"That's an unusual name. Is it your real name?" I decided to answer with candor. No, I told him, it was my married name. I was married to the saxophone player, Nick Note.

"I've heard of him," said Roger, and I thought I saw, for only a fraction of a second, a look of pain cross his face.

"We're divorced now," I added, feeling an unusual sympathy for this man. He must have felt something for me, too, because we talked for at least a half-hour. He told me that his friend's sister was in the dance company. He pointed her out—she was the dancer with long dark hair who played the cantilever. Roger asked if I would like to have a drink with him. I said yes, I'd love to.

Steve, our drummer, agreed to stay till the end of the performance and pack up our equipment. He didn't mind. He liked the dancing. I took my guitar and effects pedals and left with Roger.

ק ק ק

"Are you sure you're a financial analyst?"

"Absolutely," said Roger. "Why?"

"I don't think of financial analysts hanging around in places like this." After we left the benefit, Roger took me to a Russian bar on the Lower East Side—a real Russian bar, not the kind of esoteric theme restaurants they have in lower Manhattan, where patrons pretend they're in Provence, Barcelona or Odessa while they laugh at people at the Hard Rock Café. Roger knew where to find the real thing.

I would never have known the place existed. The entrance was just a doorway next to a lighting fixture store on a street full of lighting fixture stores. A Russian Johnny Cash stood in front, dressed in a black shirt, a black jacket, and a bandanna. He looked at Roger, then nodded us in.

On the other side of the nondescript doorway was the equivalent of an Atlantic City lounge with smoked mirrors, glass chandeliers, red roses, and black leather upholstery. Large groups of people sat at every table.

"How do you know about this place? This is definitely not Wall Street." Roger directed us to a dark corner where we pulled two barstools up to a black marble bar.

"We have a Russian guy in the office. He takes us here about once a month."

"You don't feel strange coming here?"

"No, why should, I?" he said, signaling the bartender.

"It feels like a private club." Over the sound of decades-old disco music I noticed no one was speaking English.

"Maybe. But no one cares if we're here." Roger ordered two straight vodkas from the stone-faced bartender. "I go where I want to, and if someone doesn't like it, they tell me." Roger smiled. Here was a man who didn't spend a lot of time worrying about where he did and didn't belong.

In the dim light of the bar, Roger's brown eyes and gold hair were smokier, darker. Roger wore glasses, narrow rectangles that had a distinctly 1960's feeling. His beard was starting to grow, and the coarseness of it contrasted with the fine line of his lips. His dark blue suit gave him a formal look at this late hour, like a man not yet off-duty—a detective or a body guard. In fact, everything was a touch more manacing in this place, including Roger. He had an aura of nervous energy about him, and I watched his hands, strong and covered with flaxen hair, as he played with a matchbook on the bar. Roger stared at me with as much interest as he had earlier. "Grace, you were great up there tonight," he said.

"Thanks. I'm glad you enjoyed it."

"I really did. I love your music, it's so original. What was that song? Clear it with Doreen?"

"Maxine. Clear It with Maxine. The song where people started dancing?"

"That's it. I loved that one. And I can't believe we're sitting here now."

"Why not?"

"An hour ago you were up there singing. I was a guy in the audience."

"And you didn't expect to be out with the entertainment."

"I guess that's right." He laughed nervously, then recovered his cool and looked at me. "It's exciting." I felt a warmth spreading through me, starting in my face and working its way down like a heat wave spilling through me. "Sorry, I didn't mean to embarrass you. So tell me, what's it like being in a band with you and three guys? Who's in charge?" Guys always want to know who's running the show. Before I could answer, Roger, who seemed slightly excited by the whole idea of one woman and three guys, continued, "The thing that really amazes me, is how you can get up there in front of all those people like that. How do you do it?"

"Are you kidding? That's the best part. We spend so much time rehearsing. Performing is the payoff. I like to play in front of people."

"You're not nervous?"

"Sometimes. It depends who's watching. I wasn't nervous tonight. No one important was watching."

"Thanks."

"If I'd known you were there..."

"Well, you looked like you were having a great time. I couldn't do it."

"I'll bet you could."

"No. I'm terribly shy," said Roger, leaning close to me and looking into my eyes. In spite of his self-proclaimed shyness, I believed he could do anything he wanted to. He had a kind of sexy self-confidence, the kind you see in certain men who know their whole professional life is a game. Yet in Roger's case it was not an aggressive confidence; he had a cheerful, natural authority. As if to prove my point, he reached out and casually touched my hair, the warmth of his fingers brushing across my forehead as he pushed back my hair. He narrowed his eyes as he looked at me. Then, just as casually, his hand went back to the bar.

"You're good in front of a crowd. I prefer making things happen behind-the-scenes," he said, ordering another round.

"Like what?" It was past midnight and the music in the bar had turned from disco to slow, overheated Italian ballads, adding a layer of warmth to our words.

"I like to paint," he said. I smiled. "Is that so unbelievable?"

"No, not at all. It's just that I saw you taking notes earlier. I thought you were a journalist. You were drawing."

"Yes. Something caught my eye."

"Can I see it?"

"No."

"Please?"

"Maybe later, Grace."

By two o' clock in the morning most of the tables were empty. The night coasted into the timeless hours when everything stands still and you feel as if you could go on forever. Roger wanted to keep going, to another bar or even his place. His hands encouraged me, his lips helped him make his case. I sat on the barstool while Roger stood in front of me, his arms circling me now. I leaned against him, feeling his body through his blue suit, inviting me to come closer. But after a hard show, and even harder vodka, my body told me to just go home and sleep. Roger whispered his urgings to stay; our compromise was dinner the next night.

It wasn't until the next afternoon that I found a piece of paper in the pocket of my leather jacket. I pulled it out and unfolded it, thinking it was someone's scribbled phone number. It was a little sketch of my band, on stage. We were minimal, a few strokes at a microphone, lively forms with instruments, yet I recognized each of us. Underneath the sketch it said "Grace, see you tonight—Roger."

ๅ ๅ ๅ

People who know us say Roger and I are an unusual combination—he's so cool and logical; I'm so creative. They don't realize even financial analysts have a creative side. For example, not many people know Roger loves to paint. He's turned the dining area of his co-op apartment into a studio. He paints eerie scenes of brightly lit windows glowing in dark, urban landscapes. His paintings are rich and layered, as if he's studied every brick and stone in the buildings he paints. They seem to glow with a light of their own.

Roger is artistic in other ways too. His closet alone is a masterpiece, full of ties that are works of art, shirts folded like origami, and suits in infinitely subtle shades of blue and gray. From his toaster to his telephone, everything Roger owns shows an appreciation for the art of daily life, not to mention the power of credit.

Roger is hopelessly fascinated by the fact that I'm trying to make it as a songwriter and musician. "I wish I had the courage to give up Wall Street and just be an artist," he must say at least once a week. I tell him it's no thrill singing your heart out for $40, then driving home from the Jersey shore or Delaware at four in the morning, but he won't listen. Roger won't forgive himself for not having pursued art more seriously. Knowing how hard it is for him, I encourage his painting. Thanks to my influence, Roger has been painting more dread-filled landscapes than ever. I cultivate the painter in him, and in exchange Roger has been teaching me the ABCs of finance. He says I need to know them if I want to get anywhere in the music business. Nothing he has taught me has done me any good, but the day will come when Swan Venom will be big and I'll put my new knowledge to use. Until then, economics is fascinating and I pursue it as a hobby, although I wouldn't tell anyone in the band.

Roger has made the subject exciting. Lying in bed and talking late at night, he's managed to make his definition of a profit and loss statement surprisingly stimulating. The sheets move over his strong legs as he sketches invisible columns in the air. Sometimes he gets so animated he walks around the room, often wearing nothing but a wristwatch. I could listen to him for hours.

Roger's job as a financial analyst is to keep his ear to the ground. Listen to hearsay and get the lowdown. He says the economy is the real news. "Read about business if you want to know what's going on in the world," he says, and I remind him that not everyone wants to know what's going on in the world and that's why we have cable television. When I say that, Roger just laughs and tells me about no-load mutual funds. Over candlelit dinners we discuss futures. Sometimes he tests me just to make sure everything has sunk in.

"Grace," he says, "tell me about options."

And I, who always thought an option was whether to use reverb or not, who thought the Big Board was a table, can now confidently define a put and a call, selling short and buying long. Now I watch the news and I know what the Wiltshire 5000 is. I can tell you which Friday of the month is known on Wall Street as the "witching hour." I feel more involved with the real world.

ʸ ʸ ʸ

Roger's financial tutoring had an effect on Swan Venom. I started to take a more commercial view of the band. I began to notice that while musically we had developed a lot of excellent material and a distinct sound, financially we were going nowhere. Thanks to Roger, I felt the tickle of an ambition that went beyond music. I started to look for our bottom line, and I realized we didn't have one. Like so many bands, we were stuck, hovering at a low level of the New York music scene, making no real money and getting no closer to a record deal.

Sure, we had our regular gigs; every other Sunday night at Fernando's 57, once a month at JoJo's, and a Saturday jazz brunch that helped pay for rehearsal studio time. Sometimes the promoter at Mantis Praying Mantis—a club on Tenth Avenue designed like the inside of a hive—calls us to open for a bigger band. The guys and I know we can't count on making a fortune in the music business. Still, it's hard to keep your enthusiasm up when you earn only tips playing for people who care more about what's in their omelet than they do about you. It wasn't enough anymore. I wanted better gigs. We needed to make a serious effort to get some record company attention. And before we could do that, we needed a new demo tape—one that really captured the Swan Venom experience.

I brought the matter up at rehearsal.

Three days a week, Ray, Geoffrey, Steve and I meet at Fat Boy Rehearsal Studio to practice and work on new material. After two and a half years, we've developed a certain routine. Ray and I work out arrangements, while Steve and Geoffrey bicker. Then we practice. We stop for coffee, and in the last hour we work on new material.

It was Wednesday afternoon. The guys were already in the rehearsal room when I arrived. Ray, our guitarist, was on his knees in the corner playing with his overdrive pedal when I walked in.

"Grace, did you get a chance to work on 'Walls of Forgiveness?'" he said as soon as he saw me.

"I came up with a few ideas for the chorus. The bridge needs work," I said, dropping my guitar.

"Let's hear what you got."

I write most of Swan Venom's material. Ray does the arrangements and deals with our tone. He and I are the brains behind Swan Venom. I'm ultimately in charge because I handle the band's business, make arrangements for gigs, and deal with the money. And I sing. Geoffrey plays bass, Steve plays drums, and that's the band, the four of us, with a keyboard player when we have the money for one.

"I want to talk about something before we play," I said.

"What's up?"

"Everyone should hear this."

Behind us Steve and Geoffrey were tuning up and arguing over who was dragging the rhythm down in "Soaked by Tomorrow." "Yo," said Ray loudly. They stopped talking.

"Guys, I want to talk about something. I've been thinking about where we should go with the band in the next few months."

"Can we get a gig on a cruise ship?" said Geoffrey. "I want to go somewhere warm."

"No, I don't mean it like that. I mean where we should go with the band, professionally. We're making almost no money. I've been thinking about trying to get us better gigs."

"Cool," said Steve.

"We sound good. We can do it. Also, I want to start shopping around a demo. Not the one we have. I want to do a new demo." I let this sink in. There was some nodding and quiet plucking.

Finally Steve spoke. "That's cool," he said, then he returned to tightening his tom-tom. Years of drumming have jarred Steve's brain, and I knew in five minutes that he wouldn't even remember this conversation.

Geoffrey, on the other hand, looked profoundly disturbed by what I had said. Geoffrey is always disturbed, so this didn't mean much either. He stared down at his hands, which rested on his bass.

I waited for Ray's opinion. "What's wrong with our last tape?" he said. "We made it only six months ago."

"It's not good enough."

"You don't like 'Soaked by Tomorrow?'"

"We have better stuff now. And I don't like the mix on it. We can put Soaked on this one, too, if you want, but I think we should include "Reverse Mr. Fortune" and "Clear It With Maxine."

"Digital?"

"Twenty-four track digital. Four songs," I continued, shifting on the amplifier where I sat.

"Who would produce it?"

"That's another thing. I want to have a really great producer this time." We had done the last demo ourselves with help from Steve's cousin, Tony, who wants to be in the music business. He's a cop and it caused problems when it turned out he was scheduled to testify in court on the same days we had booked studio time. This time I wanted a pro.

"I'm thinking of someone in particular."

"Who?" said Geoffrey.

"Jetty McPhereson."

"The guy who produces Tabular Zero?"

"That's him."

"Are you crazy?" Geoffrey cried hotly, his eyes wide, magnified by his glasses. "What makes you think he would be interested in us?"

Jetty McPhereson was the hottest producer in New York, responsible for a wave of hits. He had single-handedly created what was being called the "Delancy Street Sound," by converting a former delicatessen on the Lower East Side into a state-of-the-art, post-production facility. Having Jetty McPhereson produce your demo was like being given the key to the front door of every record company in New York.

"I know he's interested in us, because he told me."

"When has he even heard us?" said Steve.

"At Jojo's a few weeks ago. He came over to me between sets one night when we were playing. He said he liked our sound, and asked if we had ever worked with a producer."

"Why didn't you tell us, man?" Steve continued with exaggerated shock, his head dangling over his drum kit like a dog in the back of a car window.

"She did tell us. You just don't remember," said Ray.

"I ran into him again the last time we played and he gave me his card. He said we should get together. He's into new bands now," I said.

"Didn't he produce that Virtue album, *Feel This*?"

"That was him."

"Jetty McPhereson. Heavy," Geoffrey continued, bursting into a bass-line. Steve joined him, his curly hair flipping over his sticks. Steve and Geoffrey are opposites in many ways, but they have one thing in common; they both make more sense when they play than they do when they talk.

"Shut-up," shouted Ray. Steve and Geoffrey stopped in mid-groove. "Before you get too excited, let's talk about the price tag."

"Doesn't it depend?" I asked. "Maybe Jetty would do a spec deal or an independent production deal."

"Let's just say we at least pay for studio time," said Ray, calculating. "Four songs. Let's see." He sat still and closed his eyes. Ray is very handsome and when he concentrates—also when he does a wailing solo—the muscles on the side of his face stand out smooth and definite, like a marble sculpture.

"Maybe four thousand dollars," he said, "not including a fee for Jetty. He would probably want a royalty if we get a deal."

"No problem," I said. "We can get four thousand dollars." My role as leader of Swan Venom is to be positive in spite of reality.

"Four thousand is no problem?" said Steve. "You just said we have no money."

"Steve, man, I said I'll get the money."

"You're dreaming, Grace."

"You want to keep playing jazz brunches?"

"No, man, but four thousand dollars."

"So don't be a jerk. Have some confidence."

Insulted, Steve broke into an aggressive beat.

"Okay, Grace," Steve shouted over his drums. "And when you get the four thousand dollars, let's record the demo in a studio down in St. Croix or the Bahamas. Just us and Jetty, as long as we're dreaming. How about that?"

"At least it's warm there," Geoffrey added.

"Fine. Can we rehearse now?" I didn't mind Steve's bad attitude. I never take drummers seriously.

❧ ❧ ❧

A band is not a good place to be if you need money. Nobody starts a band so they can buy a house or a car. You do it because you love music. I did it because as a songwriter, I needed an outlet for my material. A band is fun. But a band is not a place to go for financing.

I realized this after I figured out that to earn the money for a top-quality demo, we would have to do 20 weddings, 50 bar gigs or 175 Saturday jazz brunches. I couldn't wait that long.

Our next option, after earning the four thousand dollars ourselves, was to go to relatives. It wouldn't be the first time we had done that. I had already gotten plenty of support from my two uncles, Maurice and George, in upstate New York. They play piano and accordion together at family gatherings. They're proud to have a professional in the family and are always giving me gift certificates to help me with what they call "the little extras." Gift certificates are good but I knew they couldn't afford more than they were already giving.

Steve's family was no help, even though they would put up as much money as we needed. They always wanted something for it. I think every relative he has wants to be in the music business. We could always go back to his cousin Tony, the cop, but that would be a last resort since he didn't actually like our music and kept telling us to add disco whistles.

Geoffrey's family couldn't help us, either. They had already lent him a lot of money to replace the bass he lost when he left it outside a hall in Massapequa. We were doing a wedding, and someone on the groom's side took it while Geoffrey was getting the car. And Ray's family lives out West somewhere and is not about to put money into anything taking place in New York.

The guys were right, four thousand dollars was a problem. Some good news came our way, however, when I called Jetty McPhereson; he said he would work with us in exchange for a royalty. But we would have to cover recording costs. It looked as if we were going to have to strike up some kind of relationship with a studio, maybe do a barter deal or record in the middle of the night for a reduced price. Either that or go back to Ray's eight track and record it at his place, which would make the quality I had hoped for impossible, especially if his five roommates were around.

It was around this time, over dinner one night, that Roger mentioned Punch and Torkney.

❧ ❧ ❧

A year ago, I would have thought Punch and Torkney was just another English pop duo. It's only since Roger has taken me under his financial wing that I know Punch and Torkney is an advertising agency—one of the biggest in the world.

He first mentioned Punch and Torkney over dinner at the Golden Pear.

That day, the band had been working on a melodic ballad which we were using to explore the possibilities of Brazilian percussion. I remember because I was carrying a calabash and the Maitre D' asked me to put it in the coat check.

I had come directly from the rehearsal studio to meet Roger. We met at the bar. Roger kissed me hello, then we settled in a warm corner of the Pear to chat about our day.

"I heard an interesting rumor today," Roger said, tucking his tie into his shirt.

"About who?" I replied.

"Not about who, about what. Someone is buying up shares of a company called Punch and Torkney. There's a lot of movement in the stock. This means a takeover might be in the works."

Roger explained this was surprising since P & T is one of the most established companies in advertising, and if it were indeed true that someone was trying to buy it, it would mean we were seeing a whole new kind of leveraged buy-out. Naturally, I didn't know what kind of buy-out we had been seeing till then, but to sum it up, there have been few successful takeovers of service companies like ad agencies.

"This would be the largest," said Roger.

"The largest what?" I said.

He explained again. The largest hostile takeover of a creative company. By dessert I understood exactly what he was saying and I felt something stir in me, a tiny thrilling flame. The very thought of the turmoil to come, of the uproar in the marketplace, of men in expensive suits running down corridors intrigued me.

"I've been watching this company for a long time. It's very undervalued. That makes it a perfect target." Roger said we had to be patient. It might be days before anything was announced. The buyers would be forced by law to disclose their intentions to the public when they acquired five per cent of the stock. Until then, we would simply have to wait. We ordered coffee.

The interest in the matter was not mine alone, in case you are wondering whether Grace Note, in a burst of short-lived enthusiasm, embraced the rumor like a supermarket tabloid. Hardly. Everyone wanted to know more.

In fact, in the next days both networks and cable stations invited Roger to appear on their business programs and discuss rumors about Punch and Torkney. Roger's specialty as an analyst is media and communications. He racked up four or five business shows in a few days. Sometimes I think Roger performs more than I do.

Sure enough, Roger's nose for a takeover is as good as my ear for music, and that's good. I can hear the root note in a chord the way other people hear car alarms. I guess Roger can do the same in his profession, because by the end of the week events with Punch and Torkney were unfolding just as he predicted. He brought me up to date when I came up to his office late Thursday afternoon.

I had gone up there to meet him for dinner. I enjoy visiting Roger in his office. Roger works on a high floor of a black granite building that overlooks New York harbor. You can see the tip of Manhattan from his window and if you stand against the glass and look down, you can see docks and piers curving around the end of the city, a tangle of yellow lines running between them.

I stood by the window and stared out over the water. The Hudson was silver in the November dusk. Roger sat at his desk behind me in a black leather chair, his back to the window. "Grace, take a look at this," he said, swiveling his chair to face me. He saw me looking out the window. "Gorgeous, isn't it?" he said, paying his respects to the view. He stared, then he stuck out his hand, which held a folded *Wall Street Journal.*

"Here, Grace. Read the highlighted part."

I took the newspaper, folded to show a single column of stock prices. A bright yellow line ran across an item near the bottom of the page.

"PTP," I read aloud. "What's that?"

"Punch and Torkney, PLC. The stock I've been telling you about. Look at the last column, under 'change in price.'"

"'Plus 7 points,'" I read.

"That's right," said Roger with satisfaction. "How's that for a jump?"

"I don't know, you tell me," I replied, sitting on the arm of his chair.

"Very nice. Especially since I just got a few investors into it." Roger leaned back in this chair and looked up at me, his lips curling into a grin. Behind him, the sky had turned to deep blue. It was almost dark in the room now. The only light came from a small bird-necked lamp on the corner of Roger's desk. In the dim light his eyes seemed brighter, shining like the plane lights that gleamed over the harbor. From above him, I could see the netting of Roger's pale eyelashes like a canopy over his eyes. His hair, straight and gold, fell over his eyes and I pushed it back.

"That's great news. It looks like you're on to something." I got up from the arm of his chair and walked along the edge of the room.

"I might be. It's still a little too soon to be sure." Roger swiveled his chair to follow me as I strolled. On one of the shelves was a photo of one of Roger's paintings, lights burning in the windows of a dark building.

I continued to stroll around the room until I arrived back at Roger's chair, where I stood between him and his desk. I put my hands on his shoulders. "You're so talented, Roger."

"Did you ever doubt me? Here, sit down," he said, and not waiting for an answer he lowered me onto his lap, facing him. "Do you know what this means?" he continued. He put his hands on my waist.

"What?"

"It means people are starting to buy in. If a takeover really happens, my clients are going to do very nicely."

"Really?" I shifted on his lap.

"Yeah," he said. "Move closer. It looks like Punch and Torkney will be in play any day now. And if that happens, when everyone else jumps in I'm getting my clients out. You know why?"

"No, why?" I whispered. I watched Roger's lips as he spoke. Pleasure moved through them as he recounted his news. Even though I could see he was excited, his voice remained low and steady. Suddenly Roger's lips felt like a magnet. I leaned forward and as I got closer, Roger's hands tightened over my waist.

"I'm getting my clients out, because in the market you should always get out when you're on top, Grace."

"Like right now? I'm on top."

"No. Stay right where you are," he whispered, leaning forward and kissing me with surprisingly romantic feeling for someone talking about a hostile takeover.

"Your job is so exciting, Roger."

"I know. I love my work," he said, kissing me again. I let my arms fold over his shoulder. His chair tipped back giving me a dizzying sense of imbalance. I held on to Roger, and he put his arms around me, pulling us closer.

ᚐ ᚐ ᚐ

The financial world exerted its stimulating pull on everyone. By our next dinner at the Golden Pear, even Monsieur Paul, the Maitre D' wanted to know more.

"Mr. Roger," he said, "I saw you on *Around Wall Street*. You were superb."

"Thank you, Paul," said Roger, pleased by the attention.

"I loved your remarks to that gentleman from *Barron's*; the stock is definitely undervalued. And you looked fabulous."

"I was trying a new tie. Did it pick up all right?"

"Terrific."

Everyone seemed pleased. With a flourish, Roger picked up his menu. He was feeling giddy from the rush of live television. He flipped open his menu grandly, giving me a handsome view of the way his wristwatch met his white cuffs. It was a surprisingly masculine sight, given that no hunting or gathering was involved in Roger's profession.

But soon it was back to business and Roger, who loved Wall Street gossip, filled me in on the day's events.

"Grace, it happened," said Roger, as soon as Monsieur Paul returned to his podium.

"What happened?"

"The group buying up shares of P & T has reported to the SEC. It looks like it's a takeover," he said with a taut smile. "Now the most interesting part of the P & T story is about to unfold." Roger looked at me intently with his brown business-school eyes.

"What could be more interesting than what happened so far?" I asked, thinking that business was only interesting when large sums changed hands.

"Let me ask you something, Grace. What is something that separates a great musician from a mediocre one?"

"Talent?"

"What else?"

"Feeling?"

"Something else."

"Experience?"

I think he was getting frustrated that his analogy wasn't catching on because he didn't bother to ask what else.

All he said was, "Character."

"Character? You mean like Vladimir Horowitz was a character?"

"No, I mean a musician plays with character, with a depth of style uniquely his or her own. And that's what makes things interesting in business, the characters of the players involved. So I'm trying to tell you that this Punch and Torkney takeover is interesting because of the players."

"Tell me more," I said, sensing that Roger would not drop the subject until he had told the whole story.

Roger stared into the distance as he solemnly considered the tale he was about to tell. I felt closer to Roger then, knowing he cared enough to let me in on things he wouldn't even mention on television.

"There are two Englishmen," Roger began with a whisper as if he were telling a campfire tale, "One is named Geoffrey Isaac Robbins and the other is Anthony Punch. Punch is a typical British aristocrat. He founded Punch and Torkney in 1925.

"Robbins is a middle-class nobody, the son of immigrants who rose through the business world to head a gigantic holding company. He owns everything from silver mines to newspapers. And he earned every penny himself. Robbins wants to own Punch and Torkney," Roger continued. "That's who's been buying up shares. He wants to add the world's most elite advertising agency to his holdings. You can imagine the uproar."

Actually, I couldn't. "Who cares?" I asked. Roger likes me because I'm not afraid to ask the tough questions.

Roger attempted to underscore the clash of values at play here. "Don't you see," he said excitedly, "It's the old against the new, the upper class against an upstart, and it's all being played out in the personalities of these two men."

He lowered his voice. "Grace, this is beyond buying and selling companies. Anthony Punch created some of the most famous campaigns in advertising. He's been knighted. Punch and Torkney is his baby. Robbins is a raider. If he gets his hands on P & T, he would just as soon sell off the parts as not."

"But doesn't everyone make money?" I asked.

Roger looked at me as if he pitied my shallowness. I made a mental note not to be so tolerant with him next time he asked me to explain Bebop.

"Grace, I'm trying to explain to you that Punch already made his fortune years ago when he took the company public and sold most of his stock. It's a matter of ego now," said Roger impatiently. "He doesn't want to see his baby auctioned off."

The fact that Anthony Punch was only a minor shareholder did not stop him from whining publicly over the fate of his agency, nor did the fact that he was 93 years old. He was everywhere, making grand statements to anyone who would listen, saying things like, "It's a tragic day for civilization," and, "The art of advertising will be transformed into a carnival sideshow."

Geoffrey Robbins' comments could be summed up by "If successful, we will preserve the integrity of P & T's standards," and "I'll be laughing all the way to the bank."

"Robbins will have to make an offer to tender all shares soon, if he's serious," said Roger, "but for the moment, P & T is still a very good value. Big investors are keeping their distance because they don't think Robbins can pull it off. I think he can. I've been watching him for years."

Roger put down his silverware and leaned forward. "There's a lot of money to be made here," he whispered.

So the fundamental question was whether a brash and shallow newcomer could conquer the traditional, a question I've often asked myself when considering the merits of a Fender Twin Amp versus a Rochester Redstar Digital 5000.

But the financial markets of America and Western Europe were not the only place where big things were happening.

"Roger, I have some news about the band. We made a big decision the other day."

"What's that?"

"I've been inspired by all this talk about business. I've decided to making a serious effort at promoting Swan Venom."

"Really? That's great."

"First we're doing a new demo. Then I want to work towards getting us a record deal," I announced, borrowing Roger's assured tone.

"Good for you, Grace."

"The time has come. We're sounding good."

"You sound fantastic. I always tell you that. You guys really have your own distinct sound."

"You do tell us. And I'm ready to do something about it. I want a new demo because if I'm going to go out there and sell us, I want the most professional tape we can make. What do you think?"

"I think that's smart. You need to do whatever makes you feel comfortable about what you're selling."

"I think so too."

"Hey, this is exciting, Grace," said Roger, a little squeak of enthusiasm in his voice.

"I know. I don't know why I didn't do this before. I've been putting off shopping around our tape, but it's time. We're ready for the next level."

Roger picked up his wineglass, and looked at me with a perky expression. He likes it when I get ambitious about my music. "Here's to the next level," he said raising his glass.

"Thanks."

"I know if you put your mind to it, it's going to be great," he said earnestly.

"I hope so."

"It will. You have an intensity about you. It's why your songs are so good. You really concentrate. I could never be as focused as you," said Roger, looking downcast for only a fraction of a second

"I like what I'm doing. That helps."

"And it helps that you're good at it."

"There's something I want to ask you. It has to do with something you're good at." I looked down at the roll on my bread plate. I had given my next question a lot of thought. "Is there some way I can invest in this thing you're telling me about?"

"What thing?"

"This Punch and Torkney thing?"

"It's not a thing, it's a risk. And why would you want to do that?"

"Because right now we can't afford the kind of demo I want to make." I nudged a square of butter around the plate with my knife. "You know how I am, when I get in the mood to do something I plow right ahead because I don't like to wait, and I get impatient and I thought maybe I could give you two or three hundred dollars and you could invest it—"

"—To make money for your demo?"

"Yes."

"Are you kidding?" Roger dropped his hands in his lap and gaped at me, just to make sure I knew he was surprised.

"No, I'm not. Why are you so surprised?"

"Because this is not a way for you to make money. Investing in the stock market is a huge risk."

"So?"

"It's not a good idea."

"Why not?"

"It's a risk that you can't afford to take."

"Roger, I'm not afraid of a little risk. If I lose it, I lose it."

"Grace, you say that now, but when you lose it I guarantee you're not going to be happy, and this will come between us."

"That's not it. You don't want to do it because you think it's more glamorous for an artist to struggle."

"Grace, that's ridiculous. You know that's not true. You're making this personal."

"No I'm not, Mr. King of Wall Street."

"Do you think this is some magic way to make money? It isn't, and I don't want to see you lose what you do have." Roger's voice took on an almost professional tone, which annoyed me even more.

"Then why are you so interested in Punch and Torkney? Didn't you say there's a lot of money to be made?" I said, flinging his words back at him.

"Come on, Grace, you know it's my job to be interested," said Roger pushing back his hair with an exasperated swipe. "I make recommendations to people who *do* have money to invest. Lots of it. I tell you because I think it's a dramatic story. I thought you would enjoy hearing about it. I listen to your stories about the band. I don't ask you if I can come on stage and sing with you."

Roger and his logic. I could never argue with him. And acting childish was getting me nowhere. Roger folded his arms across the table and looked at me. He had taken his jacket off and rolled up his white sleeves. His gold and blue tie was tucked between the buttons of his shirt. He looked like a croupier.

"I would let you sing with us if you wanted to."

"Big mistake." He reached across the table. "Give me your hand, Grace." He smiled. "If you want to take risks, go to Las Vegas."

Sometimes I think Roger considers me entertainment. "Go ahead and make jokes about my life," I said.

"Grace, you're a talented musician. Stick with that and everything will work out."

"Positive thinking doesn't get you four thousand dollars, Roger. I need money."

"I'll help you think of something. I'll even be an investor. How's that?"

"I liked the idea of investing in Punch and Torkney. It seemed like a good idea. I even like their name."

"It is a good idea for someone. But not for you."

ᖶ ᖶ ᖶ

I lay awake in bed that night and thought about Roger's words. I always lie in bed awake when I stay at Roger's apartment. He does everything two hours earlier than I do, including sleep. Sometimes I go into the other room and look at Roger's paintings. They looked especially real in the middle of the night. It's like looking into the windows of a whole miniature universe. I almost expect someone to move inside the windows. Staring at them stimulates my imagination if it doesn't frighten me first. In the morning Roger is always excited and wants to know how they looked.

Other times I get up and work on a song or thumb through Roger's books. But tonight I was thinking about a world where the clashes of a few can influence the fortunes of thousands.

My world is hardly so dramatic. The unexpected happens now and then. Ray breaks a guitar string on stage, or I might meet someone interesting, like the time I ran into Tino Del Rio, Count Basie's clarinet player, subbing in a wedding band. But generally upheavals are few and far between, and pretty minor at that.

I got out of bed and walked to the window, staring through the venetian blinds at the mist shifting over the Hudson River, thirty-seven floors below us.

Roger lay quietly in bed on his back, one arm folded over his chest, his head sunken in the pillow. Roger looks younger when he sleeps, and his brow was smooth and untroubled. His glasses rested on the night table next to him, along with his watch. Roger looked like he knew more about what was going on in the world asleep than I do awake. He was born to know what's going on. I walked over and touched his forearms. He moved.

I know about music. I can hear the ninth in a thirteenth chord. I took two years of counterpoint. But where was that getting me? Perhaps it was the late hour or the sense of winter approaching, but I felt a little downhearted. Nothing in my lifestyle allowed me to join in the high stakes excitement that was all part of Roger's job. I couldn't even scrape together the money necessary to take a simple step forward in my own career. All around me was opportunity and I couldn't take advantage of it. In fact, I could barely understand it. Everyone was busy moving fortunes around, and I couldn't even get my own boyfriend to buy me a few preferred shares.

Perhaps it was wrong to ask Roger to get involved. But that didn't mean it was a bad idea to make an investment. Even Roger agreed. "It's a good idea for someone," he had said. Just not for me.

If I couldn't participate, perhaps I knew someone who could. I may not have the capital myself, but I had what I've heard about so many times before—a hot tip. That had to count for something. Maybe I could still make this work for me.

I climbed into bed again, next to Roger. As awake as ever, I racked my brain for names and faces. I realized that all the people I know put together count for very little in the overall economic picture. There was my closest friend Natalie, an actress and poet who made her living word processing. My other friends, the guys in Swan Venom—all just barely paid their rent.

It was no good. I was doomed, at least for now, to a life of fighting over whose turn it was to buy coffee during rehearsal breaks.

I sat up again and looked out the cold window. Roger stirred. He sat up, his eyes half open and looked at me with a squint.

"Getting tired yet?"

"No, I've been thinking."

"It's getting late, even for you. Come to sleep," he said pulling me towards him and putting his arms around me. "Don't you have to get up early tomorrow?"

Then I remembered—breakfast with Zermin.

ᛉ ᛉ ᛉ

Of all my friends, Zermin Lengenstaff was the one who could most benefit from my recent insights into the stock market. Zermin inherited a business from his father. He imports children's socks from the Far East.

Zermin's life is like a quest. His dream is to be in the right place at the right time. He's a little like Roger that way, except Roger knows it's all a game and can quit playing at any time and pick up a paintbrush. Zermin, on the other hand, spends everything he has on this quest. He owns good clothes, a big apartment, an exotic dog, a lot of strange art collections, and expensive shoes. He wears a gold bracelet. He eats dinner out every night. Although he gets no satisfaction from any of it, he's always hoping someone will finally notice him and invite him to the party. I always tell him there is no party and no one is having as much fun as he thinks they are but he doesn't believe me.

Zermin has aged in the five years I've known him. As we sat together in the Athenian Corner, our favorite diner, I noticed the dark rings around his eyes and the gray flecks in his beard. He looked fatigued, as if even the weight of his own body was too much for him. I remember Zermin when he was slender and young, brimming with health. Not even the two packs of Chesterfields he smoked each day could diminish his vigor.

He was in the music business when we met. Zermin managed a few bands, which he rotated through clubs and colleges. He was devoted to his musicians and worked on their careers with limitless enthusiasm. Though he never managed Swan Venom—we're still looking for the right person for that job—we often turned up at the same events and became friends.

Zermin had one month and three weeks of success. A musician he handled, Vrig Zyland the avant-garde guitarist, got invited to a new music festival in North Carolina. Vrig got a record deal out of it and immediately broke his contract with Zermin. That's when Zermin became disillusioned and went into the sock game. He's kept his distance from the music business since then, but he enjoys watching the twists and turns of my career. I, in turn, appreciated his advice and enthusiasm. I felt sure that with his keen sense for business, Zermin would appreciate a timely stock tip.

I presented the matter to him over breakfast. To my surprise, Zermin received my suggestion that he sell his collection of contemporary altarpieces and put his money in the stock market with skepticism.

"Grace, what do you know about money?" he said to me over his sixth cup of coffee.

I didn't answer. I just stared profoundly into his right eye as if I had all the time in the world. Then I said simply this: "Punch and Torkney."

It was early in the day for both of us. We had met at 9:30 as an experiment to see whether we could make our day more productive. Even though he was in business for himself, Zermin did not operate at conventional hours. My mornings usually start in the afternoon. It made it difficult for me to deliver my proclamations to their greatest effect but when I said, "Punch and Torkney," I conveyed a certain sense of gravity.

Zermin didn't know what I was talking about. He shook his head and mouthed "What?" silently.

"Punch and Torkney. The ad agency. You want to buy as many shares of it as possible. I would do it myself only I'm putting all my money into Swan Venom right now."

I wished Zermin would stop gnawing on his bagel since it was diminishing the seriousness of my proposal. Here I was at breakfast with a real businessman, which was as close to a breakfast meeting as I would ever come. I leaned across the table. "Zermin, sell one of your art collections. Sell the altarpieces. The dried chicken bones aren't going to last anyway, so get rid of them now while you can still get something for them."

"My altarpieces are a spiritual investment."

"Go to Lourdes if you want to make a spiritual investment. I'm talking business here." Zermin has a whole wall of his apartment filled with little boxes made by artists who spent too many years in parochial school. Each box was decorated with the usual curios— pastel figurines of saints, plastic roses and plenty of thorns, combined with cryptic items like microscopes and barber tools, x-rays, and class photographs with someone's face mysteriously circled. I didn't know what it all meant, but I often told Zermin he should move to Spain or Sicily if he likes relics. He says he prefers the kind they make in Manhattan.

"Sell your spiritual investment. Be a businessman."

"Grace, what do you know about stocks?" This was the question I had been waiting for.

"I know there's a British holding company that wants to take over a major American advertising agency. They've made a rights offering in England to raise cash. Any day they're going to announce their plans and make an offer."

Zermin looked at me suspiciously. I continued. "The ad agency is called 'Punch and Torkney' and they have a very low price earnings ratio which makes them attractive to a foreign company looking to buy an American agency."

"What are you talking about? Are you possessed?" he exploded. People don't like it when you reveal different sides of yourself, especially when they rely on you for a certain experience. Zermin was disconcerted to find me giving him financial advice. He comes to me for glamour.

"Do you even know what a price earnings ratio is?" he cried, nearly hysterical. People at nearby tables looked at us. Zermin is outwardly very respectable, not at all the type to be yelling in a small coffee shop. I told him to loosen his tie.

"Yes, it's the ratio of a stock's current price to its earnings over the past year."

"Grace, how do you know this?"

I said simply, "Roger."

Zermin was silent. Then, lowering his voice almost to a whisper, he leaned across the table and repeated, "Punch and Torkney?"

"Exactly," I said. I could see by the look on his face that his altars were already up for grabs.

ᛩ ᛩ ᛩ

My plan was simple; Zermin would make a lot of money. Then Zermin would lend us the money we needed for a demo. Ordinarily, I would not borrow that kind of money from a friend. But in this situation, I was more like a partner. After all, hadn't the tip about Punch and Torkney come from me? I didn't need to explain any of this to Zermin. I knew him well enough to know he wouldn't miss an opportunity to throw himself in the middle of the action. And as if sensing the logic of my plan, Zermin moved fast. By breakfast the next morning, he was in for two thousand shares.

"Let's see," said Zermin taking his small electronic notebook out of his briefcase, "Here it is—two thousand shares. I paid $8,231.65, including commission," he announced with pride. It was day two of our experiment in early rising. I still felt tired, but Zermin's news opened my eyes.

"That's half a year's salary for some people," Zermin added, savoring the thrill spending money gave him. He punched the little keys with his thick fingers and closed the notebook.

I recalled Roger's words for Zermin. "Buying stock is more than a matter of dollars and cents," I said, spooning up some poached egg. Zermin looked disturbed when I said this, perhaps because he had just sold not only his collection of altarpieces, but also his 1939 World's Fair souvenirs, his French rain bonnet collection and a whole series of Asanti fertility dolls to raise quick cash.

"I sold half my art collection for dollars and cents," he said, "What do you mean it's more than that?"

Patiently, I tried to explain. "What's the difference between one hundred percent cotton socks and cheap polyester socks?"

"Price?"

"Something else."

"Natural fibers?"

"No, Zermin, it's character," and although he didn't immediately grasp my point and chopped up his omelet in frustration, I told him about Anthony Punch and Geoffrey Robbins, and he soon understood that the drama in which he had invested was much richer than he had dreamed.

"That's all very interesting, Grace, I see what you mean," he said, trying to appear casual. "By the way, I wanted to tell you that P & T opened half a point higher today. "

"Wow, Zermin. That means you already made a thousand dollars."

"Exactly. But that's pocket change, Grace. I'm thinking of buying a few thousand shares more. Would you mention it to Roger? Ask him what he thinks and give me a call later today."

"I don't know, Zermin. Roger is sensitive about people plying him for information." I wanted to make him pay for his skepticism of the other morning.

"Please, Grace, I beg you," Zermin hissed. He lowered his head and stared at me as if he were about to fall into a trance.

A desperate Zermin was not an attractive sight. "Okay. But not now. I'm late for work. I'll talk to Roger tonight." I threw a few dollars on the table and left Zermin grimly leafing through a footwear catalog.

♩ ♩ ♩

When I'm not busy practicing, writing or jamming, I supplement my income from music by working a few days a week as a waitress in an Italian cafe. The money I make helps offset the cost of rehearsal studio time, and pays for my little luxuries like expensive moisturizer and boots. The place is called the Café Capri in Greenwich Village. The owners of the Café Capri are two Italian gentlemen, Mr. Rocco and Mr. Zuccaccia, and their wives. They employ an all-female staff to sling espresso. Every waitress is an actress, musician, writer, or painter. Between all our shifts there's enough talent to keep an arts center booked for a year.

When I first started dating Roger I felt insecure about this. How would a professional money-watcher feel about the fact that I worked as a waitress? On this subject Roger says only, "Grace, you're doing what you need to do to be an artist. I admire you. You won't be doing this forever." He should know, since he makes his living predicting the future. I suspect Roger actually likes the idea I work as a waitress because it keeps him in touch with his wild days before Wall Street, when he would stay up for days at a time and paint. He should try serving cinnamon toast to four hundred teenagers on their lunch break if he thinks the wild days were so good.

♩ ♩ ♩

I went straight from breakfast with Zermin to the café. Though it was only mid-November, the holidays were well underway at the Café Capri. The windows sparkled with garlands of gold and silver, and rows of poinsettias. A few hundred strings of Christmas lights twinkled across the ceiling. Mrs. Zuccaccia had also purchased cheerful Christmas aprons for all the waitresses.

"It's my favorite holiday, Christmas," said Mrs. Zuccaccia as she tied my Christmas apron in a bow behind me. "Spray this on the window. Make it look good," she ordered, handing me a can of Readi-Sno.

Mrs. Zuccaccia really ran the show at the café. Her husband, Ennio, spent most of his time leaning on the tables, chatting with customers, and staring out the window, spying on girls behind him in the reflections in the glass. Mr. Rocco on the other hand, always remained behind the counter with his sleeves rolled up to his elbows, ready to help. He and Mrs. Zuccaccia were on duty tonight.

I decorated the front windows, adjusting the height of snow in the two big picture windows on either side of the entrance until it looked like a blizzard had hit the cafe.

The hours passed quickly after that, as crowds hurried in and out for cappuccino. The Christmas season is demanding and by ten o' clock the room was a coffee-colored blur. The customers' faces had started to look like pignoli cookies in the twinkling of lights and their voices seemed to rise in a coordinated roar as if someone had told the same joke at every table. I stared at the field of café tables in front of me as if it were an endless lake of white marble lily pads with coffee cups on them, when a familiar face caught my eye. It was Zermin. He waved to me.

He was more excited than a table full of students from Saint Anthony's on double espresso. His body twitched with nervous energy; he drummed his fingers on the table and tapped his feet. I went over to him.

"Hi. I thought I'd surprise you," he said. "I have some interesting news."

"You look terrible," I responded. The dark rings under Zermin's eyes had grown to noticeable depths.

"I know. I have a lot on my mind. I came by to tell you that after I saw you this morning, I bought another two thousand shares of P&T. I didn't want to wait, the stock is hot. It's up another two points. Guess what I paid?" Behind me a customer waved at me. She smiled and I smiled back.

"Fifteen thousand dollars isn't funny, Grace."

"I'm not laughing at you, Zermin, I'm smiling at a customer. Get a life."

Zermin ignored me. I think he was in some kind of altered state. His eyes bulged as he whispered to me. "After our talk this morning, I decided to take the plunge. I sold my antique thermometer collection and the snuff boxes and some paintings, I just did it. I feel great."

"Congratulations. You're a man of action."

"I feel great."

I didn't know what to say. I hadn't counted on Zermin getting in so deep. "You have a lot of guts," I said, not really sure whether his plunge into P & T was a good or bad thing. More customers were drawing invisible checks in the air. "Zermin, I can't talk now."

"Okay, Grace. We'll talk later. When you have a chance, get me a decaffeinated double espresso," said Zermin, unfolding a newspaper and making himself comfortable.

I hurried away.

I didn't really want to talk to Zermin anyway. I watched him as he flipped through the Living Section of the New York Times, pretending to read the shrimp recipes. He didn't fool me for a second. He had only come tonight to ply me for more information about P&T.

It made me determined to stay busy in spite of my aching feet. I even asked Mrs. Zuccaccia if she wanted to take a break. I would handle the dishes. "Thank you, dear," she said, promptly dropping her sponge and heading to the back of the cafe for a glass of wine. Mrs. Zuccaccia had been on the job since ten that morning. She didn't seem to mind the hard work and remained good-natured about her labor—after all, she owned the place. I think she realized that if it were another time and place she would have been washing dishes anyway, except it would have been for twelve or thirteen children instead of a roomful of students dressed in black. At least this way she could afford a video camera and a month in Taormina with Mr. Zuccaccia and their grandchildren.

I washed the cups and saucers, then walked through the cafe, handing out checks to the last lingering customers. A couple of regulars asked if they couldn't have one last cup of coffee and I told them they had enough caffeine for one night. I, Grace Note, try to handle my customers with just the right mixture of discipline and kindness.

By staying busy, I was not merely avoiding Zermin; I had problems of my own to think about. My ambitions for the band had exacted a price; my recent song writing efforts were a mess. I hadn't practiced the guitar for weeks and my eighth notes were sounding sloppy. And it didn't help that I had canceled a rehearsal this week and last week in order to watch *Around Wall Street*. I told myself all this was due to the pressures of our trip into the studio. I was spending a lot of time in meetings with Jetty McPhereson and the guys in the band, arranging and planning our demo. But it wasn't just that. I was so caught up lately in Roger and his world, so busy advising Zermin and keeping up with the financial news; in short, so preoccupied with minor things that I was neglecting my music.

And it wasn't a one way street, I continued to myself, dropping a cup on Zermin's table without stopping. My own lack of discipline was affecting Roger. I noticed he rose a little later in the mornings. He was buying strange ties. He even started to complain about the brokerage firm where he worked.

"But Roger, you like what you do," I reminded him. He just said, "So what," and asked me if I could teach him to sing.

I wasn't worried about Roger so much. With his lifestyle he can't afford not to do a good job. But I, Grace Note, am the type who needs to work very hard to get anything done. My gift is inspiration. The ideas came first; to realize them takes months of hard work. Didn't it take me half a year to finish, "I Seem to Love Him," which won first prize in the Public Libraries of Iowa Song Writing Competition? I needed to get back to music.

Behind me another waitress, Jessica, steamed a café latte at the big copper espresso machine on the counter. "You don't look so hot," she said. "What's up?"

"I don't know," I said, not knowing where to begin.

"Is it band stuff?"I nodded no and she continued to guess. "Men? This place?" Jessica is an aspiring jazz singer who at 6' 1" really stands out when she's walking through a cafe with a tray full of cups. Add to her height a pile of black hair curling high on her head, and cat's eye glasses, and you have someone waiting to be discovered for the kind of Italian movies they made before she was born. Jessica was a terrible waitress but the owners kept her there because the regulars liked her. I think she was on her way to obtaining cult status among our foreign customers.

"I haven't been working on my music as much as I should lately," I sighed. "It's getting to me."

"What's causing it?" she asked, her voice sailing over an octave.

"It's a concentration problem."

"I get that a few times a year. It usually means I've been drinking too much." She waved to a few regulars who had just walked in.

"I haven't been drinking too much. It's this thing I'm involved in. I had an idea about how to raise money for a demo tape and now I'm a little more involved in something than I wanted to be."

"What, drugs?"

"No, the stock market."

"I wouldn't know anything about that."

"Me neither. Let me ask you something." I leaned towards her at the counter and lowered my voice. "Does this happen to you when you don't do enough music? I feel irritable and nervous. Depressed."

"I'm like that all the time."

"I want to get in fights. For instance, right now if Mr. Zuccaccia grabbed me like he usually does when he squeezes behind us at the counter, I would break his knees."

"He's so annoying"

"I don't feel like myself."

"Your problem is you're getting caught up in something that's taking you away from music. You're out of touch with yourself. You need to play more." Women are great at restating their friends' problems.

"You think that's it?"

"I can see it on your face," she replied with a maternal nod. Jessica has a wisdom about her and maybe it's the fact that she's tall. It gives her a sense of authority. "You need to cut back on some of these projects. Like say, for instance, your hair. Is that curl natural?"

"Yes."

"Okay, so that's not a time problem. And you don't wear lots of make-up. That can eat up hours every day."

"So how do you fit everything in?"

"I take my own advice. I only do one thing at a time. I'm into schedules," said Jessica, shaking some cinnamon onto her latte with determination. "I schedule everything. Practice, auditions, meals, sex, socializing, everything."

"And you stick to your schedule?"

"Of course I to stick to it," she said looking at me through the thick lenses of her glasses. "It's all part of a larger plan. I'm taking two years, to do music only. At the end of two years, if I'm not booked in the Oak Room at the Plaza, I'm out of here."

"A schedule is a good idea," I said.

"Of course. You can't just drift along trying to do everything."

"I'm doing too much, that's the problem."

"It catches up with you. You start to break down from all the distractions. One minute you're the next Thelonius Monk, a musical genius, and the next minute you're crying into a mirror because your make-up base doesn't match your blush. You're overwhelmed."

"It's true. I'm caught up in this stock market thing. I mean, I only know about it because of Roger."

"That cute guy who come in here sometimes with all the magazines and papers? Sits by himself?"

"That's him. Then there's all the band business, and this new demo."

"Cut back, Grace," she said, sauntering off towards a table full of Italians who had come in to order coffee from her.

I collected the last check of the evening and cleared the cheese-cake crumbs from the empty tables. A few customers remained deep in conversation. Mrs. Zuccaccia sat in the back sharing a glass of wine with her friend, Mrs. Ludovici. A sense of peace pervaded the restaurant, as long as one didn't look at the front windows onto Sixth Avenue where a neighborhood lunatic had his face pressed up against the glass.

"Cut back," I thought to myself, repeating Jessica's philosophy as I dropped the last dishes in the sink. I would have to talk to Roger about this.

Zermin, meanwhile, noticed I had finished my work. "Join me," he called out. He was feeling expansive and offered to buy me a drink.

"Zermin, you don't have to buy me a drink. This isn't a bar."

"Well, join me with something anyway."

I made myself an ice cream soda and sat down.

"So what do you think? I did it," he said, continuing the conversation from earlier as if there had been no interruption. "Two thousand shares."

"That's great. I hope you make a fortune," I answered.

"I paid $5.25 a share. If it only doubles, I'll be happy."

"You'll be lucky. There's a lot going on behind the scenes. It can all change dramatically at any moment."

"Don't worry, I know what I'm doing."

"Don't get greedy," I warned. I know Zermin. He doesn't like to let go of things, which is why he has so many collections to begin with. "Don't hold on to your shares forever. It's not art," I said.

"Relax. It's just a game, Grace." He laughed insincerely.

"It's not a game, so don't pretend it is. Just pay attention and you'll do fine. Remember, stock prices rise slowly, but when they drop, they drop fast." I felt as if I had been possessed by a stock-broker.

"Grace, I want to share something with you." Zermin lowered his voice and looked in my eyes. "I've given a lot of thought to this. If this works out, I'd like to do something for Swan Venom. I think you guys are terrific and I want you to be successful. So if I make some money, I want to pay for a really top quality demo tape for the band."

"Really?"

"I've heard you talk about doing a new demo. I would like to see you do something great."

"You would do that for us?"

"Of course. You're worth it. Plus you gave me this tip, right?"

"Thank you, Zermin. I can't tell you how much this would mean." Once again business and music were hopelessly mixed up. I had only wanted to borrow the money from Zermin. Now he was handing it to me.

"Don't forget to tell Roger I bought more P&T."

"I won't. I'm meeting him in a half hour."

Zermin leapt up from his chair, excited. "Oh good," he cried. "Do you mind if I come along and talk to him?"

"Yes, I mind. We're meeting at the Trocadero and guess what? We have other things to talk about besides Punch and Torkney."

"I'm sorry. I need some sleep. I'm getting cranky. Can I walk you there?"

"All right," I said, feeling a little sorry for Zermin.

ʔ ʔ ʔ

For as long as I can remember, I've wanted to be a musician. It's the only career I've ever had, not counting all the things I've done to earn a living—waitress, piano-bar hostess, gift shop salesgirl, art gallery receptionist, recording studio production assistant, flower arranger, au pair girl, tugboat chef. It's all part of being an artist.

It was my grandfather who first noticed my interest in music. He loved Harry Belafonte and Calypso music. He tells me that whenever he played "Hold Him Joe," I would drop my toys and sit by the record player. When I was seven years old, he gave me a toy guitar. It had pictures of cats on it. He thought it was cute. I told him I wanted the real thing, wood and steel, no cats and plastic. I got it. By eight years old I was composing my own jump rope tunes.

But above all, I've always wanted to be a songwriter. There's nothing like the simplicity of a good song, the deep feeling of order and truth you got when rhythm, melody and emotion are perfectly matched. I could spend hours studying a well-written composition. While other kids were going to make-out parties, I was transcribing Burt Bacharach songs.

My first experience in a band came at age twelve, when I formed a group with my neighbors, the Bernard twins, John and James, and Pandora Cathcart, who played bass on her mother's Hammond organ. It was a time when anyone who didn't do sports had a band. Our band—we called ourselves "Electric Chocolate Pie" —played at all the school dances and parties. At our peak, we played school assemblies. Then I got my first taste of band politics.

Pandora said James played the drums like a nerd and he bit her. We broke up.

It didn't matter because soon after, I fell in love with jazz and I spent hours and hours listening to music, practicing progressions, and learning scales. I realized then that I needed to know more about music, so my formal training began in the form of guitar lessons with Jimmy Castralino, a friend of Pandora's brother with his own apartment in Albany. My mother drove me from North Gaylordsville to Albany once a week for lessons. I also took theory classes at the local college. At 16, I got a scholarship to the Northport School of Music, and spent the next few years learning the basics: harmony, rhythm, and melody. When I felt I knew the rules well enough to break them, I came to New York.

Though I don't make my living yet from music alone, everything I've done contributes to my experience. That's where I get my ideas. My best friend Natalie says my experience needs to be deeper; she won't let me forget the songs I wrote about home furnishings when my ex-husband Nick moved out. He took all our stuff and moved to New Jersey, leaving me an empty apartment, which I used as an excuse to write terrible songs that revolved around wall units, kitchen appliances and lost love. At the same time, I wrote a song about Nick called "Free for Now," which we still perform, because it's got a great hook and nice lyrics. So sometimes personal experience leads you somewhere and sometimes it doesn't.

My goal for my current project, Swan Venom, is to create a truly original sound that can best be described as alternative-world beat-rock-jazz-twang with Spanish influences. I'm focused on writing a solid hit. I know it's going to happen, if Swan Venom can just stick around long enough. In the music business, if you can hold out, sooner or later you get a break. I believe we can make it, as long as Geoffrey doesn't lose his bass again.

ᚉ ᚉ ᚉ

The Trocadero on Church Street in Manhattan and the Trocadero in Paris have absolutely nothing in common. The one in New York is located on a street no one ever goes to, in a neighborhood no one lives in. People aren't happy there and no one wants to dance at the New York Trocadero.

Everyone goes to the Trocadero for the neon sign. It's been intact since 1942. The letters are fat, hissing, and red. They glow for blocks through the dark empty streets as if inviting you back in time. Everyone who comes there for the first time stands in front of the place and says, "it looks like a movie set." The second "o" in Trocadero is extinguished.

Zermin walked me to the bar. Light poured from inside, through the front window and onto the sidewalk.

"Do you mind if we skip breakfast tomorrow? I have a lot of things I need to take care of," I said, my hands in my pockets.

"No, that's fine. I want to stay on top of this P&T business." He shuffled awkwardly.

"Okay, I'll call you later in the day."

I went in, leaving Zermin standing outside in the cold night, awash in red. As if he knew how forlorn the effect of this was, he turned up his collar and put a cigarette in his mouth. He couldn't find a match. I waved to him through the window and he waved back silently. He walked off towards Canal Street.

Roger was already inside, perched on a barstool about ten seats in from the door. Around him, the usual customers lined the bar busily stirring up senseless debates with whoever was near. Some stared dumbly at the television, watching a karate movie with the sound turned down. No one in the bar had less than two drinks in front of him; a whisky and a coke, a tequila and a beer, a scotch and a ginger ale, or some other alcoholic chemistry poised on tattered coasters that said, "Trocadero." Each customer also seemed to have his own personal overflowing ashtray. Two different sets of patrons shared this bar—eccentric retirees and downtown professionals. It was not always possible to tell the two groups apart. One clue to the difference was that the eccentric retirees talked more about Florida. The downtown professionals consisted of art directors, speech writers for the mayor, film editors, and jewelry designers, and they came in at eleven o' clock, just about the time the retirees were starting to talk to themselves.

I hurried towards Roger and waved. He mouthed something to me but all I heard was "Rosalie, my daughter, says it's freezing."

Roger looks good dressed casually. Tonight he wore blue jeans and a tumbled Khaki shirt with metal buttons. His hair, which he wore combed back in the day, was now light and mousseless, and a wisp of it hung over his eyes. I think Roger sees himself as a man of many personas. He believes he's only passing as a financial analyst, as if he's actually something different. He even talks about quitting Wall Street, going back to painting, and taking out time to figure out his inner mystery. I don't think he has one. Luckily he only says this rarely and late at night.

In any case, there was something distinctly two-sided to him tonight, Janus-faced you might say, if you had watched as many public television programs on art history in the middle of the night as I have. Perhaps it was the spot of zinc white on his $200 shoes.

"Roger, how did you get paint on your shoe?" I asked him, after we kissed each other hello.

"I was almost out the door when I saw something I absolutely needed to do. I was in such a rush I dripped paint on my shoe."

"I did the same thing tonight with some whipped cream." It was good to see Roger. There were no complications in his eyes as he pulled over a barstool for me, no interior doubts. He was simply glad to see me after a long day.

Still, I felt tense. I wanted to talk to him about the pressure I felt. We chatted about the day's news but my mind would not stay on whatever it was we talked about. Finally, unable to help myself, I blurted out my feelings. "Roger, I was a little disturbed tonight."

"What's wrong?"

"I realized I haven't been getting anything done lately. Do you feel like that too?"

"No, I've been getting a lot done."

"Well, I'm not getting anything done," I continued, "I'm not disciplined enough and I feel like I'm not spending enough time at my music lately." The words started coming faster and faster as I realized how much I meant what I was saying.

"You get up and go right to work but I get a slow start. I sleep late, then have breakfast and organize, and it's five o' clock before I even get going. I haven't worked on a new song in weeks. And then I'm thinking about all this financial stuff you keep telling me—"

"Grace, relax, it's okay," said Roger, putting his hand on my arm.

"It's not okay," I snapped back. "I'm not practicing. I should be practicing. I should be working on songs. I should be taking singing lessons. I'm not doing any of it. I'm thinking about this demo tape all the time, and all the stuff you've been telling me."

"Fine, fine," said Roger, tensely. He clasped his hands and stared at me, waiting for me to tell him what I wanted to do about it. Men like Roger are fine in the high risk, knife-throwing games of Wall Street, but when faced with personal complexities, they freeze. Not that I wanted an argument—I only wanted a solution.

After a moment Roger spoke. "It's true you're doing a lot these days. But I thought you wanted to get serious about band business."

"I do. But I don't seem to be able to do both the business and the music. And there's this whole stock market thing."

"What stock market thing?"

"Punch and Torkney."

"What does that have to do with you? It's just a story I told you."

"I didn't want to tell you this," I began nervously, "but I told Zermin to buy Punch and Torkney. And he did."

"Are you kidding?"

"No."

"How deep is he in?"

"I don't know." I looked up at the tin ceiling while I tried to remember what Zermin had told me. "Four thousand shares."

Roger was speechless. He just looked at me and shook his head.

"Say something."

"You're unbelievable."

"In a good way?"

"No."

"Well, I didn't think he'd get so involved, and now I'm involved, too. He said he would pay for a demo for us when he gets out. He's going to give us the four thousand dollars we need."

"How did you get so deep into this, Grace?"

"I'm passionate about the things that interest me."

"You're not supposed to be passionate about stocks. You're supposed to be passionate about art."

"That's such a cliché."

"It happens to be true. Anyway, Grace, no wonder you're anxious. Who wouldn't be? You got a friend into a very risky situation."

I didn't say anything. Roger was slipping into his responsible mode again. I was embarrassed. Now that Roger pointed it out, the idea of my giving anyone stock tips seemed ridiculous. I just sat quietly on my barstool, feeling I had made all the announcements I needed to make that evening.

"Maybe you'll all get lucky," said Roger, seeing my downcast look. "P&T is doing very well."

"I heard."

"Zermin should get out soon."

"I told him that. He's not listening to me."

"Grace, you shouldn't have gotten him into it, but he's in and there's nothing you can do."

"I know, but meanwhile, I want to get back to my own stuff. I need time, more time," I said, feeling slightly hysterical. I think Roger was right, I was more anxious about Zermin than I had realized. Over Roger's shoulder I recognized a drummer I knew who has a dragon tattoo on his back. It didn't seem like the right moment to point him out to Roger.

"So take more time. See me less then, is that what you want? Because that's not what I want."

"No, that's not what I want either," I said, frustrated.

"Then what do you want me to do? Be reasonable. I can't read your mind. I love spending time with you, but I don't want to make you unhappy."

I hadn't thought this far ahead. I felt worse than ever. We sat quietly for a few moments.

"Grace, tell me how I can help. I'll do whatever I can." Roger reached over and touched my hair. Then he leaned forward and kissed my forehead.

I stared out the window into the night, needing a moment to think. I looked across the street into a darkened Heidi's Dress House, but there were no answers. I turned back to Roger. At least I felt he was on my side.

"I don't want to see you any less. I'm just feeling overwhelmed." I thought of Jessica from the café. "Maybe it would help if we had a schedule. I might end up spending a few nights less at your place, but I'd rather enjoy the time I do spend with you, than always feel like I should be somewhere else."

"A schedule is a good idea. If I didn't have to be somewhere at a certain time everyday, I wouldn't be so disciplined either."

"I could schedule a time to work on music, a time to work on band business and a time to see you. What about something like this?" My mind raced through the possibilities. "When we meet on week nights, we'll only get together after ten o' clock, provided my practicing is done."

"That's a good idea."

"And if we want to, we can meet for dinner, but not more than twice a week. We can eat between seven and ten o' clock."

"How about a weekend date?"

"Okay. Friday or Saturday, if I'm not playing. Holidays follow a weekend schedule."

"By the way," said Roger, taking my hand with both of his, "Can we change that to dinner between seven and nine? I don't like to eat too late."

"Sure. Do you think we can do it?" I asked.

"I'll do my best. The question is, do you think you can?"

"Enough fooling around. I have to."

"Don't cut back on fooling around too much," said Roger, smiling.

The conversation turned to lighter matters. I felt hopeful. Things seem so easy with Roger. Overcome with good will, we stayed at the bar a little too late, and I just barely made it home the next morning in time to begin my new schedule.

❦ ❦ ❦

The following days were filled with music, song writing, and club owners. As planned, I began to practice regularly. I organized a new press kit for Swan Venom, and even found time to work on a new song whose working title was "Borrowed Reserves." I also began the next stage of work on our demo tape. It was time to go into the studio. Jetty McPhereson said we could probably get the whole thing done in six or seven sessions. After that, we would do the mixing down at his place. I came up with a schedule and started to book studio time. Zermin's promise to pay for our demo made everything easier. I was moving fast and people noticed the difference. Even Ray noticed the difference.

"Grace, what's up?" he asked one day, feeling unusually chatty. I was over at his house using his midi keyboard. Ray doesn't usually ask questions. He's known as "the quiet one" in Swan Venom. I told him we had a lot of work to do.

"Excellent," he said, and went back to playing with the phase reversal on his mixing board.

I didn't have a moment to talk to Zermin, and he didn't call me. Our breakfast club was on hold. I assumed that his love affair with the stock market had become too hot to include me, and that he wanted to savor every shifting point in privacy, without my nagging. On Tuesday afternoon, after a week of no communication, I decided I better talk to Zermin. I wanted to check in with him and let him know we were moving ahead with the demo. I phoned him at his Happy Feet showroom.

He sounded distracted, not well somehow. He spoke quickly and his thoughts were disjointed. He said he really didn't have time to talk to me and then he mumbled something about a bidding war. He said P&T was trying to buy itself back and take itself private. They offered fifteen dollars a share. Then Zermin rattled off some numbers.

I was surprised. I thought he would have been out of it by now. Roger hadn't explained the part about a company taking itself private, so finding myself at the limits of my experience, I kept my remarks general.

"Fifteen dollars a share sounds pretty good. Why don't you sell?"

"Because they're going to raise their offer, I'm sure of it."

"Zermin, you're taking a chance, aren't you?"

"Don't worry," he said with a nasty laugh. "I know what I'm doing."

ץ ץ ץ

There are a few things in this world that amateurs should not be involved in; one of them is the stock market. The others are drug smuggling and spying, and, if I may add, the music business.

It's not that your chances of success are low. It's that the stakes are too high. Only those willing to lose time, money and health should put themselves in high-risk situations.

Although the stock market is a calculated risk—you can only lose health and money—amateurs are at a particular disadvantage. No one tells them anything. The important news always comes too late. And expert or amateur, no one can predict the future. Take Punch and Torkney, for example.

It happened Thursday morning. My clock radio went off and I had just covered my head with a pillow when the phone rang. I picked it up.

"I have to talk to you," a voice cried frantically.

"Hello? Who is this?" I asked, frightened by its intensity.

"It's me, Zermin. Grace, it's an emergency."

I sat up. "What happened?"

"Punch and Torkney dropped twelve points. It's down to three and a half. It's a disaster. I'm dead." Zermin was beside himself. "Look at the front page of *The Wall Street Journal*," he shouted.

"Zermin, I don't have *The Wall Street Journal* here in bed, tell me what happened," I shouted back.

He answered me with what sounded like gibberish. "The Canadian government is suing. A huge scandal. My sell order isn't going through."

"I don't understand, Zermin."

"Meet me at the diner in fifteen minutes. I need some air. I can't talk now." He hung up.

I jumped out of bed, wide awake now, even more awake than the time my cat brought me a live waterbug in bed. Like then, it was a hideous way to start the day. Judging by the sound of Zermin's voice, the day hadn't gotten off to a good start for him either. I had never heard him so deranged. I dressed quickly and in a few minutes was ready to go.

I stepped out of my apartment. The dull sky hung low over Canal Street. It was cold. I pulled my coat around me and thought of my comfortable bed, probably still warm. I cursed Zermin, Punch,

Torkney, Robbins, and Zermin again, as I threaded my way between the cars waiting for the light to change. I hurried to the newsstand.

There it was, just as Zermin had said, *The Wall Street Journal* headline blazed across the first column: "Canadian Government Sues Takeover Target." Then came the whole story: "Punch and Torkney Charged with Illegal Accounting Practices by Canadian Government. Twelve Million Dollar Suit Freezes Assets." I purchased the paper and hurried towards the diner.

As I squeezed between the vegetable stands and street vendors of Chinatown, a thousand questions flooded my mind. Could Canada really sue someone? Was it all my fault? Did this mean the end of our demo? I was filled with doubts. Ten minutes later I stepped into the Athenian Corner, halfway between Zermin's place in Greenwich Village and mine on the edge of Chinatown. I looked for Zermin. He was already at a booth with a cup of coffee in his right hand and a newspaper in his left.

"I read the headlines," I said, sliding into the booth across from him.

"My god," he said, "Can you believe my luck?" Zermin looked terrible. I could see he had no plans to go to work today. He wore a faded college sweatshirt, sweat pants, and an old red wool scarf instead of his usual suit and tie. He was pale and the hair on one side of his head stuck out, uncombed. His face wore the expression of a man obsessed with a process gone out of control.

"Terrible news," I said.

"It's a mess. Robbins withdrew his offer. Everything fell apart."

I shook my head while Zermin continued. "The price dropped so fast that the exchange stopped trading on it. That means too many people wanted to sell at once. They won't reopen it until the situation stabilizes. Oh, God." He leaned back in his seat and looked up at the ceiling. "I'm stuck with four thousand shares and it's going to drop again before I can sell them. My broker couldn't get my order through before trading stopped. Damn, damn, damn," he said, as the waiter put down a plate of fried eggs in front of him. I was glad to see Zermin's sense of tragedy allowed for food. I ordered coffee and a roll.

"Tell me exactly what happened, from the beginning."

Zermin took a deep breath. "Punch and Torkney is being sued by the Canadian government for tax fraud. It's got something to do with the records of airtime purchases they kept for Canadian television. Their accounting company in Toronto turned in the books. There are all kinds of allegations. Naturally, Robbins withdrew his offer. Who would buy a company with a twelve million dollar lawsuit?"

Zermin sipped his coffee. "Twelve million dollars in fines and taxes," he said, a faraway look on his tired face. It was as if I wasn't even there.

"That should make you feel better," I volunteered. "You're only going to lose a few thousand."

"A few thousand?" he cried, "You lose a few thousand and feel good about it. I don't feel like feeling better."

"Don't yell at me, Zermin. I told you not to be greedy, didn't I? And what did you say? You said, 'It's just a game,' remember?"

"I'm sorry, I'm at the end of my rope," said Zermin miserably.

I sipped my coffee and we sat quietly for a few moments. Then I borrowed another phrase from Roger and his pals. "So what's the bottom line?"

"I'm going to sell as soon as I can. All I can do is wait and hope it doesn't drop much more."

$$\gamma \; \gamma \; \gamma$$

By the time it was all over, Zermin had lost exactly $16,925.03, including commission and taxes. Zermin doesn't like to lose money and he calculated the value of what he lost in a variety of ways in order to maximize his unhappiness. He figured out that for the money he lost he could have paid seven mortgage payments on his apartment, taken three cruises, girlfriend included, or bought an etching of Napoleon.

"What a waste," he said.

I told him not to think of it that way. "You're only going to make yourself miserable." Then thinking of his offer, I asked, "Does this mean the demo is off?"

He hung up on me. The stress has been too much for him, I guess.

Deep down inside, I suspect Zermin is glad this all happened. He would rather lose money and have a little excitement than sit alone in his showroom. He'll cool off in a few weeks and then find something new to build his dreams on.

I didn't care if he cooled off or not. I was as mad as he was. He may have lost money but we lost a career opportunity. I had to cancel all the studio time that had been carefully negotiated and booked for Swan Venom. We couldn't afford to move ahead without Zermin's support. Weeks of planning and scheduling were wasted. Worst of all, I also had to call Jetty McPhereson and tell him the demo was on hold. It was one of the most horrible moments of my professional life to date, even worse than the time we were accidentally hired to play at a kid's birthday party because Nicky Joel, the booking agent, mixed Swan Venom up with Swan & Brennan, a clown act. I hope I never have to see Steve perform the Itsy-Bitsy-Spider again. Jetty was nice about the cancellation and said we could try again, but for the next four months he would be in Cap Ferrat recording Virtue's new album. Then he was off to London. Maybe next year, he said.

Ray wasn't too upset about the change in plans; he takes everything with the same measure of tranquil indifference. As long as he gets to play, he's happy. But Steve and Geoffrey were mad. They felt as if I had gotten them all excited for nothing—even though I assured them we would do the new demo anyway, with or without Jetty McPhereson.

"Grace, man," Geoffrey said, relishing any opportunity to complain, "I had to turn down a lot of gigs for this."

I just said, "Since when is substitute teaching a gig?"

I understood they were annoyed, and so was I. We lost the chance to work with a top producer. Who knew when we would get another break like that? I felt bad too. But that's the music business. I would try to make it up to them.

The only thing that worked out right was my new schedule with Roger. That, combined with our canceled demo, left plenty of time to concentrate on music. As I put more time into my music, Roger had more time to paint and we both felt better for it. He started a whole new series of window paintings; eerie nighttime scenes of windows glowing in dark urban landscapes, but now there were people in the windows. They were just shadowy silhouettes, but it was a step forward. And his pictures were getting bigger. He even talked about going to life drawing classes. Things were going so well, Roger asked me if I wanted to come with him on a trip to Palm Springs, California.

He had been invited to speak at the American Conference of Investment Bankers. He told me the name of his speech: "Service Company Takeovers; Debt Suicide or Just Bad Judgment?" Roger asked me not to mention it to Zermin. He said it might upset him.

Roger had only this to say about the P&T affair: "Grace, don't give tips. You don't know what you're talking about."

He's right. I should never have gotten Zermin involved. I understand now that the stock market is a private matter between a man and a woman. Anything Roger tells me now stays between us, although he talks less about economics and more about colors.

I told Roger I would love to go with him to Palm Springs. It would give me time to reflect on how I might have handled things differently with Zermin. And I could also take some time to consider Swan Venom's next move. One thing is certain; when I come back we're moving full steam into the new demo. My new approach is total determination combined with extra waitressing shifts. I'll get the money myself. We'll have to find someone else to produce it. I don't think I can top Jetty McPhereson, but we'll find someone.

First, I'm going to Palm Springs. It sounds like the perfect place for some serious thinking.

2

THERE'S NOTHING MORE UNNATURAL than the sight of Harvard men broiling in the desert sun. The light glints off their brass buttons and you can almost feel the threads of their navy wool blazers expanding in the heat. Their hands and faces turn hot pink merely upon contact with bright light, making them look as if they're hurtling towards spontaneous combustion. I, Grace Note, never dreamed I would see such a sight. Yet this is what I witnessed as I watched the members of the American Conference of Investment Bankers stream from the ballrooms of their Palm Springs Hotel.

It was their lunch break. They had just finished their morning sessions. Exhausted from discussing topics like "World Economy and the Future," "Global Energy Policy and the Future," and much more and the future, they poured from the hotel and hurried towards the Salad Oasis for a poolside lunch, thinking only of their pineapple shrimp salad.

I attended no sessions myself. I watched the conference from the pool where I was Roger's guest. He accepted the fact I didn't want to attend any of the conference, as long as I promised to sit with him at the big black tie dinner. I looked for him in the crowd that poured from the hotel and spotted him hurrying out one of the doors, a pink ribbon dangling from his name badge with the word "Speaker" on it in gold script. It flapped in the breeze. He stood for a moment on the other side of the artificial lagoon, next to the mock totem pole fountain, and squinted in the bright light as he searched for me. I waved. It took a moment to get his attention, but as soon as he saw me he waved back, then started in my direction over a footbridge that crossed a tributary of the hotel lagoon.

I was surprised to find a lagoon in the middle of the Palm Springs desert, but it was the centerpiece of the California Club and Spa. The resort and all its restaurants, spas, facilities, and ballrooms swung in a huge horseshoe around this man-made body of water, which was further subdivided into coves, streams and waterfalls.

Nature may have declared the Coachella valley a dry zone, but the California Club decided it was a Caribbean island. Walls of flowers crept up the buildings and over fences, and bright green patches of grass, bordered by petunias, surrounded the walks. Everywhere you looked the land was lush with palm, date, and lemon trees, ivy, shrubs, and flowers; in short, all forms of life alien to a desert, including bankers. The lagoon was the final insult to nature, filled with enough water to float boats of guests from one side of the hotel to the other.

In spite of the effort to make the hotel tropical, no matter where you looked in this garden, no matter where you sat, the California desert stretched bare and dry just beyond the hotel fence dwarfing everything. In the distance, the flat plain of the desert gave way to pale mountains. They appeared cool and indifferent next to all the botanical fuss of the hotel. Distance softened everything, as if there were no time or space.

I turned my attention back to Roger and watched him as he crossed over bridges and a waterwheel, like a ball in a gigantic miniature golf course. Finally he arrived at my lounge chair.

"So you made it out," said Roger. He sat on my chaise lounge and put his hand over mine, leaned over and kissed me. I hadn't seen him since he left our room at eight that morning. We had arrived at the California Club late the night before. Roger looked neat and handsome, dressed to face a day of work in any financial market on the planet. His hair was combed straight back over his head and he wore sunglasses.

"I woke up about an hour after you left," I said. "How's it going?"

"Great. I enjoy sitting in a dark ballroom all day," he said.

"Why don't you skip the afternoon acts?"

"They're not acts, they're speakers. And I go out of professional courtesy."

"Will you be finished by midnight?" I said, teasing him.

"I will be finished in two hours," he replied looking at his watch. "I'm going to one more session and then I'm taking off."

"Good. I'll save you a chair. It's beautiful here, isn't it?"

"I'm not even going to look until later when I can enjoy it."
That's Roger. He likes to keep his five senses organized and not
squander them. He stood up and shook the wrinkles from his suit.
His tall shadow fell across my knees and zigzagged over the empty
lounge chairs next to me.

"By the way Roger, you look great today," I said, shading my
eyes with my hand and looking up at him. He wore a beige linen
suit with a pale blue shirt. The light colors suited him; he looked
elegant and slightly colonial.

"Thanks."

"Let's pretend I'm a Las Vegas showgirl and I just came to meet
you here for the weekend."

"Fine. You be a showgirl and I'll pretend I work on Wall Street.
We'll start later. For now, I'm on a schedule and I must join some of
my dear colleagues for lunch. I'll look for you here in a few hours.
Bye." Roger blew me a kiss, then headed back towards the snack bar
where his chums were starting to realize they would be more comfortable with their blazers off.

From my position near the towel hut, I noticed the women in
Roger's group were better off than the men, enjoying the advantage
of dresses in 96-degree heat. Even so, some of the women insisted
on wearing sports jackets like the men. At least they got to wear
colors like cantaloupe and lime.

Soon it was time for everyone to return to their ballrooms.
Once again tranquillity overcame the pool as it was left to non-fin-
anciers, spa-lovers, children, and me.

♩ ♩ ♩

Barnett McWilliams, the saxophone player, said, "All things can be
reduced to the saxophone." I read this in chapter six of his autobiography, *Big Barnett,* which I had brought with me to California.
The words made me think, and I put the book down next to my
lounge chair as I stood up to consider his words and stretch my
legs.

I walked to the first step of the pool and felt the cool water wash
over my feet. The pool sparkled blue in the bright sun. Small paths
led away from it in several directions. Not thinking, I strolled down
one of the cement walks.

I knew what Barnett McWilliams meant, even though I'm not
sure I agree. He meant all things have their counterpart in musical form. Rhythm and harmony can convey complex meaning, the
tone of a particular instrument and player allow for subtlety and

nuance. Put it all together and you have the power to communicate almost anything.

But is the saxophone enough? It was certainly better than a bassoon. Still, there was something off-center about the whole state-ment; it was one of those grandiose proclamations that never matter to other people as much as they do to the person making them.

It reminded me of my friend Natalie's boyfriend, Massimo Vitello, the painter, who says, "All things can be reduced to an im-age," which contradicts the idea that all things can be reduced to the saxophone. Or of Roger, who says all things can be reduced to eco-nomic necessities, or M.C. Romald, our bass player, Geoffrey's brother and a successful rap musician, who says all things can be reduced to selfishness. Or as he puts it, "Let's iterate the axiom that vanity is maximum." They're all pretty sure of themselves.

I was thinking about how I, Grace Note, am not at all sure what everything can be reduced to. The few times I thought I had it all figured out, it all changed by the next day anyway, or else some-thing would come along to distract me and I would drop my amplifier down the stairs and suddenly things weren't so clear. Why reduce things to just one truth, anyway? Infinite possibilities exist, constantly and in every second, so why deny it? Roger says I wouldn't think that way if I had a real job. Being an artist gives you the impression you have choices.

The desert brought out these kinds of thoughts. It's what I thought as I walked along the edge of the golf course and looked out at the empty plains. The lush green curved around the outside of the hotel, a grassy border between the California Club and the outside world.

People were playing golf nearby and a man waved to me in a hostile way which distracted me from my thoughts. He screamed "Fore." I think he wanted me off the course. I didn't want to get hit by a ball, which would certainly clear my mind before I had a chance to jot down my thoughts.

I walked back towards the hotel, having already wandered by the spa, tennis courts, fitness center, men's shop, ladies' shop, gift shop, golf course, and putting green. This had taken nine minutes. I continued along the edge of the golf course on a cement path, en-joying the cool air and warm light, until I found myself at the pro shop on the far side of the hotel.

This was a remote part of the California Club and I viewed the distant mountains unobstructed from here. Thin palm trees lined the smooth green of the fairways, forming a feeble barrier between the hotel and the immense desert. All was silent here. The only guests in sight were small, bright golfers in the distance. The pro shop was shut tight. Everyone was at lunch. Rows of empty golf carts stood quietly aligned on a cement driveway in front of the pro-shop. A white stucco staircase next to the golfer's boutique led to the upper level of the hotel. I had nowhere special to go, so I stopped and leaned against the base of the staircase.

Waves of heat rose from the ground and wrapped me in a blanket of warmth. I felt as if New York were not only far away, it had never existed. Space and quiet overpowered everything. Feeling sleepy, I stared at the golf carts. How did they manage to line them up so perfectly? I wondered. Just then, footsteps interrupted the otherwise motionless scene. A man approached appearing from around the corner of the hotel on one of the cement walks. I was instantly alert.

He walked quickly towards the staircase as if he were in a hurry to get somewhere, and as he came towards me, his eyes, clear and green, met mine. I remember I opened my mouth slightly and I felt something move inside me. His face was a face I had imagined, a perfect face, round, taut, familiar. I stared at him, astonished. He smiled imperceptibly. I had the disorienting feeling that he was coming towards me and not the stairs.

He blinked in the bright light. Our eyes met for only a moment, but I was sure he felt a shared curiosity. I wanted to say, "You, I've thought of you before," because that's what I felt. But that wouldn't have made any sense. Had I just been walking in the sun too long? He continued past me and hopped up the stairs.

I turned and watched his back, his jeans and dark blue shirt, and the back of his straight brown hair, streaked with gray. I didn't just watch; I stared, and as he arrived at the top of the steps he twisted back, looked at me once again, then disappeared.

I felt strange. Did he turn back to see if I was looking? Did he recognize me too? The experience felt like a dream; it had that irrational quality, the way something completely meaningless, like a tangerine, can provoke an intense emotional reaction.

But he was gone and there was silence once again. A lizard moved across the hot ground and disappeared under a golf cart. The sun burned overhead. I was surrounded by the midday lethargy of the desert. Life had just disappeared up the stairs. I turned around and followed.

At the top of the stairs, I found myself on the terrace of a restaurant. This was the Putter's Snackbox where guests and golfers dined quietly at tables shaded by white umbrellas. In front of me was an archway sheltering a double glass door. This led inside the hotel. To the right were the outdoor tables of the Snackbox, then a doorway leading to an interior restaurant. The man with the green eyes had gone through one of these doors.

I had to decide whether I really wanted to make a search out of this. I was charmed and curious. I wanted to see more. But following people wasn't something I wanted to encourage in myself. The light chiming of silverware, plates and voices soothed me. Suddenly I felt tired and immobilized by the potential effort of my search. What was I looking for, anyway? So I had seen a sexy, not too tall, nicely built stranger who had walked out of my fantasies. This was just the kind of thing that happens when I have too much free time. My practical side spoke up. I decided the most logical thing to do was to stop here at the Putter's Snackbox, have lunch, and if at all possible, get a grip on reality.

᭙ ᭙ ᭙

"Hey," said a voice behind me. I turned around to face a hearty blond specimen of California wellness in a yellow polo shirt and checkered shorts.

"Hey," I replied.

"I'm Rick. How 'ya doin'?" he inquired, lifting his sunglasses and grinning at me.

"Okay. One, please," I said, hoping I was correct in assuming Rick worked here. He didn't wear an apron or a uniform, just a nametag that said, "Rick." He looked like a lifeguard.

He led me to a table by the wall, which allowed me to view the hotel grounds from yet another angle.

"I'd like an iced coffee," I said.

"Absolutely. Be right back." He bounced away into the shadows of the restaurant.

The canvas umbrella above me sent a hard-edge angle of shadow across the table. The air was fresh and cool in the shade. Birds hopped around the walls of the terrace and pecked at crumbs on the empty tables. Rick brought me my coffee quickly. "Yell if you need anything," he said. He leaned over me and I thought for a moment he was going to give me a hug. He went away.

As I looked out over the lagoon, which shone white like a mirror in the afternoon sun, I realized that putting a man-made body of water in the middle of a dusty plain was what made California the great state it is. Perhaps I should try and learn something from the way Californians never let reality get in the way of a little pleasure. Hadn't I already seen a kind of mirage today? Just enjoy it, I told myself.

I let my mind travel. I sipped my coffee and watched ice cubes melt in my glass. Rick came over every now and then just to say hi. I leaned back in the chair so my face was in the sun, and closed my eyes feeling the warmth wash over me. When I opened them, I started; the man in the blue shirt stepped out of the shadows of the archway that connected the restaurant to the hotel, and stood in the doorway.

His hair blew in the breeze. He remained motionless. I realized he must have gone into the hotel before. As I watched, another man joined him. Together they stood in the shadows, talking quietly. The second man was older, his skin brown with a California tan. He leaned over and whispered a few words to the first man and they both smiled. They began to organize themselves, each putting on a pair of dark sunglasses. They looked like they were about to do something important, like plant a bomb or make a documentary about Marilyn Monroe.

The older man looked as if he might be in the film business. He was conservatively dressed, yet there were a few casual touches—the pricy kind. He wore a smart black leather jacket and his gray hair was just a touch on the long side. He had an expensive watch, which he looked at repeatedly as he flipped open the date book he had taken from his leather satchel. The desert breeze stirred the pages of the book and they rippled in the wind. The two men glanced at the book, then at their watches. Plans were being made and I felt sure I was witnessing the beginning of some significant West Coast activity.

I didn't feel shy about staring, mainly because they didn't notice me. I, Grace Note, confess I could not take my eyes off the man I had seen earlier. He was as good as I remembered; his face and eyes were shadowed in pleasing shades of gold and gray. It was a rugged face, delicate in the details. His hair was brown and short, with a little gray, and it moved in the soft desert wind.

They finished their arrangements and his companion put the diary back in his bag. The two men shook hands. Instead of departing together as I had expected them to, the older man disappeared into the hotel while the younger man remained in the doorway, once again still, as if he were contemplating a stroll to Nevada.

He must have stood there for two full minutes. I couldn't tell where he was looking behind his sunglasses. Then he started to walk. I decided I ought to look at him as he passed; after all, if he were walking off forever I would like him to know I noticed. It was a little something he could take with him.

To my surprise, he walked not towards the stairs but towards the tables. Was he actually going to eat here? Perhaps he was just taking the long way around, passing close enough to me to give my imagination a jolt. Men do little things like that although they'll deny it every time.

But he walked right up to my table, and stood in front of me, casting a shadow across my condiments. I felt paralyzed. Then he spoke. "Excuse me. I don't know you—I guess you know that— but would you mind if I joined you?"

His voice was soft and he spoke quietly. He peered at me through his round, green sunglasses and I looked back at him in disbelief.

"Please do," I said finally.

"I hope I'm not interrupting you." He pulled a chair around so that the umbrella's shade fell on him. "I noticed you earlier when I was walking up the stairs." His politeness offset the boldness of walking up to a total stranger.

I didn't say anything. He didn't seem to need me to say anything.

"I thought I'd be brave and say hello," he continued. "After all, we both have something in common."

"What's that?"

"We're among the few non-bankers in the entire resort."

"How do you know I'm not a banker?"

"I'm not positive. I just don't think of bankers as wearing an earring like yours." I had forgotten I was wearing a single, shoulder-length dolphin earring. It gave me away.

"I'd love a cup of coffee," he said, looking out over the golf course. I liked the way he spoke, in short sentences that were clipped and rich, as if words were merely a convention and the real action was inside. He seemed totally at ease, yet at the same time watchful. He had a self-contained poise that contrasted with the people around us who were busy gobbling burgers and comparing handicaps.

I signaled Rick. He was in the middle of demonstrating a surfing technique to a family from Oregon. Rick came over, looking cheered by the fact that I had found some company. We gave him our order and he hurried away as if he were on staff in cupid's own dining room.

"I'm Paul Teagarden." My companion extended his hand across the table to shake mine.

"Grace Note," I said. "I noticed you, too, by the way."

"Grace," he said, as if he had just learned a new word. "What brings you way out here?"

"How do you know I'm 'way out' here?"

"I'm only guessing, of course, but you look like you're from the East."

"That's right," I said, appreciating his eye for detail. "What else do you know?"

"That's the limit. You'll have to tell me the rest."

"I'm on vacation. My friend is actually attending the conference. But I'm going to try to get a little work done while I'm here."

"What kind of work do you do?"

"I'm a musician." There was no point in going into more detail. In New York you could say something like, "I'm a musician," and it would be the equivalent of saying, "I'm a postman" anywhere else. But who knew what it implied here? "What about you?" I said.

"I'm working on a film. I'm here to meet with the producer and the studio executive. He has a place out here. That man I was just talking to was one of the producers."

So he knew I had been watching them. I wondered if he were an actor. That would mean all of this—the strange attraction, the familiarity—was just the product of an actor, that is to say, acting. Yet he didn't seem like an actor and he certainly wasn't good looking in any traditional way. He just happened to be my type.

"What do you do?" I asked.

"I direct."

"Really? That's interesting."

"Unfortunately, not always. That's partly why I stopped to talk to you. I need to think about something else for a while."

"What kind of film is it?"

"It's a television movie."

"You don't sound very enthusiastic."

He leaned forward slightly and lowered his brow, directing his gaze right at me, as if he were sharing a secret. "It's about a twelve year old who becomes principal of a school." He raised his eyebrows.

"Oh, I see," I said.

"I'm doing this for practical reasons. They want me to direct it so I'm doing it. I mean, it's not that bad, but I have another project I really want to do. I'm working with the studio because I'm hoping they'll pay for another film. One I wrote."

Things were getting interesting. This Paul Teagarden had a lot of irons in the fire. In fact, he was just like everyone else I knew; he had a project. I don't think I know anyone who doesn't have a project. I felt at ease. I could relate to someone with a project because they always have direction in life. It's only chance that allows you to cross paths with people who have projects since they're always in motion, and now that I think about it, I'm lucky I have any friends at all.

But why did I find him so appealing? I had the same mysterious feeling of familiarity as when I first saw him. Talking to him only intensified the feeling. He spoke quietly but there was something exciting in him. He knew exactly where he was going. I felt shy in the presence of such clarity. All I could think to talk about was whatever happened to be in my field of vision, and I must have said at least four times how I had never seen such a big sky. After a while, I loosened up and told him about Swan Venom.

He seemed interested in my songs. "What are they like? Are they like you?" he asked.

"That's a strange question." I paused to think. "They're a lot like me. Original. Memorable." He laughed. "What's your film about? The one you're writing."

"I'm working on the script now with a friend. It takes place in the fifties. It's about an old man who's been around long enough to remember the last of the Indian wars. He was once a soldier but now, in his old age, he works in a barbershop in San Diego sweeping the floors in order to support his grandson who lives with him."

"That sounds different."

"I think it's an original story. The grandson doesn't really comprehend what his grandfather has been through. So it's about the tension between them, and the way they eventually come to some understanding."

"And the movie takes place in the past as well as the present?"

"Yes. I want to contrast two centuries meeting. The older man is from a completely different world from his grandson, literally a different century. The only modern thing this guy knows how to do is turn on a radio. He's the past."

"It sounds like you can do a lot with that idea."

"I can, if I can get a studio to pay for it."

"I know the feeling."

Below us, golfers dressed in lemon yellow and watermelon red stepped into their carts. Lunch was over. Paul didn't seem to be in a hurry to work or run off, or even talk. Calmness prevailed. If I were with Roger now, we would have played three ping-pong games, gone on a sketching walk, talked about undervalued blue chips, gone to the men's shop and bought a watch—Roger loves buying watches—and gone swimming.

That wouldn't be bad either. It was a different way of passing time. Now, without even moving I felt a charge between us and for a second, I felt as if it were really Paul and I who were on vacation. I imagined that we would go our separate ways for a few hours, he to his producers and me to the pool, and we would rendezvous later in the afternoon for dinner. It was as if we had done this before.

When not listening to his words, I absorbed his image. His eyes were slim and deep. He was taller than me, but not by much. He wore pale blue jeans, not tight, but with a very personal fit.

I stopped myself. What was I thinking? I was getting romantic. As harmless as it all seemed to me—after all, what was wrong with a pleasant encounter over coffee, especially on vacation—this couldn't be right. Roger wouldn't have liked it. He would not have wanted to exit from his grand ballroom to find me lounging at an umbrella-covered table with another man. I was Roger's guest and as long as I was here in Palm Springs and not Manhattan, I had to be considerate. I decided I should leave.

But I was unable to walk away. Another part of me declared it impossible. I argued with myself. I insisted. I declined to leave. Then Paul solved the problem for me. We had been sitting together for about forty minutes.

"Grace, I have to go. I wish it weren't true, but I'm expected at someone's house."

I didn't say anything. "Stay with me forever," was the only thing I could think of saying, and I knew that was premature.

"Listen, what are you doing tomorrow afternoon?" Paul asked.

"I don't have any plans yet. I thought I would do what I did today."

"What did you do today?"

"Sat by the pool. Talked to you."

"I'm doing lunch tomorrow and then I have a free afternoon. I wouldn't mind doing something in Palm Springs. In fact, there's something I've always wanted to try."

"Is this an invitation?"

"Yes," he said, in his direct way. "Join me tomorrow."

"What do you want to do?"

"There's a cable car here that goes up to the highest spot in the desert. I've wanted to do it for years and never had the time. Let me take you on a cable car ride."

"That sounds good." I think I even said, "I'd love to."

I admit I felt a little guilty. What would Roger think? On the other hand, I had nothing else to do. I didn't really do sports. I didn't convene. The spa was too expensive. One body buff or skin-nourishing facial cost more than I made in a week. Why shouldn't I have a harmless afternoon of sight seeing?

His departure was fast and clean as if he already sensed Roger's eyes upon him. He signaled for Rick to bring him the check, signed it with Rick's Snoopy pen, then stood up.

"I'll meet you here tomorrow at two o' clock. Is that good for you?"

"Two is good." Roger's afternoon meetings started at two. I could have lunch with Roger, disappear for a few hours and be back by dinner.

"See you tomorrow, then." He smiled. He walked away.

❦ ❦ ❦

Life was good, I decided. Of all the places in the world, this was just where I wanted to be. Having acknowledged my good fortune, it was time to get moving. I couldn't spend the whole afternoon here drinking iced coffee with the birds.

I picked up my bag, straightened my harem pants, said adios to Rick, and marched off towards the pool, following the maze of sidewalks lined with flowering bougainvillea and oleander that led back to where I had started. I passed a few lonely crows pecking at the lawn and some uniformed hotel employees who brightly shouted "Good afternoon" at me as they trotted towards their stations, which no doubt had something to do with hospitality.

To tell the truth, I needed a walk to calm myself down. My encounter with Paul Teagarden left me feeling exhilarated—more than I could account for. My plan was to put everything out of my mind by replacing it with a project of my own.

The project I had in mind was my musical, a kind of side project I'm working on with my friend Natalie. She's writing the lyrics and I'm writing the music. Natalie usually writes poetry, but she wanted to try her hand at something longer, so she suggested a musical. She urged me to put some time into it while in Palm Springs. This was the perfect moment; the effort of providing the music for her odd lyrics was guaranteed to bring me down to earth, if not to another planet altogether.

Natalie's lyrics are on the cosmic side. She's into spiritual development and her lyrics are always about "becoming," which isn't a hot commercial topic unless you're an English pop-mystic. She believes you have to look beyond everyday reality for inspiration. I tell her that it's a matter of individual style and I'd rather look in my own backyard for material, than write about angels from another solar system, like she does, so we've come up with a motif that satisfied Natalie's need to explore transcendent subjects. The story concerns a socialite and time traveler, who goes back in time to parties in other ages. In her adventures, our time traveler learns that every party—and every age—has inherent in it the notion that the world is about to end. She comes back to the twentieth century and tells everyone they can relax.

We call it, "When Matter Meets Doesn't Matter." Natalie wanted a title that was a little more serious. She suggested calling it "The Blue Glow that is the Trace of Neutrons," but I told her not to get too heavy. There are more than enough brain teasers in the art world as it is. We're not getting a grant so there's no reason to be grandiose.

Natalie and I complement each other. She's very intense, especially about things which I tend to take for granted, like gravity. She's working on some of the heavier characters, like the physicist our heroine falls in love with in the nineteenth century. He tries to convince her to stay, but she has a date during the Inquisition. I, on the other hand, notice details so I'm working on the character of the socialite. Natalie helps me to see the big picture while I teach her to notice the little things, like haircuts and bus schedules.

We're trying to make a statement about the truths that endure through every era. Everyone thinks their party is the latest and the greatest. Everyone thinks they've broken all the rules there are to break. Everyone is at the center of time. Our socialite does her big number on the patio at Versailles, which we call, "In My Next Life, I'll Stay Home."

It was the perfect day to work on "Matter." Roger would come to the pool and find me absorbed in my work. He would attribute my inordinate good mood to musical progress. I settled down by the shimmering water of the swimming pool.

I was outlining the scene where our heroine goes to a masked ball in fifteenth century Florence. I'm using our project as an excuse to explore different musical styles. I was trying to decide whether something bluesy was right for the scene or whether something more worldbeat, like a mambo or a sword dance, might be in order.

I hummed quietly. The warm air curled around me like perfume, making me sleepy. There were few guests at the pool this afternoon and the air was peaceful. The quiet was broken only by whistling birds, the steady click of a ping pong ball, and the splashing of children at the shallow end of the pool.

The other guests by the bright blue water were mostly woman whose husbands attended the conference, and who now lay stretched out on lounge chairs, dressed in tiny gold and black bikinis. There were also a few young couples here to take a break from their LA routine, and they lay side by side, their hands locked between their chaise lounges.

I closed my eyes. In the dark, behind the speckled shadows that moved across my lids, I had hoped to picture our work in progress. Instead, images of Paul Teagarden wearing his dark green sunglasses appeared. Once again, he looked at me a few seconds longer than I expected. I reenacted stretches of our conversation and watched him for a long time, tracing the outline of his face with my eyes. Then, I don't know why, I imagined we were in a car driving somewhere. Perhaps I was thinking about the next day. The car was a convertible because the wind blew back Paul's hair. He said something to me, but before I could hear his words everything changed, and then it was Roger sitting there in my mind. Some kind of romantic safety valve must have opened, because Roger sat there, happy as you please, right where Paul had been. I was surprised. I had forgotten about him.

You may be getting the impression that I, Grace Note, am not the ideal date for a spa weekend. It's not true; I just have room for all kinds of feelings, for all kinds of people. My heart is roomy. It comes from years of connecting to people through music. When you spend a week or two on the road with four or five inarticulate strangers, you really have to learn how to see the best in them and forget the rest. You get close to people. That's part of the reason Nick and I didn't work out. He didn't like it when I got close to people. But the fact is, I enjoy different people for different reasons. Whatever attraction I had for Paul had nothing to do with the way I felt about Roger.

Anyway, conventional things simply never worked for me, as my one marriage to date had taught me. The current situation—being here with Roger on what was essentially a four day date—just didn't seem to produce the conventional results with me. Hadn't I just made a date to climb a mountain?

❧ ❧ ❧

Across the pool, next to the Salad Oasis, two musicians were setting up. It was 4:30 in the afternoon, and the sun was now heading towards the mountains. Soon the sound of fifty instruments poured from the musicians' synthesizers. The melody of "Yellow Bird" wafted over the pool, then moved away over the golf course where it distracted anyone who happened to be on the sixth or seventh hole. After that, I imagined, it floated off into the distant mountains where it annoyed the spirits of dead Indians.

It was cocktail hour.

"Hey, Grace." Roger waved to me as he strode along the edge of the pool. His meetings were over.

"Hi there," I called back.

"May I join you on your vacation?" he said merrily, sitting down on the chaise next to me.

"Please do," I answered. He had already gone up to the room and changed into his bathing suit. He pulled off his tee shirt revealing an expanse of white chest that rivaled the desert for unbroken lack of color.

"Boy, you're pale."

"I haven't been in the sun for months. Have patience." Roger leaned back and closed his eyes. "By the way, have you been out here since I last saw you?"

"No. I took a walk and stopped for something to drink."

"Tough day."

"I've actually been trying to get some work done," I said, rustling my tablature book and papers in case Roger didn't get the idea.

Roger didn't say anything. He took in the sun, sighing and stretching, his arms behind his head.

Ten minutes passed and Roger reached his limit for sitting still. He sat up and surveyed the premises.

"Grace, look," he said directing my attention to the outdoor bar at the side of the Salad Oasis where a number of people had now gathered. "It's Jack Waldorf. He was my boss at Stein Oriole. Come, let's say hello."

"Do I have to?"

"Suffer a little. I've hardly spent any time with you, and I'd really like you to meet this guy."

I groaned and stood up. Only a few minutes before I had been lost in pleasant thought. Now I would have to smile and act interested and end up talking to someone's wife about her interior design business or some other business and she would ask what I did for a living, and after I told her she would say 'Oh, my son or daughter is in a band,' and I would have to hear about it.

"What do you want to do for dinner tonight?" I asked, putting on my sandals.

"I made reservations at Il Crostino," Roger said, pointing across the lagoon at an Italian restaurant with huge canvas umbrellas in front of it. He started singing along with 'Lemon Tree,' which ricocheted across the pool.

"Fine," I said as dully as possible. But Roger was in one of his unshakably cheerful moods. He was glad to be here and he was even glad to be with me. I remembered why I liked Roger so much. He didn't take me too seriously. He was completely honest. He enjoyed himself.

I put my notebook away, and we walked over to the bar where Roger greeted a number of comrades who always seemed to be named Jack or Dick. Briefly, between Jack from First Investors, and Jack from Arnold, Mitchell and Cleeve, I wondered whether Paul Teagarden was behind one of the shaded windows that looked out over the lagoon.

"By the way," said Roger between Jacks, "Don't forget my speech is tomorrow. You're coming, right?"

"When is it?"

"Two o' clock."

A tiny traffic accident only I could hear took place somewhere in my brain. "Great," I said. "Two o' clock is perfect."

𐤊 𐤊 𐤊

My options were few and unrealistic; I could have a fight with Roger, tell him I was going back to New York, take another room and be free the next day. Or I could tell him the truth, that I had a date with a film director to go sightseeing.

I certainly didn't want to let this new complication ruin our evening. It was my problem. It was Roger's problem, too, but as long as he didn't know it, I wasn't about to bring it up. Perhaps I could get Rick at the Snackbox to give Paul Teagarden a message. Yes, I thought to myself over Rhum Baba at Il Crostino, I could write a note, give it to Rick, who could pass it on to Paul.

The note would explain why I couldn't make it. I could leave Paul my phone number in New York and casually suggest we stay in touch. Or maybe it would be better to keep things local and suggest we meet for coffee later in the afternoon. No, that was too complicated. Maybe I just should just leave a note, say 'ciao' and forget the whole thing.

"I've never seen the mood so down at one of these events," said Roger, jabbing his spoon into his tartuffo. "But then it's no surprise, given the numerous banking fiascoes following in the footsteps of the go-go nineties."

"You sound like you're on a television show."

"Just practicing for tomorrow. And recent years have brought little relief with their periodic global banking crises," he continued.

"What time did you say your speech was?"

"Two o' clock. Right after lunch, so everyone can doze."

"That's what I thought."

"As I was saying, the mood is really down this year."

"What has it been like in the past?" This was our first conference together.

"Very upbeat."

"I can see it. Everyone pushing each other in the pool."

"This year they're all worried about whether they'll even have a job come the next conference."

"Well, they're all getting what they deserve as far as I'm concerned."

"Oh, really? You've been studying the banking industry?" Roger didn't indulge my off-the-cuff analyses. "Please explain."

I was pleasantly distracted for a while as I reviewed the various factors—the scandals, the mergers, the bad Asian investments, the over-leveraged loans, and the greed I felt had accounted for the current crisis.

Roger listened attentively. At the end of my speech he said, "Not bad. Are you sure you didn't go to any of the meetings today?"

"I was working on my musical most of the day," I replied. I knew Roger was kidding, but I wanted to make it extra clear I had nothing to hide.

"How are Natalie's lyrics working out?" asked Roger.

"They're a little weird. But I can work with them."

"You would think living with Massimo would bring her down to earth," said Roger. Natalie's boyfriend is a very successful painter whose value for material comfort is second only to his love of painting. Material comfort would have been first, but it's the painting that got him the material comfort. He's a regular in Architectural Digest and all the other magazines that go for photogenic artists. Ever since Natalie moved in with him, she's been living the life of New York royalty of the downtown sort.

"Does Natalie talk to Massimo about your musical?" continued Roger.

"I don't think so. I don't think he's interested in anything he can't sign his name on."

"Maybe to be a professional painter you have to be that way."

"You have to be a jerk?"

"No, I mean really committed. Egocentric. Maybe that's the difference between him and me. I'm not really committed as a painter. Basically, I could take it or leave it."

"That's okay, Roger, some things are meant to be a hobby."

"I know. But I would like to experience that intensity that you guys feel. That commitment." I think Roger was in one of his self-pitying moods. It happens whenever he spends too much time around financial types. I would have to remind him what a thrill it is to be in his shoes.

"Let's get out of here," I said. "We'll go somewhere else and relax." The restaurant was too artificial. It was a brass and chrome backdrop for everything unnatural; fish that had come by plane, perpetually blooming plants, pale tourists dressed in polyester.

After seeking out one of the discreetly stashed hotel bars where the less active guests gathered, we settled down for an evening away from the anxieties of banking and finance, and we talked about art and commitment the way only the well-fed can, interrupted occasionally by the nagging question of what I would write in my note to Paul Teagarden.

❡ ❡ ❡

I awoke at dawn, or at least it felt like dawn. Roger was yelling into the telephone. "Are you kidding?" he shouted. "You must be kidding."

He was sitting on the second of the two double beds in our room wearing a pair of gym shorts. It was 6:50 AM.

"This is too much." He paused, listening fixedly to whoever was on the other end of the phone. "Sure I'm upset, but what can I do? I mean the whole thing is rather incredible, don't you think?"

I perked up. This sounded exciting. Roger looked over at me but said nothing. He was absorbed in his phone call. "Okay, Jack, I have no choice. Will everyone know by then? I mean, who's going to even listen to me at that point? Ten-thirty. Yes, fine. Bye, Jack, see you then."

He put down the phone and then leaned back against the pillows and closed his eyes.

"Is everything okay?" I said, lifting up my head.

"Sorry, I didn't mean to wake you."

"Don't worry about it. What's up?"

"The strangest thing just happened," said Roger, getting up and padding around the room once before getting back into bed next to me. The room was frosty thanks to the roaring air conditioner and I shivered under my three blankets. Roger sat on top of the blankets and folded his arms.

"You know the chairman of the conference? Phil Edelweiss? He's the president of the Detroit People's Diamond Savings and Loan. Well, he was scheduled to make a major address this morning. It turns out he flew back to Detroit last night. His bank has been shut down by the FDIC."

"Wow."

"It seems one of their top executives is an arms dealer."

"Is that a problem?"

"Not generally, but he's been using bank funds. I don't know exactly what's going on but it's something big. Anyway, the convention organizer, Jack Rotondi, said he wants to move my speech from two o' clock to the ten-thirty spot."

"Why?"

"Everyone is going to be there expecting Phil Edelweiss. Someone still has to speak."

"But why you?"

Roger moved closer to me, and stretched by my side. "In case you don't know it, Miss Note," he said with a smile, "I'm a very popular speaker. Jack knows I can handle this crowd. He would rather move up my speech and leave the afternoon slot empty, than have a full house and no one to speak. It's going to be tough. The place will be in an uproar once everyone finds out what's going on. Jack doesn't want to deal with it, so he asked me to move up my speech. It's going to be a wild morning." With this, Roger rolled over and dialed room service.

While Roger ordered breakfast, I considered this lucky turn of events. It wasn't lucky for Phil Edelweiss maybe, but it was good news for Roger and me. He could be a hero, I could watch him be a hero and still keep my afternoon appointment without having to resort to anything underhanded. I could live life in the sun again.

I would have to find some excuse as to why I wanted to be alone that afternoon, but that would be easy.

It was as if fate had reviewed my situation and acted in my favor, benefiting everyone except, again, Phil Edelweiss. Even the conference members would benefit. They may have lost their leader, but now they had an extra hour and a half to practice for their round robin golf tournament.

Roger got up and started reviewing his speech. He wanted to make sure he was prepared. Anything could happen once the conference members got wind of the Phil Edelweiss affair.

We talked a little longer and by the time Roger disappeared into the shower, I had fallen back asleep.

ካ ካ ካ

Roger had nothing to worry about; his speech was a hit. He made it look easy. Without a hint of nervousness, he appeared relaxed and witty, forward looking and insightful. I can honestly say that when he thundered, "Ask yourself whether that Cezanne in the conference room was worth the long term payback we've demanded from the nation," I would have sworn Roger was running for office. And Roger not only sounded good, but he looked fantastic in his Valentino suit complemented by a pastel floral tie I had picked out. I was proud of him.

The bankers united in their thunderous approval of Roger's speech. Roger managed to take all their anxiety and fear at the news of their chief executive's crisis, and channel it into an excellent presentation, including slides. By the time Roger finished his speech, they were back on track, ready to address their industry-wide problems and focus their attention on the task of figuring out who to blame.

Those who didn't rush off to lunch swarmed by the podium to talk to Roger, Jack Rotondi, and a few other ACIB luminaries. I moved to the front of the crowd as the ballroom emptied, inching forward, smiling and nodding with the rest of the insiders.

I joined the circle of people around Roger. When I judged the moment to be appropriate, I appeared by his side. "You were fabulous," I whispered. He glanced at me but was quickly distracted by a big shot from Sandwich Brothers who had come to compliment Roger on his speech.

I waited for another break so I could tell Roger my afternoon plan. I had thought the whole thing through; I would tell Roger that I needed to run into town after lunch to the drugstore. Roger would ask me why I couldn't just go to the hotel drugstore, and I would say because I needed something special that the hotel drugstore won't have. Roger would assume I was referring to some mysterious feminine item that he didn't need to know about.

It was a while before there was another lull in the congratulations but as soon as there was, Roger turned to me and put his arms on my shoulders as if to steady me. "Grace," he said quickly, "I'm really sorry, but I'm not going to be able to have lunch with you. Is that okay?"

I gave myself a moment to look disappointed. Roger continued, "I'm going to have lunch with Jack and some other people."

"Too bad," I replied, thinking on my feet. "I was hoping we could go into town and look around. Maybe I'll go now while you're at lunch. Would you mind if I used the car?" The drugstore story was out.

"Sure, go ahead. The keys are on the dresser by the lamp."

"Thanks. I wanted to do a little sightseeing."

"Sure," said Roger, only half listening.

"Okay, great," I said. "I'll see you later."

"Just be back by six," said Roger. "We have a cocktail party. Don't be late," he warned. Then he said, "Bye," and nearly shoved me off the proscenium. Obviously, we both had bigger fish to fry.

♪ ♪ ♪

According to my plan, our rented car would never leave the hotel parking lot. I had to take the keys and make a show of borrowing the car, otherwise Roger would wonder how I got around town. He would notice if the car keys never left the dresser. Roger has an eye for those kinds of details. Now, as far as he knew, our white convertible Le Baron was on the road with me in it.

I went back to the room. It was 12:30. I wanted to change out of the skirt and blouse I had put on for Roger's speech, and into something more casual. I tried on a few of the outfits I had brought, a one piece body suit with shorts, then a velvet tank dress. I finally settled on jeans and a tee shirt, deciding this would be most practical for hiking. I also called room service. Even though I was too excited to eat, it would be best not to undertake anything on an empty stomach. I ordered a plate of croissants and some coffee and put it on the room bill. It was almost two o' clock.

♪ ♪ ♪

Paul sat at a table, the shadow of a yellow umbrella darkening his face. He was dressed much the same way he had been the day before, in jeans and, this time, a dark green shirt over a white tee shirt.

"Good afternoon," I said sitting down with him.

"Good afternoon, Grace," he answered. "Good day for climbing a mountain."

"Are we actually going to climb it?"

"No, not actually. We'll be taking the 8,516 foot aerial tram," he said, handing me a brochure that said "8,516 Foot Aerial Tram." Once again, I noticed his particular way of speaking. He moved and gestured little, as if giving every word his full attention.

"What did you bring with you?" he said, pointing to my large shoulder bag. "Is that our lunch?"

"No. I have my camera, a map, my notebook, bug spray, a harmonica, band-aids, a sweater. Things you need on a hike."

"Thank God we're prepared."

"If we need anything else, I'm sure we can get it up there."

"I'm just bringing myself. And you," he said, looking into my eyes.

I sighed, inside. Outside, I looked away towards the mountains. "Are we ready to go?"

"Ready," he said.

We walked through the hotel lobby together. Our first step was to stop by the Courtesy Desk for directions. I wore my sunglasses into the hotel, a scarf wrapped over my chin and a straw hat with the brim pulled down low, just in case I ran into anyone familiar. Paul was discreet enough not to ask why I looked like a burn victim.

Soon we were sitting in Paul's car, a Chevy Cavaliere that the producer had rented for him. Across my lap, I spread a map of the area. Wendy at the Courtesy Desk had outlined a route for us in yellow highlighter. We began by winding down the long driveway of the California Club, before joining the highways of Palm Springs.

"This is Palm Springs?" I asked, eyeing the panorama of fast food joints, patio furniture outlets, pet centers and mobile home parks.

"This is Highway 111, the commercial part."

"So where is the famous part? The posh part?"

"That's over towards there," he said, pointing past me to the right. "We can go back that way. This is the original Palm Springs."

I admit I was a little disappointed at first, but then I wouldn't have gotten to see places like "Bowl 'n' TV," the "Rio Grande Drape Center," "Yucca Bowl Barbecue," and "The Lamp Ranch." This was the American part of town.

"Look at that. 'Covers for Lovers'. That could be a song," I said as we passed another broken-down shopping center. The buildings were all styled in the architecture of Palm Spring's original heyday, the fifties. The modern shops that once thrived here had long ago turned into second hand stores, social service organizations, and strange churches, like "The Church of Mental Physics." It appeared as if time had stopped in 1955. Downtown Palm Springs was a motionless strip of barely stocked shops where the inventory was older than the patrons, and that was old.

Paul said in the summer it was too hot to go out at all, but at this time of year you could see people strolling around. I saw two pedestrians in half an hour, but by California standards that might be considered a crowd.

We followed the route indicated on our map, moving slowly through local traffic. We talked and commented on the scenery.

From the passenger seat, I could take a good look at Paul. It was just like my fantasy of the day before, only the car wasn't a convertible. His cheeks were lit by the bright sun pouring through the window. He squinted a little. Sometimes Paul looked over at me and I felt a lazy wave of desire run through me.

After twenty minutes we came to a billboard with the words "Turn here for the Palm Springs Aerial Tramway" written in swinging script. A big arrow pointed to a small turn-off.

The scenery changed instantly, from tattered commercial zone to moon landscape. We found ourselves driving through hills of boulders with not a living thing in sight, not even a weed; just huge rock piles rising steeply from the earth. The sun burned directly overhead and we wove between the boulders on an incline that took us higher and higher. It was a spooky place and I had never been anywhere so devoid of living things, unless you count the time we played The Knife and Fork Pub on the Jersey shore in January.

After a few minutes, we arrived at a parking lot where eight or ten cars and a couple of buses were parked at scary angles. A sign welcomed us to the base lodge of the Aerial Tram. We pulled into a spot and I reminded Paul to use the emergency brake.

The Aerial Tram is a major stop on the tourist trail in this part of California. The base, called the "Valley Station," is a log cabin lodge, and it offers a variety of activities to keep waiting tourists occupied. Most of the attractions were closed. A velvet rope hung across the doorway to The Tramway Restaurant, with a sign that said, "Closed for Renovation."

Almost everyone in the waiting room of the Aerial Tram seemed to know each other. I looked out the window and figured they all belonged to the two big buses that said "Minnesota on Wheels." The tourists hollered and joked as if they were having the time of their lives. But in spite of them, I felt as if we were somewhere terribly remote, like an outpost in Alaska or the Yukon. The waiting room was rustic and bare, and this single room served as ticket window, gift shop and tram museum. It was all supervised by a woman who looked as old as the mountains themselves.

We looked at a wall of black and white photos of workers toiling on the mountainside, colored geology charts, and a display of local flora done in the style of a junior high school bulletin board. After studying a few fir leaves glued to construction paper, we sat on a bench by a row of windows.

"Look at that," said Paul. He put his hands on my shoulder and directed my view out the window. A giant cable car flew down the mountain swinging towards us between huge pine trees. It dangled from steel ropes. I watched it grow in size as it moved towards us.

The members of the tour group, all fit-looking middle age couples, were laughing loudly. Someone yelled, "Hey Jerry, how'd they get your picture here?" pointing to a picture of a rattlesnake on the bulletin board. The tourists roared. But when the cable car pulled up to a cement platform outside the waiting room, there was silence as everyone realized the seriousness of our situation. We were about to be suspended in a glass box thousands of feet above the earth, attached to life by a few steel cables. We crammed into the car, and I only hoped these were not the people I was going to die with. The machine lurched forward with unexpected speed and everyone said "oh" at the same time.

We rode over steep rock ravines and the desert below spread into a huge plain. We had the distinct sense of leaving one land and entering another; the world beneath us was gold and flat as far as the eye could see, the world ahead craggy and shaded, carved out of stony gray cliffs and hidden by layers of dark green pine trees. I was impressed by how inaccessible our destination was. We sailed upwards between walls of sheer rock, in an alley that had been blown into the mountain forty years earlier.

I stood by a window. Paul and I had gotten separated in the rush of fellow travelers all looking for a spot with a view. I strained to see where he had ended up and found him between a pair of tall men in v-neck sweaters. I smiled, and he smiled back. There were moments during the day, like this one, when, awkward and unsure, I realized I didn't know this man. What was I doing here? As I looked down into an eight thousand foot valley, I reminded myself that we were here to have fun.

𐤉 𐤉 𐤉

We stepped off the tram and moved with the crowd into what looked like an old ski lodge. Here I found Paul again.

"Hi. Are you all right?" he said.

"I'm fine. I thought I lost you on the way up."

"No, I'm right here. Ready to explore?"

We walked through the lodge, past aging maps and photographs. There were old plaques commemorating some forgotten dignitary's visit, a dusty pair of antlers, a totem pole, a letter from an ex-president, a menu from a restaurant now gone; I had a feeling that I often had in California—that a place had been abandoned for something more promising, with everything left perfectly intact. It was as if we had gone back in time.

"This looks like the kind of place where the guy from your film—the grandfather—would feel at home," I said to Paul.

"That's true. I'll bet he was here."

Our eyes adjusted to the darkness, but our gaze was drawn to a huge glowing window at the front of the lodge. Outside, the world was covered with snow.

"Look at that," I said, rushing to the window.

Paul was already by the door. "This way," he said.

The air was still and cold. In front of us stretched deep woods speckled with sunlight and snow.

"Breathe," said Paul.

I breathed. "It's so beautiful. So perfect." The air was fresh and chilled, like a sunny day in February. We were so high, the snow never melted here. I put on my sweater. A wooden staircase led from the deck outside the lodge to the ground, where one could follow a sidewalk past picnic tables into the woods. It was as if no one had ever been here before, though our friends from the cable car were already dotting the brown and white floor of the forest with their colorful presence.

We walked over the snow that stretched evenly in bright patches between large flat rocks. The trees stood far apart, making the forest feel airy and bright. We tread on a muddy path, towards a wooden trail guide. Here the path forked in three directions.

Paul pointed to a long blue line on the trail guide that corkscrewed up the mountain. "Here's a five mile trail."

In the snow was a sign that pointed to the left, painted with the words, "Two Mile Trail." "What about this?" I said.

"That looks fine to me. Let's start with that. I can get lost just as well in two miles as I can in five," said Paul.

"Do you plan on getting lost?"

"The moment the lodge is out of sight."

"You're not a woods person, are you?" I asked as we started down a small path in the snow, lined by a wooden rail.

He looked ahead of himself, considering the sunlit woods in front of us, as if he wouldn't mind being lost at all.

"No, I'm not," he said. "I like the beach. Maybe it's because I grew up in LA not far from the ocean."

"Really? I would have thought you were from the midwest. You're not the way I pictured a typical Californian."

"I am. The people you think of as typical Californians are not necessarily the ones you meet every day. Most people are just average. Isn't that true for New Yorkers?"

"I guess so, although not in my neighborhood. People generally live up to the stereotype. Usually they're beyond it."

"You don't seem like a stereotype. You seem different."

"I am. In New York, being different is just another type."

Our path cut to the left across a rocky glade, curving around slender trees. We stepped across the muddy patches where snow had melted, crushed by other outdoorsy Americans. Our companions from the cable car were nowhere in sight now. They hadn't ventured past the picnic tables. We were almost completely alone in the forest. Now and then a cross-country skier in a bright ski-suit appeared from behind a tree, then zipped away to another part of the forest. The smooth marks of their skis criss-crossed the ground.

We walked side by side with plenty of room between us, making the most of our 13,000 acres. We pointed out fallen trees, bird's nests, and tracks in the snow. The sun fell in patterns at our feet.

Alone like this, I felt comfortable with Paul; we were sharing a hidden part of the world. I think Paul felt it too. Now and then he would say, for no particular reason, "I'm glad we're here," and then look at me as if he had just made a confession. But other than this, he remained distant and polite.

"So where do you live in L.A.?" I asked him, after we had lost the trail of a deer we had been following.

"I have a small place up in one of the canyons."

"A canyon. That's exciting."

"I love it. It's in a pretty remote part of Laurel Canyon. It's very private, with lots of trees and wildflowers growing everywhere. How about you?"

"I have a small one bedroom apartment downtown. The building is beat up, but the apartment is all right. I have too many musical instruments taking up space."

"What do you play?"

"Guitar. I also play the piano. But I don't have one. It would never fit in my apartment."

"Sounds fun. Very New York."

"It's a little tight."

"It's amazing the way people in New York compress everything into a little space. I'd like to see it sometime," he said, looking at me. Did he want an invitation? I didn't say anything. Why get too personal? Here I was, a long cable car ride away from the earth, alone with him. I meditated on the taut line of his jaw and how it was cut by a single wrinkle on each side of his mouth. Wasn't that personal enough?

"Do you think your boyfriend minds your coming up here with me?" Paul asked, getting even more personal.

"How do you know I'm here with my boyfriend?"

"It's obvious," he laughed. "You said you were here with a friend, but you didn't mention the friend again. You're discreet. Besides, this hotel costs about $350 a night, not in the budget of a struggling songwriter."

"You're right, it is my boyfriend, and no, I didn't tell him I was coming up here with you."

"Would he mind?" I looked over at Paul and my eyes met his clear green eyes.

"I don't know. I don't want to complicate things and find out," I said, stepping over some branches. "I don't have to account to him for everything I do," I added. "I felt like coming up here, and that's that."

"I'm sorry. I didn't mean to imply you shouldn't be free to do what you want to do. I admire your independance. Lots of women aren't like you."

"Lots of men aren't so free either," I said, thinking of Roger and his love of plans. I didn't like these questions. Why did I have to think about Roger now anyway?

"Want to sit down for a while?" said Paul. I followed him onto a wide boulder that sloped upwards from the snow at a comfortable angle. Gold light poured over the rock unobstructed by the treetops. We sat down side by side. The natural curve in the rock tilted us back and we looked up at the sky.

"What about you?" I said. "You obviously do what you want." I hesitated. "Are you married?"

He laughed. "No. I'm not."

We sat quietly for a few moments. "Sorry I ask so many questions," said Paul. He stretched on his side facing me, taking a moment to rearrange his ribs on the hard surface of the boulder. "I'm glad you decided to come with me today."

He looked so young for a moment, my tension dissolved. I felt like a kid. Then, he reached over and slowly touched my lips with his fingertips.

He stayed reclined on the rock and let his fingers move over my lips lazily, as if he were absorbing me. The air was chilly and he put his hand on my cheek.

"You're cold," he said. "Maybe we should go."

He stood up, then helped me up. But standing on the rock, we didn't move apart. It seemed natural, instead, to lean forward and put our arms around each other. I felt his warmth, and it felt good in the chilly air. His kiss was also warm. We leaned into each other, feeling the world spin around us as if the rock we stood on were at the center of everything.

I closed my eyes. When I opened them I felt as if I were in a soft dream. Long shadows stretched over the ground like dark thread laid down between the trees. There was yellow in the sky. The woods were quiet. It was late afternoon. I held Paul's arms to stay balanced on the rock.

"What time is it?" I asked, suddenly alert. I remembered Roger's cocktail party at six.

"It's five 'o clock," he whispered.

"Oh no," I cried, nearly falling off the rock. "I'm late." I would never be back by six. Roger had asked me not to be late. Paul made a stab at looking concerned, but I sensed he was too absorbed in the moment to really care about my cocktail party.

"Where do you have to be?" he asked, not letting go of my arm.

"I'm supposed to be back at the hotel by six," I said, feeling like part of me didn't care that much either. "We should rush." I took his hand and stepped off the rock.

We walked the remaining quarter of a mile back to the cable car, then had to wait fifteen minutes for the next car down. We leaned against a tree and I leaned against Paul, who put his arms around me as the sun went behind the hill and the air turned colder.

ᴎ ᴎ ᴎ

It's easy to be carefree on top of a mountain. But the closer we came to the ground, the less magical it all seemed. At two thousand feet above sea level, just about the time the fellow at the tram controls was pointing out the general direction of Mexico, I started to panic. The snowy forest where we had recently rollicked seemed about as distant to me as Central Park. Did we imagine it? The air was hot once again, and the plains of the desert stretched out in front of us, vast and golden in the hot dusk. It seemed to extend forever in every direction, like a dry yellow planet.

It was five-thirty. Just about now, Roger would be standing in front of the mirror, carefully attaching the gold cufflinks made of his grandfather's Knights of Malta pin. He was probably studying his reflection, tall and neat in a white shirt and tuxedo pants.

My dress would be hanging in the closet without me in it. I could picture Roger methodically assembling himself, not even bothering to look towards the door. He was pretending I would walk in any minute.

"You're thinking about your boyfriend."

"How can you tell?"

"You're face is changing. You look troubled."

"He hates it when I'm late."

"I'll get you back fast," said Paul, as we sailed towards earth.

By the time we got back to the parking lot, most of the cars were gone, although there were as many rocks and boulders as I remembered.

"This is not good," I said, as we rushed down the steep incline towards the car. Paul unlocked the doors and hot air poured out.

"You'll only be a little late," he said as we held our breath and climbed inside the car. "Maybe fifteen minutes."

"You think so? Even though it's rush hour?"

"I know a short cut back."

"You do? How?"

"This is my neck of the woods, remember? I live in L.A. and I come out here pretty often." He started the car and then shifted and twisted the wheel with confidence. He swung the car out of the lot and we shot down the winding road that had delivered us here earlier.

"Relax, Grace," said Paul as we slid through the now shadowy hills. He looked over at me and smiled. The road soon released us back onto the flat streets of Palm Springs. I sat quietly in the seat, mentally urging us forward.

I was right about the traffic. Cars, shiny, bright and hot like toaster ovens on wheels, slowly trailed each other over the bleached pavement. The sun burned low in the sky, blinding us with its light. We inched forward.

"Okay, tell me about the shortcut," I said. "What's the plan?"

"The plan is we head for the interstate. It runs parallel to the road we came out on, but people don't use it for local travel. We bypass Cathedral City and Palm Springs. Our hotel is in the next town after Palm Springs."

"And we're back at the hotel fast," I added.

"Exactly. We have you back a few minutes after six," said Paul as he directed the car onto the road that would lead us to the interstate.

ﻻ ﻻ ﻻ

I would have been back by six, too. I don't know what made me
insist we get off at the exit for Desert Hot Springs. Paul told me
this was not the way back to the hotel, but I was sure that was the
name of our exit. I let my intuition guide me. It didn't guide me
too well; it was only on a dusty road about five miles past "The
Hootenanny Inn," I realized I had made a mistake and we were completely lost.

"I was positive that was the exit," I said.

"We're staying in Palm Desert Springs, not Desert Hot
Springs."

"How was I supposed to know everything around here has the
same name? Who could tell these places apart? Palm Desert, Desert
Palms, Desert Hot Spring, Spring Desert Palm, can't they think of
different names for things? Why don't they give towns numbers if
they can't think of names?" I was starting to rave. We had been
driving on a flat two lane road for twenty minutes, searching for the
highway again. No one, not the cashier in Junior's Liquor Mart nor
the deaf mute at the auto body shop, could tell us how to get back
to our hotel. There was nothing but rocks and an odd trailer as far
as the eye could see. I was pretty sure that every twist of the road
was taking us farther away from the California Club.

"I told you it was the wrong exit," said Paul, his eyes on the
road ahead.

"So why did you listen to me?"

"You sounded pretty sure of yourself. I thought you knew
something I didn't."

"Why would I know something you didn't? I don't even know
where I am," I said, slumping back in the seat.

"Then stop acting like you know what you're talking about
when you don't. I don't know why you told me to get off in the first
place."

"I was anxious."

It was a friendly fight and it kept us going until we arrived at
the actual town of Desert Hot Springs, whose name had lured us
off the interstate in the first place. Our plan was to find someone
who could point us in the right direction.

Desert Hot Springs is the kind of place I thought you could
only get to by time travel. Single story buildings, each one set at
least fifty feet from the next, line the one big main street. Behind
these buildings, both on the left and the right side of the street,
there is nothing right to the horizon. The place conveys a singular feeling of indifference, as if someone had randomly dropped
down the pieces of a play village and then lost interest.

The wide empty avenue stretched pointlessly onwards, with stop lights at the end of each long block, though no one was coming or going. The main street arched upwards slightly, giving us the feeling of being suspended in air. We passed an empty Grand Hotel and a Robertson's Department store; all deserted, if not boarded up. The red sky and distant blue-gray mountains loomed behind everything, silently making a joke of whatever impression the town did manage to make.

Maybe I was in a bad mood, but this was exactly the last place on earth I wanted to be.

"Where are we?" I moaned.

"Desert Hot Springs."

"But why? Why here?"

"Because we're even more lost than we thought."

"Look, all the motel signs say 'Natural Hot Springs'," I said, momentarily distracted by the local sights.

"I think this place was popular before they started building in Palm Springs." Big neon signs swept towards the sky, all advertising vacancies in looping script. I pointed out an oval shaped diner and a beauty salon in the shape of a pagoda.

We pulled into a gas station. A tall weather-beaten man strolled out to our car and peeked inside. We repeated our list of familiar locations—The California Club, Country Club Road—but nothing stirred his memory. He just smiled, and asked us whether we wanted him to look under our hood. We said no. The best he could do was give us a set of instructions that would take us back to the interstate. Apparently, we were on the wrong side of the highway and we needed to get back to it before we could even begin to look for our hotel.

♩ ♩ ♩

"I guess when he said, 'Turn left at Utah' he meant the road and not the state," I remarked, as the abandoned resort town faded away behind us. It was 6:30 now. We were driving directly into the still setting sun. Perhaps it was the nature of the terrain here, but everything reflected light and the sun never seemed to set. Though barely above the horizon, the sun still burned through the window, blinding Paul. He had no choice but to drive slowly and now and then he veered off onto the dirt on the side of the road.

This was the final insult. I had already gone through all the phases one can go through when impossibly late; desperation, denial, anger. Now, thanks to the fact that we didn't dare go faster than twenty-five miles an hour, I was entering the hopeless stage. I pondered the fact that the man at my side was a completely different man from the one I was supposed to be with at this very moment. He was a nice man, but the wrong one all the same.

Of course, he might be the right man at some other time and place, I thought to myself. The sun visor shed a strip of deep brown shadow across his red face. He had the beginnings of a beard. There was a relaxed friendliness about him now, as if he were not shy so much as quiet and comfortable.

We were getting giddy and found increasingly silly ways to pass the time. We had just finished a game where we named things that live in the desert. After naming four things, we agreed we were ignorant about natural life in this part of the world. Paul asked me where I was originally from and I told him I was from North Gaylordsville in upstate New York. I described it to him as we traveled across shadeless plains. We passed a few houses which all had satellite dishes. I told Paul about the houses of my town, close to each other on small streets, with overgrown trees that broke through the sidewalk. I thought of New York City, crowded with strangers living yards apart from each other. Here, the houses were barely in sight of each other.

Every road seemed to end in a T-shaped intersection with both sides of the road disappearing infinitely into the desert. All the roads seemed to be called Indian Road.

I was just starting to sing my high school anthem when we came to a stop sign. "Stop at the intersection," I ordered, realizing we were as lost as ever and might never find our way back if we didn't take action. It would be dark soon. "I'm getting out and stopping a car. Someone has to know where we are."

Paul didn't argue. He pulled over. I climbed out.

A moment later a red pick-up truck pulled up to the stop sign. At the wheel was a man who appeared to be about nineteen, with short blond hair and a navy blue tee-shirt. He looked at me in wonder as I flagged him down with a Chinese fan I had bought on Canal Street for a dollar.

"Excuse me, but do you know where the California Club is?" I asked. I might as well have asked him for our longitude and latitude. He looked at me.

"No ma'am, I'm sorry," he answered.

"How about Country Club Road?"

"No, sorry, ma'am."

"Palm Desert?"

"Somewhere near Palm Springs."

Suddenly my memory snapped into action. I remembered the peculiar names of Palm Springs Streets. Surely one of these would sound familiar to him.

"Gerald Ford Drive? Frank Sinatra Street? Bob Hope Drive?"

"Sure. Bob Hope Drive—that's an exit off the interstate."

"The interstate?" He had said the magic words. "How do we get there?"

"Just go straight down this road here," he said, pointing out the window of his truck at the road behind him. "You'll come to Indian Road. Make a right. That'll take you back to the interstate. Make a left onto the highway heading east, and go for about ten miles. You'll see an exit sign for Bob Hope Drive."

I thanked him. He drove off.

"He told me how to get to the interstate!" I cried joyfully as I climbed back into the car. How little it took to lift our spirits. I was nearly overcome with happiness when I spotted the familiar Hootenanny Inn. Soon we were passing the same now-welcome sights we had passed on the way out, Junior's Liquor Mart, Mr. Meat, Jimmy's Targetland. In no time we were back on the highway.

We sped towards the hotel, singing and sighing and laughing as if we had just returned from a foreign war. Within twenty-five minutes, we were sailing up the long driveway of the California club, past the lush, floodlit lawns and fountains.

"I have never been so happy to be somewhere I can't stand," said Paul.

"Home, safe. It's a dangerous world out there."

"Indeed it is."

"And I'm only an hour late." It was seven o' clock. "I'll say farewell now, because my boyfriend is going to kill me."

"Don't let him do that," said Paul, looking at me. We pulled into a spot in the lower parking lot. In front of us was a big pond with flamingos milling around the edges.

"I'm really more upset than I seem," I said, gathering my things and collecting the soda cans that had accumulated on the floor. "If he finds out I was with you..." I felt a little embarrassed. Without thinking, I suggested that Paul and I had something to hide.

Paul turned off the engine and we sat for a moment in the dark, with the lights off. "Leave that stuff," he ordered. "You go ahead. I'll stay here for a little while."

"Thanks."

"I had a great day. I feel like I've been gone for weeks. You're fun to get lost with." He put his hand on my shoulders.

"I enjoyed it too. Thank you." I moved closer.

"So. Tomorrow morning on the terrace?"

"You want to meet?"

"Yes. You're going back tomorrow aren't you?"

"Tomorrow after lunch."

"I'd like to say good-bye."

I was quiet for a moment. "I'll meet you there at eleven," I said.

He leaned towards me and kissed me. Then, I picked up my bag, whispered good-bye, and hopped out of the car. I ran fast towards the main entrance of the hotel.

י י י

I flew past the doormen, who for some unaccountable reason were dressed in Bedouin costumes, and ran into the hotel lobby. It bustled with cocktail hour activity. A crowd of guests lounged near a white piano by an indoor waterfall—older men in blue and green sport jackets and women in summery two-piece outfits, usually with a flower attached somewhere around their breasts. I rushed by them all, noting as I passed the distinctly polka-like feel the piano player was giving to his version of "Every Breath You Take." I would have to stop by later to hear more.

I hurried upstairs, my sneakers pounding quietly against the orange plush carpeting, and let myself into the room, out of breath. All was silent. Roger was gone.

Not permanently, of course, just downstairs to the Lincoln Room, as I learned when I found his note on the marble counter in the bathroom, held in place by a tiny complementary container of baby powder. 'I'm in the Lincoln Room,' said the note, with a simple 'R' tersely confirming the note was his.

This news was both bad and good. The fact that he had left a note addressed to no one in particular, was bad. However, the fact that I got a note at all was good, since it meant Roger wanted me to join him. I was not totally lost.

I jumped in the shower and then quickly slipped on the black dress I had purchased especially for Roger's special events. I combined stages whenever possible, putting on jewelry while I dried my hair. It wasn't easy, but I was soon dressed and ready to go. I held my shoes in my hand and ran down the hall as fast as I could, surprising a night maid who had been peacefully wheeling a towel cart down the hall.

I put my shoes on just as the elevator's chimes announced its arrival.

❧ ❧ ❧

The unctuous concierge, the psychotic elevator attendant, the evil gift shop owner, the big blonde from the South at the Courtesy Desk; hotels are all the same, wherever you go. Not that I've enjoyed such fine hotels on any of my road trips with Swan Venom, with the exception of the week we opened for Glare on their New England tour. It was one of the happiest weeks of my life. Usually, Swan Venom is relegated to the ground floor of a cheap motel, with an occasional night at a Ramada Inn when the price is right.

Nicky Joel, the booking agent who sometimes finds us gigs out of town, always says, "You're lucky you don't sleep in your car like we did in my day." I guess it's true, except for the time the motel in Poughkeepsie caught fire. Then the car would have been a very good place to be.

No, my knowledge of good hotels has come about primarily through my now jeopardized relationship with Roger. We've traveled together several times, once to a wedding in Cleveland and many times just for the fun of it. My flexible schedule allows me to join Roger on these weekend trips. He's flexible enough to pay for them.

Roger likes luxury. I've told him we don't need to stay at such fancy places, but Roger says he's paid his dues and now wants to live comfortably. We don't talk about what my dues have bought us, but I don't think they've earned the mints on the pillow yet. I tell Roger those are from his dues.

My dues have earned me the right to sit in with the hotel band, and this makes Roger simultaneously proud and a little jealous.

I could see that The California Club wasn't the kind of place where I would be making much music. The easygoing California style of the lobby, with its interior waterfall and white grand piano, gave way to grand European style in the east wing of the hotel. I walked under frescoed ceilings, decorated with pale pastels and trimmed in gold, down a wide promenade. There would be no jamming here.

Rich and ornate carpets covered the floor, in elegant oriental colors like slate blue, plum and deep yellow. At intervals along the hall, glass showcases displayed African masks and statues. The works of art were poised with care, suggesting that each piece was hand-picked by some eccentric hotelier who had been a mercenary before settling down in the hotel business. In reality, the hotel was a public company owned by thousands of faceless shareholders, but the company's strategy was to give each of their prize hotels a unique and personal touch. Roger explained this to me last night, after he attended a seminar called "Hard Times in the Hotel Industry."

I enjoyed the display as much as I could while trotting down the massive hallway in high heels. I wasn't sure whether the ballrooms were named after presidents or money; I passed The Franklin Room, The Madison Ballroom, and The Washington Suite. The rooms were all occupied, and bands of insurance salesman and opthamologists traveled the hall with me, looking for their own ballrooms.

As distracted as I was by the problem at hand, I admit I had not completely put my afternoon with Paul Teagarden totally out of my mind. On the contrary, the nervous energy which now propelled me towards the Lincoln room was more the result of my afternoon with Paul, and the prospect that I might run into him again right here in the hotel, than it was from my fear of Roger's temper. I was thinking about Paul, not in any specific way, but in unclear and exciting images that slowly came into focus like Polaroid snapshots. Paul and me on a rock. Paul's arms slipping around me, his hands warm. Paul and me pulling into the parking lot of Mr. Meat to ask directions. Us, above the desert looking down.

I felt guilty about these little snapshots. On the other hand, they would make it much easier to be truly wretched and humble when the time came to apologize to Roger. At exactly 7:25 I pushed open the ten foot doors to the Lincoln Room and stepped into a sea of black ties and gray heads.

ℽ ℽ ℽ

"Grace, you made it," said Roger. He squeezed me on the shoulder like I was an old teammate. It was a bad sign. It meant Roger was feeling formal.

He had probably been here about forty-five minutes. The party was in full swing. He held a vodka drink in his hand. He was talking to a short man with glasses.

I decided to start right off by groveling. Introductions could wait.

"I am really sorry I'm late," I said quickly.

"We'll talk about it later," said Roger, not meeting my gaze. "I'd like you to meet Jerry Offenbach," he said, indicating the man by his side.

"Jerry," said the man, extending a plump hand to me with a thick ring on his pinkie.

"Grace," I answered. "Sorry I'm late."

"Jerry is an old friend from Roland and Lussingi," said Roger.

Jerry stood just close enough so that my eyes met his forehead. "Roger tells me you're a musician," he said, grinning. "I play a little guitar myself."

It was difficult to jump full steam into a polite conversation, but no one seemed to want to listen to my apologies. I moved ahead.

"Really? Do you play in a band?"

"Yes, just for fun. I play with a few other guys in my firm, you know how it is."

"Sure. You do songs like 'Money,' things like that."

"You got it," said Jerry, pointing his cocktail at my chest.

"Jerry lives only two blocks from me in the city," Roger remarked.

"That's right. Roge and I are both city boys, " Jerry said, leaving half of Roger's name off in friendship. Jerry didn't look like much of a boy to me, but as long as he kept "Roge" occupied, he was all right.

Jerry made a few more excited remarks about the Rickenbacker he played, then swiveled towards Roger. "What did you think about Horton's tirade about the Fed?"

"Fascinating," said Roger. This meant my part in the conversation was officially over. People were here to talk business, and introductions and pleasantries were kept to a minimum. Those who couldn't contribute were expected to stand by silently or else stay in the spa. I did the former, tilting my head in a way that suggested I was captivated by the conversation.

Dick from United Republic Resources joined the conversation and soon he and Jerry spun off together on a subset of the main topic, while Roger found himself engaged with Dick from Rilroth, LeTrege, and Klieg. The conversation then split again, like two cells splitting into four, and then four into eight; in this way Roger and I moved slowly around the room.

Now and then someone would take me for a financial professional and ask me where I thought interest rates were going. I always tried to answer as best I could. But the person would soon realize I didn't know what I was talking about and he or she would smile, a glazed expression on his or her face, and I might as well have been talking about modal linkage.

Whenever I had the chance, I tried to make contact with Roger and let him know I realized I screwed up. I apologized frequently, at the bar, between hour's d'oeuvres, by the bandstand, but all Roger would say was, "Not now, Grace, we'll talk later." He obviously wanted to avoid the subject and preferred to concentrate on work. He only said one personal thing all evening. "You really fucked up," he intoned, giving me a pretty good idea of how he really felt.

I like watching Roger in action. He's very smooth. He projects security and ease, and this attracts people. Since Roger was an outsider, people were especially interested in his opinion; this group looked for direction wherever they could get it. Everyone had one mission and that was to beat the competition to the next deal. Anyone could see behind the handshakes, name cards, and ribbons, the instincts of starving sharks were at work.

In fact, by this time next year half this crowd would be serving the salmon finger sandwiches instead of picking them off the trays, while the other half would be shopping for houses in Aspen or the Hamptons. I could feel the tension and it made me glad I had never gotten used to so much luxury that I couldn't afford to lose what little I had. This thought made me feel more relaxed, and I became less shy about sharing my opinion when solicited. In fact, I was in the middle of explaining to two bankers from Kansas City that the hard times in their recently merged banks were their own doing, and they had no business extending credit to so many fly-by-nights around the world, when Roger told me it was time to go.

❧ ❧ ❧

He walked quietly next to me down the wide carpeted hallway, his hands in the pockets of his tuxedo pants. He seemed preoccupied and didn't even look at me. In his fancy dress and black bow tie with little red dots, Roger looked like a sad Armani model.

We made small talk about the cocktail party until we came to some glass doors that led onto a terrace. "Let's take a walk," he said. We went through the doors and found ourselves on a wide patio that extended from the hotel. Far off in front of us we could see the distant lights of town and beyond that, the glow of the airport. The hills around us were dotted with villas and condos.

The darkness came as a shock after all the activity inside the hotel. Fuschia, green and blue outdoor lamps glowed among the shrubs, lighting up the grass and palms trees. A boat drifted quietly across the lagoon, carrying guests to the Italian restaurant.

"It's just like Venice," I joked. I wanted Roger to talk.

"Grace, what am I going to do about you?"

"What do you mean, 'what are you going to do about me?' What am I, some kind of problem?"

"When you show up hours late for something important you are." I didn't say anything. I continued to stand with my face towards the night, watching the boat on the lagoon. "Help me out here," Roger continued. "I'm really at a loss."

I turned to him. "What do you want me to say? I know you're mad. I also know 'I'm sorry' isn't good enough, right?"

Roger looked pained. "That's right. It's not good enough. I'm so pissed off at you. I asked you for something very simple. Be back at the hotel by six. That was too much for you." Roger doesn't raise his voice when he's angry or lose control; he just reasons. The inevitability of his logic makes me feel as if I broke some cosmic laws.

"I told you I got lost on the highway coming back from Palm Springs."

"So why didn't you leave earlier?"

"I didn't plan on getting lost."

"I don't plan on getting lost," Roger replied intensely, "and I don't. So why are you always getting lost and screwing up?"

"I don't know, that's just how I am, why are you always complaining about waiters?"

"Oh please, Grace, I'm not the problem here. The problem is I can't trust you."

How could I argue with him? And he didn't even know the whole story. Roger was right, there was no way around it.

"You can't trust me," I said. It was all I could think of saying.

This only seemed to make Roger more frustrated and his irritation poured from him. "It's always the same thing," he said angrily, "You have to be late, whether I'm meeting you at the Golden Pear or the airport or anywhere. Why can't you make more of an effort, for me, just because I ask you to? It's not so much being late that's the problem, it's that I've told you how much it bothers me, and you don't seem to care."

I could see now this was about much more than being late. "I don't do this to hurt you. Maybe you've just come up against one of my limitations. There are some things I can't change no matter how hard I try. Maybe it's just one of those things I can never completely control."

"That's an excuse. I don't believe it, Grace. You have amazing will power when you want to."

"Then maybe I don't want to change."

"Maybe you're doing it on purpose."

I turned to him. "You think I'm late to spite you or something?"

"I don't know what's behind it Grace, I'm just telling you I'm sick of it." We were getting to the heart of the problem. In Roger's mind, I was late on purpose. I was late because I didn't care.

It was just like him to think that everything can be controlled, that I was late on purpose, that it was an act of will.

On the other hand, maybe I didn't care.

I felt the breeze gently blow my hair and dress. "I was just plain late, and I'm sorry, Roger. Can't you just accept that?"

"Maybe I can't. This really bothers me." He looked away and I felt I had hurt him somehow. I even had the feeling that somewhere inside him, he knew I had spent the day with someone else. I stood next to him and looked at his face. He looked away. Roger didn't deserve to feel sad. I felt sorry I had caused him to feel this way.

"I'm going to take a walk," he said. "I'll see you back at the room."

ใ ใ ใ

Roger had left his tee-shirt draped over the back of a chair. It was one I had given him. It said, "Glare: The Double Vision Tour." On the bed was Roger's folded bathing suit and on top of it, a tube of sp35 suntan lotion. He must have gone to the pool this afternoon while I had been away. I sat in an armchair by the window. I was glad to be alone for a few minutes. Outside our room I could hear deep voices and bursts of laughter from conventioneers passing in the hall. Their voices faded and it was quiet again, until the phone rang. It must be Roger, I thought. I picked up the phone.

"Hi," said a voice. It was Paul Teagarden.

"Hi. I can't believe you're calling me here."

"Do you mind?"

I didn't say anything. I did mind slightly.

"I just had a feeling you were alone," he continued.

"You're right. How weird that you knew."

"Where's your friend?"

"I don't know. Walking around. He's furious at me for being late today."

"I got you in trouble. I'm sorry."

"No, it's my fault. I'm always doing things like this." I sat back in the armchair, letting my head fall against the back of the chair.

"Will he forgive you?"

"Usually he does. But maybe not this time. He's sick of it. And he should be."

"Don't be so hard on yourself."

"But he is right," I said angrily. "I was over an hour late for his party. He shouldn't forgive me." I wanted to regret spending the day with Paul.

"Well, I forgive you," he said softly. What a delivery. Even if the line meant nothing—Paul was in no position to forgive me for any-thing—he was very convincing.

"You? What can you forgive?"

"Nothing. But I don't want you to feel bad."

"Thanks," I said quietly. Paul was not exactly impartial. But talking to him reminded me today had been important. As much as I was attracted to Roger for the charm of our differences, so I was attracted to Paul for our sameness. He seemed to believe, like I did, that being late doesn't matter, as long as you show up.

ᵞ ᵞ ᵞ

Roger came in during the night and didn't say much. In the morn-ing, I woke up to find him preparing for the final hours of the conference. I tried to start a conversation. I asked Roger who was speaking today, and when we were going back to LA. His answers were terse. I even asked him whether he was still mad at me. "Yes," was all he said, and he picked up his five complementary newspa-pers and lost himself in breakfast.

I didn't worry about it too much. We had a long drive back to Los Angeles. Somewhere between here and LA we would have to work this out. How long could he go on without talking to me? At the very least, he would have to ask me to look at a map.

The room was silent except for the voice of an anchorman on the television. After breakfast, Roger packed, then dressed. The only thing he said before he left the room was "Be ready to leave at one o' clock. If you're not ready, I'm leaving without you." He shut the door with a slam. Then he came back again because he had forgot-ten his "Guest Speaker" badge. He left again.

ᵞ ᵞ ᵞ

At exactly eleven o' clock, I went downstairs to the Putter's Snackbox. I put on sunglasses and pushed my hair up underneath a big straw hat. Emulating the trim look that prevailed among spa-

goers, I donned black slacks and a green, short sleeve satin shirt
with a Japanese collar. I would have fit right in if it were 1962. I may
not have been incognito, but at least I looked snappy.

"Hey, how's it hangin'?" said Rick, seeing me at the entrance
to the terrace. Paul was not there yet, so Rick showed me to a table
on the terrace where I had a full view of the golf course below. I
ordered a cup of coffee and hid behind a copy of *Desert Life*.

Twenty minutes passed and there was no sign of Paul. Roger's
last meeting finished at eleven-thirty. I knew he would come
straight to the pool and look for me in order to ignore me some
more. I couldn't hang around much longer; the last thing I needed
was to have Roger spot me dining al fresco with another man.

I wasn't annoyed Paul was late. I, of all people, accept the ec-
centricities of time. Yet with every passing second I felt increasing
panic. I felt there was something important about seeing Paul before I left. I had to say good-bye. I couldn't say why I had such a
sense of urgency, but if the Putter's Snackbox were serving fortune
cookies that day, mine would have read "Your destiny will be transformed by the arrival of a stranger." That's how strongly I felt
about it.

Paul appeared in the doorway. I felt that same intoxicating mixture of attraction and surprise.

He put his hand over his forehead to shield his eyes from the
light, and he scanned the tables, looking for me. He saw me and
walked towards the table.

"Good morning," he said. "I'm sorry I'm late. I had my producer on the phone and I couldn't get him off."

"It's okay. I can't stay long, though."

"I can't either. I had to tell them to go to hell just to get a few
minutes with you now. I wanted to see you before you left."

"I'm glad."

Paul looked very good this morning. I looked in his eyes and he
looked back at me with peaceful intensity.

"Tell me, how are you today? Were you forgiven?"

"No."

"I really am sorry."

"It happens. We'll work it out on the way home."

"Listen, before I forget, I'm going to give you my number
in LA. Do you have some paper?" I pulled out my notebook and
turned to an empty page. "This is my number," he said as he
wrote, "If I'm not on a shoot, that's usually where I am. I also
have an office in town. I'll write both numbers for you. Will
you write down yours?"

"Yes," I said. I pulled a page out of my notebook, wrote my phone number and handed it to him. After that we sat quietly for a few moments. I played with the spoon in my coffee cup.

"I may be coming to New York in the next few months," said Paul.

"Really?"

"Yes. I have a meeting coming up. I'll give you a call if I do. I'd like to get together in New York."

"That would be great."

"I want to know more about you. About your music. I'll take you to dinner."

"I would like that." Time was running out. "I really enjoyed yesterday."

"I did too," he said quickly. "Very much. I'm glad we met."

"Paul, I'd better run now. I have to pack. We're leaving for LA soon. If I'm late again...."

"Right," he said. I folded the paper with his phone number and put it in my notebook. We both stood up. We shook hands.

"Bye, Paul," I said. I left first.

In the elevator, I pulled out the piece of paper where he had written his number and looked at it. I folded it in half and slipped it back into my notebook.

♪ ♪ ♪

The sun hung like a hot, red disk at the end of the highway. It burned through the windshield. On either side of us, bare hills stretched indefinitely, giving us the illusion if we turned off the highway we could drive forever.

I stared ahead. The minimalist scenery of California Highway 10 flew by. I felt as if the world were a projection around us, a thin film of bright reality. Looking out the car window, I pretended there was nothing beyond the dry hills; no resistance or change, just more desert. The sky was clear and light with no clouds. We were hours away from dusk, though it would be night by the time we got to LA.

Roger didn't say anything. The sunshade cast a shadow across his forehead, and beneath the dark stripe of shade, the sun blazed across his cheeks. Again it was like my fantasy, only instead of Paul here was Roger. He wore sunglasses and stared impassively ahead.

Roger was finding himself after days of being in a business mode. These events took a toll on him. It was as if he had been at a three day costume party and could now finally abandon the outfits.

Another day of Roger in a blazer and even I wouldn't have recognized him.

I didn't say anything. The quiet was good for us. I closed my eyes, comforted by the knowledge that whenever I opened them the landscape would be the same brownish dirt hills dotted with billboards. As we neared L.A. there would be more towns, more developments, more highways. But right now we were suspended between places at seventy miles per hour. We drove at a constant speed and I felt as if I were simultaneously flying and not moving at all. It was the kind of feeling you never get in New York except for those rare moments when, speeding down an avenue in a taxi in the middle of the night, you make all the lights. And even that wasn't close to the feeling I had now.

I felt free. It was as if everything I owned was right here in the car with us; I had my notebook and a suitcase full of clothes, as well as some souvenirs, including a pair of cable car earrings and a Palm Springs shot glass for my grandfather. We never had to go back to New York if we didn't want to. But in case we did, we had tickets on a flight to New York tomorrow at three.

I wouldn't have minded talking to Roger, but there was so much I couldn't tell him. And he didn't want to listen to me anyway. He was still mad. When I got home, there would be plenty of people to tell about my trip. I could tell Natalie or Ray. Even my neighbor, Mrs. Chu, would want to hear about my adventures.

I think I fell asleep because when I opened my eyes, the sun was down. Cars on the highway had their headlights on, and the dark sky was touched with gold and magenta on the horizon. Roger had taken off his sunglasses. He looked more like himself again. He saw me looking at him.

"Want to stop and get something to eat?" he asked.

"No. Let's wait until we get to Los Angeles. Is that okay with you?"

"That's fine. I know a few nice restaurants."

"We could even eat at the hotel."

No one said anything for a few minutes. Then Roger spoke.

"It's too bad we have to fight, isn't it?" he said.

"I don't know. It just happens sometimes."

"I guess so. We're so different, I guess it just has to happen."

"What do you mean?"

"You do things I wouldn't do."

That much was obvious. I hoped he didn't plan to start another big discussion. "That's part of what makes it fun, isn't it?"

"Sometimes." He was being mysterious today. It wasn't like him.

Neither of us said anything for a few minutes. Then I spoke. "So we're different. Does it bother you?"

"It bothers me when you do things that are so alien to me, like showing up hours late for a party. You can be incredibly selfish. But it doesn't bother me so much that I want to stop seeing you. At least not yet."

I got his drift. I could have let it upset me. I could have felt threatened, allowing Roger's remark to mean that he was planning an imminent break-up. In fact, I, Grace Note, could have gotten upset enough to get out of the car right then and there, and find some other means of transportation back to Los Angeles, where I would have gone directly to the airport to wait tearfully in an empty lounge all night, watching airport employees sweep and wax the floors, and early morning ground crews arrive for the day shift, feeling sorry for myself yet finding it all kind of fascinating. I could have done all that but I didn't. It may seem cold, but at that moment I didn't care.

I had two gigs with Swan Venom next week, a wedding date Saturday, two rehearsals, and a musical to write. I put my hand on Roger's leg. He put his hand on mine.

"I'm sorry," I said. "I was selfish."

"Let's forget it for now."

I squeezed his hand and he squeezed back. "Let's eat in the hotel," I said, turning on the car radio with my other hand.

"That's a good idea. I'm a little tired," he answered. And except for the phone number in my bag, it seemed as if everything had returned to the way it had been.

3

"I WOULD NEVER KNOW you were at a spa, from the way you look," said Natalie, puffing on a cigarette and blowing out smoke in a long stream. She posed on a stool in her kitchen as if she were waiting for someone to take her picture for a downtown magazine. She held her cigarette in one hand and a paper cup of coffee in the other, which she sipped languidly. Her long brown hair was pulled back in a tight ponytail.

"I don't do sun. You know that," I answered. I, Grace Note, inherited the fair complexion that runs in my mother's family. None of the Cherokee on my father's mother's side found its way to me. "I burn like a match."

"Did you at least get to relax?"

"Sort of."

"What do you mean, sort of?"

"Well, there was a lot going on."

"A lot going on? At a convention of bankers?"

"Not everyone there was a banker, Natalie."

"Grace, stop being so mysterious. Something happened. Now tell me what."

Water boiled in a kettle on the stove, and I poured myself a cup of Ylang Ylang tea, adding to the mystery.

"Grace, talk."

"I met a guy out there. I spent some time with him."

"Really?" said Natalie, her naturally bored look turning to curiosity for a moment. "Tell me about it."

I proceeded to give Natalie a detailed description of my vacation, exaggerating only when it came to how much time I spent working on our musical.

Natalie considered my story for a moment. Then she asked the only question one can possibly ask after hearing such a tale. "Do you think he'll call?"

"I think so. But I'm not going to worry about it." I just didn't have the time. Besides all our gigs and studio time, I wanted to spend every free moment working with Ray on our newest tune, "Walls of Forgiveness."

"Good for you. You're not getting caught up in some guy's problems," said Natalie.

"What problems?"

"Whatever his particular set of problems are," Natalie replied with authority.

"I don't know if he has problems or not. I'm saying I don't have the time to worry about it. Did I tell you we're playing at the Box Factory next Thursday?"

"That's great. Sheldon and Harvey just played there." She was talking about Bagg and Rhombus, or "The Shredders" as Ray calls them.

"Really? How was their show?" Natalie used to date Sheldon Bagg, but they broke up when he wrote a piece called "The Big Heat." It was a tribute to fire worship. She got tired of helping him rehearse and she especially hated the fires in her studio apartment. If Sheldon had been a mime, I think things might have lasted between them.

"They were very good," she said. "Perfect for the Box Factory. Depressing and funny at the same time. They even got reviewed in the *Downtown Moon*. I cut it out. Want to hear some of it?"

"Sure."

She picked up a blue note book and flipped through clippings that included reviews of all her friends' and lovers' various works. She began reading. "Here's what they say:

> 'Few acts plunder the playroom as they declaim high culture, but Bagg and Rhombus have spliced the cross-talk of the high and low into a narcotic evening of performance. Their piece, *Rabbit, the Morning*, is a breakwater whose waves wash over the audience with the salty, unpleasant flavor that is inevitable when truth meets calamity. The team retreads the classic theme of alienated man in search of *das Ding an sich*, stamping the piece with their trademark sentimentality and quenchless sense of mockery. For those looking to enter into an evening of great performance, the password is refulgence.'"

"Is that a good review?"

"I think so. Sheldon says it is."

"Good for them. I hope we get reviewed."

"I bet you will. Leave a message for one of the music reviewers at the *Moon* with an invitation to the gig."

"This is the first time we're playing the Box Factory. I want to blow them away. If they like us, it could be a steady gig." The Box, as it's called, is the place for new acts and alternative performers. Any day of the week you can see something incoherent and marvelous there. Critics love the place. We only got a date because Ray has been subbing in Styrene Dream, one of the Box Factory's regular bands. Ray talked the guy who books the place into giving us a date.

"I'll come down and see you," said Natalie. "Maybe I can even get Massimo to go."

"Massimo would actually come hear us? I thought he doesn't like us."

"He doesn't. But the Box Factory is near his gallery. I'll get him to meet me there. I won't tell him it's you. By the way, exactly how far did you get on the musical while you were in California?" said Natalie putting out her cigarette in a crystal ashtray.

"I worked on the bit that takes place during the Inquisition. I did it sitting by the pool. Nice, eh?"

"You worked by the pool? That's a waste of time."

"Why? I enjoyed it."

"How can you get anything done by a pool? You need stress to be creative. Everyone says so. I read an interview with Nick Hake and he said he got the idea for his best album when he was drunk and locked in the trunk of a Ford."

"That's ridiculous, and anyway, what do you know about stress?" Natalie lives in a loft that makes any normal apartment look like a slum. Massimo brought in a team of Italian builders to renovate every inch of their gigantic place. Ever since she's moved in with Massimo and his builders, Natalie has become an expert on creative ambiance, even though her apartment is about as much of a stress-free environment as you get in Manhattan. Her kitchen, done in white oak and finished with iron hardware imported from Portugal, is larger than my entire apartment. "Don't talk to me about stress, Natalie, you live in a private health club."

"I do not."

"Yes, you do. Even your roach motels have been renovated. Guess what else," I continued, having heard enough of Natalie's theories on creativity, "I decided to go ahead with the new demo, even though Zermin won't pay for it. I'll just have to raise the money for it some other way."

"How are you going to get four thousand dollars?"

"I don't know yet. I'm working on it. Right now I figure if I act like it's going to happen, it will. Man, you just can't let money stand in your way sometimes," I said with enthusiasm, trying to charge myself up for the extra waitressing shifts I knew it would take to pay for it.

"Do you think that's realistic?" asked Natalie.

"Sometimes momentum is all it takes, Natalie. Everything else follows."

"I know what you mean. It's an attitude thing. I never let money stand in my way."

"What money does it take to mail out poetry?"

"Stamps, Grace."

"Oh. Well, studio time is really expensive. Much more expensive than stamps."

"How about my word processor?"

"Okay, but you only needed to buy that once. And you could have used a pencil."

"True, very true. In any case, equipment aside, you're getting me excited. I think I'll go write after you leave." Natalie didn't look any more excited than she had a minute before, but if she was in the mood to write, that was fine with me.

"I'll let you get on with it," I said, preparing to leave. "I have to meet Ray at the studio in an hour."

"Listen, Grace, let me know what happens. It all sounds very interesting," she said, walking me to the door. I wondered whether she meant interesting musically or romantically.

♩ ♩ ♩

I arrived home to find my answering machine flashing peacefully. Thinking it must be Ray or Roger, my usual mid-day callers, I pressed 'play' and went about my business, brushing the cat off my amplifier and packing up my guitar effects pedals. This is what I heard:

"Grace. Hi. It's me. Paul Teagarden. I was thinking about you and wanted to know if you got home okay. When you have time, give me a call. I'm in my office." There was a pause and I heard him breathing. Then he said "Bye," and hung up.

I got very excited when I heard this message. It had it all; mystery, sex appeal, promise. But I also felt shaken. I didn't expect to hear from Paul so soon. We had only gotten back to New York a few days ago. I had been happy with the possibility, the idea of him. But this was no fantasy; Paul Teagarden's voice was in town.

I listened to the message a few more times. When I felt one more play would qualify as an obsession, I turned off the machine and paced my apartment, considering what to do.

Should I call him back or not? By calling him back I sensed I would set something in motion, but I did not know what. Perhaps it was better to wait a few days. That would give me a feeling of control. On the other hand, why call back at all? Where could things possibly lead? But I was being too serious; why did they have to lead anywhere?

Then, as if there had never been any doubt about what I would do, I pulled his number from the top drawer of my dresser. I wasn't afraid to face my fate or Paul Teagarden.

I sat on the couch. Then I sat on the bed, and then back on the couch. I felt this call needed just the right setting; it was the performer in me. I decided the couch was right for a friendly call. When everything seemed to be in order, with the pillows arranged and a glass of water by my side, I picked up the phone and dialed.

He answered. "Hello?"

"Hi, it's Grace."

"Hey," he said, his voice warming, "How are you?"

"I'm fine," I said a little too explosively. "And you?"

"Very good. You called just in time. I was just about to leave to go look at locations."

"Is this a bad time to talk?"

"No. Talk to me, Grace," he said hurriedly. "I have a few minutes. How was your trip home?"

The sound of his voice paralyzed me slightly. I was glad he asked about my trip home. It gave me some direction. "It was fine," I replied, "We stayed in Santa Monica, and the hotel gave us a suite because they had given away our reservation."

"That's the kind of mistake I like."

"It was good, especially after the scene in Palm Springs. We had two rooms, and a great view of the ocean. And an excellent minibar." Suddenly all sorts of details seemed enchanting.

"So I take it your friend is talking to you again?"

"It took a few hours, but he loosened up."

"I felt bad about that."

"Next time we'll leave for our adventure earlier."

"It's a deal."

"And how was your trip back?" I asked.

He told me about his flight home from Palm Springs. We had shared enough so that I could even ask him a few questions about his film.

The telephone brought his voice into focus. I could hear every grain, every layer of sound. His voice was sharply defined and had texture, like a piece of slate. It was good to talk and I was pleased to discover a new setting with Paul Teagarden. Now I knew we could handle long distance. We talked for half an hour. Soon I was stretched out on the couch, the pillows piled under my knees, my finger swirling in the glass of water at my side.

"So, Paul," I said, knowing our conversation would have to end shortly, "I'm surprised you called me so soon."

"I was thinking about you a lot after we met," he said, his voice getting softer.

"Why?"

"I don't know." He was quiet. "I find you very attractive." I could hear him breathe.

"Thanks," I said.

"You probably hear that a lot."

"You're kidding. I don't hear that a lot. Anyway, you live in LA where everyone is attractive."

"And you're talking in clichés. Not everyone in LA is attractive. I mean it. There's something about you."

"There's something about you, too, Paul," I said. I paused, wondering how much I should say.

"So now you know why I called," he said. "I was pulled. Anyway, I should go. There are people here waiting for me."

"What kind of locations are you going to look at?"

"High Schools. The twelve year old principal." He paused. "I'll call again soon."

"Bye, Paul," I said.

"Bye," he said quietly.

We hung up. I stretched out on the couch, a tickling mixture of words and voices twirling in my mind. Then I realized I had ten minutes to get to the rehearsal studio. I got up, finished collecting my things, and ran out the door.

♪ ♪ ♪

Our three o' clock rehearsals at Fat Boy Studio give my week order. Every Monday, Wednesday, and Thursday, I count on being there. Ray and I have no problem meeting in the afternoon because we have flexible job schedules. I make sure I never take a waitressing shift on those afternoons, and Ray doesn't have a job, so he's always available. He makes his living playing and repairing guitars.

Ray is a genius when it come to guitars. He only has to look at a guitar to know its pick-ups are out of phase or the frets need a grind and polish. People come from all over the five boroughs to have him work on their guitars. They say that when Ray works on your guitar, you actually play better. I don't know how it happens, but he's well paid for his talent which leaves him plenty of time to devote to Swan Venom.

Ray is quiet, and he uses language sparingly, which is good because when he does talk, it's usually about state-of-the-art digital recording equipment or his dog. This can be a disappointment to any girl who's been hanging around a bar all night waiting to get to know the moody-looking guitar player who holds his instrument as if he's just spent the weekend in bed with it. They don't realize that in fact Ray has spent the weekend in bed with his guitar because it's the only thing he's truly interested in. Ray has dark hair and a clear, handsome face that projects depth. Not a gig goes by without a pile-up of young girls in heavy make-up trying to get to know him, inviting him back to their friend's place in Jackson Heights or Fort Lee, begging him to visit them when they're on duty at the jewelry counter at Macy's.

Once in while there will be a woman who succeeds in bringing out Ray's interesting side, only by doing all the talking herself. They go off in the night together to spots that are only open to people who look good for a living.

Ray is our lead guitarist. Steve and Geoffrey make for a very tight rhythm section, which is important in our music. They're always together, right on the beat, easing in and out of grooves with unbelievable timing. It's strange that they're so tuned in to each other because they're opposite personalities. Geoffrey is very serious and sensitive; you have to be careful what you say to Geoffrey because he looks for hidden meanings in everything. Steve, on the other hand, isn't into subtlety. He's not too bright, and as long as he gets to play his drums, everything is fine. Geoffrey has to struggle to get something right. Steve just gets it, although he can never explain how.

I worry about Geoffrey sometimes. We found him through a classified ad in the Downtown Moon. He's the best bass player I've ever met who actually shows up on time. His big problem is that something always goes wrong. Either his bass gets stolen or he loses his car keys or he gets a parking ticket; if he stays around to collect our money from a club owner at the end of the night, it's always short. Like Ray, what he likes to do best is make music. He went to all the New York music schools and he's very devoted to his instrument. I think that's one thing everyone in Swan Venom shares; we all take music very seriously, except for maybe Steve, who says he wouldn't mind being a florist if the band doesn't work out.

Steve has a hard time making it to rehearsals, not because he has a job, but because he forgets things. I leave messages on the machine at his girlfriend's house every hour on the days we have rehearsals, starting in the morning. Steve is a living example of the joke, "What do you call a musician without a girlfriend?" The answer to that is "Homeless," which is what Steve would be if it weren't for his girlfriend, Diana. She has a loft in the East Village and looks after Steve and his drum kit.

Of all of us, Geoffrey is the only one with a regular job; he's a substitute teacher in an elementary school in Queens, which may explain why he's always so tense. He finishes at three o'clock and comes straight from P.S. 127 to us, and Steve always says, "Good afternoon, Mr. McCoy," to annoy him.

Each of us plays with other bands, but we all have ambitions for Swan Venom. I think we all realize there's something special about the band. Our individual differences make for an interesting mix and our sound is unique. Because I write the material, our songs have very strong melodies. I really know how to get a harmonic foothold when it comes to crafting a tune. I'm into big, open chords lately, which is making our music a little more powerful. I listen to all kinds of music from unusual, avant-garde stuff like Reynolds Boolaneau and Jacob Nostranovich, to down-to-earth Ghanaian Highlife and Spanish Bulerías. But as far as my songs go, they're pretty traditional. My best songs are a kind of Leonard-Joni-Miles-John-Paul-Keith kind of thing, if you know what I mean. I have to be careful of letting my melodies get too soft, but that's where Ray comes in. He knows just how to keep a song ruthless. He knows when to add an interesting effect, and he always resolves his harmonies to the least expected places. Ray uses his knowledge of electronics to add texture to our songs. Geoffrey and I both come from a jazz background, so we know how to improvise and go places musically. And Steve is a rock 'n' roll animal; he gives our music a touch of fear. People remember our songs.

I was fifteen minutes late for rehearsal the day Paul called. On top of that, I was unusually excited. Everyone in the band could tell something was going on because I kept speeding up. We started off by working on a new song called, "Your Bag is Open" which is our experiment with a Ragamuffin Hyperthrash kind of sound, so luckily the speeding up fit right in. Most of the rehearsal was spent working on our new song, "Walls of Forgiveness." I like it a lot because it has a haunting feeling, yet you can dance to it. When I told the guys I definitely wanted to put it on the demo, they gave me a hard time.

"I don't want to hear anymore about a demo," said Geoffrey. "Not again. Not until I see the pile of money to pay for it."

"Geoffrey, we're doing it," I replied, exasperated. "I have to earn the pile of money first."

"And what superstar are you going to get to produce it this time?" said Steve.

"Look, I'm doing the best I can. I can't help it if Jetty McPhereson had to go make an album with Virtue."

"I knew it was too good to be true," Steve mumbled, playing a roll on his snare drum.

"Hey, Jetty McPhereson can't just wait around for us to come up with four thousand dollars. He had to go. Are you saying you don't believe he would have worked with us?"

"Yeah," he answered, shaking his head.

"Great. I'm glad you have so much faith."

"It didn't happen," Steve exclaimed, "It didn't happen, so it didn't happen. What does believing have anything to do with it?"

"Nothing, okay? I'm just saying we're going to do this demo. Do you believe that?"

"I believe in action, man." I couldn't argue with him.

After rehearsal, we sat in front of the Bobbin Building—buildings in New York are often named after industrial parts—and waited for Steve to bring his van around. One of Steve's important contributions to Swan Venom is that he has a van and doesn't mind taking each of us home after rehearsals.

Ray sat on a brass water duct with his guitar between his legs. "I like what's happening in 'Walls of Forgiveness'," he said, staring straight ahead over 30th Street, talking to no one in particular. "What if we ended the song with the bassline and took out all the other instruments at the end and just let it go, dee, dee, dee, dum, dee."

"Doable," said Geoffrey.

"You know, just keep going, dee, dee, dee, dum, dee"—here Ray played an invisible bass as he worked it out—"dum, dee, da, and I could sample some percussive crashing sound, like someone crashing into a wall. It could come in real suddenly at the end."

"I hear it," said Geoffrey, repeating the line.

"We could try it tomorrow. Geoffrey, are you teaching tomorrow? Maybe we could meet a little earlier and work it out." Geoffrey always comes to rehearsal late on the days he teaches school.

"Yes, they called me for tomorrow. Damn," he said, pushing his glasses up on his nose. Geoffrey wears little round glasses, and always dresses in a shirt and tie. His idol is Jimmy "Serpent Handler" Mitchell, the famous Chicago bass player who said, "If you don't look good, you don't play good." He repeats this every time we tell him not to bring his cashmere overcoat to gigs. It always ends up covered in beer. Geoffrey won't listen because he believes in dressing well, 24 hours a day. It's hard to believe that his brother is D.J. Romald, who claims he started the fashion of wearing sneakers hanging around the neck.

"It's no big deal, Geoffrey, man. We'll do it when you get there," said Ray. Then looking over at me, he added, "Maybe we can get the new ending together for the Box Factory."

"Let's try it. But I don't want to do it unless it's perfect. We have a lot of people coming," I replied.

"No problem," said Ray. "I can get it together. I also want to put together a sample for the introduction. It should start with a roaring sound, which I can get if I sample a bus or a truck and put it onto an S770 with the fan control switch flipped, and then do the whole thing in stereo, with a positive aftertouch into the left sample, and a number 11 cross-town bus, and a negative aftertouch into the right."

"Cool," I said. Even if I didn't know what he was talking about, I knew if he said we could have the song ready by Thursday, we would. If one of us has an idea, the others help make it happen.

♩ ♩ ♩

Our show at the Box Factory was a big success. It's true that most of the audience was composed of our friends and acquaintances; Ray's five roommates, Steve's relatives from Bay Ridge, Geoffrey's girlfriend and her friends and their friends, and of course the 500 postcards I sent out to our mailing list brought in a few familiar faces.

Besides our regular fans, someone from Tremendous Records was there to talk to us about doing a month in Europe. The critic I invited from the Downtown Moon actually came to review us, and a few musicians stopped by to sit in. Swan Venom is getting a reputation.

For me, a good audience makes the show much more exciting, and this audience was hot. I put on the best show I could, working a lot of magic despite the fact that Ray had to stand behind a column because there was no room on the stage. We were really on.

After the show, James, who books the place, gave us another date. Unfortunately, it was eight months away. But we got an excellent review from the guy at the *Downtown Moon,* who called us "melody anarchists" which I think he meant in the best sense possible. To quote a little more of the review, he said, "Swan Venom goes on a midnight blue rush, swinging through modal architecture with an urgent combination of Spanish off-treble octaves and hard rocking chops, bending notes into a mutiny of sound. Fronting the band is Miss Grace Note who really dishes the kasha, setting timber afire in unblushing improvisation. Long live rock."

Between sets at the Box Factory, I stretched out on an old, red velvet couch the club keeps in the dressing room. The dressing room had once been an office and it looked like it hadn't been cleaned for years. The club must have thought this contributed to the artistic atmosphere, because they didn't even bother to remove the sign that said "E-Flute Cartons Made to Order" which dates back to the days when the Box Factory was a box factory.

I lay back on the couch and looked up at the walls. They were covered by at least a decade's worth of graffiti. I saw the words "The Big Heat" written in thick black magic marker, telling me that Sheldon Bagg had indeed been here like Natalie said. There were other familiar local names scrawled across the walls — Lenny Rollings from the Pantry Dwellers, Crispy Gerber and Vinny Dimarchio from Carving Knife, and Samantha Kerr from Barbie Without a Head, who had done a very lively sketch on the wall next to her name. I even saw the great blues singer, James "Hollow Leg" Wilson's name, lettered carefully above one of the windows.

Geoffrey and Steve liked to stay in the club between sets and sit with their friends or play video games, but I prefer to rest between sets. I give a lot to the audience and I need to recover my energy. I was meditating on the walls, lulled by the tones of a pounding bass vibrating through the room, when Ray walked in. Wordlessly, he flopped down on the other end of the couch. He picked up my feet and put them in his lap.

"Grace," he said.

"Ray. What's happening?"

"Someone wants to talk to you," he said. He put his head back and stared at the ceiling.

"Yeah? Who?"

"Guess."

"Give me a clue."

"Who's your best fried in the universe?"

"I don't know. Roger? Natalie?"

"No, c'mon," said Ray, slapping my leg. "Who comes to every show just to see you?" Then I knew.

"Tell him I went home," I urged, rolling on my side and covering my head with Geoffrey's homburg, which I picked up from the top of his bass case on the floor next to me.

But it was too late. For at that moment, the door opened and Walter Wiener, candy salesman, walked into the room and headed straight for me.

ᛉ ᛉ ᛉ

He stood over the couch. "Fantastic," he pronounced. "That's all I'll say and now I'm going." He didn't move.

"Hello, Walter," I said, sitting up.

"As usual, you were exceptional," he continued, "I'll leave now, I just had to come back here and tell you that new song, 'Walls of Forgiveness,' is very powerful. It builds. I love it."

Walter showed no sign of leaving. "Have a seat," I suggested, pointing at a yellow vinyl bean bag chair. The pleasure of watching Walter Wiener splayed in a beanbag chair would be some consolation for having to undergo a visit from him. We like Walter because he's such a good fan, but he's made being a pest into an art form.

Walter Wiener sits in the front at every show and nods along happily with each song. Between sets, he comes back stage to let us know how we're doing. Walter is fairly new to pop music. It's something he discovered after his divorce when he was trying to carve out a new life for himself. He moved into the city, and as he puts it, has been making up for lost time. I think he somehow imprinted on Swan Venom, the way baby birds do when they attach themselves to the first living thing they see. Maybe we were the first band he saw in his new single life; he remains totally loyal to us, no matter how much we discourage him.

"Did you ever think about maybe doing something with horns on that one?" he said, as he sunk into the beanbag chair, which had long ago lost most of its beans. He began to sketch out a careful plan which had to do with a trumpet and a tenor saxophone.

Walter Wiener tries to contribute whenever he can. He isn't afraid to be frank with us. He feels it's his duty to let us know when the sound man did a lousy job, when my singing is less than perfect, or when Ray's solos are not coming across. He takes our music almost as seriously as we do.

Walter also loves telling me his ideas, which are more suited to a Las Vegas variety show than a seedy club in downtown New

York. I ignore most of them, but I don't mind his company. It's strange, but he relaxes me. Even after a drop dead set climaxing in "Shine It This Way" and "Clear It With Maxine," our most hard-rocking tunes, talking to Walter made me instantly sleepy. In fact, I felt myself relaxing more with every word he spoke. Now and then one of the guys in the band would open the door and come into the dressing room and the roar of music would pour in, drowning out Walter. I admired the way he kept talking, whether anyone was listening or not.

"...then you have a drum solo, and some dancing thing with you and Ray..."

"I don't dance."

"Okay, something with lights, then."

"Walter, I can't talk anymore. It's time to do another set." I stood up and picked up my guitar.

Walter hoisted himself out of the beanbag chair, falling on his knees for a moment before he stood up.

"Grace, listen. I want to ask you a question."

"What, Walter?" I replied tensely. I had been hoping he would go quietly. He seemed especially pesky tonight.

"Later, after the show, could I talk to you for a few minutes?" He shifted back and forth for a moment with his hands in the pockets of his ski jacket. A squarish clump of lift tickets hung off the zipper. "Please."

I looked at him and he gazed back at me. Walter was two inches shorter than me. I could see his head shining where his curly hair began to recede. "Okay, Walter. I'll look for you when the show is over."

"Fabulous. I'll talk to you later," he said, waving to me as he stepped out the door.

💥 💥 💥

Our second set was even better than the first. I was glad Roger could make it in time to see it. He couldn't be there for the first set. There was a birthday in arbitrage and he had to celebrate with some people from the department.

After the show I made the rounds of tables and greeted Swan Venom's friends and relatives. It's important to mingle with the crowd, and thank people personally for coming. It helps bring them out the next time. I was sitting with Steve's girlfriend's sister, and Geoffrey's Aunt Gladys, when I spotted Walter alone at a table on the other side of the room. I waved to him and signaled that I'd be over in a minute.

After chatting with some musician friends, and saying hi to Roger and a few of Ray's roommates, I made my way to the table where Walter sat.

۲ ۲ ۲

Walter Wiener beckoned to me with a grand wave. He waved as if he were surrounded by an invisible entourage. I must have a soft spot for Walter Wiener, I thought, if I were willing to leave a crowd of friends just to sit in a dark corner with him and listen to what I thought would be more silly ideas for our show.

Walter didn't view my presence as a sacrifice. "Let me tell you something," said Walter, before I had even completed the act of sitting down at his table, "A good salesman is natural around people. He's a natural. Let me tell you a little story. I was in Portland a couple of months ago and I was talking to a wholesaler who's hobby, interestingly enough, was collecting matchbooks."

I, Grace Note, was not sure why this was interesting, but I knew Walter would tell me if I could stand the wait. Sipping a club soda, I leaned back in my chair, wondering if it were dark enough to fall asleep without Walter noticing.

"So by chance, I happened to have eaten two days before in New York at Da Venitia, you know, off Sixth Avenue and I reach in my pocket and what do I find but a matchbook. So I waited and then, at a certain point I said, 'Barry, listen. I know you collect matchbooks, and I happen to have something here from a very nice, very famous New York restaurant' and I explained to him about the place and I said, 'Barry, why don't you take it for your collection?' And I gave him the matchbook." Here Walter opened his eyes wide and stared at me with a grin full of wonder.

"That's great," I volunteered.

"He was thrilled."

"So did he order anything?"

"Did he order anything? He said, 'Give me 65 gross and we'll talk some more.' Let me tell you something, Grace, you have to know how to communicate with people on their level. I made him feel comfortable."

"Walter, is there a point to this story?"

He threw his eyes back and made what seemed like fifteen or twenty different gestures all conveying embarrassment, and then he put his hand on mine and said, "Forgive me. I have so much on my mind sometimes, I forget where I'm going at times." He looked so upset I thought he was going to give me a matchbook.

"Don't worry, it's no big deal."

"Grace. What I'm saying is I'm a salesman and I can sell anything. I would like to try representing you and your group. I have
some money to invest and it's a thing which excites me very much."

I was glad our table was removed from all the activity, from
the laughter and chatter of the other tables. This discussion would
take all my concentration. Walter was no longer content being a
fan; he wanted to be a player. I sat quietly as I considered how to
handle this. Walter stared at me brightly, waiting for me to speak. His
face shone in the glow of sharply focused track lighting, his skin the
color of a conch shell. The interior of the club was done entirely in
black, making Walter look for a moment like a painting on velvet.

I wasn't surprised he had come up with such a crazy idea. It
was the natural consequence of attending every show of ours for
the last year. Well, I wasn't interested. We weren't looking for a
manager right now. Ray and I had already decided that when the
time came we would go for experienced, high profile management
and not a novice.

And even if we were looking for an agent, Walter had some big
strikes against him; his expertise was in candy, not music; he wasn't
polished enough to handle some of the music business sharks he
would have to deal with; and most importantly, he didn't make sense
most of the time.

"May I tell you something?" Walter continued. "And whether
you believe it or not, I must tell you that I don't snack, ever. Why
am I telling you this?"

"Because I have snacks for you?"

"No, I'm telling you this because I want you to know how very
serious I can be. I am not a man who is easily distracted." Here he
looked at me in a way that I found ominous. He looked at me as if
I were wearing nothing but a bra, which as a matter of fact I was,
although technically it was my costume.

"I have plans for you," he declared.

"You mean Swan Venom."

"I mean Swan Venom, of course. But I will tell you something.
I have plans for you. You meaning you. Personally." He gave my
hand a tap, as if he were putting a spell on me. "I want you to
know I think you are very talented."

"But right now I'm very happy with Swan Venom. What kind
of plans do you mean?"

"I'll get to that, but let me tell you a story; I was in Colum-
bus and I went into a restaurant. Beautiful place. I wanted to take
this customer to a very nice lunch. And we had a very nice lunch, even

though I never eat fish, and the customer said to me, 'Walt, do you really enjoy yourself as much as you seem to be enjoying yourself?' And I said, 'Absolutely. I can't hide things, if I look like I'm enjoying myself, then I am. I'm natural. What you see is what you get.'"

"Why are you telling me this?" Walter's soothing effect was beginning to wear off.

"Grace, I'll get to the point. I sense a chemistry between us. I think you know I find you very attractive."

"That's nice," I replied, inwardly dreading the turn this conversation was taking. "But I don't think our relationship is heading anywhere romantic, if that's what you're suggesting."

"I'm not surprised to hear you say that. I sensed that you're holding back. You're afraid of being hurt."

I, Grace Note, am afraid of many things. I'm afraid of what would happen if I dropped one of my compact disks on the floor. I'm afraid of having a Japanese beetle fly into my mouth. But I am not afraid of being hurt by Walter Wiener, candy salesman, unless you include his potential as a serial killer. What could I say? I knew Walter well enough to know that any answer, to him, would mean yes. If I said "no, I'm not afraid of being hurt," he would take that to mean yes, and next thing you know I would be walking down some hideous aisle with him somewhere. If I said I only go out with men who wear their own hair and don't have an ex-wife named Mindy, I would have come closer to the truth. But how could I say that? As annoying as he was, Walter was a nice person. He said so himself. I paused to choose my words, which probably made him think I was reconsidering.

"Walter, you know I like you. But we're really talking about business here. I would like to keep it that way and not confuse things."

"I am able to separate business from my personal life. Are you able?"

Again, an impossible question; any answer, to him, would sound like "I love you, Walter." How could I tell him that me and him as a romantic pair was as likely as the earth falling into the sun?

"Walter, you're asking me to explain a feeling. It just won't work. I don't want to mix business and my personal life. And it's not just that. We're just too different. Our lifestyles are too different."

"Isn't that a good thing? Opposites attract."

"That may be, but I'm not that interested in candy."

"I'm sorry to hear that. I really felt as if you and I were getting to know each other and now I feel as if I'm getting mixed signals."

"Mixed signals?" I was amazed. I had no idea Walter had taken our backstage chats for flirtations. I knew he liked talking to me better than he liked talking to Steve, for example, but so did everyone. It was time to spell it out for him. "You're not getting mixed signals. Walter, you're not getting any signals. I'm saying no. I'm not interested."

"Maybe you should relax and take a chance. Give in to your feelings. I sense you're fighting them."

"I don't have the feelings you think I have."

"I hear you making excuses. Do you hear that?"

What could I say? I just looked at him, stunned by his persistence.

"I know you're scared. You've been hurt and now you're being cautious," he continued. Walter didn't want to listen to reason; after all, he was a salesman.

I only had one more option; I remained quiet, letting Walter absorb the image of the track lighting sparkling in my hair. Finally, I spoke. "Walter, I'm seeing someone."

He bent his head back and closed his eyes. He laid his hands flat on the table. He shook his head. He sighed. He was a regular catalog of comprehension. He looked up a few more times with a knowing expression, as if he and God had just shared a joke.

"Now I understand. This makes everything clear. I didn't understand that before." He looked at me with sympathy and leaned forward. "I want to tell you something. I would never do anything to interfere in your life. I didn't know you were involved."

"Yes, I have someone I've been seeing for a while now."

"Grace, I understand. You're involved and I wouldn't want to get in the middle. Just remember one thing. I can wait. I'm the kind of person who is patient, and six months from now, if you change your mind, I'm not going to throw you under a truck."

"Thank you. I'll remember," I answered.

"Now I'll get going. But I want you to consider my offer. I am very serious about it. I want to represent Swan Venom to some of my connections."

"What connections, Walter?"

He put up his hand. "Enough. We've said enough for now. We both have a lot of thinking to do." He stood up and put on his ski jacket. He zippered it up and wrapped a scarf around the outside of the collar.

He stood in front of me and sighed. "Before I go, I have one favor to ask." He could tell by the look on my face I was about to tell him to do something rude, so he spoke quickly. "May I at least have one of your demo tapes? This connection I'm referring to—he's a friend in the music business—is only in town this week. I'd like him to hear some of your songs.

"You just want a tape?"

"I swear, just a tape," Walter declared, solemnly placing one hand on his chest and the other in the air like a middle-aged boy scout.

"We're making a new one soon."

"Give me an old one, a new one, whatever. I just need it by to-morrow."

"You better not be wasting my time, or I'll never let you into another club where we're playing again. Ever."

Walter closed his eyes, his hand still in the air, and said, "I swear. You will not regret this, Grace."

"Fat Boy Studios, 251 West 30th Street. Tomorrow at three."

"Grace, I love you, so to speak," said Walter as he bundled up and headed out.

❧ ❧ ❧

When I told Roger about the interest Walter Wiener had taken in me, Roger wasn't the least bit jealous. Being jealous of Walter would have been like being jealous of a really great kitchen appliance. No one lacked that much confidence. But when I told Roger that Walter claimed to have some connection in the music business, Roger perked up a little. I always forget how insecure men can be.

"Walter knows someone important in the music business?"

"He claims he does."

"Who?"

"I don't know who. He won't tell me, he just says it's a friend."

"I wonder who he could know," said Roger, balancing a letter opener on its tip. Roger was at his desk. I sat in an arm chair with my feet on his coffee table eating grapes.

"Well, just be careful."

"Be careful of what?"

"He may be after you."

"Right. And you think that I'm going to suddenly get inter-ested in Walter because he knows someone in the music business?" I tossed a grape at Roger.

"I don't know. No, I guess not."

"You've met Walter. Is he my type?"

"No."

"Okay then."

"Am I your type?" asked Roger. I stopped to think about it.

"I wouldn't have thought so. But you are now."

"See? Things can change." Roger was smiling. I knew he was kidding, but it was a good point.

"Anyway, don't worry about Walter Wiener. I'm not so shallow that just because someone helps me in business, I'm going to have a relationship with him. That's such a guy thing to think. It's just business."

"Okay, okay. I trust you completely, although I'm not so sure about Walter."

"I can handle Walter. I mean, give me a break. It wouldn't be the first time I had to deal with someone like him." As soon as I said this, I regretted it. Roger has a morbid curiosity about the past relationships of women he dates, and I had to review a good five years before I could get Roger to turn his attention back to his expense report.

˹ ˹ ˹

The neon clock in the studio had no sooner glowed three o'clock when Walter Wiener stepped into the room. We were in the recording studio, working on a rough pre-demo. Ray and I wanted to work out some ideas for the final tape and get a feel for how to handle the newer tunes.

We were laying down rhythm guitar tracks when I saw Walter through the studio window. He jogged into the control room as if the world were his game show. He was dressed casually, in slacks, a dark blue sweat shirt and sunglasses that said, 'Ferrari' in the corner. He looked as cheerful as ever, and I was glad to see he had snapped back, at least outwardly, from his romantic disappointment. He waved to me and smiled. I was busy playing the guitar so I nodded back. He watched us through the glass as we finished running through "Walls of Forgiveness."

When we finished the tune, I excused myself and walked out to see Walter. The guys gave me a funny look. I could have told them Walter was there to pick up a demo tape and shop it around for us, but no one would have believed me. It was too implausible. Instead, I let them make goofy noises, and think whatever they wanted.

When I came into the control room Walter pulled me over to one side and spoke in an urgent whisper.

"Grace, I have something for you," he said, handing me a big white trash bag. Inside was a giant candy basket. The candy lay in a circular design, nested in shredded green cellophane like an Easter basket. There were boxes of Chocolate Joy Birds, a few rolls of Zwangles, some dietetic jellied pretzels, and in the center, a marshmallow pumpkin with a bow.

"Let's go into the other room where it's quiet," I said, sensing that contrary to my instructions, Walter was about to say something that only I should hear. I directed him into the empty reception area. We sat on a brown couch under a Joan Jett Calendar.

Walter lifted his sunglasses and looked at me. He held his hand up as if to silence me. "Before you say a word, I just want to let you know I'm only here to pick up a tape. That's all I'm going to do, don't worry. I just wanted to give you this little token because I feel bad about yesterday. I was insensitive. I didn't know you were seeing someone and if I had, I wouldn't have pushed things the way I did. Forgive me."

"Don't worry about it." I could accept his strange flaw of being unable to absorb or hear the truth. It just seemed unusual that someone who didn't listen very well wanted to invest in music.

"I want to tell you something, Grace. I don't like to push. I'm not a pusher, and I feel bad that maybe I overstepped my limit with you. I know you're on a merry-go-round right now and you don't need me in the middle to make it more confusing."

I was wondering if it would take him long to apologize, when he put his hand on my arm and looked at me with his 'Let me sum it all up for you because time is money' face.

"I can't stay," he began, "but let me say one thing. I'm going to leave you alone now and not mention this personal matter again except maybe in the future, after July, but no later than November. You're on a roller-coaster right now. I think we could have a lot of fun together. But not while you're involved with someone else. Meanwhile, we'll be friends, we'll be what we are, associates, whatever you call it, and that's that. I'll live with it. How does that sound?"

"That sounds fine."

"So now we won't talk about it again, and you get back to work and enjoy your candy. I'll go quietly," he said standing up and putting on his sunglasses.

"Walter, didn't you forget something?"

He slapped his forehead. "Where's my head? The tape." I handed it to him. "I'll let you know what happens with it." He smiled at me wistfully. I pulled my candy towards me, as if it were a shield between his karma and mine.

The price of doing business is high, very high, I thought to myself as I walked Walter to the door. He walked down the steps, looked back, and winked. It was the kind of wink that told me he would be back for me—and long before November. I would have to remember to ask Roger whether this kind of thing ever happened to him.

❡ ❡ ❡

I didn't think about Walter's offer again until I received a phone call in the studio a few days later. We had already eaten all of the candy, so there was nothing around to remind me of Walter. Burton, the engineer, picked up the telephone at the console and handed it to Ray. We were listening to the vocals on "Walls of Forgiveness." Ray looked over at me and said, "It's for you. Some dude."

People rarely call me at the studio. My friends know it's my prized, not to mention expensive, creative time. It couldn't be Roger because he was out of town at a meeting in Boston. I thought perhaps Zermin had relented and wanted to come around and visit, like he used to before our stock market debacle. Zermin can spend all day in the studio, doing nothing.

Ray handed me the phone. "Hello?" I said.

"Grace, it's Walter Wiener," said Walter with urgency.

"Hi, Walter. What's doing?" I signaled to Burton to turn down the sound for a moment.

"Grace, I'm in the neighborhood. Can I come up and talk to you?"

"We're working. Where are you?"

"I'm actually downstairs in the lobby."

"Okay, I'll take a break. Come on up," I sighed, trying to convey my impatience. I would have to have a talk with Walter. It was one thing for him to be poking around backstage all the time, but another for him to be interrupting us at Fat Boy where we paid for our time. Besides, I was afraid that the guys were really starting to believe I had a thing going with Walter Wiener.

Walter came rushing in a minute after I hung up the phone. I directed him to the battered reception area, where we sat down. "Grace, I have a question for you," he began. "Have you ever heard of the band Death Threat?"

"Of course I've heard of them."

"What do you think of them?"

"That's what you came to ask me?" I said, annoyed.

"Trust me. I'm asking for a reason," he urged.

"Okay, okay. Death Threat. Let me see." I thought for a moment, trying to find just the right words to sum up my feelings. "Sleazy popstars."

"No, I mean what do you think of their music."

"Music has nothing to do with it, " I replied, in no mood to be academic. "They're an act. Their act is being disgusting and stupid and having a lot of hair. They've been doing it for years and they're good at it. They've sold a lot of records by acting nasty. Who cares about their music?"

"No, that's not what I'm asking," whined Walter, sounding unusually exasperated. "Let me put it like this, Grace. Do you think Death Threat is a successful band?"

"In pop music, yes. They're very successful. They must be zillionaires. They have gold records for breakfast. Is that what you want me to say, Walter?"

He ignored my sarcasm, and pursued his as yet unrevealed point. "Have you ever heard of Hunter Burns?"

Another silly question. Of course I had heard of Hunter Burns. He was Death Threat's front man, the subject of hundreds of scandals and biographies, backstage legends and mad rock 'n' roll fantasies. He was the unchallenged icon of fifteen year-olds around the globe. He was huge. Hunter Burns invented power pop. "Sure I've heard of him." I figured that Walter had only heard of Death Threat because one of his kids had a Death Threat poster. Or maybe he had seen them on the news, dressed in their cutaway leather tuxedoes.

"Grace, what if I were to tell you that the music business connection of mine I mentioned was Hunter Burns?"

"I would say welcome to Venus."

"No, really, Grace, I want you to be totally serious with me here. What would you say if I told you that my music business friend is Hunter Burns."

"Walter, cut it out. I don't know what I would say."

"Grace, it's Hunter Burns."

"Right, Walter." We went back and forth like this for a while, but soon I realized Walter was dead serious. It was not his words that finally convinced me, but the look on his face. It was aglow with a kind of self-satisfaction that could only mean he was telling the truth.

I was truly shocked. I could barely get out my first question: "How?"

"I know the guy from the time we were seven years old. His family and my family are very close. We used to go on vacations together, his family and mine, to the Adirondacks. Lake George. We were in school together, the works, until we went away to college."

I just stared at Walter. He continued.

"His mother and my mother are best friends. Grace, stop staring. He's a Long Island kid like me," Walter continued. "He dated my sister in high school."

I looked up at the acoustic tiles on the ceiling, feeling that very little in the universe was secure anymore. Walter Wiener knew Hunter Burns, the sleaziest rock and roll bad dream. "I can't believe this. Does this mean you're the same age as Hunter Burn? How can that be?"

"So his hair didn't fall out. The guy ages well, what can I tell you. And anyway, who wouldn't look good in videos, with all the effects. Put me in pants like that and I'd look good too."

Even that seemed possible at the moment.

A look of power crossed Walter's face. I didn't like it. It was as if Hunter Burns' aura had suddenly attached itself to Walter. Walter lowered his eyelids and stared at me lasciviously with a slight smile on his lips, as if he knew he had something I wanted. As if he had some kind of candy exclusive.

"Walter, why are you staring at me?"

"Grace," he began, savoring every word, "What would you say if I told you I think I can get Hunter Burns to listen to some of your songs?"

"I would say what would Death Threat possibly want with my songs? I don't write about teenage hookers." I regretted saying this. Walter looked hurt. Fortunately, the hurt passed quickly. Walter's strong point is that he rises from defeat instantly; Walter Wiener, candy salesman, is a Phoenix rising from a pile of M&M's.

"Grace, be serious. I think I could do it."

"Walter, of course it would be incredible. But I really don't think Death Threat would be interested in my kind of music."

"I talked to Hunter last week, he was at his mother's house in Bellport, and I stopped by to bring Mrs. Burns some candy for her synagogue, which is having their annual fund-raiser carnival. Hunter's mother is the co-chairman and I always like to contribute something."

"Walter, please get to the point."

"Anyway, I knew Hunter, whose real name, by the way, is Gary, would be there, because he's leaving for Japan on Tuesday and I knew he would want to stop by his mother's house before he left so I thought, I'll go and say hi. To make a long story short, he was there and I told him what I was doing and I told him about you in very enthusiastic terms. Gary is about to start work on a new album and I thought maybe he would be looking for new material.

We listened to a little bit of your tape and he was impressed. He said he was only interested in ballads and suggested that if I could get something together with just ballads, I should drop off a tape with him before he leaves for Japan. He said he'll listen to it. And let me tell you something: I know Gary for many, many years, and he's the kind of person who is very up front. If he says he's interested, he's interested. He doesn't say things he doesn't mean."

How many times I rolled my eyes and dropped my jaw in this conversation, I cannot say, but anyone who was watching me might have thought I was a mime. I couldn't believe what I was hearing. There's no doubt Walter Wiener had just delivered the opportunity of a lifetime for a songwriter. As much as I disliked Death Threat, nothing could compare to the exposure I would get if they did one of my songs. These days it was trendy for even the nastiest band to throw a power ballad into the mix. It gives bands a shot at a huge chunk of the market they would otherwise miss; ballads are much more likely to make it onto the charts. Death Threat could probably give an interesting edge to one of my more commercial tunes. And in fact, the more Walter talked, the more I recalled Death Threat's virtues. Sure, their music was completely commercial, but at least they didn't pretend it was anything else, like some musicians who act as if they've just rewritten the Messiah. And they did lots of public service announcements. There were worse bands, that's for sure. In any case, I, Grace Note, am not one to throw away an opportunity. If Walter wanted to do his job as our honorary manager, I would do my job as a songwriter.

"Walter, this is unbelievable. Obviously it's an incredible break."

"I think so too. But what I need to do is get a tape with some ballads on it. Pick out some of the slower songs you guys do, you know the ones I like — 'Under the Lights too Long,' 'She Wouldn't Say A Word,' 'Hopeless In French.' Those kinds of songs."

"I'll get a tape together. When do you have to get it to him?"

"There's a little bit of a time problem. I think I should get it to him tomorrow. Today is Monday and Gary said I should drop it by his office before Tuesday so his manager can take it with them to Japan. Can you handle this?"

"I'll mix something from the demos I have around the house. I can do it tonight on my four track," I said breathlessly, my mind racing ahead to review the tunes I had lying around the house, already on tape. I could mix something up with at least six songs on it.

"Walter, I want you to know how grateful I am. I admit, I never dreamed you could come through this way."

"I'm glad I could help. You know how I feel about you and Swan Venom. If I can help out a friend, why not? Anything you need, you just ask," said Walter, patting my leg. "And besides, I have a selfish motive. I told you I wanted to be your manager. This gives me a chance to try it out, to be a kind of agent at large, whatever you call it. I help you, you help me. We help each other," he added, just in case I didn't get the idea.

"We can work out the details," I said. I certainly owed something to Walter for this.

"Absolutely. Meanwhile, I'll stop by tonight to pick up the tape."

"Tonight? Tonight I'm making the tape. I won't be finished till late, maybe about one or two in the morning."

"Grace, let me tell you something. You wouldn't know it to look at me, but I'm a night bird. Night is no problem. I'm up. I'll drop by tonight."

"Are you sure you wouldn't rather come by in the morning?" Something about the idea of Walter and the night, together in one place, made me feel panicky.

"Grace, relax. I don't bite. Not hard, anyway." He laughed. I laughed. As soon as he left, I called Natalie to tell her the news, and ask her if she wouldn't like to come over tonight and help me with my tape.

𝄞 𝄞 𝄞

"It's your boyfriend, the candyman" said Ray, stretching the phone cord across the console, then over Burton, the engineer, who passed it to me.

"Thanks," I said taking the phone from him. I didn't say anything about Ray's little joke. I hadn't told him about Walter's offer to take my songs to Hunter Burns. Ray had no idea why Walter was calling so often.

I also didn't tell Roger that Walter came over to my house at one o' clock in the morning. Natalie couldn't be there, but Walter behaved himself. I knew he would. Walter is ultimately practical, and there was too much at stake for him to be pushy. I could learn to live with his wistful looks.

The secrets were piling up. I didn't want to tell anyone about Walter's offer, though, because I didn't want to jinx anything. I know it's superstitious, but musicians are like that. Once I started telling people what was going on, word would get around and some complication would ruin everything.

I also didn't want to upset anyone in the band. Even though the guys know that the songs I've written for Swan Venom belong to me, they might feel I was cutting them out of something. I didn't want to upset anyone by announcing I was about to sell one of Swan Venom's better numbers. The guys know that I will pursue anything that comes my way as far as songwriting is concerned, but there was no need to remind them of this until I had some concrete news.

"I'll take it in the office," I said.

Steve looked at Ray, then at me. "Grace has a thing with the candyman?" he marveled. "Really?"

"Looks like it," said Ray, fiddling with some knobs on the board.

It was difficult, but I didn't say anything as I closed the door behind me. I went into the office, which was piled high with papers, tapes, and trade magazines. Tina, a part-time receptionist, sat at a desk. I asked her if I could use her phone for a second and she said yes.

I picked up the telephone. "Hi, Walter," I said, quickly. He didn't bother saying hello.

"What would you say if I told you I had some very good news for you?" he said.

"I don't know, Walter, what would I say?"

"You would say, 'Walter, I was wrong about you.'" As usual, Walter expressed himself in the most indirect way possible, in this way maximizing the time people had to spend with him. At $50 an hour in studio time, I didn't have the cash to be polite.

"Walter, I was wrong about you. Now what is it?"

"There's somebody who is very fond of your songs and would like to meet you."

"Really?" I felt my breath catch in my throat.

"Hunter Burns likes the tape. His manager called me today at the office."

"That's unbelievable. He liked it?"

"Let's say he is extremely interested."

"Great, this is great."

"I'm not surprised. Grace, they're terrific songs."

"Thanks." I was so excited I could hardly speak. "What do we do now?" I asked, unexpectedly finding myself completely in Walter's hands.

"Hunter is in Japan till the end of the week, then he's stopping in L.A., and then he's coming back to New York. I wanted to check in with you. I'm supposed to call Jerry, their manager, back and make an appointment to meet with Hunter towards the end of next week."

"Call him. Make an appointment. Anytime is okay. Call me back and let me know what the plan is."

Walter called me back within an hour. I saw now that what he lacked in presentation he made up for in efficiency. Everything with Walter was smooth, casual, and easy. From his manner, you would have thought he was arranging a dentist appointment instead of lunch with Hunter Burns at Le Papier Maché, on Thursday, one o'clock.

When I hung up the phone, I felt myself nearly overcome by the potential of the situation. Anything could happen, and my mind was filled with fantasies of hit songs and recording contracts. But I also had to be practical. Between now and next Thursday, there was a lot to do. I couldn't go into this meeting without a little preparation.

I needed to know something about selling a song to a group like Death Threat. I had a shelf full of books on how to make it in the music business, but none of them had anything to say about lunch. I would almost certainly need a lawyer. But where to get one? Everybody said there were a lot of them around, but I didn't know any personally.

Roger was able to give me a little push in the right direction. I told him the news over dinner at Filomena's, a little Italian restaurant in the Village.

"Roger, it's incredible, isn't it?"

"Isn't Death Threat the band that did that tour on a stage shaped like a breast?"

"Yes, that was them. That was a few years ago."

"They want to do one of your songs?"

"I think so. They're considering it."

"Fantastic. Who would have thought Walter Wiener had those kinds of connections."

"It goes to show that absolutely anything is possible."

"You are really getting a break. I'm proud of you. Death Threat," Roger mused. "Do you know they've been big since I was in college?"

"Do you still have any of their records?"

"I think I might. I definitely had their really big one. 'Revolting'."

"It was that bad?"

"That was the name of the album."

"See if you can find it."

"I'll look for it."

"Roger, if they want to use the song, I'll need a lawyer. Do you have one I can borrow?"

"You'll need an entertainment lawyer."

"You're right."

"Don't get ahead of yourself. You're not supposed to count your profit before it's made."

"I learned, remember?"

"You must know other people in the music business who have lawyers. What about Massimo, Natalie's boyfriend?"

"What do you mean?"

"Doesn't he have a lawyer? His lawyer might deal with musicians as well as artists."

"I'll find out. Now that you mention it, I remember Natalie telling me that Massimo was suing his art dealer to get out of his contract. He must have a lawyer."

"Start there. Talk to him. Meanwhile, I'll ask around."

"Thank you," I said, spontaneously reaching over and putting my arms around Roger. I hugged him. He smiled at me, happy to see me so excited, not to mention friendly. The good news made me feel warm, and Roger and I held hands as we discussed copyright law over coffee and dessert.

♪ ♪ ♪

Hunter Burns is very tall, if you add his natural height to the height of his hair. He doesn't wear it as high as he does in his videos, but it's still pretty big. Let's just say you notice him when he walks into a French restaurant in midtown.

I saw him as he entered the restaurant. He wore a very stylish, long white raincoat, but other than that, his dress was not exceptional. He was outfitted casually, in blue jeans, a rust colored, very expensive sweater, and a silver bracelet on his wrist. I also noticed that around his neck hung a small piece of leather with a little gold symbol on the end. It lay just inside his collar, but I could see it as he leaned towards me to shake my hand. I thought of one of their recent albums, called "The End of Magic." The symbol was probably a tribute to alchemy or Druids.

I had chosen to keep my dress low-key, yet with a touch of individuality. I wore a simple black sweater and black pants, with half my hair up and the other half down in a long braid. The individuality in my outfit came from the orange silk smoking jacket I wore loosely over the sweater. Around my neck was a long ribbon with a key on the end. I wanted to look mystical yet professional. Walter, as usual, looked like he was on his way to a hockey game, in a short sleeve sport shirt and a waist length jacket.

Walter and I were already at a table when Hunter arrived. I was a little nervous, yet when he sat down with us, the familiarity of his face made me feel more comfortable instead of less. I felt like I knew him and in a sense I did; Death Threat was a regular on every video television show, music award show, and record store promotion. I had seen his face a thousand times, although in person he didn't look so hot. Sitting across a table, you could tell he and Walter were the same age after all. He had a fine net of wrinkles spread across his forehead and around his mouth and eyes. They were fine enough for the camera to miss but across a table, they could not be hidden. His hair was dark brown, and his skin olive, made darker by a slight tan. Hunter has the kind of dark good looks that can look positively evil with the right make-up.

"It's good to meet you," he said to me as he sat down. "Hey, Walter." He gave Walter a light punch on the arm.

"Gary, how ya' doing?" Walter replied.

"Man, I am really beat. We've been traveling for two months."

"So how was Japan? Good?" asked Walter.

"Walter, do I know? I go and I'm in hotels and arenas ninety-five percent of the time. I wouldn't be able to tell you the difference between Osaka and Minneapolis. Usually I do some sightseeing, but on this tour I really didn't have time," said Hunter as he picked up his napkin and smoothed it across his lap. "I spent most of my free time working on our next album."

"That's wonderful. I'm glad to see you're so productive." If I closed my eyes I could have been listening to two guys from the garment business.

"We try to keep to a tight schedule, because everybody's all over the place and it's hard to get together. In fact, Rudy just left for Montana yesterday. He's into this ranch thing."

"Rudy is into cows?"

"Horses. Don't ask me where he comes off owning a ranch, but he loves it."

I figured they were talking about Rudy Rude, the lead guitar player in Death Threat. Rudy Rude was just like Hunter Burns only with a stupider name. They were both tall, lean, and good-looking, and they put on a lively show together, playing off each other and performing the usual lewd, heavy metal band high jinx.

"Is Rudy from your neighborhood, too?" I asked Walter.

"Are you kidding?" Walter answered. "Rudy was a year younger than us. We knew him because his older brother was on our little league team."

"That's wild," I said, but no one was really paying attention to me. Walter and Hunter were busy talking about Rudy, and how it was a good thing he had given up drugs, and speculating whether or not he was the most famous heroin addict to ever come out of Great Neck South High School, when a waiter came over to take our order.

I noticed that Hunter Burns hadn't even looked at me since he had first sat down at the table. I figured this was his way of coping with the attention brought on by his fame. He probably just ignored anyone up till the point he actually wanted them involved. I could wait. I knew the whole point of his being here was to talk to me. And the few words he had said to me—"Good to meet you," and "Are you ready to order?" had been friendly enough, so I had no reason to feel insecure.

We all had salads and after the busboy had taken away the plates, Hunter Burns decided the time had come to address me. He leaned back in his chair and shifted so he could see me. Looking straight into my eyes, he said, "So, Walter gave me your demo. I think he mentioned we're considering doing one of your songs on our next album. Would that interest you?"

"Yes, of course I would be interested. Which song did you like?"

"The one we're considering is 'Let Me Show You.' I really like it and so does Rudy. Our producer says he wants to think about it a little more. We need to see if it fits in with the overall mood of the album."

"What's the overall mood? "

"Something to do with destiny. We're working on it now. I felt it was time for us to do something a little more thematic, some kind of 'suite' thing so I'm trying to tie the songs together. We're thinking about something along the lines of the four seasons or the seven ages of man. I'm interested in the idea that there's some greater force that directs us, even when we think we're making our own decisions." I was impressed. I never knew so much thought went into a Death Threat album. Hunter took a sip of his water.

"So, the theme of the album will be destiny, making choices, and I really like the way your song ties in with that," continued Hunter, as the waiter put our main courses in front of us. "I like your whole idea of having this guy walking along, kind of lost, then seeing a doorway, and choosing to go through it. Then on the other side he finds his romantic destiny waiting for him. That's very good. I think we could do a lot with that."

"Thank you."

"Yes, and it's a good ballad. That's really what we're looking for. We write all of our own material but ballads are difficult for us." With no warning, Hunter suddenly turned away from me, called the waiter, told him his fish was cold, and then turned back to me, as fixedly as ever.

"What made you write it?"

"What, 'Let Me Show You?'"

"Yes, I'm just curious, did something inspire you? Because I feel a lot of power in this song."

What had actually inspired me was a song writing contest. Ray was entering it, so for fun, I thought I would, too. I tried to write the most commercial, uncomplicated song I could think of, with the most meaningless lyrics, a good hook, and tons of emotion. A pure product. Ray helped me make the demo. I had him stick in a lot of fast riffs and feedback-drenched chords. I just wanted to see if I could write a hit, nothing more. I got an honorable mention.

"It had to do with this dream," I said. "I had this dream where I was walking through the streets confused until I came to a door. And my whole future was on the other side. It was so intense, I thought maybe I could work it into a song."

"But why did you write it from a man's point of view?"

"It just felt right. I wrote it first from a woman's point of view but it just wasn't working, so I tried it from a man's point of view and it worked." That was true, although the reason I preferred it was because it was more commercial this way. Hunter didn't need to know any of this. If he saw destiny in it, that was fine with me. Besides, he was right, "Let Me Show You" was perfect for Death Threat. Even I imagined it as a hard-rock ballad. That's how I heard it when I wrote it; a moody acoustic beginning, building to a big orchestra sound with a wailing guitar solo over it, cellos in the background carrying the theme, and vocals sung in a screechy scratchy heavy metal voice that goes nuts in the final chorus. And there was plenty of room for the power chords and pomp that had made Death Threat famous. This song was made for them. In the end, I liked the song myself. It was very catchy and after I wrote it I went around humming it for days, which is always a good sign.

"So what we have to do," said Hunter, "—that is, if we decide we're definitely going to put 'Let Me Show You' on the next album—is have you work out a contract with our management. I'm going to have Jerry, our manager, talk to your lawyer. I don't really want to get in the middle. I try to stick to the music," he said, giving me a smile. I had almost forgotten he was a musician, he seemed so business-like. "It would be a standard arrangement with royalties paid to you as the writer, and an advance for publishing rights. We would definitely want the publishing rights. Jerry will send you a contract to look over and you can show it to whoever you want."

I nodded along as seriously as possible. Hunter didn't leave me much to say. I noticed I had completely lost my appetite. I was too excited to eat. I glanced over at Walter who serenely chewed on a steak. The waiter had returned Hunter's trout, and he too was eating briskly.

"Hunter, I'm really pleased about this," I said when he had finished rattling off his terms and conditions. There was no point in asking questions now, I would deal with his lawyer for that. I wanted to see if I could get things a little more personal. "I'm very excited."

"You should be," said Hunter, his dark eyes focused on the dish in front of him. "In eighteen albums, this is only the third time we're doing an original someone outside the band wrote."

"Wow," was all I could think of saying.

"Our last two albums have sold three million copies each. You're going to get a lot of exposure," he said scooping the last grains of rice off his plate. "Right, Walt?"

"You better believe it," said Walter. "Not to mention you'll be earning some bucks."

"It's just good timing," continued Hunter. "We were actually looking for a whole new direction when Walter happened to mention you. I'm really interested in trying something new, working with some younger performers. You're totally unknown. There's a freshness in your work. We can use that right now." It sounded as if he were talking about a blood transfusion.

We ordered coffee and at the same time Hunter asked for the check. Hunter asked me a few questions about Swan Venom. He didn't seem disinterested as much as distracted. He looked away now and then as we chatted, as if he had something on his mind. He was really very handsome, I noticed, with the kind of sensuous lips that are de rigeur among high profile rock stars. His stack of hair didn't look quite right against his strong, soon-to-be-middle-aged face, but it was part of his image.

The only time he seemed to perk up was when a lady came over from another table and asked Hunter for an autograph for her daughter. He grabbed one of the leather-bound menus, signed 'To Betsy, from Hunter Burns' across the whole menu and handed it to the woman, much to the waiter's dismay.

The check came and Hunter insisted on paying it. He was in a rush, and by way of an explanation he turned to me and put his hand on mine as if truly noticing me for the first time and said, "I'm sorry if I'm a little distracted, Grace. I've got to run. I have a meeting with my lawyer about our next album. And then I have to be at some awards thing by eight. Maybe we can meet again when I have less on my mind. Provided everything goes the way I'd like it to, we'll be in touch." He turned to Walter.

"Babe, I'll talk to you," he said. He stood up, put on his trench coat and gave Walter a slap.

"Be good," said Walter, returning Hunter's friendly punch.

"Okay, Walt. Grace. So long," Hunter said, and with that, he turned around and walked out, leaving a trail of turned heads, gaping waiters and a few busboys discussing in Spanish the identity of the man in the white trench coat.

4

I walked all the way home from Le Papier Maché after leaving Walter Wiener at the subway. It was a long walk from 56th Street to Chinatown, but the February day was clear and bright, and I wanted to be outside as I replayed every word of my lunch with Hunter Burns.

I had an overwhelming desire to shout to the people hurrying down Sixth Avenue with me, and tell them where I had just been. I looked at the men in dark suits and overcoats and at the trimly dressed women; like them, I was going places. Would I be as successful in my own career as they were in theirs? How could I not be, I mused, I just came from lunch with Hunter Burns.

I walked past the office buildings of midtown, the Public Library, down to the Village and then through Soho. When I got to Canal Street I turned left and headed east to Chinatown, and as I passed the People's Bank of China, the Tai Tai Dumpling Palace and the Jing-so Tea Shop, I felt power. I admit that I indulged myself in a feeling of total self-satisfaction. You could do that when you lived on Canal Street because the neighborhood kept you honest. No matter how great I thought I was, it was hard to forget that not one of the 150,000 residents of Chinatown could care less about me, Hunter Burns, or guitars. My neighborhood was the crossroads for a thousand cultures who all had one thing in common—their lack of interest in American pop culture except to the degree it affected their merchandise. And so the Korean lady in the deli, the Senegalese watch seller, and the Chinese fish merchant all said hello to me with no more enthusiasm than usual and if they noticed my bigger than normal smile or excited step, they said nothing. I could have told them I was probably going to sell a song to one of the biggest bands in America, but not one of them would have said more than, "that's nice" and continued to wrap my fish or whatever I had bought. I smiled at the world, indifferent as it was, and squeezed through the clusters of tourists and shoppers as I made my way to my front door.

Once upstairs, I applied myself to the task of calling everyone I knew. I flopped on the couch, picked up the telephone and dialed Roger first.

Unfortunately, he was out. Denise, his secretary, told me that Roger was taping *Marketwatch* where he was guest analyst this week. I left a message for him to call me. Next, I phoned Natalie. I got her answering machine. After waiting patiently through the lengthy new age musical segment that introduced her beep, I left a message for her to call me. I thought about calling Ray but decided against it. It was early afternoon. Ray would still be asleep.

I wanted to talk to someone who would appreciate the weight of my good news. This meant I wasn't ready to call my relatives yet. Like my neighbors in Chinatown, they would all say "That's nice," and secretly continue to wonder when I would become a music teacher.

No, I would first call someone who could share my excitement, someone who understood the whimsical nature of the arts where a single day, apparently no different than the day before, can elevate you from a toiling worker, invisible as an ant, to the status of artistic royalty or at least partners with Death Threat. I wanted to talk to someone who could appreciate a lucky break. I called Paul Teagarden.

It was two-thirty in New York. That meant it would be eleven-thirty in the morning in California. I dialed Paul, positive I would get another answering machine. Instead, Paul answered the phone.

But I should take a moment here to mention that my phone conversations with Paul Teagarden had taken a very personal turn in the last few weeks.

ᛆ ᛆ ᛆ

Our first phone calls after Palm Springs had been friendly talks, the telephone equivalent of pen pal letters. Except for the tone of his voice, which was always a little on the intimate side, they could have been conversations with any friend or acquaintance. After that first phone call to me in New York, Paul began to check in regularly, calling me once or twice a week. We would talk for an hour or so, covering topics with the range of a radio talk show. Between our two cities, we had plenty of fires, mudslides, shootings, and explosions to keep us occupied. There were also the advances in our own ambitious projects—my band and Paul's film. I liked the fact that

Paul asked a lot of questions about my music. And he liked to laugh. There was nothing in these conversations I had to hide.

But certain casual discussions advanced our talks in small romantic steps. For instance, Paul told me about a job he was on one week. "I'm shooting a commercial," he said, "it's for a brand of wine, and the client wants a romantic setting. They want me to use a fireplace but I'm a little tired of that scene. It's been done. Do you think that's romantic?"

"I think a fireplace can be romantic in real life. I don't know about a commercial."

"Imagine it, you're in front of the fire..."

"Are you there too?"

"Of course I am. We're in front of the fire, and you're stretched out on the couch."

"Is this a commercial or your fantasy?"

"Both. It's dark in the room, and we each have a glass of white wine. The flames are shining in the glass..."

I was starting to feel a little warm, even without a real fireplace. Paul's voice became softer as he spoke, as if he were trying to create the effect of being there beside me.

"The only light in the room is coming from the fire. I'm with you on the couch and you're next to me, close. "

"I like this commercial," I said.

"Now it's more a fantasy," he whispered back.

We were having this kind of conversation more and more often. I would say it was flirtatious. And our voices were getting more familiar to each other. This meant a lot, because voices replaced touch and all other senses. Voices were all we had.

Paul started to call more often, late at night instead of during the day. If Roger was at my apartment I would let my answering machine take the call. Otherwise, I talked to him. The calls at night were relaxed and they strengthened our connection.

When you talk to someone for hours in the dark it's a little like falling through space with them. Your words and thoughts become sharper, more focused. Breathing becomes a whole new vocabulary. We were getting good at the phone. As the talks became deeper, I told Paul more about my life, from the smallest detail to the grandest plan. I answered all his questions, sending out my story in signals to be picked up at his end of the phone, three thousand miles away. The talks were a stream of consciousness jumble, sometimes silly, sometimes deep. "What was the first song you learned to play on the guitar?" he asked one night.

"When Johnny Comes Marching Home."

"Hurrah, hurrah."

"You know it."

"When you were married, did you and your husband play music together?" he asked.

"We did. Not professionally, but at home. He was great."

"What would you play?"

"Oh, mostly jazz." I was stretched out on my bed, my feet against the wall, my hair falling back over the edge of the bed. "Standards. Old ones like 'Stardust.' 'How High the Moon.' 'Green Dolphin Street.' We did a mean 'Killer Joe.' "

"I know that song," Paul said dreamily. "Can you play 'The Nearness of You'?"

"That's a gorgeous song. Sure. You're into music, aren't you?"

"Yes, I am. I think it goes with being a filmmaker. Music is so evocative, it helps me see a scene in my mind. Sometimes the music is inseparable from the scene itself. It all goes together."

"I'll make you a soundtrack. Tell me a story."

And then he would spin a tale and I would pick up the guitar and play while he talked. Our worlds seemed to intertwine in a way they never did with Roger.

As Paul stretched across the sleeping country into my bedroom, I told him stories about the clubs I played in, about the Italian weddings and the Jewish weddings I did, about the guys in Swan Venom and about my college roommate who I hear all the time on light jazz stations. Even a little about Roger.

I noticed Paul never told me that much about the people in his life. We talked about his projects. I assumed this was because his projects were most important to him. Perhaps he didn't have much of a personal life. He shared some gossip about the actors he worked with and stories of life on a film set. We talked about the videos he had directed and I was surprised to learn he had done a video for Band of Rags and Abish. He had done a lot more than these but he said he didn't really enjoy them; the shooting schedule was too hard and the results chaotic.

He shared a few anecdotes about his personal life. He told me a story about an ex-girlfriend who followed him around for a year after they broke up. She watched his house and waited for him at the airport when he flew into Los Angeles, until he had to get a restraining order and to this day she still sent him letters. It made me wonder if Paul was the kind of man who caused obsessions.

As I talked to Paul on the verge of sleep, I noticed a growing desire to see him. His presence seeped into the day. Our words and stories started to saturate me. I thought about the things he said, sometimes even when I was with Roger. I was sure I wanted to get closer than a telephone. It became harder not to acknowledge this. One night Paul broke the ice.

I lay on my bed. The only light in the room came from a small lamp at the other end of the bedroom. I had draped a mustard color Russian scarf printed with flowers over it. It made the light in the room dim and soft.

"I wish you were here," he said, after we had talked for a while. Usually I let remarks like this pass. Tonight I pursued it.

"What would you do if I were there?"

"Hmmm," he said languidly. "First I would take my clothes off, because you have all yours off. Don't you?" There was a boldness in his voice tonight.

"I don't now," I said. "But if I were there it might be different."

"Yes. It would be very different. I want to see you naked."

"Then what would you do?"

"I would put my arms around you and kiss you. Like I kissed you standing on that mountain. More," he added, in his terse way.

"I would like that," I said.

"I've been thinking about this lately. I want to touch you again." I was a little nervous about where this kind of talk would lead. What if all of this had been just a build up to an obscene phone call? But no, how could that be? Whatever he was saying had evolved out of a growing feeling. "We've been talking on the phone so long, it al-most feels as if you're next to me," he whispered.

"Is this what you've been thinking about while we've been talk-ing?"

"Sometimes. It's been building up."

"I know what you mean," I said, rolling on my back.

"Let's imagine you're here. My bedroom is on the second floor and there's a big window along the right wall," said Paul. "It faces the trees. The tree tops actually."

"What color is the bed?"

"I have a white blanket. The sheets...let me see...they're blue and white stripes."

"How do they feel?"

"Nice. Warm. If you were here, I would start by kissing your neck."

"Where are your hands while you're kissing my neck?" I whis-pered.

This conversation was the turning point. From then on, each call found us both a little bolder, a little more explicit. The question, "what would you do if I were there?" was answered with more detail every time.

It had happened so naturally, I really didn't have the chance to start wondering whether such conversations were right or wrong. Besides, I was still aware of the safety factor; California was far away. I told myself it was all just fun. Passionate fun with a new friend. And I didn't tell Roger about it.

Soon our conversations had an entirely different tone from our original discussions about the changes in the California senate. Except for the fact that we never actually saw each other, things were heating up.

۲ ۲ ۲

By the time my lunch with Hunter Burns came around, Paul already knew everything about it, including where and when it would take place, who would be there, and what I planned to wear. Details are the essence of long phone calls.

As soon as Paul answered the phone that afternoon, I broke the news.

"Hi, it's me. I just came from lunch."

"And? How did it go?"

"It looks like Death Threat wants to record one of my songs."

"Congratulations!"

"Thank you. Isn't it unbelievable?" I sat on the worn couch in my living room, a few pillows piled around me.

"It's not unbelievable at all," said Paul. "You deserve it."

"Death Threat is not exactly my ideal."

"So what, it's fabulous anyway. This is going to be the start of great things for you, I can feel it."

"Do you think so?"

"Yes."

"It's not definite yet. Hunter Burns wants to talk to their producer about it and see if it fits in with the rest of the stuff on the album. They're doing some kind of theme album. They're into destiny now."

"Hunter said he would get back to you?"

"Yes, next week. Actually, he said his manager would get back to me. They're in a hurry to move on this."

"That's good. I've met Hunter Burns a few times. From what I remember, he's a pretty straight guy."

"You met him?"

"Actually, I was going to do some work with them."

"Paul, why didn't you tell me?" I said, my grip on the phone tightening.

"Because I didn't want to give you any ideas about what to expect. It was backstage at an Abish concert, a couple of years ago when I was doing their videos."

"And?"

"And Hunter was there. He's a good friend of the lead singer of Abish, Arnie Saint Jones. At the time Hunter wanted to do a documentary of their next tour and he wanted to talk to me about directing it."

"Really? I can't believe this."

"Hunter liked the stuff I did for Abish. Nothing came of it, though. I met with him and their manager—what's his name?"

"Jerry Saltstien?"

"Right. Jerry. We had one meeting and it looked promising. But the timing was bad. A week later Rudy went into rehab and Death Threat stopped touring for a year."

"So you met Hunter Burns. That's funny." Actually, it wasn't funny at all. I was annoyed. He kept the fact that he knew Hunter Burns a secret while I rambled on and on about him.

"I'm sorry I didn't tell you, Grace. I just didn't want to ruin anything for you."

"Thanks, I guess."

"Anyway, Hunter is a decent guy," Paul continued. "He called me himself to tell me the tour was off. He's tough when it comes to business, though, that I remember."

"I guess I'll find out soon enough." I paused. "Still, what a coincidence."

"Not really. The entertainment business is smaller than you think, Grace."

"Imagine if you had done the film. We could be working with the same people."

"That's nothing. We could be sleeping with the same people," he said with a laugh. I didn't laugh with him. "I'm sorry, Grace," he continued. "Maybe I should have told you sooner."

ɣ ɣ ɣ

The fact that Paul had met Hunter before I did took some of the edge off my good news. Part of the thrill for me had been that I could report such impressive news to my friends. My competitive spirit was glad to show I could play in the same league on the creative circuit as Paul. Career-wise, Paul—and for that matter, most of the men I know—are further along than me. I don't know if it's because of gender, or age difference, or opportunity, but the arts are a difficult place to make headway. In many arts, you can be forty-five and still be considered new on the scene. And if you're a woman, you can be new on the scene right up until you die.

Having told him the news, I wanted to keep the phone call brief. I didn't have the money for a long call to California in the middle of the day. "I better go," I said, standing up. "I just wanted to give you the news."

"Well, congratulations again, and a big hug and a kiss."

"Paul, why don't you come out here and give me a hug and kiss in person?" I was sick of hugs and kisses over the phone. "Aren't you getting tired of just talking all the time?"

"I'd love to come to New York," he said, lowering his voice as if to convey his earnestness. He didn't seem surprised by what I had just said. "I've been thinking about it myself."

"Really?"

"Yes. I may be shooting a job in New York very soon."

I was a little disappointed he didn't consider visiting me unrelated to his career, but he was a busy person. Whichever way he got here, I wouldn't complain.

"When do you think you could come?"

"Next month. I'm talking to my producer. And if the job doesn't work out maybe I'll come to New York anyway."

"You have to get out here. I can't take much more of these phone calls, Paul. I need to see you."

"Mmmm. Just your voice turns me on. What am I going to do with the rest of you?"

"That's up to you."

"Can you meet me at the airport with no clothes on?"

"Okay," I murmured. "Paul, try to come out here."

"Definitely. I have plans for you," he replied. Another man with plans. I wondered if he had been talking to Walter Wiener.

"Grace, I better go." His voice was so physical, I could almost feel it. "I'll talk to you soon. I'll work something out." Now I had even more to be excited about.

۷ ۷ ۷

By the next day, I had broken through the busy signals and phone machines to report the good news to my friends. I even called Zermin. We hadn't talked much since the Punch and Torkney affair, but I knew he would want to hear the news. He went wild when I told him I might have a song on Death Threat's next album. He asked me if I still needed help with a demo. I told him no, thank you, he had his chance.

I had to remind myself that excited as I was, the deal was still only speculation. There would be no guarantees until I got the official word from one of Death Threat's people. To help me stay calm during the wait, Walter Wiener telephoned daily to inform me of my ever-improving odds. On Monday, the week after lunch with Hunter, Walter reported that the chances of having Death Threat record my song were seventy-thirty; he had talked to Hunter Burn's mother, Marilyn. By Tuesday, he phoned in the odds at eighty-twenty; Jerry Saltstien, the band's manager, said things were looking good. On Wednesday, Walter called me to say, "We're 97.51% there."

The big call came Thursday, exactly one week after I had lunch with Hunter Burns. Jerry Saltstien telephoned me at home.

"Gretchen?" he said, when I picked up the phone.

"Do you mean Grace?"

"Yes, right, excuse me. Grace, how are you."

I had no idea who was talking but I allowed him to finish his pleasantries before I asked who was speaking. He introduced himself, then gave me the news.

"The boys want to use the song," he said. "They'd like it for their next album."

"That's great."

"We'll want the publishing rights," said Jerry. "I think Hunter mentioned that. I'm going to send you a contract. Look it over and get back to me soon. We'll be taking care of all the arrangements with the record company, but don't worry about it, we're talking full statutory rate here."

"Oh, good," I said, not knowing exactly what that meant. "So do I need to meet with you?"

"No, that's not necessary. First look at the contract. Give me your address," he ordered.

As soon as I had finished giving him my zip code, Jerry announced he had another call and had to go. I could tell by his tone of voice I was just another item on his to-do list; there was no point in getting too joyous with him.

I thanked him for the news then put down the phone. I jumped on the bed. My song would be on Death Threat's new album. I had actually gotten a break. It's one thing to work and struggle and hope that one day you'll get somewhere, but now it was going to happen. Why me, I wondered, as I threw my cat in the air. Was it some kind of repayment for how serious I had been about my music? Was it my persistence? Or was it just because Walter Wiener liked women who were taller than him? Whatever the case, I was in with Death Threat.

ɣ ɣ ɣ

Geoffrey and I both arrived early at rehearsal Thursday. I was tuning up while Geoffrey sat in a corner and changed his strings. When he was done setting up, Geoffrey leaned his bass against the wall, put on his sunglasses, and sat in the corner, his hands around a Styrofoam cup of tea. He remained that way until I spoke to him.

I hated to bother Geoffrey because he looked like he needed rest. He was having problems with his girlfriend, Joanne. She worked late almost every night and came home at two or three in the morning, which was odd because she worked at a bank. But he had promised to bring me the phone number of an entertainment lawyer. His Uncle William, who plays the clarinet in the Buddy Rodriguez Big Band, said that the band's manager, Sid Flough, knew a very good entertainment lawyer. It was his daughter, Lisa Flough.

"Geoffrey, are you asleep?" I said in a hushed voice.

"No."

"Did you remember to bring me that number? The number of the lawyer?"

"Yeah," he replied listlessly. Geoffrey leaned forward, and reached into his leather Coach bag, rummaged through it and pulled out a pad. "Here it is," he said, sighing. He ripped off the top sheet and handed me the piece of paper that said, 'P.S. 127 Loves You,' at the top. Lisa Flough's number was on it.

I appreciated Geoffrey's effort to help me find a lawyer. Massimo wouldn't give me the name of his lawyer, claiming he only handled art, and Paul didn't know anyone on the East coast who specialized in music. Only Geoffrey had connections to a professional.

In fact, all the guys in the band were extremely supportive once they found out Death Threat was going to record one of my songs. I was worried there might be some resentment at first; they might think I was losing interest in Swan Venom. Or there might be some jealousy. My status in the music business was definitely going to shift up a notch.

But I underestimated the guys. Jealousy has never been part of the Swan Venom experience. As it turned out, everyone was happy for me and Steve even shook my hand after rehearsal one day, and said, "Good deal, Grace." I think he was relieved I wasn't dating Walter Wiener. Anyway, they had plenty of reason to be positive; any attention I might get would translate into more work for Swan Venom.

"Lisa Flough-Delgado," I said reading from the pad. "Who is she?"

"Her husband is some rich South American producer dude. Roberto Delgado."

"Oh, sure. I've heard of him. He does a lot of Latin stuff, right?"

"Yeah. And he produces all of Buddy's albums. That's how they met. Lisa does all the legal work for The Buddy Rodriguez Band."

"How romantic. So can Lisa help me with my contract?"

"I think so. My uncle says she's really good. She did his will."

"That's not what I need a lawyer for."

"I'm just trying to help," said Geoffrey, glaring at me, the muscles in his neck tensing up. "Call her or don't call her, it's all the same to me."

"Geoffrey, lighten up. I appreciate the number. Thank you."

"Sorry," he said sullenly. "I didn't get much sleep last night. As far as Lisa goes, all I know is I met her a couple of times and she seems like a smart lady. Even my brother uses her. Lisa did the contract work for his last album." Geoffrey was referring to his brother, D.J. Romald's, last release, "Gangsta' Bakery."

"He uses her? That's a good sign. He's doing really well, isn't he?"

"Oh, yeah. And she's tough on him, too, man. She even made him start a retirement account, so he wouldn't blow all his money."

"She sounds serious."

"Yeah, I think she is." I noticed he was wearing a very handsome jacket today, a dark brown tweed with flecks of color and patches on the elbows.

"Maybe she can even do some stuff for Swan Venom when the time comes. By the way, I really like that jacket. We're going to have to start calling you, 'The Professor,'" I joked, trying to cheer him up. He didn't answer. He was already on his way out of the room, hurrying to leave another message on his girlfriend's answering machine. "Thanks for the number, man," I called after him.

᠀ ᠀ ᠀

Lisa Flough-Delgado has long, brown hair that falls in tight ringlets over her shoulders, and piercing lake-blue eyes which are the result of the fashion contact lenses she wears.

"How are you?" she pronounced in a throaty New York accent, when I walked into her office. She stared at me as if she wanted to make sure I got the full effect of her blue eyes and her highlighted corkscrew curls. Then she stuck out her thin, bony hand to shake mine. We shook hands and she pointed to a small arm chair on wheels parked in front of her desk. "Have a seat," she said. She sat down in her own chair.

I sunk into the arm chair, nervously clutching my manila envelope full of papers. I had called Lisa the same day Geoffrey gave me her phone number; I didn't want to waste a second. I felt that if I didn't act quickly, my opportunity might vanish. She gave me an afternoon appointment at her comfortable office on the forty-fourth floor of the Manhattan firm of Berman Whippe & Slotnick Law Associates.

The roofs of the theater district spread beneath her window, soot-covered and brown. Lisa's office, by contrast, was decorated in clean, pale colors like sand and cream, with wood furniture. The brightest thing in the room was Lisa herself, and she shone in an orange suit and oversized jewelry that peeked from beneath her collar and under her cuffs. Coins, charms and chains jangled whenever she moved. I guessed Lisa was somewhere in her late forties, although it was hard to tell because of her layers of make-up and accessories.

"I understand you're a friend of Geoffrey McCoy," she began. "I've known his uncle for a long time and his brother too. Sweet kid. You're in a band with him?"

"Yes. He's our bass player." I shifted in my chair, which was uncomfortably small for me, my coat and my envelope.

"That's lovely. Grace, you look like you've just been shot. Relax."

"Sorry. I'm a little nervous." I had explained to Lisa over the phone that I needed help in looking over a contract. Jerry Saltstien had sent me all the paperwork as promised. It might as well have been written in Dutch. I hardly understood a word. "I'm a little overwhelmed," I added.

"Maybe I can make things less overwhelming. Did you bring me something to look at?"

"Oh, right. The contract. I have it here." I fumbled though my folder. "I looked it over but I don't know what any of it means."

"You're not supposed to."

"They want publishing rights to my song."

"Naturally."

"But why?" I hadn't understood the gravity of Hunter Burn's demand that Death Threat own the publishing rights until I had read the contract; owning the publishing rights meant they owned the song.

"It's simple," said Lisa, "the writer's income from a song is broken into two parts. One of those parts is the publisher's share, the other is the writer's share. The publisher controls the copyright. The songwriter gets fifty percent of the royalties and the publisher gets the other fifty percent. It's like a fee for managing the business of the song."

"So who's the publisher now?"

"You are, more or less. Right now you own the song completely. But once Death Threat owns the publishing rights, they receive fifty percent of the income from your song. Many established songwriters publish their own music so they get the full royalty. But bands as successful as Death Threat demand the publishing rights to songs they record because they want the control that comes with those rights. And they have the power to get it."

"So do I have to give it to them?"

"Given their status? That's their deal, take it or leave it," said Lisa, brushing some lint off her orange suit. I had hoped she would show a little more zeal on my behalf.

"So what's all the other stuff in the contract? Like this, right on the first page..." I read from the contract. "'The Composition, Let Me Show You, which title may be changed by the Publisher, including the title, words, and music thereof, and all rights therein, and all copyrights and the rights to secure copyrights and any extensions and renewals of copyrights in the same and in any arrangements and adaptations thereof, throughout the world and any and all other rights that the writer now has or to which he may be entitled or that he hereafter could or might secure with respect to the Composition, if these presents had not been made, throughout the World and to have and to hold the same absolutely unto the publisher and its successors and assigns.'" I took a breath. "What does that mean?"

"All that means is that publishers can do what they want with their portion of the rights," said Lisa cheerfully, "for instance, should they want to publish sheet music, or sell their catalog. It means that you are transferring the complete set of rights that come with ownership of the copyright, and that includes the right to change the title and lyrics if necessary."

"Why would I want them to do that? I don't want them to change the lyrics," I cried.

"Grace, it's normal. Something may come up and they may need that right to protect themselves. Let me look at the contract, please," Lisa said, extending her hand. I gave her the papers.

She began scanning the pages, pronouncing "uh-huh" and "yes" as she read. She smiled as she came upon familiar phrases, nodding at some and smirking at others as if they were old friends and enemies. A cluster of silver frames took up the corner of Lisa's desk.

While Lisa read, I looked at the pictures. In one school photo, a chubby boy grinned against a colorful autumn background. In another, two dark-haired girls, both wearing wide headbands and checkered skirts, smiled. These must be Lisa's children, I thought. Another frame displayed a man I took to be her husband, Roberto Delgado. He stood on the roots of a big tropical tree. In another, the same dark haired man had his arms around Lisa on the deck of a sailboat. I noticed there was the smell of hairspray in her office. Lisa probably kept a big can right in her desk drawer. I looked at the picture of her on the sailboat. Then, like now, she had a dark tan and freckles. I guess Lisa didn't worry much about wrinkles or skin cancer. My reverie was interrupted by her sharp voice.

"It's aggressive. But there's nothing unexpected."

"So?"

"So we can work with it." She tossed the papers on her desk. "It's a boilerplate agreement. The royalty rates are standard. To sum it up, the contract says you license Death Threat to publish and record the song. You're entitled to fifty percent of all mechanical, or recording royalties, and fifty percent of all performance rights. And you get a cut of royalties for sheet music, synchronization rights, and anything else they do with it. Death Threat gets the publisher's share."

"For how long?"

"For the rest of your life and then fifty years after you die."

"Is this a good thing?"

"No," said Lisa. Then she stared at me and added, "But that's the music business," and began noisily sorting through the papers she had thrown down a minute before. She had a great sense of timing. It didn't surprise me that both she and her father were involved with the music business.

Lisa spoke as she sorted out papers. "Look Grace, you're completely unknown. You have no bargaining power." I listened to her glumly, not thrilled to be reminded of how low I was in the music business kingdom. "This is not a bad contract, as things go. They could have been much tougher on you. All they have to do is change a line in the lyrics and they get writing credit too, and there goes another 25% of your royalties."

Lisa explained that the most important right I had was the right to collect a small amount of money every time "Let Me Show You" was played on the radio, on someone's tape deck, in a bar, in a dance club, at a skating rink, in a hotel lobby, on a jukebox, or in the circus if it should come to that. There would also be royalties from songbooks, sheet music, and other arrangements. The performance royalties would be collected every time the song was played in some commercial establishment. These were not counted one song at a time; it was all done with statistics and random samples collected by the organizations that represent artists, Lisa explained. I would have to join BMI or ASCAP, the performing rights organizations. They figured out how often your song was being played around the country and paid you a royalty accordingly.

I would get three and one half cents for every CD or tape that was purchased with my song on it. That meant if they sold a thousand albums, I would get thirty-five dollars. It didn't seem like a lot, but then Lisa reminded me I needed to be realistic; "Death Threat usually sells several million units," she pronounced. On top of that, I would get an advance as soon as I signed. "It's in your contract," said Lisa. "You're getting a two thousand dollar advance for these rights, which will be collected against incoming royalties. Your royalties will be paid to you semi-annually."

Death Threat would be free to use the song any way they wanted. This was the part of my contract I found hardest to accept. I had never given up creative control before. I would have no say in what they did with my song. They could play it on spoons or record it as a cha-cha. They could use it in a popcorn commercial, or to sell frozen dinners.

"They can sell it to a movie for a theme song. A movie about Spring Break. A karate movie. Anything."

"And they don't even have to ask me?"

"No," said Lisa. "They call the shots. You can refuse to sell the song of course."

"What do you think I should do?"

"Honestly? Thank your lucky stars."

"I can do that."

"I can make a few suggestions, however," said Lisa, swiveling in her chair. "I see no major problems with what's here, but I think there are a few things missing. Some small matters to protect you. You'll want a right of reversion clause in case they don't use the song. You'll want to keep the advance if they don't record the song. I'd like to get something in this that protects you from having them issue any licenses that don't produce any financial benefit— for instance, in case they want to use the song as part of some giveaway or charity concert. They would need to negotiate with you first. Also, I'm going to try and see if I can get something in about the writer's consent to licenses, which would allow you to approve of certain types of uses they might want to grant, for instance, should someone besides Death Threat want to re-record the song for an advertisement. That one is tough, I can't guarantee anything, but I'll try to get you as much as possible."

Finally, I felt as if she was on my side. "What do we do now?" I asked. "Do you want to get in touch with Death Threat's lawyer?"

"Yes. Let me work on the contract first."

"But you'll let me know what you're going to ask for, before you talk to them, right?"

"Of course. I don't do anything without talking to you first. You're the client, right?" she said with a deep laugh.

"Right," I said, doubtfully. She stood up at her desk and dropped a paperweight on my file. I think this was her signal that it was time for me to go. I felt there was a lot more I would like to have clarified but the fact that I was paying her more an hour than I earned in an entire day at the Café Capri gave me incentive to limit my curiosity.

"It's the little things that catch up with you later," Lisa said as she stood up. "That's what we're looking for. Come, I'll walk you out." We walked from her office and down a quiet corridor to the reception area. Two big glass doors led out of the firm and back to the elevator. Lisa walked me through the doors.

"Grace, everything will work out fine," said Lisa, reaching out her hand to shake mine. I grasped her hand, feeling her cold rings against my skin.

"Thank you, Lisa," I said. "I'll talk to you soon." Although I felt more secure, I didn't feel happy. I felt I was drifting into deep water. There was much going on here I did not comprehend.

"I know you're a little nervous," continued Lisa, not letting go of my hand. "Don't worry. I've been doing this for many years, and for many, many people. I think you know my father is in this industry and so are my two brothers. One of them is a lawyer like me. The other is an agent in LA. My mother works for Warner Brothers. My husband is a producer, and even our son is in the music business. He plays the tuba in his school orchestra," she said with a laugh. He looked like he would play the tuba, I thought. "You're in very good hands," Lisa concluded. I thanked her again, and with a small cloud of Lisa's perfume and make-up clinging to my clothes like a constant token of her presence, I stepped into the elevator.

ን ን ን

Roger and I had a date to meet after my appointment with Lisa. The timing was perfect; dressed in dark blue pants and a silk striped shirt I had borrowed from Natalie, I was ready for an evening out.

I found a working telephone, and called Roger at his office. We arranged to meet in the Village.

Roger was eager to hear about my meeting with the lawyer. I think it was because he finally found something in my life he could really relate to. Though he tries to understand song writing issues, he just can't get excited over questions like, is it okay to modulate after a bridge and should you ever substitute a ninth for a flat seventh? A meeting with a lawyer was something he could sink his teeth into.

At 6 o' clock I walked into Mikonos Gardens, a small bistro with blue and white tiles and scenes of Greek ports painted on the walls. The room had a twilight glow thanks to lights hidden behind rows of flowers against the wall. Black iron lanterns with amber glass shed a warm light on the tiled floor. The lamps, along with the relief archways lining the walls, made patrons feel as if they were sitting on a terrace overlooking the Mediterranean, instead of staring into plaster on Fourth Street.

I saw Roger at a table in the corner near some fishing boats. He already had his napkin spread across his lap and a glass of red wine in front of him, as if he had been there for a while.

"Hi, Roger, am I late?" I said joining him. I looked for a clock.

"No, you're not late. I'm early. I ran out of the office right after we talked. It was crazy today, I had to get out of there."

"So it's not me," I said with relief. Since Palm Springs, I had been making a special effort to be on time, and be nicer in general to Roger. This was due as much to guilt over my stimulating talks with Paul Teagarden as it was to a desire to please Roger. Once I even made the bed before leaving his apartment in the morning.

"I'm beat," I said sinking back in my chair. "This legal stuff is very stressful." Tension stretched across my neck.

"Me too. At least your stuff is in the works now. You should feel relieved."

"I am, I guess."

"Have a glass of wine." Roger picked up the carafe on the table.

"What about you? Why was it so crazed at work?"

"An employee of one of the biggest communications companies brought a class action suit against the company's chairman. It's a mess."

"Why are they suing?"

"The chairman plans to move the entire company from Manhattan to the edge of a golf resort in New Mexico."

"So?"

"It's not good for business and no one wants to move to New Mexico except the chairman. The company is going to be tied up in court for years." Roger was once again called upon to make the rounds of business programs, and was already booked on both *Around Wall Street* and *Newman Onofrio's Financial Report.*

Ordinarily, a lively week at work gave Roger a contented glow. It was one of the few times he stopped lamenting the road not taken and enjoyed his work. But today I noticed an air of preoccupation around him. I can always tell when Roger is upset, sometimes before he can. There was a darkness around his eyes and a tension in his hands, which he held clasped in front of him.

"Roger, you seem down. Are you okay?"

"Sure. Why?"

"I don't know. You seem like something's bothering you."

"I'm concerned about this New Mexico thing. I have to find an angle. It's the castle being stormed by the peasants. Or no, it's an overthrow of the czar," said Roger, looking for just the right metaphor. He paused. "And how about you?"

"Me? What do you mean?"

"You seem very, I don't know... " Roger looked at me as he searched for the right word. "Different. Something."

Here was the problem. Roger sensed something was going on; he just didn't know exactly what. It wasn't his style to come right out with it.

"What do you mean?"

"You're so excited all the time. Almost hysterical."

"I am? Maybe it's all the incredible stuff happening with the song and all. It's been hard for me to sleep." I tried to look extra weary, just to show it was not preoccupation with something else that was keeping me awake at night, for example, burning, late night phone calls. I was not about to tell Roger about Paul Teagarden.

"Maybe that's it," Roger said. He looked only slightly relieved. Sadness still hovered over him.

And now that I thought about it, there were other signs that Roger was troubled. His paintings were getting smaller again. Not only that, they were getting darker. The lights in his windows had faded to a pale 25 watts, losing their former bright glow.

Roger may be easy-going, but it had been wrong of me to assume he didn't notice something had changed. After all, my phone calls to California had been going on for a few months, how could Roger not notice?

"I'm under a lot of pressure," I said hoping this would satisfy him for now.

"I know," he said. Like a child with a puzzle who has come to the limit of his powers, Roger stared at me. I didn't say anything else. He decided to let it go, at least for now. "So tell me about the lawyer," he continued, shaking off his melancholy mood.

"She was very intense. Very fashionable, too. Kind of a music lawyer Barbie. But she really seemed to know what she was talking about."

"What did she say about the contract?"

"She said it was all standard. It gives a ton of rights to the band. But on the other hand, it could have been worse."

"Can she do anything for you?"

I repeated what Lisa said. "She plans to concentrate on getting me a few key points. She says I don't have a lot of room to make demands. I have no bargaining power, but she'll go after what she can."

"Sounds sensible."

"I got the impression she's been through this a million times."

"That's good. Experience is important when it comes to making deals." Roger reached across the table and took my hand. "Grace, I'm proud of you. This is really exciting. I'm almost excited as you are. Can you believe it?"

"Sure. I've been bothering you enough with all the details."

"It's hardly a bother. I like it. It makes me see what can happen with a little persistence. Maybe I'm even more excited than you," Roger mused, and I think he was right. He kept fidgeting and taking his glasses on and off as we talked about my contract.

"It could be. I'm too caught up in it all. There's so much to do. Jerry asked me to get him lyrics and lead sheets, and he wants two more copies of the song on tape. He also wants the contract back as soon as possible."

"If you're too busy, I'll be excited for you. You know me, I can't get enough," said Roger, picking up a piece of squid from a dish the waiter had just placed on our table.

"You're pretty popular yourself this week. When are you on *Around Wall Street*?"

"Tomorrow or the day after if I'm not bumped."

"Tape it for me in case I forget."

"Okay. And speaking of forgetting, I have something for you." Roger pulled a small box from his jacket pocket.

"What's this?"

"I bought you a little present."

"Really? Why?"

"Just to celebrate. Nothing special. Go ahead, open it." He handed me the box.

I pulled off the white ribbon that held it closed. Inside were gold earrings, thin threads wrapped around three stones, each a different shade of red.

"They're beautiful," I exclaimed.

"We've both been so busy lately, I wanted to let you know I was thinking about you."

"Thank you, Roger" I said, holding them up. "I don't know what to say. It's not even a holiday."

"You don't have to say anything. Anyway, they're not just for you. They're for me too. I'm the one who gets to look at them."

Roger could not have made me feel more guilty if he had recited Paul Teagarden's phone number. Was it only that morning that I had been stretched out on my bed talking to Paul, dizzy with excitement? I looked at Roger and he smiled back at me, his shiny glasses reflecting the red stones of my new earrings as I held them up in front of him. He looked pleased; he was the picture of a man who had done his part, at work, in the world, and now with me. It wasn't a smug look; rather, it was a kind of calm, as if for the moment, he felt secure.

Roger's generosity touched me. I took off the earrings I was wearing and replaced them with his gift. "How do they look?" I pulled back my hair.

"Beautiful. A perfect choice."

"Thank you, Roger." I stood up and put my hand on his cheek and kissed him. He put his arms around me. Embracing Roger, I felt a unique mixture of pain and pleasure. Pain, because I had said things to Paul Teagarden fifteen states away I had never said to him. It would hurt Roger if he knew. Pleasure, because I was truly glad to be exactly where I was, and how often do you feel that in life?

The night ended at his apartment where I slept soundly, still wearing the earrings Roger had given me. I could afford to sleep sloundly. Life was moving forward smoothly, like a stream down a mountain. I felt I had little to worry about; with my legal work in the strong and skinny hands of Lisa Flough-Delgado, with Walter Wiener as a surprisingly competent middleman smoothing the road between Death Threat and me, and with Roger and Paul in the background supplying good-looking emotional support, I settled back to enjoy the blossoming of my career.

5

SOMETIMES WE DON'T SEE THINGS CLEARLY. Even if the whole story is there for us to see in black and white, or in flesh and blood, as the case may be, we don't always see truth. And there's a good reason why; seeing things as they really are might get in the way of our fantasies.

I think that's what happened with me and Death Threat. I didn't want to see things for what they were. The potential rewards, the promise of a big launch into the music world clouded my judgment. Instead of seeing Death Threat for what they were—the musical equivalent of that candy that sparkles in your mouth for a second before turning hard and tasteless—I had convinced myself that they were roguish, professional naughty boys who I would come to appreciate over time. I had started thinking of them as musicians.

If I had thought about the whole thing clearly, I might have remembered this was the very same band that did, "Anywhere, Anytime," along with a video that had more girls in their underwear than a lingerie shop. I would have remembered this was the band that recorded, "Turn Over and Turn Me On," "Let's Do It On My Desk," "She's Bad, Bad, Bad,"—parts 1, 2, and 3—"Ain't Had Enough and Never Will"; in short, that included enough sex in most of their songs to satisfy the average high school music consumer and that's a lot. This is the band whose last album, which sold about four billion copies, was called *Slippery When Hard*. When they're not including references to cherries, sticks, cucumbers, flashlights, tunnels, and candles, they're singing about doom. Knowing this, you're probably wondering the same thing I am; where does Grace Note fit in?

The answer is, I didn't even stop to think about it. I only thought this was my big break. What did I think Death Threat was going to do with one of my songs, wear flowers in their hair and sing on a beach? Turn into four sensitive guys? In my defense, even if I had stopped to think about what Death Threat was going to do with "Let Me Show You," I would not have been prepared for what I saw in the screening room of Hyperion Productions, the production company that had just completed the shooting and editing of the "Let Me Show You" video.

Walter Wiener had invited me to the screening. It was late spring when he called with the invitation. Death Threat's recording of "Let Me Show You" had been wrapped up months ago, and their new album, *Tomorrow Never Cares*, had been released in April with my song on it. Since the release, I had followed the album's progress almost day by day. *Tomorrow Never Cares* received a surprisingly warm welcome from the music press. Although it was strictly more of the same from Death Threat—grandiose compositions that swung between pompous and rude, this time organized around a theme of destiny—several critics approved of the band's more thoughtful approach. The recording got reviewed everywhere.

Of all the things I read about *Tomorrow Never Cares*, though, nothing shocked me more than the review in the *Downtown Moon*. Ordinarily, no alternative paper in New York would even acknowledge Death Threat's existence. My band, alternative and unknown, was more likely to get a review than Death Threat was. To an inflated downtown weekly like the *Moon*, Death Threat was a fragment of pop culture beneath consideration, worth mentioning only as a reference point for the base and absurd. Hunter Burns was a musical untouchable to the New York music critics who thought playing a toy xylophone and a penny whistle deserved more space than a new Death Threat album did.

Perhaps it was the thematic nature of the album, or maybe Death Threat was so out of fashion they were allowed back in—whatever the reason, someone at The *Moon* loved *Tomorrow Never Cares*. Walter Wiener sent me the review. Amazed, I read the columns of praise:

> "Just as water finds its own level, so the turgid, swampy pop-metal ooze of Death Threat keeps on flowing, forming new in-roads into the kingdom of loud. With their newest release, *Tomorrow Never Cares*, Death Threat has finally hit solid ground. Teeming with bulging rhythms, and ripe with lyrics that revolve around the theme of destiny, Death Threat has brought grown-up fire power to the business of pop rock.

"But first: how does a band whose trademark is over-blown tunes and underworked craft turn out an album this good? The answer is, by sticking around long enough. Twenty years has brought Death Threat full circle, back to their early days in London and Pittsburgh. Death Threat has given us fourteen tightly-crafted tunes performed with power and ve-locity, beginning with the very first track, 'Start Monday Without Me.' This tune kicks in where your Testarosa leaves off, zooming smoothly around the hairpin curves of sound. Salaaming to the bass in a searing act of respect, the incessant beat of Death Threat's drummer, Frisk, carries the album forward, driven by the sheared vocals of Hunter Burns. Burns has never sounded more hazardous, and he delivers each tune with a sincerity not seen since his days as lead singer in Ant Farm. He attacks each song with a brick-in-your-shoe, kayak-in-the-rapids, art-metal compulsiveness. The harder tunes throb with an in-tensity that makes you feel as if you're heading for a bad finish, only to be redeemed by the thaw of a mel-low ballad. If hard rock is poison ivy, this album is pure irritation. In a track that shows the forty-some-thing Burns is not beyond a little self-mockery, "Harder and Harder to Get Harder and Harder" evokes Burns' own encounter with passing time. It's a gauzy wash of regret, coming from the libido of a generation.

"Like the petrified forest, nature has turned some-thing damp and green into solid rock. Anyone who wants to add a natural wonder to their CD collection should start here. Death Threat has found the exact point where hankering meets rage, where cacoëthes meets malice. My advice: let them take you there."

ᛉ ᛉ ᛉ

Since the album's release, Walter and I had been talking regularly, both of us enjoying our new professional link to the higher spheres of the music industry. Walter still had plenty of plans for me, al-though now they were mostly connected to the music business. We had finally finished recording our new demo, paid for in large part by my advance for "Let Me Show You" and a lot of extra afternoons at the Café Capri. Our tape sounded great, I thought, original yet commercial. Walter wanted to shop it around for us using Jerry Saltstien and Hunter Burns as his entree into the record companies.

Taking into account his success at placing "Let Me Show You" with Death Threat, the guys and I were willing to give Walter Wiener a try, even though he had spent most of his professional life as a candy salesman. But first he needed some serious training in the particulars of the music industry. We had to get him away from concepts like new flavors and creme-filled centers, and get him to start thinking in terms of hit songs and hooks. We had Walter come to our rehearsals once a week. We wanted him to be part of the process and learn the business from a musician's point of view.

When Walter called me at home one evening in early June, I thought it was because he had a question about something he had seen in rehearsal that week.

"Grace," he said, when I picked up the phone, "It's me, Old King Cole."

"Hi Walter, how're you doing?"

"Very good. Making headway everywhere."

"Did you read that book I gave you, *This Song is for Sale?*"

"It's my airplane reading. I'm flying to Dallas next week to see a customer. It's my in-flight entertainment."

"Good. You'll learn a lot from that book."

"But I'm not calling to bug you about the usual thing, although as far as I'm concerned a little bugging now and then is good. I am calling you on behalf of some friends of yours."

"Who?"

"They're four guys, who share the initials DT."

"Death Threat?"

"Exactly. They shot the video for "Let Me Show You" and are going to have a screening of it next week. And you, my dear, are invited."

"Really? That's great!" Walter had told me that "Let Me Show You" was going to be the second single released on Death Threat's album. The first release, a hard rock number called "Love On My Back" had made it quickly into the top forty, where it reached number 6. The record company wanted to follow up with something a little slower and "Let Me Show You" was their choice. It would get more exposure than I even imagined.

"They made a whole big thing, a rock video with the works," said Walter as if he were talking about a sandwich. "Hunter tells me it's very good."

"I can't believe they're inviting me. That's really nice of them."

"Did you think you wouldn't be invited? Grace, you're part of the Death Threat family. Of course Hunter wants you there. Listen, I told you from the start, Gary is a very loyal person even if he intimidates people."

"I'm there, Walter. I wouldn't miss it."

"I thought you would say that. And let me say, good. I'll pick you up." With that we made plans to join Hunter, Rudy, Frisk and Regbert in a private screening of "Let Me Show You," the video. My video.

ッ ッ ッ

The last time I had seen the guys from Death Threat was at a small party thrown by their record company to celebrate the album's wrap several months ago. As I got ready for the screening, I imagined what it would be like to meet them again.

It wouldn't be at all like the first time I met Hunter Burns, that day at Le Papier Maché. Then I was intimidated by Hunter Burns. Now we were more like colleagues. I would tell Hunter I read all the great reviews. We would talk about them, and laugh at the critics' change of heart. Maybe they would want to use another one of my songs on their next album. This could be the beginning of a long-term collaboration, I mused, as I tucked my black knit shirt into my organza skirt. Hunter might even consider letting me perform one of my songs with them the next time. I could be a guest artist. There would be a special thanks in the CD booklet, "Special thanks to Grace Note, appearing courtesy of Tralala Records." If that didn't work out, maybe I could just sing back-up.

In short, I had big ideas. I managed to keep my illusions about Death Threat intact right up to the moment I saw the video.

But first, let me give you an idea of what they had to work with—the lyrics to my song.

Let Me Show You
by Grace Note

I was walking,
just before the day,
going nowhere in the night, on a midnight flight,
I knew that I had lost my way.

And I was looking,
Through time and space,

I saw a light in a window sayin' "com'on in",
I saw the outline of your pretty face.

I knew I didn't have to knock and the door was unlocked,
I walked inside, I just couldn't stop.
You were leaning on the ledge in a long white dress,
I wiped your tears away and I heard myself say,

[Chorus:]
Let me show you, let me show you,
Just how much,
I can give you if I know you,
How much love.

Let me feel it, let me feel it,
The light from your star,
I wanna meet you halfway babe,
I wanna know who you are.

There it is, your classic rock ballad. In the next verse, the singer
in question looks back over his life and realizes how empty it has
been:

Lookin' around me,
Through the colored light,
I saw a face in the mirror I had seen before,
I knew that I was finally right.

Leaves of forgiveness,
Blew across the floor,
You swept them up with your love and you threw them away,
You forgave the pain I wrought before.

On a table in the hall was a crystal ball,
You held it in your hand like you were holdin' the world.
I looked inside, I saw the time gone by
I knew that I was home and I heard myself cry,

[Chorus:]
Let me show you, let me show you
Just how much,
I can give you if I know you,
How much love.

Let me feel it, let me feel it,
The light from your star
I wanna meet you halfway babe,
I wanna know who you are.

Hunter Burns really liked what he called the literary feel of the song and the way I used words like "wrought."

As in my original arrangement, after this second verse and chorus, the song goes into a wailing solo. It modulates back to the chorus, repeats a verse, then fades out with vocal improvisations. The song has a big sound. As I told Hunter, I had always imagined it with an orchestra accompaniment and lots of cellos doing the bassline. The orchestra part, which I put onto my demo with the help of a synthesizer, creates a contrary motion to the melody, giving the song a feeling of truthfulness tinged with agony.

Now the video. Here is what I saw from my comfortable, swiveling seat in the Hyperion screening room.

Picture Hunter Burns in his signature, calf-length, white trenchcoat walking down the dark streets of a city. We see him before any music starts. A white aura of light outlines his long hair, created by gas-lit street lamps. His footsteps echo on the pavement, loud reverb-enhanced clicks. It's the middle of the night. The streets are deserted and the lamps cast long reflections across the wet pavement. It is raining. Hunter is lonely.

During this walk through what looks like a cross between eighteenth-century London and downtown Cincinnati, Hunter sees a light in a doorway. The song's intro begins with a kind of wistful simplicity, provided by an acoustic guitar. Hunter walks towards the light, and begins to sing the first verse. So far the images are true to the song.

When he arrives at the door he finds it ajar. Slowly he opens it. The music builds, and Hunter steps inside to find himself in the middle of a gigantic, roaring, swinging-from-the-chandelier costume party. There was nothing about any of this in my song, I thought to myself, as I watched trapeze artists float over Hunter's furry head. This tremendous bash was shot with a swirling psychedelic feeling. The camera tipped and swerved as it followed Hunter into the heart of the party of the century. Staying true to their image, Death Threat employed the same rock video staples they had used for years. The scene was thick with fire, explosions, and snakes. Colors flashed everywhere.

People awash in patterns of light press up against Hunter, wearing strange costumes and wigs. He doesn't really see them; he is driven forward as if he is looking for something. Metaphorically, I think this is meant to symbolize that Hunter has come in from the cold to a warm interior place; a place where he finds life but also chaos. To me, it looked like Hunter has wandered into a New Year's Eve party in Miami Beach.

But most of all, what Hunter finds in this mysterious sanctuary are women. There are women everywhere, in every shape and size, and all of them with big breasts and little costumes. There were strippers and snake charmers, women in French maid outfits, cafe hostesses in leather get-ups, California girls in thread-like bikinis, go-go dancers, motorcycle chicks, burlesque queens, dominatrices, cheerleaders, hookers, geishas, schoolgirls, cowgirls in cutaway chaps, contortionists, and fan dancers. The camera traced each of their bare thighs and shoulders lovingly.

I wasn't happy to see this, but it was still pretty standard as videos go, particularly for bands of Hunter's generation. Although there was more skin than I had expected, I reminded myself that a video is nothing more than a way to sell records. The producers do whatever it takes to capture the public's imagination. They were just following a formula, I told myself. I tried to be positive and looked for the romance in the story. Yet I felt despair creeping close to me, and it wasn't just Walter Wiener on the seat next to me.

I watched, waiting to see when the heroine of my song, the woman in the long, white dress would arrive to spare my song from total meaninglessness. Hunter sang as he strolled through the fleshy mass of mostly female humanity. He bumped up against breasts, his hips met the hips of sequined bikini bottoms. The camera recorded the mix of bodies with unapologetic detail. The video had a dark, moody quality and stringy shadows cast patterns across Hunter's face. He sang to the camera, his black eyes peering coldly out at us. When he sang the words about seeing her "leaning on the ledge in a long white dress," a woman differentiated herself from the crowd; the camera lingered on her face with a moist blur. She was blonde and pale and she sat on a window sill, a mystical wind ruffling her dress and hair. At last, I said to myself. The hubbub of the party seemed to recede. The camera focused in; her dress blew around her in rippling layers and her eyes twinkled with recognition as Hunter Burns strode towards her.

Then the first chorus began. And as Hunter sings, "Let Me Show You," as a wind wildly blows his hair, Hunter takes off his trench coat. The camera zooms in on the blond woman, examining her in faster and faster cuts, first her lips, then the line of her jaw, then her hand on her collar bone. Hunter takes off his vest. Then he takes off his denim shirt. He's at the woman's side. He's showing her.

The next thing you know, he's pressed up against her. There are fast ambiguous shots of Hunter's jeans; his hands running over her bare arms; his lips on her neck; her nails on his back; and he's singing, "Let Me Feel You, Let Me Feel You," which for the record, was never meant to be taken literally. The music vibrated through the walls of the screening room and quivered through the seats.

They were having mock video-sex, judging by the quick cuts of hands on skin, thrusts and falling bits of clothing. Ambiguous body parts filled the screen and Hunter did things with his tongue that must have taken a lot of practice. Hunter is now into the second verse—the part of the song where he acknowledges he is home at last. The camera pulls back to a long shot of Hunter and the blonde groping each other under a spotlight. People churn around the couple and leaves blow through the air. Those must be the leaves of forgiveness, I said to myself, although no one was sweeping them up. Hunter and the woman see only each other, which I think was supposed to signify that Hunter has found stability where he had previously found only confusion. Of course it might have meant that the director had a few seconds to kill before Rudy's guitar solo.

When Rudy's moment came, the video cut to a concert shot of the band on stage, swinging their hair, followed by an angled shot of Rudy Rude ripping into a burning guitar solo. His high notes were drenched in overdrive and his face was contorted in a grimace of rock ecstasy. Hunter swayed in the background like the holy at a revival meeting, a bank of lights blazing behind him. Then he swaggered over to Rudy where they exchanged a knowing look as they leaned against each other in a traditional rock 'n' roll gesture of male bonding. Music filled the screening room and, as in my own arrangement, the song changed key, building tension as the melody returned to the chorus accompanied by a frenzy of images— more leaves, more strippers, a shattering crystal ball, the silhouette of a woman running her hands over her breasts, Rudy walking in a wheat field, go-go dancers pressed up against bars, more bikinis, lips and thighs spinning in a tilt-a-whirl blur of sex, vice and fire.

Then, suddenly, there was quiet. With rock-opera theatrics, the hubbub ceased. We were left with the lonely strumming of the acoustic guitar that had opened the song. We were ready for the final chorus.

Hunter and the woman in white are together now on a giant bed. Actually, she is behind him, chained to the bed post. She wears a white collar. It looks like all the guests at the big party had gone home. Flaming torches on the walls give the room a quivering, eerie light. Hunter looks out, and recaps it all for us musically in one last chorus, as the woman slithers towards him like a hungry leopard. The camera disappears into the darkness of her cleavage.

I tried, but I could not find one shred of meaning in any of this. "What is this?" I hissed to Walter, next to me. The music was vibrating through the room so loudly, I couldn't tell whether Walter heard me or not.

"What do you mean?" he whispered back. "This is a video of your song, what else?"

"My song isn't about boobs, Walter, is it? So what the hell are they doing?"

"Grace, I don't understand," Walter whispered, without taking his eyes off the screen.

"Let me explain it, Walter," I said, leaning into his shoulder and practically shouting in his ear, "I hate this video. Why are there a million girls in this video? What do they have to do with anything? What, Walter?"

Walter put his hand to his ear and turned towards me, missing the poetic moment where a white dress floats through the air in slow motion before catching fire.

"I don't understand," said Walter with a wince, "can we please talk about this later?" The video was almost over. I leaned back in my seat and bent my head back as I listened to the familiar music, while on the screen Hunter ran his hands across the silver satin sheets as the words "Let Me Show You," faded from his lips in a suggestive coda.

๚ ๚ ๚

I was sure there was nothing about a naked girl in bed sheets with a dog collar anywhere in my song, I thought to myself, trying to keep my cool as I made my way to the front of the screening room. I was mad. But I could tell by the mood of others around me that this was not the moment to lose my temper; everyone was busy congratulating each other and people were feeling positive.

The approximately thirty people in the screening room included representatives of all of the forces that had come together to create this opus; three or four people from the record company, most of Death Threat, some of their friends and kids, the director and a couple of other people on the production side. Everyone seemed pleased with the results and I overheard Jerry Saltstien marveling that the video really had it all, which was something I couldn't argue with.

The screening room was small. I felt as if I were in the waiting room of some futuristic medical center. The walls, ceiling, and floor were all the same spotless shade of slate blue. Track lighting, aimed discreetly upwards, created regular circles of light on the ceiling. The light bounced back down, lighting everyone's face gently. The voices sunk softly into the carpet in an indistinguishable hum. I looked around to see who I knew, and how I might avoid them in order to make a quick getaway. I wanted to sort out my thoughts before I had to talk to anyone.

Unfortunately, as I eyed the exit sign, Hunter Burns spotted me standing in the upper rows of the screening room. He stood near the exit. His stony face broke into a smile. "Grace, good to see you," he called, waving at me to come down and join him. As I came close, he stretched forward until he found my cheek, then gave me a kiss.

"Hunter, hi. Congratulations." It was all I could think of saying. I noticed he was a little more dressed up than the last time I had seen him. He wore an all-black poet shirt with a brightly colored South American vest over it, and the usual charms. He looked like he had put on a little make-up for the occasion.

"Hey, incredible, wasn't it?" He seemed happy and energetic.

"Incredible," I nodded back.

"Yeah, I know," he replied with a satisfied smile. "Grace, I want you to meet someone. This is my favorite Englishman, Vince St. James. He directed the video." Hunter laughed as he put his hand on the shoulder of a thin, very tall man with a big nose. Vince stretched out his hand and shook mine. "Grace wrote 'Let Me Show You.' " Behind him I could see the red exit light over the door, its glow taunting me.

"I feel very good about this video, I think we're going to do extremely well with it," Hunter continued to our little circle. "It looked absolutely spectacular. How about you, Grace, what do you think?" Hunter looked down at me from his lofty height.

"I'm taking it all in," I answered ambiguously. He waited for more. I auditioned at least twenty other phrases in my mind, but none of them sounded believable except, "That was the worst thing I ever saw," and my instincts told me not to say it. Luckily, Hunter didn't have time to wait around for a follow up. He heard the jangling gold bracelets of his girlfriend, Varina, and looked up to find her signaling him. "I'll catch you later, Grace. Glad you could make it," he said, pushing past me. He squeezed the shoulders of Walter Wiener, who stood behind me talking sales with Jerry Saltstien.

Vince St. James instantly jumped into conversation with Frisk, Death Threat's drummer, and Frisk's wife, Kathleen; they all knew each other from Death Threat's days in London. This left me free to make a move for the door. I caught Walter's eye, and mouthed, "I'm leaving." Quickly, Walter ended his conversation with Jerry.

"Grace, what's the big hurry?" he said, as he stepped into the hallway. I pounded the elevator button.

"I want to get out of here. Do you want to come with me?"

"Look, I know you're upset, but don't get so worked up," said Walter. I didn't say anything. I just stared at him. If that was his advice, I decided it was better to just pretend he was invisible. I stepped into the elevator. "Okay, let me get my jacket, I'll come with you," he said.

ᛉ ᛉ ᛉ

The fresh air of 38th street came as a relief. The screening room had felt stuffy and unnatural. A breeze moved through the empty street, cooling the June night. There was no one else in sight except a guy in a big cardboard box, and he seemed to be asleep. There were no cars and Walter and I walked in the street under the pink street lamps.

I walked quickly. Walter trotted by my side trying to keep up with me.

"I'm glad I'm getting some exercise here so it's not a total loss," he joked. At the end of the block a traffic light changed from red to green giving a strange glow to the scene ahead. "Want to go someplace and talk?" he asked, puffing.

"Sure." I nearly spat out the words.

"Where would you like to go?"

"There's a restaurant with a bar a few blocks from here," I said, not looking at him.

"If I make it without having a stroke."

"Wait until we're in the restaurant before you have a stroke."

"You're all heart, Grace," said Walter.

Soon we found ourselves sitting at a table in a tiny Mexican restaurant on Eighth Avenue, drinking margaritas.

I had hardly said two words since we left Hyperion. I didn't even know how to begin to tell Walter what I was feeling, perhaps because I didn't know myself. I only knew the video bothered me. It was sleazy and I hated it.

I also didn't talk because I was sick of the sound of my own voice. All I had been doing lately was talking, calling people, tell-

ing one person after another the latest detail of my deal with Death
Threat. All my talking had led to nothing but a big mess with my
name on it. I sipped my drink. I was grateful for the quiet and the
darkness of the restaurant. A candle in a red glass flickered on our
table.

I wanted a few moments to choose my words carefully; Walter
had been good to me. I didn't want to hurt his feelings by speaking without thinking. I had to keep in mind Walter was thrilled
with everything that happened so far. He wouldn't understand
why the video bothered me. He has no idea how much my identity
is wrapped up in the songs I create, even the commercial ones. He
thinks I write songs only when I have absolutely nothing else to
do—when I can't get to Atlantic City or a video store.

Still, just the thought of that idiotic video made me wince and
I'm sure my face reflected the disgust I felt because Walter looked
at me as if the centerpiece of his candy tray had just turned into a
hideous, smoke-spewing dragon.

"Grace, talk to me. You're thinking, I can see it."

"I don't know where to begin." I paused, then blurted out,
"That video was so...."

"Loud. I know. It was much louder than I expected."

"No, not loud, Walter. Lewd. It really upset me."

"That much I know. So tell me why," he said, leaning over the
table.

"First of all, it didn't make any sense, none at all."

"So?"

"So that's not how I pictured 'Let Me Show You.' It isn't what
I wanted my song to be."

"What do you mean? What did you want, an opera?"

"No, I didn't want an opera, Walter, but I didn't want a sex
show either." I sat back in my chair. My brain was buzzing.

Walter tried to understand. "I don't see what was wrong with
it."

I leaned forward and stared at Walter. "Of course you don't see
what's wrong with it. You don't see that video the way I see it.
You're a guy. You want to see a video packed with girls in their underwear. You want to see breasts in every shot. I don't. Did you see
the girl on the bed with a dog collar? The strippers? That's for men,
Walter. But I'm not a man. I don't want to see a video packed with
women portrayed as morons, particularly since I wrote the song.
What is there for me to like in a video where women don't say anything, sing anything, think anything or do anything? Imagine how
I feel, Walter." I sat back in my seat, exasperated.

"Well, I liked it."

"Of course you liked it," I nearly shouted, "It's meant for horny guys. Why wouldn't you like it? It's a peep show, Walter. The point is *I* don't like it. It's like I've been completely excluded from my own song. Do you think I like that? Do you?" I felt warm, as if my face were turning red.

"But why are you excluded? What—are you on a prison island all of a sudden? It's your song! You were there tonight," Walter exclaimed, his little eyes wide and round.

"No, it *was* my song. I sold it, remember? It's my own fault, I gave them the right to do whatever they wanted with it. This is what they did," I declared, practically talking to myself. I took a sip of my drink. "It's typical of this stupid business I'm in."

"Grace, it's just a video," Walter whined, leaning across the table as if he were struggling for a shred of sense in what I was saying. "Why are you taking it so seriously?"

"Why shouldn't I take it seriously? I wrote the goddamn song. You think I have to like it, just because Hunter Burns made it? Fuck him, too."

"So you're saying you didn't like it?"

"Are you listening to me, Walter?" I glared at him. "It was obscene."

"I'm kidding, I'm trying to lighten things up! Grace, calm down," Walter exclaimed. He squeezed my arm. I took a deep breath. There was no one else in the restaurant except a couple of guys a few tables away. They didn't appear interested in our shouting.

I sat quietly for a few moments. Christmas lights tacked to the ceiling cast reflections on the top of our table. I stared down at the patterns of red, green, and blue that flickered in the varnish of the wood.

"Walter, it's not like I don't know what's going on," I said lowering my voice. "I realize they did what they think they needed to do to sell records. It's not just the music business, it's part of selling something, a way of giving a product sex appeal. I just wish they hadn't taken all the usual cheap shots with my song."

Walter looked embarrassed. "This is strange, I never heard you talk like this."

"Because what is there to say?" I replied. "I don't go on the rampage every time I see something I don't like. This is the way the world is, women deal with it every day. You get used to it, but it doesn't mean I have to like it."

"It's hard for me to understand. The kids have the television on at home, I see stuff like that video everyday. I don't pay much attention. In fact, I thought it was the year of the woman. That's what they're always saying."

"Sure, Walter. It's a woman's world. Except for all the money and power. If it's the year of the woman, how come rock videos look the same as they did for the past five years?" I sipped the last of the margarita and put down the glass. "I don't know why, I thought this would be different. I was wrong.

"Let Me Show You" was just more of the same; guys having all the fun while women stood around licking their lips. I was tired of it. I was tired of waifs and sexpots, hot babes and male fantasies. "It's not fair, Walter. That wasn't what I wanted my song to be." And I closed my eyes feeling that was all I had to say.

Then I had one more thought. I opened my eyes. "And besides all that, Walter," I said, "it was a really stupid video. Who the hell is Vince St. James, anyway?"

"He used to be Hunter's personal trainer."

ᚼ ᚼ ᚼ

Walter understood, as much as he could, anyway. It wasn't like he was going to stop his monthly outings to The International Club & Topless Lounge with the other salesmen. It's just that now he knew it wasn't everybody's idea of a good time. And I didn't want him to stop going anyway. I didn't want to ruin other people's fun.

I just wasn't having any fun. By the time we finished our conversation, I was too tired to even think about fun. I wanted to go home and sleep. We paid our check, left the restaurant, and walked quietly to the parking lot where Walter had left his car. We squinted under the raw, white fluorescent light of the garage.

"Thanks for talking to me, Walter. I know this isn't what you want to hear," I said as we waited for the attendant to bring down Walter's Grand Prix.

"Grace, please, you don't have to say thanks. That's what friends are for."

"I appreciate it."

"Just call my name and I'll be there."

"Thank you."

"Tomorrow you'll feel better about all this."

I thought about all the people I would have to call, the very same people I had been calling with good news day after day. As of tomorrow, the video would go into circulation on every music television program.

"I don't think so," I said.

Walter dropped me off at my place. I could tell he appreciated the depths of my unhappiness because he didn't pester me once about going with him to a ball game. He watched me from inside his dark car as I let myself into my building. I could see his silhouette and the outline of the little pine tree that hung from his mirror. The red and white lights of the traffic crossing Canal Street momentarily illuminated Walter's face as he watched me unlock the front door of my building. I waved one last time; then I closed the front door behind me.

ʔ ʔ ʔ

This evening marked a new career low. It was also one of my career highs. It was the high professionally. But it was the low emotionally. It was a high financially—the sale of my song would net me more in two months than I had earned all of last year. But it was a human low. I felt confused, and when I got upstairs I threw down my coat and got right into bed with all my clothes on, which isn't the most comfortable thing to do when you're wearing three layers of organza. I didn't even stop to listen to my answering machine; that's how bad I felt.

Although it was still early—not even eleven o' clock yet—I fell asleep right away. This was due not only to my despair, but to the three margaritas I had drunk with Walter Wiener. I tumbled into a deep, unhappy sleep and dreamed I was being tied up in wet leaves and then woven into a basket, which was probably the result of having some of the organza twisted around my knees. It was a dream of tangles and complications, of little comfort.

I awoke from a nightmarish sleep several hours later. My body must have thought it just taking a nap because it sprang awake as if it were morning. My body awoke as if it had plans. My mind wanted to go back to sleep and stay asleep. I stood up, pushed my blankets onto my cat, and walked down the dark hallway from my bedroom to the living room.

The silence in my apartment told me it was very late. I can always tell the general time by the particular mixture of creaks, squeaks and rumbles. Now there was no noise at all. I walked to the window, pushed aside the curtains and looked out. Had morning sunshine poured in, I might have felt a little more promise in the day. But the brownish night sky stretched like a dirty curtain behind the tenements of lower Manhattan. All was quiet on Canal Street. Directly across the street, at a perpendicular angle to my building, I could see the faded letters of a sign that said, "Muriel Shears." Further uptown the gold clock tower said three o' clock.

I moaned. How could it be only three o' clock? There was no chance of my getting back to sleep. I walked to the kitchen and turned on the lights. I decided this would be a good time to use the coffee-maker. Roger had given it to me. It had been a gift to him from a company he did business with and it said "Rilroth LeTrege and Klieg" on the side. This kept me busy for about ten minutes. The coffee underway, I walked to the bathroom to wash my face and change into normal clothes.

The mirror confronted me with an image that matched my state of mind. There were shadows of stress and dark rings under my eyes. My hair, laying in random strands and unformed curls, my lips, dry with the stain of lipstick, and my somber expression all told me the same thing; I was miserable. The mild throb of a headache agreed. I took some aspirin.

If I forgot why I was miserable for longer than a second—for instance, when I went back into the kitchen and admired the way my new coffee maker had three different lights on it to report its status—my memory of Death Threat's version of "Let Me Show You" would flood my mind and remind me. What I had seen at Hyperion tonight was an embarrassment. Months of expectation had collapsed in a period of three minutes. I was about to get national exposure, my name on something I would have sneered at and flipped off only the day before. A wave of nausea moved through me.

I poured a cup of coffee, then walked back to the bedroom. How does that work? I wondered. How can things change so fast? I picked up one of my guitars. Is there some formula that says the more you expect, the more deluded you'll be? Does it ever happen that reality exceeds hopes? Or is reality always a letdown? And exactly what part of my song gave them the idea for an all-girl costume party? It wasn't even logical, all those women tearing their hair out over a middle-aged wreck like Hunter Burns. The video had a serious credibility problem, I remarked to myself, and most rock and rap videos had the same flaw; it was always spooky guys surrounded by gorgeous women.

I sat on my bed to strum and think. I always think more clearly with my arms around a guitar. I played some soothing chords and listened to each note vibrate in the silence. It was time to face facts. My song was permanently linked to Hunter Burns' libido. My big entry into the music business was a humiliation, not a triumph. And disappointment wasn't the worst of my problems. The worst part was that doing what I loved—song writing—had taken me to a place I didn't want to be. Song writing itself seemed depressing and that was scary, because it was the force I had let guide my life. Which meant maybe I had gotten it all wrong.

I played quietly, con dolore. Maybe I wasn't meant to be a songwriter. Maybe I wasn't strong enough, I said to myself, running the back of my nails across the strings in a loud flourish. What can you do when you've tried hard to do everything right, when you've made an effort to live a creative life, and then Hunter Burns turns your song into an aerobics workout for his tongue? How can you keep your faith?

At least it felt good to play. I could still do that. My ears were too good to waste. I could hear every interval, every tone that resonated from my guitar. I played songs to pass the time, a few old ones, some Neil Young and Bob Dylan, some Marc Daine and Joni Mitchell. Late at night when the traffic on its way to the Holland Tunnel dies down, my apartment feels far away from New York City. With its painted floors and its skylight, it reminds me of a beach house.

I sat on the bed, plucking and strumming until about 4:30 in the morning. Still hopelessly awake, I decided it was time to call someone. I was getting tired of going around in circles by myself. It was time to go around in circles with someone else.

It was too late to call Roger. Also too late for Paul. It would be one-thirty in the morning in LA. I knew Ray would be awake, and there were a few musicians on the night shift who wouldn't mind a phone call now.

I could definitely call Natalie; as far as I knew she never went to sleep until it was light out. If I called Ray, he would listen to me, but in the end he would only have two or three words to say. Ray clarifies problems by reducing them to their simplest elements. He would cut through the clutter and come up with something like, "You've gotten your first Death Threat." Since I knew what he would say, I didn't need to call him.

I called Natalie instead. With Natalie, I can be myself; I don't have to go out of my way to be cheerful or likable, something I have to do being in charge of a band. I can be childish or anything else and Natalie just ignores it all. I put down the guitar and picked up the phone; she works until eleven each night as a word-processor in a law firm. After work, she and Massimo go out to dinner. They would surely be home by now.

"Hey!" cried Natalie when she heard my voice, "You called at the perfect time." I knew this meant I had caught them in one of their perpetual debates. "Massimo and I were just trying to remember the name of that guy in the band we all saw five months ago at The Don't Walk Bar. That guy with the cane, what was his name?"

"Frye Caruthers," I answered. Here Natalie shouted the name to Massimo.

"Massimo says he saw him on Crosby Street the other day, and I said it couldn't be him because he died. Didn't he die?"

"No, he didn't die. He just went to England. But he came back and now he plays with Lutheran Church Courtyard."

Natalie screamed to Massimo again, telling him that he was right, it could have been Frye Caruthers.

Staying up all night has that effect on you—you start to spend a lot of time talking about things that don't matter. When she and Massimo had come to an agreement on who he had seen, she turned her attention back to me. "What's up?" she cried, lively as a squirrel on a summer morning.

"Natalie, I went to the screening of the 'Let Me Show You' video tonight."

"Oh my god, I completely forgot that was tonight!"

"It was definitely tonight. And it was a total disaster."

"What? Did Walter Wiener hit on you again?"

"It's not that. The video is totally hideous."

"How can that be?"

"Hideous," I repeated.

"Oh, my God."

"I know."

It felt good talking to Natalie, and if it hadn't been for Massimo, I probably would have gone over to her place right then to talk. Natalie makes me feel secure. She has such authority about everything. I knew whatever she said would comfort me, at least until daylight.

"Natalie," I continued, stretched out on the bed, "it was the most obnoxious thing you could imagine. Totally sleazy. I didn't even think they did things like this anymore. I'm so embarrassed."

"Why embarrassed? Grace, it's Death Threat's problem, not yours."

"I know, but I take it so personally."

"They bought the song, let them make fools of themselves."

"I know, but it's still my song."

"Grace, let go of it."

Natalie was getting very Eastern lately. Her solution to every problem was to "let go of it." Not that she let go of much, especially in her fights with Massimo. Many is the time I have had to take a walk around the block while she and Massimo battled out an issue like whether it's better to put salt or sugar in the pot when you boil corn.

"It's easy for you to say 'Let go of it.' Just wait till everyone who knows me sees this. I'm going to be totally humiliated." My reputation as one of the growing lights on the downtown scene would be irreparably damaged. I winced, not having thought about this until now. I had been too upset about the global to think about the personal. This could affect Swan Venom. People thought of Swan Venom as "alternative," if they thought of Swan Venom at all. Luckily, Natalie was there to set me straight.

"Grace, don't be so self-centered, it's not like everyone is going to know you had something to do with this."

"Oh, really? Considering how many people I told about this, it's amazing if there is anyone who doesn't know. Oh, why do I have to talk so much?" I whined, falling back on the bed. "I want to give up song writing."

Natalie reasoned with me. When it became apparent to Massimo that our conversation was going around in circles he cried "Basta" in Italian. "Enough for one night. You two are talking always."

"Grace, I have an idea. Why don't you come over for breakfast tomorrow?" said Natalie. "Are you doing anything?"

"I have no plans."

"Then come over for breakfast."

"That would be nice. I have a rehearsal at three."

"Good. Come over at one."

"Thanks, Natalie. That'll be great," I said, noticing a distinctly babyish tone in my voice. I was glad to get off the phone before I had a chance to become any more whiny.

"Goodnight, and get some sleep now. We'll talk more tomorrow," Natalie pronounced, then she hung up the phone, cutting off the sound of Massimo bellowing in the background.

I put down the phone. I finally felt tired. There didn't seem to be any reason to stay awake anymore; it was time to end this day. I picked up my guitar from the jumble of blankets and leaned it in the corner, then turned off the lights and returned to my tangled and anxious dreams.

♪ ♪ ♪

The name on Natalie's bell read "Westhaven/Vitello." The words were written in neat calligraphy on the back of an index card and taped directly under the bell. I pushed the little black button and waited in front of the spray-painted, scratched, steel fire exit that Natalie calls her front door. On Greene Street in Soho, one floor below the Di Angelo Steel Die Corporation, Natalie lived the good life.

The fabulous home that Massimo had created for them used to be the headquarters for the BelleJoe Toddler Corp. Their high-tech kitchen, a Jacuzzi, rows of beautiful teak bookcases and a few healthy ficas trees now stood where twenty pedal-driven Singers used to be. There were expanses of empty space, lit dramatically by halogen lamps. Massimo claims he designed the place for thinking, although I think he was being ambitious. In the back of the loft was a separate, large room where Massimo painted.

I traveled up the freight elevator looking forward to the respite of Natalie's minimalist home. It had been a busy morning. After waking at 11:00, I called Roger. We talked for a little while, but he was busy. I try not to bother Roger with personal problems at work. We made plans to get together later in the evening.

I also spent some time on the phone with Paul Teagarden. I called him after hanging up with Roger. I felt driven to keep him informed about my life. He was like a human diary. He was glad to hear from me and he reacted to my latest news with his usual warm and comforting words. Still, I didn't have the patience to talk to him. I wanted comfort up close.

I was still waiting for him to come to New York. My attraction to him was as hot and steady as the sun over Palm Springs. I still thought of him all the time. But it didn't feel as good as it used to. Frustration and a nagging cloud of disappointment shadowed my feelings for him. I think the unnatural mixture of intimacy and distance in our relationship was causing me anxiety. I looked forward to his phone calls, but now I felt tension as well as anticipation. Paul made an effort to keep things going between us; he always said how much he liked talking to me, how much he wanted to see me. But so far, none of his plans to come to New York had worked out. And no invitation to come to California had been forthcoming. I had said to Paul bluntly several times, "If you like talking to me so much, why don't you come out here and talk to me in person?" All he ever said was, "Soon, I promise I'll be there soon." His idea of soon wasn't soon enough for me. I had met him in November. It was now June.

On this particular morning, I wasn't in the market for extra frustration. He had already picked up the phone when I realized calling him was a mistake.

"Listen," I said, making little effort to be polite, "I'm not really in the mood to talk."

"Then why did you call me? You didn't have to."

"I know. I don't even know myself why I called you. Out of habit, I guess."

"I'm a habit now. Well, I hope I'm a good habit,"

"No, I don't mean that," I said, feeling the balance of my feelings shift towards the warm side. "I'm just feeling very anxious. I wish I could talk to you in person. I'm not in the mood for the phone right now."

"I'll see you soon. I know I keep saying it, but I promise I'll come to New York."

These words did not cheer me up. I had heard them before. I said good-bye, packed up my guitar so I could go straight from breakfast at Natalie's to rehearsal, and left my apartment, looking forward to the comfort of a visit with a friend.

Yet when Natalie let me in, I felt as anxious as ever. I walked up and down their long loft, past the grouping of furniture that represented the living room. I always called the style of their living room 'Early Drop Cloth,' because the furniture—designed by one of Massimo's Italian friends—was upholstered in raw canvas. I circled their living room while Natalie sat in one of the armless arm chairs. She had put two steaming cups of coffee on the glass coffee table.

"I don't know how I let this happen," I declared, pacing her huge living room as if I were doing laps.

Natalie looked troubled on my behalf. She watched me as I passed. "You didn't let it happen," she said earnestly. "You made it happen."

"Is that supposed to cheer me up?"

"I'm sorry. I meant that positively. I mean you had this fantastic opportunity and you followed up on it. You made something happen. It was great in theory, but it got screwed up in practice. How could you know what they would do with 'Let Me Show You'?"

"I should have known. Their last big hit was called 'Disgrace Me.'"

"You can't know everything. This was all new to you."

"Come on, it's not new to me. I've been involved in videos before." I had been in a few videos made for wedding showcases.

"You've never done anything on this level before. Can't you just learn from this?"

"Yes, I can learn. I can learn that I'm so embarrassed I could die." With these words, I flopped on the couch, which was as minimal in its use of foam as it was in its design. "This furniture sucks, Natalie," I said.

Natalie didn't say anything. She puffed intensely on a cigarette and then blew out the smoke in a statuesque way she has perfected.

"I am so humiliated. He practically has sex by the last chorus."

"It sounds good."

"Oh, it's great," I said staring at the ceiling.

"Anyway, I'll see it soon enough. It's going to be a hit, Grace, I can feel it." I moaned, wondering if Natalie wasn't getting some kind of pleasure from this. Natalie asked me to pass her an ashtray and I thought about what would happen if I accidentally dropped the huge slab of marble on their glass coffee table. But Natalie was my friend, willing to listen to me as I rambled. I stayed with my central themes of professional and personal embarrassment, wandering now and then into secondary considerations to do with the fact that I had contributed to the musical degradation of my own gender.

I was glad Massimo was not around to hear this, since he contributed even more than I did to the degradation of my gender with his obsessive paintings of naked woman in elevators. He calls these "I Quadri," which in Italian means not only "paintings," but also "boxes." He claims this is a play on words related to elevators. I don't see anything playful about it, but he's the darling of the latest art wave, and is frequently praised as "cryptoerotic," which has earned him a good living.

Natalie prepared breakfast before I arrived. After we talked for a while, she went into the kitchen and brought out two omelets. We sat on the rug and ate at the coffee table.

We talked about song writing and art in general, and about what happens when something to which you've devoted yourself seems to turn against you. Natalie shared her own frustrations and bad times with me, telling me of her bitter experiences with an old boyfriend, Richie Mustard, a photographer who took pictures of Natalie when she was sleeping, then blew them up to several feet high and put them in an art show. "Believe me, I know what it means to feel exposed," she said, sympathizing with my embarrassment. Natalie, a good and true friend, listened to my problems. But Massimo would be back at two-thirty and we both knew that Massimo did not rejoice in other people's problems, especially mine. He knew I was much more interested in Natalie than I was in him, and although most people would consider this normal, it was highly unusual in Massimo's world. So at two-fifteen the pressure was on Natalie to wrap things up. Under these circumstances, she had an idea. I had already circulated through my problem twenty or thirty times when Natalie snapped to attention and declared, "Grace, I have it."

"What do you have?"

"I know what's going to help you."

"You don't have to help me, this is my life."

"No, I need to help you, that's how I am." And it was at this moment that Natalie assured me, with all the formidable authority she could mobilize, that a trip to the Mind Self institute in West Cluster, New York, was just the thing I needed. She said this just in time, because as soon as she did, we heard keys clinking in the lock of the loft door, and Massimo, Dunhill in hand, walked in.

۷ ۷ ۷

Natalie discovered The Mind Self Institute two years ago. She was working on her acting at the time. Natalie went to 127 auditions in six months. She got one callback; it was for the part of a waffle in a breakfast food commercial. She didn't get the part. Natalie was feeling down because if you can't even get a job as a waffle, what right to you have to call yourself a thespian? She hit a low point. Then, at the recommendation of our performance artist friend, Sheldon Bagg, she did a tape program called, "Let Good Things Happen."

The tape program distracted Natalie from her problems. She started to feel better, more confident. She ordered a second set of tapes, "Let More Good Things Happen." Soon Natalie was going to auditions again, getting rejected, and feeling fabulous about it.

Since then, Natalie has been regularly praising the virtues of "Let Good Things Happen," and their creator, Dino Rainwater of the Mind Self Institute. As Natalie says, "Dino Rainwater introduced me to my mind."

"It's all about gaining confidence and getting in touch with the true forces that motivate your life," Natalie had explained once, when I asked her why she was spending so much time talking to herself in the closet. We were roommates then which meant I had to witness her every flash of cosmic truth.

"Too often, we let our mind tell us what to do," she said. "Dino Rainwater says our biggest problem is we let our minds push us around."

"And we shouldn't?"

"No, because we have a higher self that's composed of many parts, and this higher self is the only one who knows how to get things done. You have to get in touch with this higher self in order to take charge of your life."

When I asked Natalie exactly how this was done, she went into several theories to do with Brain Layers, Sensory Weaving and some other things called "Coatings." Dino Rainwater's theories had a quasi-medical tone to them, and as if sensing my skepticism, Natalie added,

"Dino was a very successful psychologist before he started The Mind Self Institute. He invented the concept of emotional geometry." Then she went back in the closet to continue her conversation with her mind.

The main change in Natalie after she did the "Let Good Things Happen" tape series was that she said things like, "I'm going to talk to my mind now," and "Let me see what my mind thinks about that." Otherwise, she seemed to be the same actress, poetess, and word processor I've known for years.

Still, I make no judgments when it comes to self improvement. Natalie claims her acting has improved greatly, which is one of those things that's impossible to measure since she never actually does it. She says that The Mind Self Institute has transformed her life, and although she's said the same thing about quartz, Sheldon Bagg, datebooks, and bee pollen, she claims her life is better in many ways. She did meet, fall in love, and move in with Massimo Vitello in the last year, and for all I know she can thank the Mind Self Institute for that.

I decided to accept Natalie's offer. I, Grace Note, am always willing to try something new. The question remained as to whether I could get in touch with my own higher self and I asked Natalie, point blank, "What would my higher self do about my situation with Death Threat?"

"I don't know. You'll find out this weekend," she said.

"You think so?"

"One self, many selves, Dino says."

"That really talks to me, Natalie."

"Grace, you're too in your own head," said Natalie, with all the wisdom of someone who majored in pronunciation.

"Where should I be?" I asked.

"You need to be out of your head."

ʇ ʇ ʇ

If nothing else, the weekend would give me a chance to consider my problem without calls from Walter or anyone else. It was getting so I didn't want to answer the phone; everyone had something to say, everyone had an opinion. My phone didn't stop ringing for three days after the video hit the air. Even my neighbor, Mrs. Chu, had seen the video when her nephew, Vincent, made her watch it. She knocked on my door to say she liked the song, "but why so many ladies?"

Perhaps the Institute really could help me. I felt as if I just couldn't see things clearly anymore. If the song did well, I would have both money and success. On the other hand, I had contributed to something repellent. Maybe it was like Natalie said; maybe my mind was pushing me around. After all, wasn't it my mind that told me to sell my song to Hunter Burns? Maybe I should have listened to some other part of my body.

Being a creative individual is like traveling on a dark path; one stumbles blindly forward without ever knowing exactly where the path will lead. I put so many hours into my projects without knowing what I'll get back. Maybe the answer is nothing. Maybe one day I'll wake up in Indiana working in a garden shop, telling people I once was a songwriter. Or maybe it will be a gift shop in Palo Alto. Who knows. As I wrote in "Walking to the Corner," "I'm gonna take a chance and cross alone, because the light ain't changin' and I got to get home." Maybe I should have given Hunter Burns that song.

6

ROGER AGREED IT WAS A GOOD IDEA that I get out of town for a few days with Natalie, mainly because there wouldn't be any television where we were going. Every time I turned on a TV, there was Hunter Burns, guest-hosting, promoting, sitting in, and showing up as he pushed Death Threat's new album. Even Rudy Rude made an appearance, turning up at seven in the morning on the couch next to Jill Winslow, the host of *Wake Up New York*, trying to put his head in her lap. Roger called me to tell me Rudy was on, waking me up with the rest of New York. And Death Threat—the whole band—turned up for a record store appearance, causing a ruckus on lower Broadway.

Hunter Burns had also managed to get himself on the cover of *Grind*, the rock magazine, so every time I passed the candy store next to the Café Capri, there was Hunter, staring out at me from a row of covers in the window, a dark scowl on his face. I couldn't get away from them.

"A few days in the country will be good for you," Roger said. He thought the part about getting in touch with my mind couldn't hurt, although he was skeptical. "If it's going to make you more like Natalie, I don't see the point," he said. Roger thinks Natalie is one of those boyfriend-oriented artists who creates only in relation to the men in their lives, and now that I think of it, she's doing a series of poems that go with Massimo's elevator paintings. I told Roger he shouldn't be so judgmental, it doesn't matter what the inspiration for your art is, as long as you live a creative life. He got a little upset because he thought I was implying something about him.

In general, Massimo doesn't mind Natalie's spiritual quest. He approves of her conversations with her mind and I think it's because he knows he can't be jealous if Natalie is only talking to herself. He let it slip, however, that he doesn't like her trips out of town. It interrupts their late night routine, and he was especially unhappy about Natalie's decision to go out of town that particular weekend. He had an important dinner at Le Feu Bleu on Saturday night with one of the owners of the big auction house, Alfonse Delaneau Père. He wanted Natalie there but had neglected to tell her about it. It was too late to change our plans.

"Can't you come back Saturday?" Massimo whined, as I stood in the north end of their loft waiting for her. We were on our way to the train station.

"No, we need to do this. Grace needs to," she said, zipping up her leather shoulder bag.

"Oh. Ah. I see. Then by all means, you must go," said Massimo, barely hiding his sarcasm behind his thick Italian accent.

"Honey, I'll be back Sunday night. Can't you change the dinner to Sunday?"

"Sure," said Massimo, pronouncing the word, 'shoe-air.' "Sure, I will tell one of the most important dealers in New York to change his plans because Natalie and Grace had to go to the country this weekend."

"Good," she said.

Massimo leaned against the kitchen counter and watched Natalie as she applied lipstick in the cross-shaped mirror against the wall. "Grace," he said, "You are lucky to have such a loyal friend. For you, she won't change her plans." He looked at me, sucking on his cigarette.

"Sorry, Massimo."

"Grace, you have a lot of problems, it seems." He directed his irritation at me since Natalie ignored him, and was busily winding up the cord of her blow dryer.

"Me? I have a lot of problems?"

"It seems. The music video. That man in California. You have a complicated life. Molto complicato, eh?"

"Excuse me, Massimo, but it was Natalie's idea to go away for the weekend. Take it up with her. And my life isn't your business."

"Grace, it is my business when because of you she cannot join me at an important dinner."

"Why didn't you bother to tell me about it before, if it's so important?" Natalie chimed.

"Because I thought, like always, you would be home."

"You were wrong this time," I said. This was an impossible thing to Massimo, and he looked at me with disbelief.

"You are telling me I am wrong about my own life?"

"No, not about your life. I'm saying Natalie and I had plans. I'm sorry you're going to be lonely, but this is important too."

"This is not about being lonely, Grace. This is about my career."

"Massimo, come on," Natalie said, walking over to him, "Don't get mad at Grace. This is my fault." She put her arms around him and hugged him, pulling him close though he remained rigid, peering at her with a suspicious squint. Then he reached up and took the cigarette out of his mouth and hugged her.

"I am just disappointed you cannot be with me Saturday."

"I am, too."

"So stay."

"I can't. I'll call you."

"Okay," he mumbled. "What can I do? Nothing. Buon viaggio."

I was at the door with my bag, ready to fly. Natalie joined me, Massimo shuffling to the door besides her.

"You too, Grace," he said without conviction. "I hope you get better."

"Thanks so much."

"Have a good time, girls," he said half-heartedly.

ᵞ ᵞ ᵞ

The Mind Self Institute is located on a magnificent estate eighty miles north of New York City. It was formerly the home of railroad king Chester Wharburton, but as the age of the railroad realized its promise, the Wharburtons moved on to greater habitats—estates in Long Island, mansions on the Hudson River, and whole square blocks of Manhattan. The Wharburton estate then experienced the decline familiar to stately mansions everywhere. It first became a summer resort for the very wealthy, then a middle class resort, then a psychiatric hospital and finally, after the main house was ripped down and replaced by bungalows in the early fifties, a summer camp with socialist leanings.

Natalie explained all this to me on the Metro North train that carried us towards West Cluster Plains, the home of The Mind Self Institute. Natalie has a zeal that drives her to possess every detail about a subject that interests her. She can fill an hour and a half train ride without even a single trip to the bar car.

"Dino Rainwater bought the property five years ago," Natalie read enthusiastically from a brochure. "His plan was to create a center where people could come for introspection and self-study, and at the same time enjoy all the benefits of a weekend country getaway.

"There are volleyball courts, a lake, a baseball diamond, as well as a meditation walk and a fitness center. Guests can attend weekend seminars, enjoy outdoor activities, or just meditate."

"It's a resort for spiritual wellness," I ventured, trying out some of the lingo.

"Yes, that's exactly what it is," said Natalie brightly. I could see she was relieved to see I was getting into the swing of things.

"And they have a baseball diamond. Why didn't you tell me that before? I would have brought my mitt."

"They'll lend you a mitt if you want to play baseball. Just remember what you came here for."

"Don't worry. I couldn't forget if I wanted to."

I sat back in my seat and looked out the window. White clouds dotted the clear sky. They disappeared in the distant blue, unhurried by the oncoming sunset. The sky in the west was already turning pale gold. I felt calmer already.

It was early June, and a hundred shades of green swept the sides of the railroad tracks. Trees and plants crowded the rails like eager parade-goers, held back by rows of white flowers. The farther we got from New York, the more rural the scenery became. Cities turned into towns, towns into villages that became smaller and smaller as we traveled North. We flew past factories and old mills, farms and fields that stretched to the horizon.

Natalie put down her brochures and gazed out the window. Her bangs and straight brown hair were touched by gold in the afternoon light. I could see by her paleness that she too would benefit from a weekend out of the city. Natalie had taken it upon herself to manage every detail of our trip. Since I had agreed to join her on the weekend retreat, she had called me daily, reviewing our travel plans, advising me on what to pack, giving me special instructions on how to behave.

"Don't make fun of things while you're at the Institute, please," Natalie had said—as if I didn't know how to be discreet. Hadn't I spent a whole weekend on the road with String of Lizards without once saying anything about their haircuts? She was nervous because it was important I like The Mind Self Institute and her friends at the Institute like me.

She didn't have much chance to rest; the train pulled into the station and the conductor shouted, "West Cluster Plains. Exit from the rear and front cars."

ᛉ ᛉ ᛉ

A few taxicabs dotted the small parking lot outside the train station, but there was no one inside the cars. The drivers stood together near a clump of elm trees, watching a garbage scow sail

up the Hudson River. We stood outside the station with a few other
arrivals as the drivers strolled to their cars. A lean old man, who
looked like he might have been a pirate in a previous life, stared
at us and said, "The Institute, right?"

He threw our bags in his blue Buick, and without asking directions, took off down a two-lane road that curved between the
rolling hills of West Cluster Plains. We rumbled past farms, antique barns and hilltop houses. The country was beautiful and
Natalie and I both looked out the windows, saying little, but absorbing it all. After ten minutes, without warning, the driver made
a left onto a small dirt road. The road was rough and the car rattled
and swerved. I could see the driver's eyes in the car mirror now and
then, looking back at us.

Trees darkened the road, their leafy branches covering the sky
overhead. After a quarter of a mile, the road forked and we followed
the road marked "Main Lodge."

The taxi pulled up in front of a wooden building that looked
like the lodge of a summer camp. There was a big porch in front
where two guests sat together at a card table talking quietly and
drinking tea. A row of rocking chairs overlooked flower boxes, and
beyond them, the lawn of The Mind SelfInstitute.

"I like it. It's rugged," I whispered to Natalie. I don't know why
I whispered, except that everything seemed so quiet and I was trying to show spiritual courtesy. We paid the driver and dropped our
bags on the gravel.

What looked like a quaint summer lodge from the outside
turned out to have a snappy interior, posh enough to satisfy any
soul-searching New Yorker. A white ceiling fan turned over a comfortable sitting area furnished with a leather couch, armchairs, brass
reading lamps, and an Oriental rug. Mixed in with this decor were
a few fragments of world culture, African masks, a Buddha, and
some mysterious statuettes of Pacific origin. The shellacked pine
walls retained the summer-lodge feeling, and white curtains hung on
the screened porch windows.

"Are you here to register?" said a woman in a white beret. She
had been so still, we hadn't even noticed her. We nodded.

"Welcome. I'm Vanessa. Welcome to the registration desk," she
said, tapping on the glass desktop. "Can I have your names?" Her
voice dipped then rose at the end of every sentence.

Natalie took charge of checking in. Upon hearing Natalie's
name, Vanessa broke into a big grin and cried, "I knew I recognized
you. You were in the 'Training for Triumph' seminar with me. Remember—Friendly Energy? Last August?"

"Yes? How are you?" Natalie replied, dissolving into an equally wide smile.

"I'm just great. And you?"

"I'm great."

"Great. Hey, maybe I'll see you tomorrow. Try to take Jordan Le Shay's Creative Relationships Workshop. It's supposed to be fantastic."

"I'll try," said Natalie.

"Welcome again, and here are your packets," she said, handing each of us an envelope. I noticed she wore a tee-shirt that said, "I'm Ready."

"Have a great weekend, welcome, and I'll see you tonight at dinner, seven-thirty."

ٿ ٿ ٿ

"Friendly energy?" I said as we followed a gravel path away from the front steps of the main lodge. Other guests strolled in the direction from which we had come, gathering for dinner. A few people sat on the lawn under big leafy trees. We passed them by, continuing along the path toward a small cluster of cottages.

The keys jingled in Natalie's hands. She walked next to me, a big leather bag hanging off her shoulder. Her hair bounced neatly behind her. Natalie can look very stylish when she wants to, even when she's on a spiritual quest.

"There are different kinds of energy, Grace, and you have to learn to distinguish between them. For instance, that manic kind of energy you get in cities is a 'hostile' energy. It tires you. But the kind of refreshing energy you get from stepping outside on a beautiful day is 'friendly energy.'"

"I think I experience mostly indifferent energy."

"Grace, if you want to improve yourself you're going to have to be more serious," said Natalie, unlocking the door to our bungalow.

"I get the top bunk," I replied, throwing my bag on the bed. Natalie turned on the lights. Our cabin was like a matchbox turned on its side, with the entire floor nearly taken up by two pieces of furniture, a bunk bed and a scratched yellow dresser.

I climbed to the upper bed and sank back onto the mattress. It creaked loudly. I touched the rough wool blanket folded on my bed.

"This is really rustic. I love it here," I said.

"It's so woodsy. Smell the air." There was a musty smell of wet wood in the room.

"I feel better already," I said, leafing through the documents in my Welcome Packet. "Here's a schedule for tomorrow."

"What's on it?" Natalie said, not looking up. She was busy unpacking.

"The first thing on the schedule is 'Welcome.' Is that another welcome or the one we just had?"

"That's the welcome at dinner, tonight in the main lodge. After that, we can just relax. But I'm warning you—" Here Natalie stopped her unpacking and looked at me gravely. "We're getting up at seven tomorrow. And from then until three o' clock you're going to be very busy. The early part of the day is very actualizing. Dino likes us to really push."

ᛌ ᛌ ᛌ

The pushing begin at dinner. As we sat drinking coffee and enjoying peach cobbler, our attention was drawn to a small wooden platform at one end of the dining room. It was decorated by a single chair.

A woman walked onto the small stage. She was healthy and ruddy with long, blond hair braided in pigtails, and big, sculptural earrings. She wore a headband, and looked like someone who wished she had been born into a tribe instead of a state. She stood on the small stage beaming as she waited for the conversation in the room to die down.

"Hi there and welcome to The Mind Self Institute," she said, her face expanding in a warm grin. "My name is Bonnie Sue Orange and I am so pleased to have you here and it's so good to see you. I see a lot of familiar faces and I see a lot of new faces. I'm especially glad to see you here because you're taking action and that's good. You're here, you got yourself here because you wanted to make a change in your life and that's good, too. I know you're going to do well because you're here and that means you, your higher self, really wants to change, and that's good."

While Bonnie Sue continued to tell us what was good, I looked around the room to see what I could learn about my fellow self-improvers. I wondered if there was anything common to all the people who had traveled so far to be at The Mind Self Institute.

For one thing, it was clear there was a lot of intensity in the room. Everyone stared at the stage, eyes burning. This feeling of intensity was matched in people's features. These were not just people; these were beings. There were a lot of dramatic acts of self-definition going on here, mainly in people's hairstyles. From tight, slick-backed ponytails, to wild curls with manic streaks of gray and even dreadlocks, people's hairstyles really spoke out.

Many of the women in the room were thin and gaunt. Dressed in black, they looked like ballerinas in mourning. They sat with male counterparts who I suspected were painters or actors. More jolly were the earthier types dressed in bright colors and batik, their workshirts and sweaters hanging over their pants as if they had never seen a mirror in their lives.

Bonnie Sue Orange was finishing up now.

"I'm tremendously excited for you all, and I know we're going to have a great time this weekend. And now I'd like to introduce you to the founder of The Mind Self Institute, Dino Rainwater."

She had barely finished pronouncing the founder's name when the room exploded with applause.

᛭ ᛭ ᛭

The spiritual leader and founder of The Mind Self Institute can be recognized by his well-tailored suits, highly-polished black hair, and piercing eyes. I had seen him many times on Natalie's videotapes, and occasionally on television talk shows.

But it is only on television that he looks like an anchorperson. In the warm lights of The Mind Self Institute dining hall, Dino Rainwater was a casual man. He wore jeans and a short-sleeved, brightly colored button-down shirt, open at the neck. Around his wrist was a strand of leather with a little piece of jade. He looked sporty and fit. Even his hair was more relaxed, unstyled and a little on the long side, falling youthfully over his forehead. He wasn't bad looking, and appeared to be somewhere in his mid-forties.

I noticed Dino had a big chunk of crystal set in silver around his neck. In another age I would have called it a charm or amulet, but here, as Natalie pointed out, it was an "implement for energy concentration."

"Hello, and first of all let me thank all of you for coming," he said, his lips curling into a grin. The grin faded. "I want you to know it matters to me that you're here, and together, we're going to learn a lot of new things."

"And I want you to know something. . ." Dino looked around the room. We waited for him anxiously. "I have everything I want; and if I can get everything I want, so can you." Here Dino went into a self-effacing speech about how he ate too much chocolate as a child, and everyone called him "Rolls."

As I listened to Dino, I flipped through the brochures and schedules of my hefty Welcome Packet, which I had brought with me to dinner. Between the order forms for videos, books, seminars, tapes, and retreats, and my itinerary for self-improvement, I found what I was looking for—a biography of Dino Rainwater.

"In the quest of spiritual wellness," the brochure began, "there is one man who has combined the science of the mind with the higher consciousness of many lifetimes. That man is Dino Rainwater. Anyone who has read his books or heard his tapes—'Let Good Things Happen!', 'Let More Good Things Happen!', 'Brain Angels,' and 'Turn up the Volume on Your Mind' —knows that Dino Rainwater is a man with a sacred gift; Dino Rainwater can make people change."

Dino also knew how to blow his own horn. I read more. Like Natalie had said, Dino Rainwater had a background in psychology. In the sixties, when he was still a college student, Dino Rainwater "examined the origin and ritual of American Indian myth, learning pathways to higher consciousness." I think this means that Rainwater is probably not his real name. It was during this time, apparently, that Dino Rainwater explored alternatives in consciousness and realized rationality is not the bonanza we thought it was.

It just goes to show what you can achieve when you put fifteen years into something. As far as I could see, Dino had put together a package that had something for everyone. Dino was a new age chameleon, a mixture of shamanism and corporate culture, dry cleaners and ritual dancing, portable phones and alchemy. Maybe that's what Natalie meant when she said Dino Rainwater is a real mystery.

"I want to warn you right now; people are going to resent you for being happy," Dino was saying. "Even my wife, Tambra, can't understand why I feel so good."

"But I want to tell you something," he continued. "You can make it happen."

"Make what happen?" I whispered to Natalie, who was staring at Dino raptly.

"Whatever you want," Dino thundered, as if he had heard my question.

ๆ ๆ ๆ

I was ready for the most important ritual of initiation at The Mind SelfInstitute. This was the beginner's first meeting with Dino Rainwater, listed in the course schedule as "A Morning Talk With Dino." I had heard much discussion about it over dinner. All the Institute regulars promised me it would be a very memorable and exciting occasion, the kind that would give me energy for years to come. I would be grateful if it did, I replied, thinking that vitamins had never worked for me, so maybe Dino would. By nine o'clock the next morning, a few cups of coffee behind me, I sat in the Concentration Teepee, my hopes high.

There were fourteen of us that morning, there to get a direct blast of Dino Rainwater's personal power. Everyone looked bright and eager. Some of my fellows were even wearing the white Mind Self Institute sweatshirt printed with the Institute's slogan, "I'm Ready." I counted six of them. It made me feel a little regretful I had not given more thought to my own outfit, a tank top under a baseball jacket that said, "Yorktown Cake and Donut Supplies" on the back.

There was one free spot for Dino, and at exactly nine o'clock, he walked in the room and sat down in a folding chair in a circle with the rest of us. He bent his left leg over his right, giving us a view of the bottom of his Topsiders, and looked around. Then he spoke. "When we talk about your mind," he began, as if he had not stopped since the evening before, "we are talking about the collection of beliefs and expectations you've been taught since you were a child." He gave us a moment for this to sink in.

"When we talk about 'You,' we mean that true and transcendent part of yourself that knows exactly what is right for you. Today I'm going to show you how 'you' can listen to *you*. I want to show you how to demand the truth from your mind and not listen to the collection of Other People's Voices. That's O.P.V., Other People's Voices. I'm going to show you how to get what you want."

Maybe I was a little out of my league here, but I just couldn't keep track of who he was talking about. There were so many "yous" that by the time he was finished I felt as if I had to account for a few hundred individuals.

Still, the performer in me enjoyed Dino. He knew just when to swoop down on some unenlightened slob, and when to let things ride. And he gave great eye contact.

"Now the first thing I'm going to do is teach you to W.I.O.W.Y.S." He looked around the room at our puzzled faces. "W.I.O.W.Y.S.—Work It Out With Yourself. I'm going to teach you one of the fundamental techniques of Mind Self Therapy. So let's do it," he declared, and everyone in the "I'm Ready" sweatshirts fidgeted with excitement.

"Let's start with you. What do you want?"

I listened with interest for an answer, but for some reason, no one spoke. Dino just stared in my general direction.

"You. I'm talking to *you*," he said leaning towards me. I realized he was talking to me. It had never occurred to me I could talk to Dino Rainwater directly. Having Dino address you personally was like having a television talk back to you; it came as a shock.

"What's one thing you really want?" he said.

"A record deal," I answered.

"Okay. A record deal. Who said that?"

"What?"

"Who said you want a record deal?"

"I did," I answered, wondering if Dino thought there was something wrong with me.

"Wrong. A certain part of you said that. Are you a musician?"

"Yes."

"Okay, the musician in you wants a record deal. What do you want?"

I thought for a moment. "To get in touch with my talent?"

"What else?"

"World Peace?"

"Something else."

"Lunch?" I ventured, not sure what path I had to take in order to get Dino off my back.

"Okay. Now I'm going to teach you to Work It Out With Yourself. I want you to picture an empty room. There's no color in this room, no objects. There seems to be walls, but they have no substance. You're someplace uncluttered by images. You are there alone. Are you there?" he asked.

I pictured an old episode of a spooky TV show, where a guy accidentally wanders into another dimension. I imagined I was there. "Yes," I said.

"Good. Now picture yourself, standing in the middle of nothingness. It's peaceful. Time doesn't exist here. Everything is tranquil." I felt calm, as I allowed myself to flow with Dino's images. I listened to his voice, which had softened into a gentle monotone. The room was perfectly quiet. Dino continued. "You're at total peace as you stand in the center of nowhere. Suddenly a telephone rings. Hear it ring. Ring. Ring. Can you hear it?"

"Yes."

"You pick it up. And on the other end is your higher self. Say hello."

"Hello?" I said, feeling a little silly.

In a quiet, awe-struck voice, Dino said, "And now, you're going to ask the being on the other end a question. Whatever you want. You have your *true self* on the line. You can talk, you can fight, you can look for truth, but before you hang up the phone, I want you to come to some understanding with the being on the line. And whatever you decide on the cosmic telephone will be an agreement between you and your higher self. And this is what we mean by "Working It Out With Yourself."

"Okay, Grace," Dino said, adding to the mysterious mood by somehow knowing my name, "I want you, in your head, to talk to the voice on the other end of the line."

For some reason, I imagined I was holding a red telephone receiver. The cord curled into the distance and disappeared in the fog. I also imagined I heard music in the distance, steel drums and women singing. I held the telephone to my ear and listened to my higher self.

I heard Dino whisper, "Grace, what is your higher self saying?"

"It asked if I had a nice ride up here."

"Good."

"Something about unusually good weather." I listened. "It's talking about the music business. The universe. A little of everything."

"Excellent. Remember you don't have to be heavy with your higher self. Now, ask the being on the phone what it wants," Dino said, enunciating each word as if I was negotiating for kidnap victims.

In the beige mist of nowhere, I asked my mind what it wanted.

The voice of my higher self spoke quietly. In the background, the sound of steel drums now mixed with the noises of a beach. I listened.

"What did it say?" Dino whispered.

"It wants me to turn down the volume in the rehearsal studio, its ears are starting to hurt," I said. "It also says I should write a song about traveling."

"Excellent," said Dino. Even I was stunned. It's true my ears had been bothering me lately and I had been too lazy to take it seriously. And I had been searching for a subject for a new song. There was something to this technique.

I wanted to talk more with my higher self. There were so many questions I wanted to ask, so many things to discuss. But for the moment Dino told me to sit down, and we were soon on the phone with the higher self of a travel agent named Gloria. Excited, I sat down, looking forward to later that afternoon when I would once again have time to contact my higher self.

Ꭹ Ꭹ Ꭹ

"And then I pretended I was on the telephone," I said excitedly to Natalie as we walked down the unpaved path under the darkening sky.

"I know, Grace. This is what I've been telling you about all along."

"And I tried it again later, and I could actually hear the voice of my higher self!"

"I know, isn't it interesting? After you do it enough times you even get a kind of image in your mind of what your higher self looks like. Mine looks like a female Clint Eastwood."

We chatted this way, breathing in the night air and watching stars appear one by one. We were on our way to the big social event of the weekend—the Meeting of Selves by the Gazebo.

The sky glowed deep yellow and orange between the trees, turning to sapphire higher in the sky. It was a beautiful June night. A few other guests walked quietly on the same road, on their way to the Gazebo. The party was scheduled to begin at eight o' clock. All of our friends of the last twenty-four hours, both staff and guests, would be there.

The Gazebo stood deep in the woods, about a quarter of a mile from the main lodge on a grassy clearing cut from birches and pines. We arrived at the Gazebo, drawn by the gentle light falling from lanterns on posts. It was a very pretty sight, appropriately mysterious for people who had spent the day expanding their minds.

Guests filled the little wooden structure and spilled onto the grass around the edges of it. Just outside the gazebo, tables were set with wine, beer, soft drinks, and juice, as well as cookies and muffins which had the distinctly homespun look cherished by The Mind Self Institute. Music played, chimes and bells that repeated aimlessly.

The wooden crisscrossing beams of the little gazebo, along with the yellow lanterns, made it look like a giant beehive. Some guests hovered by the gazebo or strolled across the lawn, while others stood silhouetted against the sky by the edge of a nearby pond. A path tilted down from the gazebo to the pond, which was surrounded by a ring of trees. Natalie and I walked along the edge of the water and chatted about the day.

"Are you glad you came?" Natalie asked.

"I am glad," I said, inhaling the fresh night air. "You were right. It's good to be away from everything for a few days."

"Yes, but are you getting anything from the retreat? I mean is it helping you deal with your problems?"

"Natalie, don't be in such a rush. I'm just getting the hang of things here."

"I'm not rushing you, I just want to know if it was worth it. I know this cost you a lot."

"It's worth it, it's worth it. Just look at that pond. That alone is helping me put my troubles behind me." The water was perfectly still except for where bugs skimmed across the surface, setting small circles of water briefly in motion. The pool reflected the last light of the sky, a sliver of blue in a darkening mirror. We heard the sound of crickets and the scratching of a frog whenever we stopped talking. The night came to life, while the reassuring lights of the gazebo burned nearby. I took in the scene as we had been instructed to do in meditation class that morning.

"Being here is helping me put things in perspective. I mean, not everything is about the music business, right?"

Natalie didn't answer me. She was staring across the pond at two women who strolled by the reeds on the other side. It was almost too dark to see who it was and she peered forward.

"Is that Barbara? I think it is. I know her from the last retreat. I'm going to say hello, do you mind?" said Natalie, finding a new direction for her energy.

"No, go ahead, you're making me nervous." The good thing about close friends is that you can tell them exactly how you feel. Natalie walked off.

ۍ ۍ ۍ

I went to the gazebo, poured myself a glass of wine, and grabbed what The Mind Self Institute had named a "Lotus Muffin," but which was still a corn muffin to me. People were earnestly engaged in eye contact with their partners in conversation. This allowed me to move among the group and make my way back to the edge of the pond with my snack without having to talk to anyone.

I stood there thinking, trying to put my problems into the context of this peaceful scene. I felt as if my problems were not all that important anymore. I wanted to remember this feeling. I breathed deeply, having learned today you can "scroll through the brain layers" using breath, when someone stood behind me and spoke.

"It's beautiful, isn't it? I think this is my favorite spot."

It was Dino Rainwater.

"It's gorgeous," I said. I didn't turn around. I, Grace Note, had no intention of playing the fawning disciple like so many of my close friends.

"I'm at peace when I'm here," said Dino. He stepped over a rock and stood next to me. Together we looked out over the pond.

"Well, thanks for sharing it with me," I said, not wanting, on the other hand, to seem totally ungrateful.

"I'm glad to share it with you, Grace."

"It really helps me forget my troubles," I remarked, staring distantly over the pond.

"Do you have a lot to forget?"

"Just the usual problems. Nothing serious."

"Well, thanks for letting us help you forget them."

"You're welcome. Thank you."

"You're very welcome."

This seemed like a natural end to our exchange, yet he continued to stand next to me, his hands in his pants pockets, looking ahead. I felt a little nervous. Dino was top deity in this place, and here he was putting in an appearance by my side. He didn't say anything and I decided he must be doing something important with his mind.

Contrary to what I expected, none of the guests or staff came over to talk to Dino. There seemed to be a tacit understanding that everyone was on their own now, and this was not an occasion for the enthusiastic pursuit of self-improvement. This was down time.

Moments passed. I spoke. "So do you really get time to enjoy this place yourself?"

"Not enough. But I really get into it when I'm here." I liked the fact that Dino talked like a normal person. His delivery was a little less presentation-style.

"If I owned this place, I wouldn't want to leave, either," I said.

"I always find a little time to sneak away. I usually stay an extra night on these retreats, after everyone has left."

"That's nice. How often do you do these retreats?"

"Four times a summer. Once a month in June through September. By the way," he said, his voice regaining its booming quality for an instant, "didn't you say this is your first time here?"

"Yes. The very first time."

"I don't know if I said this, Grace, but thanks for coming this weekend. I'm glad you could make it."

"Thank you."

"You're welcome," he said with a kind of aimless enthusiasm.

Once more we were quiet. Yet he didn't move from the spot. I looked at him. He was much taller than I was and I had to look up to meet his gaze. I smiled and as he smiled back, I decided the enthusiasm in his eyes was merely a reflection of his greater enthusiasm for life. It's always easy to assign lofty motives to the behavior of advanced human beings. I decided to take a more aggressive tack in starting another discussion. I considered asking him something a little more personal. I could ask about his family.

He had mentioned his lovely wife Tambra several times. But perhaps that was just his professional technique to make himself seem warmer and more accessible. Perhaps he actually preferred to keep his family out of it.

I decided to take a chance and talk about music. I learned long ago everyone has a secret passion somehow connected to music. Maybe it's a little four track studio they built in their basement, or maybe it's a song they've been working on for fifteen years, or a special collection of Louis Prima records—everyone's got some little musical secret they're just dying to tell.

I introduced it by saying many of his theories reminded me of certain aspects of music theory.

Sure enough, Dino Rainwater opened up like a cloudburst. "That's so interesting you noticed. As a matter of fact, I'm really fascinated by music and I've found a lot of inspiration in harmonic progressions."

"I had a feeling."

We laughed and talked for at least a half-hour. Dino was relaxed and surprisingly down to earth. He seemed to grow younger by the second until I felt like I was talking to an old friend, trading stories on a summer night. He even went and got us another glass of wine.

"Listen, I'm really enjoying talking to you," he said as he handed me a little Dixie cup of white wine. "Can I share something with you?"

"What do you want to share?" I asked.

"I can't tell you. It's something you have to see for yourself. Just say yes." A mischievous look came over his face.

I hesitated. I didn't really want to share anything with Dino Rainwater. I was still hoping to experience the sense of awe everyone else at the institute had around Dino. Awe required distance. At the same time, I felt complimented Dino Rainwater wanted to share something with me.

"Why not," I finally said.

"Okay then," said Dino, "Let's do it." I really didn't know what he had in mind—I didn't think it would entail following him into the woods. But he turned around and started walking, beckoning me to follow him on a small path that ran along the edge of the pond. It was completely dark now, the sky had gone from sapphire blue to black. I could barely see where I was going and I followed Dino who tread with confidence on a tiny trail worn in the high grass. When we arrived at the far side of the pond, the trail turned sharply to the left and disappeared into the woods.

The sounds of the night were clearer suddenly, perhaps because the noise of the party had faded away. Crickets jingled regularly like little bells and a bird cried.

Instantly, I was worried. "Where are we going?"

"Someplace really special, Grace," he said, turning around and waving at me to follow. He smiled reassuringly as if sensing my fear. "Don't worry, you're safe here—this is my back yard." I felt better. Dino marched forward briskly, full of excitement as if we were embarking on a great adventure. We moved deeper into the woods, striding across cracking pine needles and snapping twigs.

It was dark now. Dino pulled a little flashlight out of his back pocket, an extremely high-tech, matte black affair which he used to light the woods ahead of us. When you took a walk in the forest with Dino, you went in style.

We made small talk and I told him it had been a long time since I had taken a walk in the woods at night like this. Moths surprised us now and then as they flickered by Dino's flashlight.

"We're almost there," Dino said, after we had been walking for a few minutes. I felt torn between childhood memories and adult realities. Half of me felt like I was back in summer camp, sneaking away after curfew, while the other half hoped Dino was not some upscale ax murderer.

I asked Dino how he knew where he was going, and he said he had come here so many times he knew the way. He still wouldn't tell me where we were headed and it remained a surprise, right until we came to the base of a big wooden tree house.

"Here we are," said Dino, standing proudly under the little cabin in the branches. "I thought you would get a kick out of this. I built it with the kids last summer." It looked like he built it with his kids plus a couple of contractors. This was not your five nails and a board kind of tree house; it was the best-made tree house I had ever seen. Looking up from the ground, I could see the underside of the floor, neatly aligned planks with a perfect square opening in the middle that served as the entrance. Dino reached up and tugged on a rope ladder attached to a pulley. It fell at our feet.

"Wow, it's fantastic," I said, marveling at what would be only a dream for most children. Dino shone a flashlight upwards and I could see a little window cut into the side of the tree house, with red dotted curtains pulled to either side of the frame. It was like a house in a fairy tale.

"Want to see the inside?" asked Dino.

"Why not?" I replied, and we climbed up.

The tree house was furnished with a roomful of tiny, kid-sized furniture. The furniture was simple—a little round table with two blue chairs, a cupboard mounted on the wall, and a free-standing cabinet with the top painted to look like a sink. Someone had stenciled yellow flowers on the front of the cupboard. All the accessories had been created with great care, and many were made out of sticks. On one of the walls a weaving hung, made out of twigs and wool.

"My daughter, Karen, made that," said Dino. A wonderful smell of pine filled the room.

Dino had been holding his flashlight and shining it around the room. He picked up a vase from the little table, and put his flashlight inside it standing up. Then he took a red bandanna from his pocket and draped it over the top of the flashlight so the room was filled with soft red light.

"There, isn't that better?" said Dino.

"This is wild. I haven't been in a tree house for years. I don't think I've ever been in such a posh one."

"Let's sit down. It's not the most comfortable place to stand up if you're my size." I realized Dino had been standing with his back arched forward and shoulders lowered, crouching to fit under the low roof. He pulled over two little blue chairs and we sat down.

"Isn't this great?" he asked, looking like a folded up giant.

"It really is." I looked around in wonderment. "How often are your kids here?" The room was neat and clean.

"They spend all of August up here with Tambra." Dino stretched back in the chair so his legs filled nearly the whole floor. "I'm relaxing," he declared with a sigh.

"It's like going back in time."

"It's true. All my problems are miles away."

"Sitting in a tree house like this."

"And no one knows where I am."

"You must work pretty hard on these weekends," I said. It didn't seem true, but I didn't feel like letting the conversation die. Dino may have been relaxed but not so much so that he ceased to stare at me with his specially developed, probably patented, "Life-Is-Full-of-Wonder" stare. It made me nervous.

"It's hard work. But I enjoy it. I get to meet all kinds of interesting people. Like you," he said, effusing warmth.

I didn't say anything. I felt a little dizzy from the swirling bands of red light thrown over the walls.

"It's not often we get rock musicians up here, especially such successful ones," Dino said.

"Do you mean me?"

"Of course I mean you," he said.

"I don't remember telling you I was successful," I said, thinking back to our conversation by the pond.

"Not everyone has a song they wrote on the radio," he said with a grin, "much less one recorded by Death Threat."

"How do you know about that? Did my friend Natalie fill out some special form about me?"

"Grace, I know about everyone who comes up here," he said with a chuckle. "I know things about people." Dino wanted to remind me who had the higher power around here. He was pulling his mystic card, although he hardly looked like one at the moment, in his neatly pressed polo shirt and khaki slacks.

"Still, I can't believe you've heard of Death Threat."

"I've even heard of your band. Swan Venom, right?"

Suddenly I felt afraid. This was spooky. How did Dino know so much about me? My own family had barely heard of Swan Venom. "How did you know the name of my band?"

He broke into a smile. "Don't get scared, I'm teasing you. You mentioned it in the seminar this morning. Remember?" He laughed.

"Oh, yeah." I had said the name of my band when we introduced ourselves.

"Don't worry, I'm not a mind reader."

"I wasn't sure for a second."

"I know about Death Threat because I have kids who help keep me on top of things. And I speak at college campuses all over the country. I pick up more than you would think about pop culture."

"I guess it makes sense. After all, you're part of it."

He gazed at me with tolerance, as if he were used to such blows. "I like to think what we do here is not just a trend. We help people transform their lives. And in order to do that, I have to know who's here. I take a personal interest in everyone visiting us. You included," he said, tilting his head in a gesture of interpersonal communication.

"Thanks."

"I would like to hear some of your music sometimes. I know I'd love it," said Dino, the warmth in his gaze heating up a degree.

"I would be happy if you did. It would be my way of thanking you for this great experience," I said in true, new age style. "I'll send you a tape. Anyway, thanks for showing me your tree house. Can we go back now?"

I felt as if we had been up there for months. I was hot, and a little queasy. Maybe it was the white wine I had drunk. Or maybe there was something in the Lotus muffin after all.

Dino was so intense he almost glowed with energy. It seemed the dizzier I became, the more focused and stationary he appeared until the whole room seemed to be spinning around him.

"Sure, let's go," Dino said. He shifted as if he were about to stand up but instead leaned forward and took my hand. "Hey, this was a real treat for me. I hardly ever get to come up here. I'm the one who should thank you," he said. "Thank you." Then Dino hugged me. Since I had no where to go, I accepted the hug.

His large body made its way around mine—not with any pressure; he just rested his head gently on my shoulder, his arms loosely around my back.

"You're welcome," I said. I held on for a moment wondering if it would help the room to stop spinning.

"Mm," he said. "This is nice."

I waited for the hug to end but it didn't. Instead, I felt that tiny flash of energy and heat in his touch, the flash that alerts one to oncoming desire.

I waited. I didn't want to say anything until I was positive. Maybe I was just not as open in spirit as Dino was. Maybe his hug simply contained more sharing and warmth than I was used to. I didn't want to jump to any conclusions.

I didn't have to. Dino ran his hand down my back and pulled me a little closer. I felt the tension in his body. This was not our spirits hugging anymore.

"Grace, I'm really glad you came up this weekend."

I started to pull back, saying something about how I was glad, too, but as I reached that critical point when my face passed Dino's as we moved away from each other, he leaned forward again and kissed me with a full blown, no-time-for-breathing kiss.

It's funny how much work your mind can get done while your body is engaged in an activity like kissing Dino Rainwater. I had plenty of time in those short moments to consider this dramatic turn in the evening. Had he planned this? Or was this just a spontaneous gesture of his higher self? Everything stopped spinning now, as if held steady by his touch. The warmth, light, scent and closeness of the little room wrapped itself around us. The red light filled the room. I tried to absorb this strange situation, but my concentration was overpowered by the smell of night and forest, by the feeling of Dino's lips touching mine.

It occurred to me that we were far away from everyone, free and alone, just two people in a tree house. But very quickly I realized this was wrong. Dino was aggressive, the way certain men are when overpowered by feelings and physical sensations. Suddenly he was kissing me too hard, holding me too tight, unable to contain his strength. His crystal jabbed me. I felt crushed. I pushed away and Dino closed his eyes and took several deep breaths.

"I'm sorry," he said. "I know, I'm too intense." He closed his eyes.

Perhaps he thought this would reassure me and allow things to continue. I had had enough. I was not interested in starting any kind of affair here in his tree house, or anywhere else. Dino was married and weird.

"Let's not do this," I said.

"Do what?"

"This. This kissing."

"I'm sorry it bothered you. I just felt close."

"I don't feel like expressing it that way."

Dino was sweating. I was conscious of his face, only a few inches from mine. He looked extremely earthy at that moment, like an actor whose pancake makeup had melted. Close to him, I could see all the marks and dents on the landscape of his face.

Rather than relent, sit quietly for a few moments and then move on like any decent man would, Dino decided to take the "What's your problem?" approach. Letting his desire borrow his method, he said, "I get the feeling your mind is telling you to pull away. That felt good, didn't it?"

"My mind is right this time."

"But you're attracted."

"That's not always the most important thing. I just don't think this is a good idea."

"But what do you *feel*?"

"I feel like this isn't a good idea."

"Is this a good idea?" Here he took my hand and pressed it up against a very substantial hard-on. His eyes narrowed as he looked at me. "Grace. It's a good idea. Take charge," he whispered.

Dino had nerve. Either that or he was uncontrollably excited, and getting reckless. I pulled my hand away. His boldness was remarkable. I felt as if I was getting a private lesson in assertiveness.

"Cut it out, Dino, right now," I said, glaring at him. "It's not going to happen, get it?" I, too, could get tough.

"Okay, Grace," said Dino, recoiling into his chair, "if you want to let your mind push you around, I can't stop you. I just wanted to feel close." He leaned back in his chair, and in a technique that was not the sole property of The Mind Self Institute, began to pout.

The warm light of the bandanna-covered flashlight shed its moody glow on Dino. He looked into the flashlight as if it were a flame. I could tell he felt rejected. He looked like a one hundred and ninety-pound child.

I would have left, but I had no idea where I was. I needed Dino and his flashlight to get back to civilization. Time passed. I decided someone should say something. "Are you upset?" I asked. Women always wonder how the other guy is doing.

He snapped to attention and looked at me. "No, I'm not upset. It's just a little embarrassing. I don't do this all the time, you know. I mean, I don't know what came over me. I'm a little overwhelmed. I just felt very attracted to you."

"I understand."

"I'm sorry."

"Fine. Can we go back now?"

Dino continued to sit motionless, with half his face in a smile and the other half in a grimace. I could tell by the look on his face I wasn't out of the tree house yet. The consequences of his actions were dawning on him. He didn't look me in the eye.

"Grace, you're not going to tell anyone about this, are you?" he asked, shifting on his chair which only held half his behind.

"Tell someone? Who would I tell?"

"I mean, anyone at the institute. I would really like to keep this between us."

"No, of course not. It's our secret. I won't say a thing."

"Thanks, Grace. I don't think anyone needs to know about my tree house. Don't you agree?"

"I agree. I won't tell a soul. Can we go now?"

"Yes, let's go back," said Dino as he despondently pulled the bandanna off his flashlight and directed it to the trap door in the floor.

❦ ❦ ❦

I walked over the dark lawn, wetting my feet in the grass. The camp was quiet. Most of the lights were off in the bungalows. I looked for ours, knowing Natalie would still be awake. I wasn't sure whether I should tell her what had happened with Dino. The Mind Self Institute is important to Natalie; she has examined its philosophy in depth, and uses it to guide her life. She has gained insight and found some degree of peace in what she has learned.

Telling her Dino Rainwater hit on me in his tree house might damage Natalie's fragile worldview.

Therefore, as I walked down the gravel path and rounded the Shack of Gladness, the glass geodesic dome where morning meditation took place, I decided I should probably spare Natalie the details of tonight's unusually friendly encounter with Dino.

The sky was nearly black. There was no moon, and stars burned white against the blackness, the cloud of the Milky Way in the middle of it all.

I saw the bright yellow light shining in the window of our bungalow. It all seemed so peaceful—the night, the sounds of the crickets. It reminded me how the night can work both ways, as a cover to hide Dino Rainwater's intentions, or to protect, as it did now.

The spring of the screen door creaked as I opened it and Natalie, sitting on the bottom bunk of the bed, looked up.

"Hey! You're back."

"Dino made a pass at me," I said. I couldn't help it. The second I saw Natalie sitting on the bed in her little traveling nightgown, the day's literature and hand-outs spread out around her, a pamphlet on Shadow Therapy in her hand, I knew I had to tell her.

Natalie looked at me with a superior look of disbelief. "Don't joke about things like that," she said.

"Natalie, why would I joke about this?"

"Because you have a twisted sense of humor."

I knew Natalie would have liked it if I just denied everything. But if she wanted to follow Dino's teaching, she would have to accept his human side. Besides, the story was too good not to tell.

"I'm telling you, Natalie. Just now I was with Dino and he hit on me in a big way."

"It can't be."

"It happened, Natalie. I took a walk in the woods with Dino Rainwater tonight. Do you want the hideous details?"

Natalie looked upset. "Yes," she said, in spite of her shock, and she pushed her pamphlets aside. I proceeded to tell her the whole sordid story, from our twilight chat around the pond all the way to our scary walk back through the woods, when Dino refused to speak one single word, even when I tripped over a fallen birch tree. I told her about the way he knew all these things about me, and how it kind of freaked me out at first, because I thought maybe he really did have some powerful higher self, but if he did, it was no better than his lower self, because he put my hand on his dick without even asking. Natalie commented throughout, expressing various states of disbelief. At first she looked pained. But soon enough her disturbance gave way to fascination.

"That is really disgusting," she said, when I had brought her up to date.

"I know. I couldn't believe it."

"I mean, I'm shocked. He's not the man I thought he was." Without thinking, Natalie closed the brochure still in her hand. "I mean, it doesn't make sense, it just doesn't. He's always talking about his wife Tambra. He's always mentioning his kids."

"He showed me Karen's wall hanging."

"I thought he was such a family man."

"People can be very different from what you see at a distance."

"Do you think he does this all the time?"

"Every chance he gets, is my guess." I wanted to be fair. "Although he claimed he never does anything like this. I don't think I believe him."

Natalie sighed. "There's no way around it. Dino is a sleaze."

I sat at the other end of the bed, some pillows stuffed between the wall and me. I looked at Natalie. I knew she felt disillusioned. Perhaps she even felt it was all my fault for getting into this situation to begin with. If I hadn't come up here, maybe everything would be as it always was, with Dino and his team taking her on spiritual outings until the inevitable day he took Natalie for a walk to his tree house. I hoped she wasn't going to allow it to affect our friendship. Natalie looked lost in thought.

Outside our cabin the crickets had called it quitting time and there was nothing but the light clicking of branches as they brushed against each other in the wind. I wondered if Natalie was talking to her higher self; she sat quietly, her eyes closed as she sorted things out in her mind. Finally she spoke.

"So, tell me. What was it like?" Natalie asked.

"What was what like?"

"You know," said Natalie, looking me in the eyes. The corners of her mouth turned up slightly.

"You mean when he put my hand on his...?"

"Exactly," she replied, the ruthless look of a truth-seeker on her face.

"Natalie, I tried not to notice. Let's just say he's closer to man than he is to god."

"I'm never going to look at him quite the same way," she said, a far-away look on her face.

I had definitely made him more human in Natalie's eyes.

֊ ֊ ֊

Let me be clear; I was not out to change Natalie's feelings about The Mind Self Institute. I don't tell people what to believe. It was up to Natalie to resolve the fact she had learned all sorts of profound things about the universe from a creep. This troubled her too, and we talked a while longer about the paradoxical nature of her situation.

"It's just all so confusing. He's always talking about the truth, the truth, the truth. I don't know how I can resolve his behavior tonight with the other stuff he says."

"It's not easy."

"Is he a fake? Did he just make everything up?"

"Of course he made everything up. This is America. The question is, are you getting something valuable from what he's made up?"

"Yes. But I don't know if I can accept the fact that he's a hypocrite."

"Is he a hypocrite? I think you have to decide whether what happened tonight directly affects his philosophy. Let me ask you this: does Dino make a big thing out of sex? Does he talk a lot about marriage or his personal life?"

"Well, like I said, he's always talking about his wife and kids, but only in passing. He doesn't reveal a lot of details about his personal life. And he doesn't talk much about marriage or sex in the abstract. His theories are more spiritual."

"So he doesn't make a big deal about relationships?"

"No, that's not his main thing."

"There, you see? It's hard to know whether he's a hypocrite or just a jerk. A person can be very evolved in one area of their life and a mud crawler in another."

"Do you think so?" asked Natalie eagerly.

"Yes, I really do. I think that's what you call an idiot-savant."

"I guess that makes me feel better. I can't stand hypocrisy. But I could live with it if I thought he was just a jerk."

"Natalie, the final call is yours."

I guess I had a special feeling of clarity that night. It's true, the weekend hadn't turned out the way I planned, but what had lately? At least the visit to the country had distracted me from my problems at home. And it reminded me no one has all the answers. Everyone makes mistakes. Even Dino Rainwater, who looks like he really has it together, especially on videotape. Even me.

We had been gabbing so long that a blue streak of daylight had appeared on the horizon and it glowed in our window. We planned to head back to New York after lunch.

"Grace, it's getting light out. I can't believe it," cried Natalie.

"I really wanted to get some sleep."

"We have to be up at seven, for the farewell session by the flag-pole."

"What's that?"

"Just some chanting, and putting our minds together."

"I hope Dino keeps his mind in his pants."

We laughed and then slept soundly for about forty-five minutes until the sounds of Balinese gamelons, Indian tablas, and an Australian digeridoo wafted in our window, and a voice over a loudspeaker cried cheerfully, "Everybody, up, up, up! Feel the energy? It's time for another day in your life!"

7

THE TRAIN ROLLED STEADILY alongside the Hudson River as it carried us away from West Cluster. By the river, birds pecked at patches of weeds, and late afternoon light laced the treetops. We were heading back to New York. I looked out the window, enjoying the final stretch of serenity. My fellow passengers seemed relaxed too. It was quiet in the car as people absorbed themselves in sections of their Sunday newspapers.

Natalie was reading a book she had picked up at the Institute's Gift Shop. It was called *Yes Without Limits; a Guide to Hope, Harmony, Heaven and Health*. She asked if she could read some of it to me. I told her no, I wanted to work on the lyrics for a new song. Perhaps she could read it to me a little later, I suggested. Then I pulled out my notebook, laid it across my lap, closed my eyes and hummed, just in case she didn't get the idea. Natalie went back to her book.

Natalie would have been surprised to learn I was not working on a song at all; I was really thinking about The Mind Self Institute. She would have been even more surprised to know I had actually learned something this weekend. I was going home with insight into the problems I had left behind.

It happened in the Sunday morning seminar called "Sacred Information." This seminar, my last activity at The Mind Self Institute, was a continuation of the basic techniques introduced in "A Morning Talk with Dino." Sacred Information exposed beginners to more sophisticated ways of W.I.O.W.Y.S.—Working It Out With Your Self.

After my Saturday night encounter with Dino, I admit I was skeptical of anything the Institute had to offer. But I remembered the advice I had given Natalie—you can always learn something, even from a creep. I went to Sacred Information with an open mind.

The first thing we learned was that getting one's higher self on the line was only the beginning of W.I.O.W.Y.S. Once you did that, there were a variety of techniques you could use to direct your Higher Self in specific ways. For instance, there was Universal 411, designed for practical problem solving. There was Heart Line Repair and Spirit to Spirit, good for more intimate questions. And there was the Energy Message Center where you could leave reminders for your Higher Self. Each method required a different visualization.

Bonnie Sue Orange was on hand to show us the steps. She gave us handouts with short descriptions of the different problem-solving methods. "These will be your tools," Bonnie Sue said, "Use them to guide you to your higher self. They will get you straight talk from your soul every time," she assured us with a wink, as if she were sharing dating tips.

The one that worked for me was Universal 411. Universal 411 is a way of letting your higher self know you're calling for information only—information as opposed to insight. You make it clear you want a simple and practical answer: no metaphors, no parables, and no long stories. It's an action-oriented approach, made for heavy-duty problem solving. And it was just what I needed.

Using this technique, I asked my Higher Self the simple question that had been on my mind. What should I do about my situation at home? I was still frustrated and angry about what Death Threat had done with "Let Me Show You." Images from their video had taken root in my mind, and I couldn't seem to get rid of them. I didn't know what to do with all my feelings. Should I stay angry? Take action? Sue?

I called Universal 411. The answer that came to me was "Say good-bye and move on."

How simple it all was. Say good-bye and move on. It was so simple I couldn't make sense of it at first. Did it mean I should stop being mad? Or could I stay mad, put it all behind me and move on anyway? And how should I say good-bye? Should I write? Chant? Phone?

Bonnie Sue Orange told me Universal 411 tends to be very literal. "It's just plain ol' information," she said. I took this to mean I should say good-bye to an actual person, as opposed to a state of mind. But to whom? I thought about all this as the train flew by New Hayward and Limerickville, Redbury and Pinecliff. Natalie was absorbed in her new book. Every once in a while she would look over at me, stare for a moment, then declare, "You really ought to read this, Grace," before returning to her page.

I did not let her distract me. Universal 411 had spoken. It was up to me to fill in the details. It was time to say good-bye. It was time to say good-bye to being angry. And more literally, it was time to say good-bye to the only people I needed to leave behind, and that was Death Threat themselves.

I decided if they would allow me, I would take a few minutes to talk to Death Threat and tell them how I felt. Part of saying good-bye, for me, meant expressing what was on my mind. That's my outspoken side. But that would be it, they would hear no more from me.

Universal 411 was right. I didn't want to be angry anymore. I wanted to forgive Death Threat. They were just doing what Death Threat does. I was the one who didn't see it. I was angry with myself and wanted to forgive myself, too. I wanted to forgive everyone. No one looking at me stretched out in my Amtrak window seat would have known such a love fest of forgiveness was going on inside my head. It was time to put bad feelings behind me and get on with the business of avoiding pop music for the rest of my life.

♪ ♪ ♪

My green canvas bag knocked softly on the steps behind me as I pulled it up to the fourth floor landing. The hallway carpet was worn down to a dirty maroon and gray, thin from decades of coming and going on Canal Street. I dragged the bag down a well-tread path in the rug. Over the weekend, while we were busy lightening our spirits, we had managed to add weight to our luggage. My bag now held an "I'm Ready" sweatshirt, two books from the gift shop, wind chimes, and some rocks I had found on a hike with Natalie.

It was late Sunday afternoon when I stepped into my apartment. Everything was just the way I left it on Friday: summer clothes in piles on the couch, microphones and guitar cables coiled on the kitchen table, dishes in the sink. On the floor were two cans of food my neighbor, Mrs. Chu, had left for my cat. Across one of the chairs was a sweater that belonged to Roger, along with a Frisbee. He had left them there the weekend before.

I put down my bag. All was quiet. On Sunday, the rumbling trucks take a break from their route across Canal Street. But it wasn't just the lack of commercial traffic that made it seem so still. The feeling of bitterness that had made me want to permanently park on the bed with a guitar was gone. I must have left all my self-pity behind me in upstate New York, because a distinct feeling of peace welcomed me home.

The bright afternoon sun poured in from the uptown-facing windows in my living room, and fell across the wooden floor like a can of gold paint spilled on the wood. Outside the window, a sparrow hopped on the rusting fire escape. My cat ran to the ledge to watch. I opened the window. The clean blue sky seemed to have traveled back with me from upstate New York.

The only sign of activity in my living room, besides the cat, was the flashing light on the answering machine. It blinked regularly, urging me to count along with it. After ten, it repeated the count as if letting me know it could handle things around the house for another few weeks.

I hadn't bothered to check in from the Institute. I had no idea who had called. The whole point of that experience had been to get as far away as possible. I stood in the warm shower of light, listening to my messages. As they played, I considered my plans for the next few days.

Two things were definitely going to happen on Monday. At three o' clock, Swan Venom had a band rehearsal. And before that, as soon as I woke up, I would call Jerry Saltstien and see if he would give me an appointment with Death Threat. It wasn't going to be easy.

First of all, Jerry would probably not take my call. He doesn't remember me even though we've been introduced several times. Jerry always looks at me as if he has a checklist in his mind he is using to figure out who I am. The list, I imagined, went, "record company personage, public relations agent, journalist, groupie, girlfriend, employee, or other." If you were in the "other" category, which I was, you might as well be transparent.

If I couldn't get through to Jerry, I could always enlist Walter to use his pull with Hunter. Walter says to call him day or night if I need anything, although I think he's referring to a back rub. Walter wouldn't mind using his personal relationship with Hunter, or Gary as he's is better known on the North Shore of Long Island, to help me connect with Death Threat.

The first voice on my answering machine cut through the quiet. It was Jessica from the café.

"Grace, Hi. Could we trade shifts this Tuesday? I know you don't usually work that night. I have an audition. It's for a jazz version of Wuthering Heights and they're looking for someone tall, so call me back." I made a mental note to tell her the switch was fine.

Next came a batch of calls from relatives. Each offered their impression of my artistic collaboration with Death Threat, which they had seen on MTV when one of my younger cousins made them watch it. A wave of shock must have gone through North Gaylordsville. Everyone up there has the impression I play in an orchestra, thanks to my family's discreet way of talking about my occupation. Usually, just telling people I live in New York puts an end to any questions. But today, aunts, uncles and cousins called in. My mother left a diplomatic message, saying only, "That doesn't seem like one of your songs, dear." She must have had a few people over Saturday night when she called because in the background I heard a number of relatives and family friends yelling hello, as well as the sound of my Uncle Maurice warming up his accordion. I received a particularly disappointed message from my ninety-two year old great-aunt Katherine. She doesn't really understand what I do for a living to begin with, and she reported in her message that "she looked for me in the movie but didn't see me anywhere."

A couple of musicians had checked in, including one who wanted to know if I could sub for him Friday night. This was good since I wanted to throw myself right into work. And Geoffrey left a message about our rehearsal. "Grace, I can't make it to rehearsal Wednesday," he said in a melancholy voice. "I have to be in court. I have to identify the dude who mugged me in the Botanical Gardens." Geoffrey got jumped one day after we did a benefit for the Lily Pond. So far, no surprises.

Roger also left a message, telling me he was in Connecticut visiting his parents. He would call me when he came back Sunday night. Roger is always a little rattled after a visit to his family. The Woodryders have been in Connecticut for generations and Roger has a lot to live up to when he goes home for the weekend. There's actually a monument to his great-grandfather, a distant relative of Peter Stuyvesant, right in the middle of town. Roger's parents don't let him relax for a second when he's home, which is probably where he acquired his own zeal for constant activity. His father adores golf and wears traditional golf clothes as a hobby, a source of great embarrassment for Roger, especially when his father wears a kilt.

There was one more message.

"Grace, it's me. How are you?" It was the voice of Paul Teagarden. "How was your weekend? I know you're out of town, but I wanted to let you know I'm coming to New York next Tuesday. Next week, not this week. Sorry it's such short notice, I only just found out. I have a meeting and I'll be there for one night. Let's get together. Call me when you come in. Bye."

I played the message again. "Unbelievable," I said, pushing over a pile of shorts next to me on the couch. This was unexpected. My cat wrapped himself around my legs. I looked down at him. "Unbelievable," I repeated. A feeling as if someone had pulled a thread through my chest from front to back gave me a fluttering sensation. I walked up and down the apartment, unpacking my bag mindlessly as I absorbed the news.

Paul Teagarden coming to New York. Could it really be? Could months of long distance phone calls really boil down to some live contact at last? Without thinking about it, I had started to believe Paul would never come to New York. It made our long-distance routine of phone calls easier to deal with. Now it was as if some miraculous incident were about to take place, as if someone had told me a total eclipse was about to happen right outside my window. Months of restrained desire caught up with me. I ran through my living room, stopping at my keyboard to play a few chords in an excited fanfare. Then I picked up the telephone. Having spent the whole weekend with Natalie, it was hard to stop talking to her. I felt as if she were still in the bunk bed below me. I dialed her number.

"Natalie, you're not going to believe this," I said as soon as she answered.

"What?"

"Guess who left a message for me on my machine."

"Dino."

"Of course not. Paul Teagarden. And guess what? He's going to be in New York."

"Really?"

"Yes. I'm so excited. The bad news is he's only coming for a day."

"Why only a day?"

"I don't know. He just left a message. He has a meeting in New York."

"Will you see him?"

"I think so. I hope so."

"That is news."

"Yes, and isn't it funny it should happen right after this weekend? I didn't even mention Paul to my Higher Self."

"What about Roger?"

"What about him?"

"Isn't it going to be complicated? I mean when Paul is here?"

"Natalie, Natalie, Natalie," I said, feeling almost hysterically cheerful, "one thing doesn't have to do with the other."

"But now they'll both be here."

"Just for a day. What's the big deal?" I said, stretching across the couch.

"You're so practical," she sighed.

"I'm not so practical. After all this time talking to him on the phone, what can I do? I have to see him. I have to."

"Well, I hope it all works out."

"Me too. Anyway, it'll be an interesting experience, whatever happens."

"Dino says every experience goes on the resumé of your higher self."

"So this will go on my resumé. Along with Dino's tree house."

"I'm excited for you. I just don't understand why it's taken him so long to get here."

"Me neither. He's busy, I guess."

"It's funny the way these guys think they can just blow into town when it's convenient."

"I don't know if Paul is blowing into town, Natalie. He has a meeting."

"Still, it would have been nice if he came here just to see you. Your phone bills alone could have paid for a few round trip tickets by now, don't you think?"

Natalie was right. Paul certainly hadn't gone out of his way to get here. And he knew I couldn't afford to fly to California. Before I could answer, Massimo joined our conversation. I heard him shouting in the background. "One hour you're home and already you're on the phone. It's incredible." He continued to marvel at us in Italian.

"Doesn't Massimo ever go out?"

"Of course he does."

"It doesn't seem like it."

"You just have bad timing," said Natalie. "I better go. Let me know what happens."

"Talk to you later," I said.

ッ ッ ッ

Jerry Saltstien wouldn't take my calls. I left three messages for him. Walter Wiener had to step in. I don't know what he said to Hunter, but as usual Walter was a bundle of efficiency because on Wednesday morning the phone rang and a sweet voice on the other end asked me to hold for Mr. Saltstien.

Jerry came on the line. "They don't have to do this," he began in an ominous tone. "I want you to understand that."

"I understand."

"They said they'll talk to you. I have nothing else to tell you right now. Thursday is the best time, if you can make it. You can thank your friend Walter for this, not me."

"I will."

"I'll call you back tomorrow. I don't know exactly what time is best for the boys," said Jerry.

It took two more phone calls—one the next day and one the day after—to detail our plans. You would have thought I was requesting their medical records. I couldn't understand why Jerry was making such a big deal out of the fact that I wanted to sit down with Death Threat. Hunter already knew what I wanted to talk about, anyway. Walter Wiener had told him. From what I understood, Hunter didn't have any problem with the fact that I hated what they had done with my song. To paraphrase what he told Walter, "I don't give a shit whether she likes it or not." Apparently, as Walter tells it, that's all Hunter had to say on the subject, and the two of them spent much more time talking about the season's baseball trades than they spent talking about me.

"Hunter really likes you," Walter added hastily in case my feelings were hurt. "That's just how he talks. It's a business to him, and the video is meant to—"

"—meant to sell records," I said, finishing his sentence. I had heard that one about a thousand times.

Unlike Hunter, Jerry was threatened by my negative feelings. He made it clear he wouldn't have been talking to me at all if it weren't for the fact that Death Threat was out of town doing a benefit concert to raise money for a drug rehabilitation center in Washington, D.C. "I don't like doing Hunter's dirty work," Jerry said, as if I were involved in some illicit deal. He felt sure I was planning something; his job was to protect the band's financial interests and stay constantly alert to scams, frauds, and phonies. To Jerry, everything in life was a financial interest.

"We've got everything on paper. That means there's nothing you can get from the boys, no lawsuits, and no extension to the contract, no bucks. They're doing this to be nice and don't you forget it, girlie," said Jerry, with all the warmth of a creature that has never left the ocean floor.

"There's nothing I want from 'the boys,' so don't get paranoid. I'm upset and I want to talk to them, that's all." I didn't tell Jerry I was just following the advice of my Higher Self.

"Okay, whatever. It sounds sick to me, but it's Hunter's decision. I want you to know that if it were up to me, you wouldn't be anywhere near them. Your friend Walter seems to have some kind of weird influence over Hunter."

"I think they call it friendship."

"Whatever they call it, I don't like it."

"Fine, you've made yourself clear. And don't worry. What I have to say will only take a few minutes."

"Be at Rainbow Head Studio on West Thirty-Seventh Street, Thursday at noon."

ʔ ʔ ʔ

Now my fighting spirit gave way to fear. Yes, I wanted to express myself. I wanted to say good-bye and move on. But it was one thing to share my feelings with friends and relatives; it was quite another to confront a mega-popstar whose face was more familiar to young Americans than the president's. I didn't mind confrontation, but the occasional pow-wow we have at the cafe when someone won't make espresso for the other waitresses just didn't compare in scale to this.

There was no turning back now. I had an appointment for Thursday, which only left a few days to practice what I wanted to say. I made notes and jotted down key words. I rehearsed speeches and visualized our conversation. My plan was to communicate as clearly and quickly as possible, to really reach out and share, and do my best to make them understand it damaged my creative spirit to see my song rendered with all those close-ups of boobs. I wanted them to know it was wrong to churn out video after video that portrayed women this way, as mindless s x objects. If I explained all this, maybe I could change them.

"Yes, and then you could start on world peace," said Roger, enjoying the behind-the-scenes turmoil of a world in which he had no personal stake. Sitting in his kitchen, we discussed my upcoming meeting.

Roger's interest in the music business has steadily grown since we've been together. It made sense he should be interested in it; the music business is connected to something artistic, yet it's also a part of the entertainment industry, which Roger follows regularly. His interest has really soared since I became involved with people he could see cardboard cutouts of in the record store.

"So you think I'm being unrealistic, wanting to talk to them?"

"Grace, being sleazy is their image. It's part of their job." Roger picked up an oatmeal cookie. We sat at his kitchen counter. A silver kettle whistled on the stove behind him. "I understand that you want to express yourself," Roger continued, "but I don't think you're going to change anyone. I definitely don't think you're going to change Death Threat because they've had so much success being the way they are."

"So what should I do?"

"I would just let them know how you feel, and be very clear about it. Don't attack, it won't get you anywhere."

Roger was so logical. I watched him as he walked to the refrigerator and opened the door. He rustled around inside, humming. He wore sweat pants and a tee shirt and it made him look exceptionally boyish. Roger is perfectly at ease in the world. He would not be the least bit intimidated if he were in my situation. I watched him pour himself a glass of milk. I had to peek over my elbow to do this, since I was now slumped at the counter, my face across my folded arms. I probably looked more despondent than I felt. Maybe it was Roger's humidifier, but I was actually starting to feel pretty good.

The whole Death Threat affair was receding quicker than I expected. It was still humiliating to be a part of the Death Threat catalog, but as it turned out, no one really seemed to care that I had anything to do with them. In fact, no one even mentioned me in any comments about the video. It's true *Music Room Magazine*, the biggest consumer rock music review, had some unkind words to say about it. To quote them:

> "Cheap shots just got cheaper with the release of Death Threat's new video, 'Let Me Show You' (Split Trouser Records). The band shamelessly pulls out every trick in its seedy trunk to sell their new song, a good, solid rocking tune that would have done fine in a more straight-ahead rendering. Unfortunately, the result of Death Threat's relentless mix of flesh and flash is a new low in meaningless rock videos.
> —Glen 'Witchy' Ottoman"

Nowhere was the name, Grace Note, mentioned. Although I was responsible for the music, I was not being held responsible for the video. And while the song was doing well, the video was not creating much of a stir. It would be played as long as the song stayed on the charts, but no longer. Roger explained these were market forces at work, which meant, very simply, that if it were a bad video, people wouldn't watch it. Furthermore, a Japanese promoter had called me and was interested in hearing more of my songs.

By the time I received my first royalty check, "Let Me Show You," the video, would be just a memory. There was a chance I could put this experience behind me with a minimum of damage and even a little gain.

"Maybe if I can make them see how one real person is affected by their crap, they'll think about what they do a little more carefully," I said to Roger.

"Don't put it that way if you can help it."

"You mean call their video 'crap'?"

"Yes."

"I'll be diplomatic about it, although I doubt they have any illusions about what they're doing."

"You would be surprised what people believe. I see it all the time on Wall Street. People believe what they want to believe in the face of all logic. A wish is a powerful thing."

"That's what Dino says. That wacko."

"Just don't assume people believe the same things you do. The universe can look very different from where someone like Hunter Burns is standing."

"Don't get so cosmic. We're talking about commercial music here, not Wall Street."

♪ ♪ ♪

Hunter looked up with a smile when I walked into the room. He and Rudy Rude were sitting together in the lounge of the studio. Regbert, the bass player and Frisk, the drummer were laying down rhythm tracks in the other room.

"Hey, Grace," cried Hunter cheerfully as if he were actually glad to see me. "How 'ya doing?" He walked over and kissed me on the cheek. Hunter Burns was not a friendly person, in general. He had even less reason to be friendly with me today, knowing I was only here to complain. It occurred to me that maybe I was the object of some sadistic joke Hunter was playing for Rudy's pleasure.

Yet Rudy sat disinterestedly on a couch with one long leg folded over the other and a magazine spread across his lap. He didn't seem to notice me or Hunter, and in fact he didn't even bother taking the cigarette out of his mouth when he looked up at me and said, "How 'ya doing?"

"Nice to see you," I said.

"Yeah," Rudy said as he folded the magazine and threw it on the cushion next to him. "I really liked your tune. I didn't get to tell you before."

"Thanks," I said. On second thought, maybe it wasn't a joke. Rudy looked at me with a friendly expression and I didn't see any derision in his slightly puffy eyes. Rudy was wearing a mechanic's shirt with the name "Chuck" sewn over the pocket. His long blonde hair fell down to his elbows. His hair looked like it had just been washed, I observed, admiring his natural wave.

Although I had met Rudy Rude once or twice before, I had never really gotten such a good look at him in bright light. He had a long slender face with pock-marked skin. I couldn't help but notice his fat, sensuous lips among his other undistinguished features. They just screamed collagen treatments. I, Grace Note, had similar lips only after an unfortuitous swelling due to an attack of sun poisoning during a gig at Club Med.

As I stared at Rudy, Hunter spoke. "Grace, why don't you sit over here," he said, pointing to a couch that was perpendicular to the one where Rudy sat. Hunter sat down next to Rudy.

I was glad Rudy hadn't stood up when I came in. I don't think I could have survived the two of them towering over me. They were both so damn tall, and besides, after years of being in the limelight, they also took up a lot of metaphysical space. I thought of the times I had seen them on stage, on award shows or in "rockumentaries," on their knees howling, sneering, and bending backwards with their instruments slung over their chest. I had seen them wrap themselves around microphone stands, slow dance with girls in the audience, fall into a rapture of screaming fans, powerful little dots on a stage in an auditorium of 40,000 people. They were used to being the total center of attention and it showed. They were completely at ease. They looked at me the way an executive who earns two hundred thousand dollars a year looks at a bicycle messenger in the elevator—a look I remember clearly from my two months at the Mr. Speed Messenger Service.

I deserved to be looked at that way, I thought. If I lived 500 years more I could never live as hard as these two. They had pushed themselves to the edge and come back from it. Now, here they were sitting next to me, their bracelets clinking, their sharp eyes staring at me unapologetically, their black boots deposited like four giant industrial parts on the floor at my feet. I admit, I was already intimidated to the point of speechlessness. That I had practiced what I wanted to say; that I was absolutely convinced I was right, all of this suddenly meant nothing.

"Grace, you want some coffee?" said Hunter. "Are you okay?" His long black hair streamed over his shoulders. I could see the small ruby earring he wore in one of his ears.

"Coffee? Sure," I stammered.

Hunter yelled, "Gino," without turning around. A thin guy came running out through a door. "Get us a couple of cups of coffee, would you?" said Hunter. Gino trotted down the hall.

On the other hand, I was entitled to my feelings. Even if I was scared, I still felt what I felt. Even if I was nothing more than a microscopic speck on Death Threat's discography, I had a right to express myself. I was proud of what I felt, and "Let Me Show You" was still my song. I had come here for a reason. It was time to get to the point. I remembered the words of my Higher Self: say good-bye and move on.

I blurted out, "Listen, I know you're really busy so I'll say what I came to say."

No one said anything to discourage me, so I continued.

"I was a little upset when I saw your video for 'Let Me Show You' and I just wanted to tell you, you know, just express myself and tell you what I felt about it. Not that you care or anything," I added hurriedly. "I mean, I guess you care, but you don't *have* to care." I was getting confused. "Okay. What I'm saying is I just want to share something that's important to me." Rudy and Hunter were leaning back against the couch staring at me. The word "share" circled around my head then crashed at my feet. I sipped the coffee Gino had put in front of me, which turned out to be scalding hot.

"Grace, relax. We're not in a hurry. Take your time," said Hunter patiently. "If it helps, Walter already told us what you thought about the video. We know why you're here."

"Oh, right. Walter said he mentioned it."

"It's no big deal," said Rudy. His voice was a little higher than Hunter's, with a nice texture. Somewhere along the line, his Long Island accent had acquired a slight southern lilt. "You hate the video, right?"

"Well, yes."

"Okay, so tell us why."

I noticed they were sunk back into the couch while I remained on the edge of my seat. I sat back. "Well, I thought it was really sleazy. I mean, there were constant shots of almost naked girls that had nothing to do with the song. I found that a little disturbing."

"Why?" asked Rudy.

I proceeded to make a speech similar to the one I had made for Walter. In fact, I was glad I had the chance to try it out on Walter because it was all I could do to get my words out. I explained to them how I resented the way they totally sexualized women. How it set a bad example for girls.

"Look, Grace, you're not telling us anything we don't already know," said Hunter, with a slight smile.

"So why do you do it?"

"It's our job. It's what sells records."

"Lots of things sell records. That doesn't mean you have to do them. Anyway, I just want to tell you, as the person who wrote the song, it's not what I wanted my song to be. It kind of hurts."

"Okay. Now Rudy and I want to talk to you about something," said Hunter briskly.

I couldn't believe these guys. It was like I told them that a light bulb had burned out in the hallway. "Wait a second. Would you just acknowledge what I said before we go on to the next subject?"

"We heard you. You want us to know that as the person who wrote the song, it's not what you wanted your song to be, and it kind of hurts. Okay?"

"Do you agree?"

"Of course we don't agree, otherwise we would have done it differently from the start. But I know exactly what you mean. You're not the first to tell us our videos are sleazy."

"Not by a long shot," added Rudy, chuckling.

"Then why do you do it?"

Hunter leaned forward on his couch. There was a look of amused patience on his face. He peered out from beneath his dark brow. "Grace, you said you know why guys like this stuff. You're right. They like it. We like it. I like it. It's our fantasy. The records sell. I don't get into the sexual politics, it's not what I do, and I'm not going to start now. And on top of that, it's really hard for me to understand why you even take it so seriously. Maybe if I had a daughter, I could relate, but it just seems like a lot of wasted energy to worry about it."

"Frisk has a daughter. He never says anything," added Rudy.

"How old is she now?" said Hunter turning to Rudy.

"I think she's fifteen. Although now that I think of it, she hates our videos, too."

"Hey, it's just business," Hunter said shaking his head.

"Humiliating women is just business?"

"If it makes you feel any better," continued Hunter, noticing my glum look, "If I were a woman I would really hate our videos, too."

"Yeah, right, you would not," Rudy said.

"I would too, man," exclaimed Hunter, twisting to face Rudy. "C'mon. You think you'd like our videos if you were a woman?"

"Hey, I'd love them, man. Put me in one, dude. I'd put on some really cool, low cut outfit, man, and show off my tits. You bet I'd like it."

"And if you were fat? Who said you could even be in the video, anyway?"

"If I were a woman I'd be in the videos no matter how fat I was. I would love taking my clothes off."

"You'd be too ugly to be in anyone's video."

"I wouldn't let looks stop me. I don't now," said Rudy and with that he gave a whoop and raised his hand for Hunter to give him a high five. Hunter slapped him back.

I could see it was totally pointless to try to talk sense to these two. I might as well talk to the ashtray. Hunter was the more mature of the pair, so I turned and gave him a full view of the expression on my face, which showed how idiotic I thought they were.

"Hey, Grace," said Hunter, turning on the charm, "cheer up. Next time we do a video of your song, we'll let you approve it."

He tilted his head a little, then slapped my knee like I was one of the guys. "Okay?" He smiled at me. He tussled my hair in a grandmotherly gesture. He squeezed my cheek as if I were a baby.

"Okay," I mumbled. I couldn't help it; I liked Hunter. There was something about him that made me feel like I didn't want to be mad anymore. He knew how to make the truth work for him. Even if you didn't like what he said, you couldn't help but appreciate his bluntness.

"Good, now on to other business," he said, flipping into his more efficient mode. His face regained its focused look of concentration.

"You have something else you want to talk about?" I asked. I thought our interview was over. Jerry Saltstien would be calling any minute to make sure I had been tossed out.

"Yes, as a matter of fact, we have something really important we want to talk to you about," said Hunter. He gave a quick glance at Rudy. I noticed even Rudy looked fairly solemn. Where he had previously been draped over the couch, he now sat upright with a look of concern.

"The fact is, Grace, you're not the only one who hates our video," said Hunter. His large hands, intertwined, rested on his legs.

"Good," I replied.

"No, it isn't good—not for you or for me."

"So who else besides me hates you?"

"It seems there's an organization called OOFF. They *really* hate our videos."

"OOFF?"

"The Organization of Families First."

"Who are they?"

"They're some kind of watchdog group. They watch TV and listen to the radio hunting for smut. If they see something they think is obscene, they start a boycott."

"And guess who they're boycotting now, dude," Rudy added. He pointed to himself and Hunter.

"Are you kidding?"

"Unfortunately, no. OOFF wants us off the air. They want us off the planet," said Hunter, his voice low and steady.

"Can they actually do that? Get you off the air, I mean?"

"They've been pretty successful with some of their boycotts. Or, I should say they scare people. They hit television sponsors, advertisers, magazines, stores, anyone who is involved with material they find offensive. They start these fanatical letter writing campaigns, and fuck knows why, people give in. They don't even represent that many people. Anyway, they've decided to boycott us because of our video. Your video."

I just shook my head as Hunter spoke. It seemed so bizarre. I didn't like the video, but I wouldn't start a movement over it.

"That is really terrible. Why would anyone waste their time?"

"I don't know, Grace, I really don't," said Hunter grimly. "Death Threat has always attracted a certain amount of fanatics."

"It's not like your video is so much worse than a lot of others."

"It's true. But they want to make an example out of us. The guy in charge of the whole thing is named Reverend Robert Bailey. He's the one who decides who OOFF is going to boycott. His latest crusade is against music videos, starting with us."

"But why a boycott?"

Hunter didn't say anything. He just looked down into his coffee cup. "The world is full of people who think their beliefs should be everyone's beliefs."

"I'm sorry, Hunter. I wouldn't have wished for anything like this to happen."

He looked away. "I know. I'm worried, though. If this organization throws its weight around and people aren't willing to fight them, we won't look too good. We're not exactly boy scouts." As he spoke his lips tightened and his eyes focused to an angry sparkle. He looked up at me. "I mean, it's good PR in a way, if all these authorities say, 'Death Threat is bad.' It may help sell records. But I have a bad feeling about this. These people are smart about it, they don't focus on the kids, they focus on the economics and get people to pull their sponsorship. They're telling their members not to buy Death Threat CDs or shop in stores that sell them, and not to watch stations that show our video. They're telling their members to send letters to anyone who does sponsor us in some way."

"It's already started?"

"You bet it has. Take a look at this." He picked up a manila envelope from the coffee table and pulled out some papers. "Reverend Bob sent this to all his members."

He handed me a letter. The name OOFF was printed in red at the top of page, along with the words, "'From the Desk of Reverend Bob Bailey, Executive Director."

This is what I read:

> "Dear Friends and Family,
>
>   This month we're sending out the word to all our members: there's a serious threat to the moral balance in your home and it's called, "Death Threat."
>
>   Maybe you've heard of them. Some of your children already own their records. Or maybe you've seen them on television. I know my own children are familiar with them. Let me make my position clear: this musical group is a magnet for all the filth and rampant evil influences that are ruining our nation.
>
>   We are writing to warn you: don't let your children listen to this depraved group of so-called 'musicians.' Don't let them buy their recordings. Their music is not just obscene and vulgar, it's a conscious attack on everything that is important to you and your family.
>
>   Their most recent video is what made me decide to take positive action in dealing with individuals I can only call warped. This musical video, called 'Let Me Show You,' is involved in all manner of sexual perversion and mockery of the beliefs we consider sacred."

The letter went on to describe the video in full and luscious detail. There were even a few repulsive details I hadn't known myself. How did they know, for instance, that Frisk had his nipples pierced? It was certainly a good way of letting people know what they missed, in case they hadn't seen the video themselves.

Reverend Bob's letter concluded with a call to action:

> "Though music videos are a common form of entertainment for today's youth, occasionally something so

vulgar comes along that I have to ask all OOFF members to take action. And so I am suggesting we add Death Threat to Reverend Bob's Boycott Roster. I am asking you, my friends who share the values so fundamental to moral health and stability in the home, to make it clear to all who trade in Death Threat music and merchandise, that you will boycott them, their store, and anyone else involved in the distribution of this filth. We want our homes clean, and if we have to clean everyone else's home to keep their filth from blowing into our yards, so be it.

In faith,
(signed) Reverend Bob

P. S. Friends, we will be launching our usual two-tiered media campaign to stop the distribution of Death Threat's material. Your dollars will help in this matter, but even more, write to your television stations and let them know how you feel."

I put down the letter. "That's scary."

"It's a freaking nightmare," said Rudy.

Hunter put the letter back in the envelope.

"I'm glad you told me about this, Hunter."

"Actually, Grace, I'm not just telling you about this to be nice. We need something from you," he said in a quiet voice.

"What do you mean?"

"We need something more practical than sympathy." Hunter stood up and paced across the lounge. Then he sat next to me on the couch, his leg touching mine. "I need you to help us to stand up to OOFF." He looked at me with his dark eyes. "I mean starting now. We've been invited on the Mimi Velaci Show."

"What?"

"We want you on the show with us."

"Me? But why?"

"Because you're a woman. Because you wrote the song."

"But—" I stopped and closed my eyes. This was a bad dream. The Mimi Velaci Show was the most infamous, raucous interview show on television.

"I'm dead serious. I am going to fight these people everywhere I can."

"But the Mimi Velaci Show?"

Not only was it television at its most harrowing, it was also one of the most widely watched talk shows in the country. Every night from 6 to 7 o' clock, the ex-baseball player Mimi Velaci hosts a hysterical discussion of the issues of the day. The discussion usually pits one group of fanatics against another, and lets them loose on each other in front of a screaming studio audience. More than one career has been damaged by a visit to Mimi's program. The show was meant to bring out the most emotional, illogical side of people and Mimi's trademark was the way he shoved a microphone in his guest's face and shouted, "Tell them what you really feel." The issues he explored usually had something to do with sex, racism, politics or baseball. Apparently, by extending an invitation to Death Threat, he was ready to get into censorship.

"Grace, I'm sorry I even have to ask you this, believe me," Hunter said with tension in his voice, "especially given the way you feel about us. But I have to. We're under attack. We have to do something. If Rudy and I go on alone, it won't look good. Part of OOFF's psychology is to take the moral high ground. Having you, the woman who actually wrote the song, on our side would make us seem less like a bunch of sleazy guys, which I guess is what we are, and more like a group that represents different kinds of people. And we're that too, because after all, it is your song."

I shook my head. "It may be my song, but you're the ones who made it into something totally different."

"That's true. But do you think it's right we're boycotted because of it? Or that a bunch of fundamentalists dictate what people can and can't see?"

"We're not asking you to like us, dude," said Rudy in a burst of energy. "We're not asking anyone to like us."

"We just don't think we should be boycotted," added Hunter, a pained look on his face.

I had hoped this would all be over and now I was only in deeper. The fear I had felt earlier talking to Hunter and Rudy was gone, only to be replaced by anger. I couldn't seem to get away from them. The more I wanted to put my connection to Death Threat behind me, the more tied to them I became.

"This is great," I exploded in frustration. "First you use women to sell records, then you use them to get you out of a jam."

"Oh, come on, Grace. Get off your high horse," answered Hunter, standing up. "We used you as much as you used us. We were a way for you to get exposure and make some money. You may not like us, but you certainly got some benefits from being involved with us."

"Even if that's true, I don't have to be involved in the mess you made."

"You think this isn't your problem?" Hunter said, his dark eyes flashing. "This isn't just about Death Threat. It's about you, too. You're being boycotted, too."

"What do I have to boycott? Nothing," I snapped.

"Grace, whether you have anything to boycott isn't the point. The point is you're under attack for something you created. OOFF doesn't make the same distinctions you make. They're after anyone who's involved, anyone who's part of our world. You wrote the song, you're earning money from what we did with it, and you're not out of it just because you don't like the way we play the game."

"But it's your video that got you noticed by these lunatics." We were yelling at each other now.

"All I'm asking you to do is take some responsibility for your part in this. We'll take responsibility for ours."

I didn't say anything. Having Hunter Burns yell at you was a paralyzing experience. "Look, you can walk away," Hunter continued, speaking quickly. "Like everything else in life, this thing with OOFF will blow over and we'll survive it. But this is important. I'm asking you for a favor."

Hunter's dark eyes burned. He walked across the room and fumed by the water cooler while I sat back on the couch staring at the ceiling.

Rudy had followed the exchange between Hunter and me without moving. He turned to me. "Grace," he drawled, "think about this another way."

"How?"

"They may be boycotting us and they may even be boycotting you. But what they're really doing is censoring what people can watch and hear and see. It's not about the video. They want to make sure no one can get our records. Even people who want them. Man, who died and left them queen?"

"Pope," said Hunter.

"What are you saying?"

"I'm saying, what they're doing is wrong," said Rudy, leaning forward and stretching out the word "wrong" as if he were about to throw up. "It's that simple. Come on with us, man. Come on and tell them what you think of it. This is not just about Death Threat."

I stared up at the ceiling and spoke.

"I've never been on television."

"So what? We'll be with you," Rudy cried.

"What if I don't make sense?"

Here Hunter walked over and sat down next to me. "Grace, you don't understand. We're asking you because we know you can do this. You may hate us, but we feel differently about you." Hunter put his hand on my arm.

Once again, I wondered if I was being manipulated, or if it even mattered. I sighed. "Can I at least think about it a little?"

"Of course. But please, think carefully," Hunter pleaded. "This is important."

"If I say yes, it doesn't mean I like what you do."

"Fine. Say so on national television if you want to, I don't care. This isn't about liking us. It's about standing up for our right to be what we are. Scumbags, if that's what you think we are."

"Okay, I'll think about it," I said, pained by the thought of such a decision. It all seemed so hopelessly twisted. "When do you want me to get back to you?"

"Call me tomorrow or the day after at the latest. We have a lot to do to get ready for this. They want us for Mimi's show next Thursday. I'm going to give you my home number. I want you to call me there. This is not business, Grace. You don't have to go through Jerry. Call me any time."

Hunter picked up a pen from the coffee table and wrote a phone number on a piece of paper he pulled from a pad. He handed me the paper and then squeezed my shoulder. I think he felt bad for yelling at me, although judging by the tense look on his face, his sense of purpose had not diminished. His expression was hard, and there was anger in the line of his jaw.

"I try to be fair with people, Grace, I think you've seen that, although you may not always agree with my choices. I don't think what OOFF is doing is fair. I had Jerry get us some material on OOFF. I want you to take it," he said, handing me a thick envelope. "You can read all about them. There are articles and brochures, and a lot of stuff we got off the Internet. There are some of their own brochures too. Read them, Grace."

"Okay. I'll call you," I said wearily.

"Thanks, Grace," said Hunter softly, as he let me out.

♩ ♩ ♩

I spun through the revolving doors in the lobby of Rainbow Head Studio and stepped onto the sidewalk. It was hot out, and the smell of warm garbage, car exhaust and pizza assaulted me as I stepped outside. I flung my bag over my shoulder. I hated Hunter Burns at that moment. Barely able to see from frustration, I asked a pass-erby for the time. It was one-thirty. There wasn't even time to go home and change after the meeting with Hunter and Rudy. I was ex-pected at the Café Capri at two o' clock, apron on, guest checks ready.

Nothing would have made me happier than to go right home, lock the doors and pull down the shades. I would have given any-thing to get out of an afternoon of waitressing. It couldn't be done. I had already traded shifts in order to go upstate. I slithered into the café feeling like a rattler ready to strike.

The café was already half-full of hungry sightseers when I joined Jessica. It was mid-June, and tourists drifted in like a scent on a New York breeze. They came in by the busloads, bringing with them wide-eyed fear and anticipation at being in New York. On that particular Thursday afternoon, a busload of tourists from Canada had taken over the café, their shopping bags piled on chairs beside them.

A few older couples shared a big table in the back where they marveled at our desserts. I think I intimidated some of them when I walked up to their table and glared at them without saying a word. What choice did I have? After what I had been through today, how could I chuckle along with them at the size of our cheesecake? It didn't seem fair that I had to make these carefree, childlike tourists feel welcome when I was nearly suffocating from pressures of my own. In front of me lay a gigantic decision and a stack of reading that would keep me busy well into the night. Behind me trailed the words of Hunter Burns and Rudy Rude, their voices whispering in my ear as I provided pastries to the genial waves of Greenwich Vil-lage tourists, hounding me as I added up checks. "Grace, please," said the voices.

The tourists moved on to Washington Square and Wall Street. The café emptied. Enjoying the lull, Jessica and I slouched against the back of the espresso maker until Mrs. Zuccaccia had to wave from the back and tell us to stand up straight

The café was particularly quiet that afternoon. Mr. Rocco hadn't put on his usual loop of Italian pop music, and classical music played softly. I stared out onto Sixth Avenue, watching people walk by. A few overheated downtowners walked by, the type that insists on wearing black leather even on a hot July day. They stopped to look at the menu in the window. I was happy when they kept walk-ing. I wanted a few peaceful moments to review what had happened today. "Think carefully," Hunter had said. "Call me at home."

Pressure. Demands from every corner. No one needs this kind of stress, I thought, banging my thigh on the corner of a table as I went to get an ice coffee. I didn't like Hunter Burns and Rudy Rude pressuring me like this. How did they get in my life to begin with? Oh right, I reminded myself, "Let Me Show You."

"Let me show you, let me show you," I hummed. It still had a nice sound, a solid melody. It really was a good little tune.

Like Hunter said, they had done me a favor by recording my song. Could I really say no to him? He had given me a break. On the other hand, this was not about music. It was about politics. Maybe. I wasn't exactly sure. Anyway, I didn't want to be seen with them in public, so what was the point? Especially not on television in front of millions of people. Especially not on the Mimi Velaci Show.

It wasn't fair. I didn't deserve to be on the Mimi Velaci Show. I haven't earned enough money in entertainment to be humiliated that way. The Mimi Velaci Show was for desperate people. On the Mimi Velaci Show, total strangers told you how much they hated you. Irrational people yelled at you. People had bad manners. I didn't want to do it. Yes, I was involved with Death Threat. But the Mimi Velaci Show? It was too high a price to pay for one bad decision. I closed my eyes and clicked my tongue against the top of my mouth.

"What's the matter?" said Jessica, hearing my disheartened sighs and noises.

"You know how you can get involved in something that seems kind of positive, and then it turns into a giant disaster?"

"Sure. Most of my relationships are like that." Jessica leaned next to me, looking like she was going to melt. She reminded me of a giant, wet clay bust before the clay had a chance to dry.

"That's what's happening to me."

"Details please."

"Death Threat. I'm talking about the guys from Death Threat."

"Oh, right. How's all that going?" I brought her up to date, concluding with the invitation to appear on the Mimi Velaci show.

"What a drag," she said, staring out the window with me. "Mimi Velaci. You couldn't pay me to do it."

"That's how I feel about it."

"I once saw that actress on his show, the one who played Doris in 'My Friend Marlene.' She was crying hysterically by the end of the show. Mimi brought in a bunch of criminals to tell her what they thought of her show."

"I wouldn't have to go on alone. I'd be on with Hunter and Rudy."

"That should shield you in some way. Next to them, you'll look like a saint."

"Oh, they're basically okay guys. "

"You've met them, I haven't," she said, sounding unconvinced. Jessica is hardened about people in the music business. I think it was from years of dating a producer who eventually fired her from her own band.

Our conversation was interrupted by an energetic figure tapping on the windows at the front of the restaurant.

Whoever it was waved, then snaked between the outdoor tables and danced in the front door. I took a few steps closer to see who it was but he was already inside.

"Surprise," said Walter Wiener, springing into the café with short little steps. "I was in the neighborhood dropping off some samples and thought I'd check in on you."

"Hi, Walter. Good timing," I exclaimed, glad to see him. I needed a little diversion.

Walter planted himself at the nearest table. "So how's it going, babe?" he said, giving my hand a friendly squeeze.

I wondered if I should give him the full story or just settle for an uncomplicated "Fine." Walter decided for me. "I heard about your meeting with Hunter. I understand you had a pretty heated conversation."

"What are you guys, twins? Does he tell you everything?"

"Before I answer that, let me get a cup of coffee and a piece of chocolate cake," said Walter, bypassing the more gourmet fare.

As I cut his cake, he filled me in on how he managed to stay so current. "I had an extra ticket for tonight's Mets-Phillies game so I called Hunter, which is how I heard about you."

"Did he tell you about the Mimi Velaci Show, too?"

"One of my favorite programs. That I heard about days ago."

"And I guess he asked you to come here and talk to me."

Walter rolled his eyes and posed for a moment in his by-now-familiar expression of disbelief. "Grace. Please. Does Hunter Burns seem like the kind of man who needs an interlocutor?"

"Yes. I thought that was Jerry's job," I said, sitting down with Walter. Jessica didn't mind attending to the other patron while I took a break.

"Well, he doesn't need help from me. I'm here because I want to do a little campaigning for him on my own. He's my friend, as you know, and I thought I could add a few words to whatever he said."

"Like what?"

"Like, careers are at stake here."

"Oh please," I said with a loud sigh. "Don't exaggerate."

"Do I exaggerate? Am I an exaggerator?"

"Don't make me sound personally responsible for Hunter Burns' career. Even he didn't do that," I said irritably. "If it were up to me, he wouldn't have one."

"This is a person who did you a very great turn in his own way."

"I know he did. But why do you have to act like this show is so important?"

"Because no one knows how this is all going to turn out. OOFF is a wild card here. The situation with these people could turn out to be a big nothing, or something serious."

"I don't see how my being there makes a difference."

"You don't have to see. Hunter has a gut feeling about this. He thinks they're at a crossroads, a fork where unexpected things happen. With you, he feels they have a little extra credibility. I don't understand it myself."

"Why can't they hire someone, Walter?" I whined.

"Hire who?"

"I don't know, another songwriter. A person to play me. An actress. Anyone."

"Grace, you're not getting it." Walter pushed aside his cake plate, put his hands on the edge of the table, and spoke slowly as if he were talking to an idiot. "Grace, this is not a pretend TV debate with actresses and lights and people winning prizes and whatnot. This is real. Gary feels they're in trouble. Do you get that?"

"I thought they liked trouble. I thought it was part of their image."

"They like trouble you can control. Manageable trouble. Not this."

"I told them I'd think about it and I'm telling you the same thing," I said sharply.

"Okay, I tried," he sighed. "It's your decision, but let me just say I'm lobbying for Hunter like I once did for you. This would mean a great deal to them. Sometimes you have to do something just because it matters to someone else. And by the way, who is that girl over there?"

"Which one?"

"The tall one, by the coffee counter," said Walter, talking out of the side of his mouth as if here were trying to sell me stolen goods.

"That's Jessica. Want me to introduce you?"

"If you wouldn't mind. She's very interesting, I can see that already."

I managed to kill the rest of the afternoon while Walter hung around waiting for the rush hour to end, passing the time by chatting with Jessica and me. By late afternoon, the events of the day had taken on a dreamlike quality. Not only did my meeting with Hunter and Rudy feel like something I had imagined, but as if hallucinating, I thought I saw Jessica give Walter her phone number.

❧ ❧ ❧

It was midnight by the time I had a chance to sit down in my kitchen and read the thick stack of papers and brochures Hunter Burns had given me. With a cup of tea next to me and silence in my apartment, I opened the envelope and emptied its contents on the table. I flipped through the stack to see what was in store; there were copies of magazine articles, newspaper clippings, network reports, and surveys as well as plenty of OOFF's own brochures and publications. I picked up a folded pamphlet entitled, "Join the Fight for Decency; The War for Your Soul is Being Fought In Your Den."

"Who has a den anymore?" I said to myself, realizing I had forgotten how much is going on outside New York City. The brochure went on to claim an ordinary evening of television represented a challenge to the moral health of the family, and included a page of statistics to prove it.

In case I thought OOFF was alone in its crusade, Hunter had supplied a range of opinion on the group. There were letters of support from people who praised the organization for its moral bravery, and a transcript of a speech by an Indiana congressman who called OOFF "America's rabbit ears, tuned in to sin."

On the other hand, Hunter had included a hefty batch of articles and editorials written by enraged first amendment defenders who felt OOFF had no right bullying people into self-censorship. There were protests from condom sellers and soda makers, as well as denials from network executives who claimed OOFF had no influence over their programming decisions. Most of the articles wrote OOFF off as a bunch of fanatics. These voices were all irrelevant to OOFF.

According to their own publications, the Organization of Families First was winning the war against smut. Every network programming change was the result of their pressure, every canceled show, their doing. Reverend Bob reported victory after victory, with a powerful sense of righteousness. To hear him tell it, the guillotine of moral devastation hung low over our necks and it was only thanks to the crusade of Reverend Bob and his followers that we had been spared.

Any good points OOFF had to make about the overheated state of television were lost in their perpetually alarmed tone. Everything was equally offensive and dangerous to them. After a few OOFF brochures, you couldn't tell whether America's problems stemmed from too much violence on the evening news, too many women in congress, or too many adult bookstores in downtown Cedar Rapids. As it said in their brochure about Reverend Bob's Two-Tiered Boycott method: "Stage Two: Boycott Everyone."

It seemed as if life itself was alarming to OOFF. Brochure after brochure described scenes of homespun family gatherings intruded on by unexpected sex and violence; debauched situation comedies that always had something to do with cross-dressing; lusty prime-time soap operas. Each offending show was described in all its filthy detail. I knew some of the shows they were talking about. It was true, they were sensational and violent. But OOFF's lurid objections were almost as unpleasant on the shows themselves. Not a lewd moment was omitted, and everything was accompanied by mind numbing statistics about how many sexual acts took place per episode of Baywatch, or how many clergymen were portrayed as adulterers per half hour of prime-time viewing. I couldn't help but wonder why they were watching these shows to begin with, and why they needed to catalog every indecent act. What about those market forces Roger had told me about? If they didn't like it, why not turn it off? Why not throw away the television altogether? If no one watched, the shows wouldn't be there. I read on, through accounts of children who listened to rock music, then sacrificed their cat, citizens turned into sex offenders, and grandmothers who had gone wild from subliminal messages in cooking shows.

After a while, I began to get a clear idea of the basis of OOFF's beliefs; I learned that the Organization of Families First is founded on the principle that an individual has no idea what's good for him or herself, and the individual needs the guidance of some higher power—namely, Reverend Bob. While many organizations, not to mention politicians, take this approach, Reverend Bob's particular tool for sorting out good from evil is the word of the bible. For people who never developed an internal sense of right and wrong this may be a good thing. But the problem with Reverend Bob, as far as I could tell, is Reverend Bob is committed to bringing the ethics of the bible into our every day life, whether we like it or not. Reverend Bob does not hesitate for a second to decide what is naughty and what is nice, and if it's unacceptable he adds it to his list and starts a boycott. He's like an anti-Santa; he's got a list with everyone's name on it and he's checking it twice, and you'd better be nice because otherwise Bob will be at your house chaining himself to your door, protesting, chanting, singing, and calling your boss, in order to save you from yourself.

"The Holy War is getting personal," said Reverend Bob in one of his pamphlets when he described how he chained himself to a radio station in Atlanta because they were playing a marathon weekend of Dr. Coco's Loveline. Thanks to Reverend Bob, radios across the city went dead and no one got to hear any more about designer condoms.

OOFF's power comes not from having so many followers. All together their members number no more than 30,000. Less than the number of members of the Florida Branch of Barbra Streisand's Fan club. Their success comes from being so noisy. If they don't like a TV program, they organize a massive letter writing campaign. If his people don't like a play, they lay down across the sidewalk in front of the theater so there's no room to walk. They surround doors and sing, they chant and shout for days. And while their main focus is entertainment—they leave abortion clinics to the specialists—they make it clear that they hold family values in highest esteem. If one cannot do something as a family then it is wayward and probably dangerous. Music is judged by whether it can be listened to as a family. Can you take your family to a certain movie? An art show? If not, Reverend Bob says, "God wants you to shut it down." Naturally, sex is out of favor with this group because it's definitely something that shouldn't be done as a family.

It also means entertainment of particular interest to women is watched with a close eye. That's because anything that concerns matters that are personal, secret, and private to women, have a good chance of running contrary to the values of the family, mainly because they exclude men. This is an anathema to Reverand Bob, who believes every man is the captain of his family ship. Shows on women's health, domestic violence, and marital infidelity are generally disapproved of. Comedies that star single mothers and powerful grandmothers are frowned upon.

OOFF's literature is very clear about the concepts they object to: acts that encourage violence and above all, sexual indecency— but it's impossible to anticipate the form this material will take. After two hours of reading account after account of OOFF's boycotts, I managed to get an idea of some of the specific things OOFF opposes. They include: programs in which children speak rudely to their parents, commercials for tropical vacations that imply sex, bawdy westerns, portrayals of religious leaders as perverts, adultery, nipples, evolution, bestial monsters kidnapping women in horror movies, panel discussions of sex, unbalanced criticism of the

American Government, shows with short, dark-haired Jewish pro-
tagonists, any program on abortion, sexy baby-sitters, bored
husbands, video games with a quasi-religious cosmology, rock
music that mentions god or the devil, Freemasons, divorce, patri-
cide, matricide, erotomania, fetishism, pederasty in any context
including news, shows about Spring Break, fashion models, women
who cheat on their husband with a priest or minister, sodomy, sa-
lacious college professors, overly loyal pets, homosexual parents,
almost anything to do with rock and roll, negative portrayals of
hunting, programs about carnival in Brazil, condoms, oral sex, insensitive policemen, amusing prostitutes, pregnant cheerleaders,
witches, cross-dressers, transsexuals, anarchists, programs about
girls' sports teams, unwed mothers, lesbianism, AIDS, meditation,
divination, necromancy, nature shows that display the sexual practices
of animals, shows that concern the sexual practices of aliens or other
cultures, and their favorite nemesis of all, jiggling breasts. This leaves
only programs about country-western dancing and gardening.

ᛉ ᛉ ᛉ

The decision to join Hunter Burns and Rudy Rude on the Mimi
Velaci show was not the hardest decision I had ever made. I knew
it was wrong for OOFF to tell other people what they could or could
not listen to. As Hunter said, I was involved whether I liked it or
not. How could I allow OOFF to tell the world they couldn't experience my song? People had the right to see the video, and hate it
all on their own.

It wasn't the hardest decision I ever made, but perhaps it was
the most serious. I would be on the OOFF hit list, probably for eter-
nity. I had nothing to boycott, although they could refuse to get
their cappuccino at the Café Capri. I would be permanently linked
with Death Threat, maybe even put in the category of rock 'n roll
babe. I would have to remember not to wear Spandex.

All I had wanted to do was say good-bye and move on. I had
wanted Death Threat out of my life. It's not that I didn't like them;
it's just that I accepted we had chosen different roads in life. I
wanted to play alternative music festivals at avant-garde venues;
they wanted to go on mega-rock tours across the suburbs of
America. Now here I was going on television with them, part of
their first amendment crisis.

I didn't want to go on television. I'm a singer, not a talker. The
one time I was on television had been a disaster. I hadn't told Hunter
about this. It was with Swan Venom. We performed on public access

cable in the middle of the night. We were terrible. We didn't have time to do a sound check, Geoffrey had an ear infection and could barely hear, and Steve was drunk. A music critic who happened to be watching wrote about us the next day, and said if music were a beach, we were a syringe washing up on the shore.

Still, I realized I had no choice but to say yes to Hunter. If I didn't go on with them, I might as well be participating in the boycott that would just as soon destroy me as anyone else who got in their way. OOFF hated everything I stood for. They didn't hesitate to ban books, music, art, dancing or anything else that offended them. They thought feminists used witchcraft. They hated sex, but tolerated violence, which was just the opposite attitude of me and all my friends, who hated violence and tolerated sex.

I thought about "Reverend Bob's Boycott Roster," the list published on the back of each OOFF brochure. This was Bob's hit list, the one that now included Death Threat. There were usually fifteen to twenty items on the list, some with a star next to them, indicating that the item was a new addition. It reminded me of Billboard's Hot 100.

It also reminded me of the rating system used in Church when I was growing up. The Archdiocese published what they called "The List." It was posted weekly on the bulletin board. If a movie or a book was on The List you were forbidden to see it or read it. The amazing thing about The List was that it wasn't just for little kids. It was for everyone.

You never actually knew why something was on The List. You only knew that someone had condemned it, and you were expected to abide by this decision. Instinctively, I knew this was wrong. I hated The List and if a CD was on it, I bought it. I remember my mother would always say, "You're in big trouble if Father Jacques hears you playing that." I played it anyway because I didn't want anyone telling me what I should listen to. Music is free. It's the recordings that cost money. You can't control the colors people see or whether they feel hot or cold, why should you control what people hear? I can't even control my own music. Why should Reverend Bob control it?

It was settled. I would go on the Mimi Velaci show with Death Threat. I would be one third of the team that included two of the world's most notorious rockers, two pop stars who were dreaded by parents and worshipped by teens from Tokyo to New York; the men who put the pomp in pomp-rock, the power in power-pop, who swiveled, rocked, screwed, drank, and sang their way to the top of one of America's roughest professions. We didn't have much in common except music—what they had blown on drugs I haven't even earned yet. What they had done in hotel rooms around the globe, I haven't even imagined. As repulsive as it sounded, we were now a team. Like Hunter said, I didn't have to like them. But together, the world loathing or loving me along with them, we would confront the righteous at the Organization of Families First and go down or rise up, in either case, in flames.

8

"HELLO," SAID THE DEEP, FEMALE VOICE. It must be Hunter's girlfriend, I thought, the Russian supermodel Varina.

"May I speak to Hunter, please?"

"Who is calling, please?"

"Tell him it's Grace Note."

"Just a moment, Miss Note," she replied, pronouncing my name, "nut."

A moment passed, there was some clattering and then Hunter picked up the phone.

"Yeah?" said Hunter.

"It's me, Grace. I agree. I'll do it."

"Great, I knew you'd come through for us," he said, his voice warming.

"How did you know?"

"I'm a good judge of character. You're okay."

"Thank you."

"Yeah. And anyone who Walter likes has to be okay."

"Right," I said, marveling at the influence of my candy-peddling friend. "So exactly when is this show?"

"We're scheduled for Thursday, one week from today. Our next step is we need to get together with our lawyer. He's going to coach us."

"Coach us? In what?"

"Grace, think about it. Thirty million people will be watching. Wouldn't you like a little coaching?"

"I guess so."

"Okay. He wants us over at his place. Next weekend.'

"Where does he live?"

"In Westchester. We'll meet there on Saturday, if that's okay with you. We'll send a car for you, and we're going to stay there until we know what we're doing."

Torn between dismay and morbid curiosity, I could now add to my achievements that I spent the weekend with Death Threat.

ʏ ʏ ʏ

Although I was consumed by my preparation for the Mimi Velaci Show, it hadn't escaped my mind that Paul Teagarden was coming to town in a few days. It was a good thing I was distracted, because otherwise I would have thought of that and not much else. Fortunately, Mimi Velaci's producers, along with Hunter Burns, Jerry Saltstien, and Death Threat's lawyer, kept me constantly occupied. You would have thought I was running for office, with all the prompting and training I received.

On Saturday, up in Westchester, we worked until two in the morning. Death Threat's lawyer, Marty Segal, briefed us on every possible issue that might come up on the show. We reviewed the history of OOFF, the Supreme Court's rulings on censorship, as well as the first, fifth, and ninth amendments, clarifying definitions of harassment, the right to a lawful gathering, and freedom to protest, as well as the three conditions for obscenity as defined in the 1973 case, Webster vs. California. We even skimmed over the definition of "the right to bear arms." It took Rudy a while to memorize "A well regulated Militia, being necessary to the security of a free State," but by the time midnight rolled around, even Rudy Rude could have stood up in court.

The whole day brought back memories of grade school, what with Marty's Xeroxed hand-out of the Bill of Rights, and Rudy throwing balls of paper at Hunter's head. Maybe it was more like reform school, considering how old everyone was. Marty had unearthed a lot of personal tidbits about Reverend Bob in order to make him more human and less intimidating. We learned, for instance, that when he was a teenager in South Carolina, Reverend Bob used to run a pinball arcade every summer at the beach. Before he went into the ministry, Reverend Bob had worked for a printing company as a salesman. This explained his love of brochures. And he was a cheerleader in high school.

We stopped for dinner, and Varina made us an excellent meal of Shashlik with couscous and cucumber salad. Later in the evening, Frisk stopped by with his wife Kathleen. We took another break while Frisk showed us slides he had taken on their recent tour of Japan, including some chilling pictures of Rudy in the bathtub with a nurse from San Bernadino. Then we went back to work.

Things happen fast in the entertainment business, and Sunday night I got a phone call from *Rock Chatter,* the premier music industry gossip tabloid. A reporter told me I had been seen checking into a Westchester motel with Hunter Burns and Rudy Rude, and would I like to come clean about the affair in their publication. I told them no.

As Hunter said, this was only the first step in my preparation. On Monday afternoon, Jerry arranged for me to meet with Lars Rudolph, an image consultant. A car came by and took me to Lars' Fifty-seventh Street studio. We spent the afternoon discussing clothes and make-up, as well as voice modulation for television and effective camera strategies. Jerry also suggested, as part of my readiness, I listen to every one of Death Threat's albums. In this way, I would really grasp the breadth and range of Death Threat's work. I asked Jerry if I couldn't just listen to their CD compilation, *Life Sentence*, and he said no, only by going through their recordings one at a time was it possible to get a complete picture of the boys. Soon, a box of 18 CD's and a few rare albums arrived at my door. Starting with their first record, a musical assault called *Disgraced, Impeached, and Baffled*, released in 1971, through *Wayfaring Blonde, Shame! Throw Down the Net, Revolting, Help It Grow, Fevertown*, right through to *Live Death*—their squalid, churning, amp blowing overstated live three-album set—I studied Death Threat.

"Eighteen Death Threat records," I said to Ray, later that day at rehearsal. "It's enough to make a person give up music."

"How far did you get?"

"I'm up to 1988. I didn't mind the early stuff. But they got unbearable in the mid-eighties."

"Who didn't?"

"I was in music school then. I didn't know this kind of thing was going on. We were studying twelve tone rows."

"I remember their stuff," he said, "I was playing in a band then and we covered one of their tunes." He played a little of "Disgrace Me," from *Throw Down the Net*. I set up by my favorite amp, while Ray's impression of Death Threat transformed into some blues riffs.

No matter what was going on, I felt it was important to maintain some degree of normalcy in my schedule and fit in the business of Swan Venom. I tried to stick to our rehearsal routine, but it wasn't easy. We managed to fit in only one rehearsal the week of the Mimi Velaci show. It was Monday afternoon. Steve and Geoffrey hadn't arrived yet. Ray and I were in the room tuning up.

"I can't take much more of this," I confided to Ray. I told him about my Saturday night in Westchester. "'I'm getting a rash on my neck from stress."

"You've gotten that before, haven't you?"

"I get it whenever I'm stressed out. The last time was on the road with Glare. Remember?"

"Oh, right." It was impossible to forget the last time we opened for Glare. That tour was in upstate New York. Their lead guitar player, Corbin Landau, fell off the stage in Buffalo. Ray covered for him for three shows, and the guys in Glare asked Ray if he would finish the tour with them. It looked like Swan Venom wouldn't exist by the end of the week, until Corbin woke up from the coma and the job offer was withdrawn. I had a bad rash that week.

Ray looked at my neck. "Yeah, I see it. Here, sit down." He pulled over a beat-up office chair and sat down behind me.

"Relax," he said, massaging my shoulders.

"Thanks. You're a pal." Ray pressed his slender fingers into the muscles in my shoulders. Knots of pain released as he touched them. "I need this."

"Is the rash going to show on TV?" he asked.

"No. My neighbor, Mrs. Chu, had her doctor prescribe some Chinese herbs for me. If those don't work, I'll wear something to cover it."

"Man, Grace. Tough week."

"Tell me about it. What time is it, by the way? Steve and Geoffrey are late."

"Oh yeah, they're not coming."

"What do you mean they're not coming?" I said, sitting up with a snap.

"They got a gig doing a trio with a guitar player next weekend. This was the only time they could rehearse."

"So why didn't they tell me?"

"Grace, they know you're busy," said Ray, his voice not wavering from its smooth monotone. "They called me instead."

"They always call me, even if I'm busy. Are they mad?"

"I don't know. Maybe a little. You know them, they're always mad about something."

"They should tell me themselves if they're mad," I mumbled.

"Grace, you haven't been around much lately."

"Maybe we can talk about it Sunday night at the Pi Bar, after the gig."

"Geoffrey will be there. Steve won't. He got someone to sub. Steve has another gig."

"I can't believe that," I said, turning around. I pushed Ray's hands off my shoulders. "He took another gig and he didn't even call and tell me?"

"He asked me to tell you."

"Man, this sucks." I slumped in my chair, irritated. "Why doesn't he just quit the band altogether if he doesn't want to come to gigs or rehearsal?"

"He said he would talk to you about that. Why don't we just work on some new stuff?"

I felt the red blotches on my neck climb a little higher.

ү ү ү

"You sure picked a crazy time to come to visit," I said to Paul Teagarden on the phone. "We're going on Mimi's show on Thursday."

"Just save Tuesday night for me."

"I will. If you're really coming."

"Of course I am. It's definite. I'll be there."

"I almost can't believe it." I held the phone on my shoulder, resting it on the pillow next to my head.

"Believe it," he said, his voice rich and delicious.

"What if you don't recognize me?"

"Don't be silly. I remember exactly what you look like."

"It's possible you won't. How do you know I haven't gained fifty pounds?"

"Have you?"

"No."

"Grace, what's the matter? You sound a little nervous."

"Maybe. It's been six months since we met."

"I wish I could have come sooner, but it's been hard. You know how many projects I'm involved in. But that doesn't mean I haven't been thinking about seeing you." His voice got softer. "Don't be nervous, Grace. I'm not." I only sighed. "Hey, I have a good idea," he continued.

"What?"

"Why don't you meet me at the airport?"

"I don't have a car. I can't pick you up."

"No, I mean just meet me. A car will be there for me. We'll drive back together."

"What time?"

"The flight gets in about nine in the morning."

"That's early for me. But so what. I'd love to come meet you."

"Great," said Paul warmly. "And remember. No clothes."

"Let me think about that one. Maybe I'll meet you half-way."

"Just a coat. Maybe you'll come back with me to my hotel."

"Maybe," I said, my voice disappearing as I breathed in.

"This will be great, Grace. I can't wait to see you."

Ꭹ Ꭹ Ꭹ

Meanwhile, the lights had just about gone out in the once bright windows of Roger's paintings. He even painted one where there were no lights on at all. It was just the side of a building, a brown wall of dark bricks with one window but no lights. Not even a candle.

I saw the paintings Sunday evening. I hadn't seen Roger for several days. We stood in his studio-dining room as he showed me his latest work.

"Roger, your paintings are changing," I said.

"I know. I'm getting darker and darker."

"I see. Subtle."

"I'm interested in exploring how much you can still see in the dark."

"How much can you see?"

"Not much," he said, looking dolefully at a canvas.

After we looked at Roger's paintings, we went out for a drink in Soho. It was a warm July evening. West Broadway was like a magnet, pulling people in, and we walked down to Broome Street where a new crop of cafés filled the sidewalks. We had to thread our way around couples who lingered in front of every glowing store, and past vendors who filled the streets with trays of sunglasses and jewelry. People moved with an easy summer patience that can be so annoying to Soho residents who just want to get to the laundry. We picked a café and found a table facing the sidewalk. Here, people-watching flourished.

West Broadway looked like a block party. It was a festival of tight ponytails, muscular legs, great tattoos, short skirts, expensive clothes, and more black than a coalmine. Hairdressers, sculptors, sportswear manufacturers, models, painters, students, doctors, and designers milled in the early evening heat. The flamboyance was tempered only by suburban couples, dressed in summery white and blue, sweaters flung over their shoulders as they too planned their next move.

"It's good to be outside, doing nothing. This is the first time in days I've sat still," I said. I was wearing a loose, white cotton shirt and matching pants whose plainness was offset by several strands of beads. The cotton moved in the breeze and the air touched my bare arms.

"When are you going to stop running?"

"As soon as Mimi's show is over."

Roger took off his sunglasses as the sun disappeared behind a building. "I've hardly seen you. It's almost like you've been out of town," he said. His features were finely cut and he looked handsome in the dusky light. Roger was wearing a green polo shirt and black pants. Roger doesn't wear tee-shirts often. He still believes in dressing for the city, even if he lives there.

"I have something booked from the minute I open my eyes. I spend an hour a day just listening to Death Threat, if you can imagine that."

"Well, I miss you," he said, reaching over the table and taking my hand. "Work's been pretty quiet too. Not much happening this time of year. And my boss is in London. Between you and work, I've had a little more time to paint. That's the good news, I suppose."

"I like what you're doing. These new pictures are more interesting once you get into them."

"You think so? I like them too. And I'm thinking of getting away from walls and trying something a little different. Maybe a sidewalk. Speaking of painting, guess who I ran into the other day?" said Roger, brightening.

"Who?"

"Massimo. Natalie's boyfriend. I bumped into him on Spring Street."

"When?"

"Friday afternoon, about five-thirty. And guess what? I asked him if he would come up and take a look at my stuff. I never had the nerve before, but I really like these new paintings." Roger looked positively radiant as he delivered this news. It gave me a bad feeling. Roger socializing with Massimo. I didn't like it. Natalie probably told him about Paul Teagarden.

"Did Massimo say he would come up?"

"Yes, he said he would be glad to."

"I'm surprised he was so friendly."

"He was very nice."

"How unusual," I said flatly.

"Grace, why are you so hard on him?"

"Because he's never nice to me." Roger didn't say anything. He looked out into the street. "So is he going to critique your work?"

"You can call it that. He'll give me some professional feedback."

I grunted in acknowledgment.

"What's the matter?"

"What do you mean?"

"You look annoyed."

"I'm not," I said, playing with my now empty glass.

"Do you think we're going to talk about you and Natalie, or something like that?"

"No, of course not."

"Or is it because you can't stand to have someone else be the center of attention?" Roger looked at me with an unexpected hardness.

"That's ridiculous," I said, sitting up with a jolt. Everything I said seemed louder than it needed it to be.

"You just can't let anyone else be an artist. It always has to be you."

"Roger, I can't believe you're saying this, it's not true. I just don't like you hanging around with Massimo. I think he's a creep."

"Well, this has nothing to do with you," said Roger with a hiss.

"Why are you so annoyed at me?"

"I don't know. There's just something about you today that's pissing me off. I don't know what it is."

"Well, excuse me for ruining your fun. I'm sorry, but I don't have to like Massimo and he doesn't have to like me."

"Don't worry, he doesn't," said Roger, a coldness in his expression I had never seen before.

"Thanks for your support, Roger."

"Yeah, and thanks for all of yours." We both turned away and looked out into the street with sullen expressions, making us look particularly fashionable at a West Broadway café.

♪ ♪ ♪

My alarm went off and I sat straight up in bed. Panic gripped me as I pictured Paul standing in the airport waiting for me. I looked at the clock. It was seven-thirty am.

I lay back down in bed, and took a deep breath. I had an hour and a half to get to LaGuardia Airport. I took a few moments to pull myself out of my dreams and connect with the morning. Daylight squeezed through the venetian blinds, urging me to stay awake. It was warm and raining out, making it the kind of mossy July morning that's best experienced at a kitchen table, peeking through a screen door. It was the kind of day that makes grass grow.

A truck clattered by in the street below. The whooshing sound of its wheels rose up to my window. I got out of bed. I didn't have a lot of time for lounging; rain meant traffic.

On the battered armchair in my bedroom, I had laid out an entire outfit, from earrings to shoes. All I had to do was stumble into it. I took a quick shower. Whatever I did had to take a minimum of thought. For me, 7:30 in the morning is not a time for thinking; it's the middle of the night.

According to my plan, I would grab a quick breakfast, then take a subway ride to the bus which would take me to the airport. But the rain changed my plans. I skipped breakfast and hurried past the one-legged newspaperman at the entrance to the subway, and went directly to Grand Central Station to get the airport bus that stopped out front. I didn't want to take the slightest chance of missing my rendezvous with Paul Teagarden.

Soon I was sitting in the middle of a nearly empty bus, hurtling towards the airport. The driver seemed to be in as big a hurry as I was. He raced over the Long Island Expressway, past the red brick projects, graveyards, and shopping centers of Queens. My coffee sloshed over the edge of the cup with every pothole. Across the aisle, a plump young businessman who looked like he was about to turn middle-aged any minute sat quietly with a raincoat folded over his lap. In the seat in front of him, a man in shorts and a denim jacket was lost in the noise of a pair of headphones. We swayed with the bus as every turn of the wheels took us farther from the city.

Outside, the rain turned an already gray world into an even more colorless sight, and I watched the rain drip down the smoky bus windows. The dark day helped me keep my excitement tempered, as if the sky were too fragile to stand too much jubilation.

All that stood between Paul and me was sixty minutes. At last, he was a sure thing. I would get to compare him to what I remembered, no long distance or answering machines between us. Just me and Paul, face to face. The plane would have to go down in flames in order for me to miss this flight, and that didn't look like it was going to happen. As soon as we arrived at the airport, I checked the arrivals screen. Boston, Burlington, Cedar Rapids, Charlotte, Chicago, there it was, Paul's flight from Los Angeles by way of Chicago. Flight 328 was on time.

I followed the signs to gate 15, where the flight would be arriving. Daylight poured in from the floor to ceiling windows. It was a long walk to the departure gates. Music played, muffled and faraway, and the air was compressed and quiet.

I looked for Gate 15, passing the busier gates where travelers waited for their flights with piles of exotic carry-on luggage beside them, scuba equipment, hockey sticks, baby strollers, and guitars. Senior citizens in jogging suits read magazines while kids

played on the floor nearby. These were the flights to Orlando and
Palm Beach.

Other gates held more professional travelers, women and men
who flew for commerce, not fun, and I passed strong-jawed vice
presidents and executives on cell phones, garment bags spread over
the seats next to them. A few peeked over their papers at me as
I walked by.

Finally, I found my gate. It was quiet. Not many people were
here yet, and an older woman read a magazine as she waited for a
ticket agent at the empty check-in desk. She was trailed by a man
in a cap and they formed a line of two. The only other person at
the gate sat in the middle of the room. He had a gray streaked beard
and mustache and he read a newspaper with an air of importance.
I walked past him and took a seat in a row of chairs by the windows that overlooked the runways.

Rain beat against the big picture windows. I felt the cool, ven-
tilated air of the terminal cut through the dampness. The
combination of emotional excitement and too little sleep gave me a
queasy and detached feeling. I took a few deep breaths. The distant
music, along with the seamless airport decor helped calm me with
its unvarying perfection. I leaned back in my vinyl chair and listened to a female voice announce flights and page travelers.
"Passengers seated in rows 16 to 32 may board the plane now," said
a voice from the next gate. Behind me, I heard the regular nasal
beeping of the carts that carried less able travelers to their gates.
It announced its nearness like a Doppler effect in the long corridor,
then faded away.

Right now, Paul was overhead somewhere. His plane would be
landing in a few minutes. I pictured him in his seat, reading a magazine. I could see him in my mind. Somehow, I knew he would be
self-contained, placid. He wasn't one of those travelers who sat in
his seat surrounded by piles of papers and blankets, tangled headphones, and cracker wrappers. Paul was under control.

I stretched back in my chair, crossing my legs in front of me.
I closed my eyes. I was ready for him. Looks-wise, things were as
good as they were going to get. I had willed my hair into perfection, made sure my lipstick was in the right state for early
afternoon, and found an outfit that matched half a year of phone
calls.

We even had a plan. After Paul arrived, we would drive back
to the city in the car arranged for him by the production company
that had invited him here. Paul's purpose in New York was to meet
with a French jeans manufacturer interested in hiring him to di-

rect their American commercials. The car would drop Paul off at his hotel, I would go home, and later, after his meetings, we would get together. He expected to be finished by nine.

He left it to me to pick a place to go. There were some bars on Lafayette Street perfect for relaxed catching-up. One had a garden and we could sit outside if the rain stopped by then. Or if Paul's hotel had a decent bar, we could go there. It might turn out to be convenient.

A textureless voice announced that flight 328 had arrived. I looked behind me to find the empty gate now filled with a cluster of shifting people. They were centered on the double doors that led outside to the plane. The crowd stared at the closed doors as if they were about to witness a miracle. I stood up and joined them. We were held back by a loose barricade of black velvet ropes.

I hoped I would recognize Paul right away. It would be embarrassing if we walked right by each other. Paul might look different in the humid New York air than he did in the clear light out west. Even if he looked the same, how well did I remember him, anyway?

People always look a little different after a plane ride. He would surely be tired from the flight, maybe a little green, with wrinkles and dents in his shoulders from the straps of carry-on luggage. I felt dread color my mood. I was so emotionally high-strung that an attack of doubt hit me while I stood among the strangers who were surely waiting for much more important reunions than I was. What was I doing here waiting for someone I hardly knew? I still had time to turn around before anyone got off the plane. But no, I told myself. This was stage fright. I had been through this before.

An airport employee in a uniform moved the rope barrier to the side, and a shudder of anticipation ran through the crowd. A moment later the doors opened and a slightly irregular trail of men and women staggered through.

I stared at every face, jumping from one traveler to the next, hyper-alert as I scanned their eyes, some fatigued, some bright with recognition at the sight of a waiting relative, some glad to be home at last. There were plenty of business travelers on this flight from Chicago, and they marched out with urgency. Many people wore the clean colors of California and the Midwest, colors that distinguished them from New Yorkers, dressed in dark, hard-to-name shades. An overweight man in a pink sweater, a woman draped in layers of cream, and a few members of a sports team, streamed out slowly. As I watched, nauseous from anticipation, it seemed like it took forever before a taut-skinned, keen-eyed Paul Teagarden stepped through the doorway. He appeared like a bobbing ball in a sea of couples, children, and carry-on luggage. He walked off the plane looking like I remembered him, sparkling to my eye in spite of being a little worse off for the ride, and with a touch of a beard growing. He saw me and his eyes held mine as he made his way to me.

"Grace," he said, arriving by my side.

"Hi."

"It's good to see you." He put his arms around me and gave me a hug, then a kiss.

I took him in with my eyes. "You made it. How was your flight?"

"Good. I was sitting next to a priest. He didn't have much to say to me."

"I wonder if sitting next to a priest on a plane is good luck."

"I got here okay, so I guess it was."

"You did. And on time too." I smiled.

"It's a miracle."

"Welcome to New York." We were surrounded by couples who now had their arms slung over each other, and by friends picking up other friends at the airport as they must have done many times before. This was a junction full of long stories. By comparison, ours was almost non-existent.

"Thanks, Grace," Paul said, and sensing we shouldn't just stand in the middle of the hall gazing at each other, we began our walk down the terminal and out of the airport.

Paul looked good. His face still had a kind of drama in it, a secret in the eyes. I tried not to stare. We both looked straight ahead at the signs meant to guide us out of the maze of escalators and moving sidewalks. I just talked. I almost don't remember what I said, I was internally so shocked that Paul was actually here. I sneaked looks at him as we walked side by side through the wide hall, taking in his every edge and angle like some kind of human scanner. I couldn't believe he was the person I had talked to so often on the phone, because in a way I didn't even know this person.

"Talk to me. I'm going to close my eyes for a second," I said, as we stood motionless for a moment on a long escalator. "I want to hear if it's really you. I'll be able to tell from your voice."

"What shall I say? Let's get out of this airport. Or how about something more personal, Grace?" he said, with a familiar whisper.

"It's you, all right."

"It is," he said and squeezed my arm. "So, am I like you remembered?"

"I think so." We arrived at the baggage claim. People from Paul's flight were already gathering around one of the carousels.

"Did you check anything?" I asked.

"I just have this," he said, holding up his brown leather bag. "Now we have to find the car that's supposed to pick me up. Look for a man with my name on his sign, and we're in business."

I was glad Paul was so relaxed. I was busy just trying to take it all in. We only had a few hours and I didn't want to miss a thing. I felt like someone on a very short vacation who has to take a lot of pictures fast.

"There," he said pointing to a cluster of drivers dressed in dark sweaters and shiny slacks, standing just outside the baggage claim area, and we scanned the cards, searching for a Teagarden among the Harpers, Fleishmans, and Blacks.

"I found him," I called to Paul. A thin man held a sign with Paul's name in magic marker.

"Mr. Teagarden?" he said. Paul nodded. The man grabbed Paul's bag. With some talk about the weather, he directed us to a dark blue Town car waiting outside the terminal on the other side of a traffic divider.

It was raining hard now. The driver stayed a few feet ahead of us as he jogged to his car. He tilted his head forward as he ran and I imagined the pockets of his black raincoat were heavy with jingling keys and change. He opened the door for us and we slid into the back seat shutting out rain with a slam of the thick door.

"What a mess," I said breathlessly brushing the water off. The gray rain pounded on the roof.

"New York in the summer. I forget what it's like."

"It's not always like this. Anyway, I don't mind the rain today."

"No, it's sweet," said Paul, arranging himself on the damp velour seat.

I was beginning to connect the voice on the phone to the man on the seat next to me. Paul's hair was a little shorter than the last time I saw him and I noticed wrinkles on his neck by the collar of his shirt. I looked at his hands. I hadn't really looked closely at them before. They were squarish and smooth with an almost childish look to them.

"You picked some day to fly," said the driver turning back and squinting at us. "I'll put the air on. You'll dry off in a second." I felt uncomfortably damp. The driver turned on the air conditioning and soon we were cool and damp instead of hot and damp.

A divider separated the front seat from the back. It was open at the top. Paul leaned forward and spoke to the driver.

"Do you know where we're going?"

"The Regency Royale, 68th Street," said the driver.

"Right," said Paul sitting back in the seat and turning to face me. He looked at me with a composure I envied. His sharp eyes took me in, yet at the same time I could tell he was considering what was ahead of him—the meetings, the travel, the hotel check-in—because he also looked away, nodding to himself as if acknowledging that so far everything was working out fine. He ran his hand along the side of his head, pushing back his hair. Neither the traveling nor seeing me had unsettled him.

"Grace, did you think about what we'll do later tonight?"

"I have a few ideas. I thought we could go downtown and see what's happening."

"Whatever you think. You're in charge."

"There are some good places where we can just relax and talk."

"That sounds good to me."

"I didn't plan anything besides that. You don't want to go to the theater or anything like that, do you?"

"No, of course not. I just want to spend time with you. By the way, you look great. It's so good to see you."

"Thanks. You look good too, I've never seen you dressed up," I said, looking him over.

"These are my meeting clothes. I'm trying to fit in in New York."

"You fit in fine." Too fine, in fact. Not only was he dressed more seriously than when I had first met him, there was something more intimidating, more powerful about him now. He wore black pants, a linen shirt, a tie with a swirling copper pattern. He looked the way I pictured the producers who usually rejected my demo tapes. He had the artsy, professional look that fits right in at certain Manhattan restaurants.

I, on the other hand, was dressed in the casual and summery combination of a sleeveless knit dress with a cotton vest over it, and sandals. My hair was down, and I had a distinctly bohemian look. Still as far as looks were concerned, I had the home court advantage; Paul looked tired from his trip.

He knew I was looking at him. "I'm a little beat," he said. "It's still last night for me. I left L.A. at 11:45 PM. I had to change planes in the middle of the night."

"You must be exhausted."

"It's just hitting me," he said, leaning his head back against the soft seat.

"Will you be able to rest before your meeting?"

"If I can. I only have a few hours and there are some people I want to call while I'm in New York."

I wished Paul would invite me to spend those few hours with him. As if he knew what I was thinking, he reached out his hand and took mine. "Grace, I'm going to get everything out of the way and spend the rest of my time here with you."

"Good."

"I'm so used to hearing your voice. It's funny to see you now."

"Do what I did before. Close your eyes. It will all make sense." He ran his fingers over my palm. His touch was full of curiosity.

"Okay," he said facing me with his eyes closed. "Say something."

I thought for a moment. "I'm so happy you're here." I don't know what got into me, but I couldn't help it. Honesty was my only choice with Paul Teagarden. I said whatever came into my head. Not only that, but while his eyes were closed, I reached out and touched the side of his face, running my fingers along his jaw.

Paul didn't say anything. He opened his eyes. He took his free hand, the one that wasn't holding mine, and lifted my hand to his lips and kissed it. It was about this time that everything became very slow and quiet. Our eyes were the source of everything. We were making up for all the time we had done without sight. We looked at each other, sitting quietly.

His fingers touched mine and he gently explored my hands, then my wrists. He put his hands around them. "You have such small wrists," he said.

I didn't say anything. I let my hands run over his, then move onto his forearms. I gripped their roundness. Every touch was rich with possibilities. The touches suggested a kiss and we both leaned forward.

When Paul kissed me I felt my mind dissolve into a million particles that flew in every direction and mixed with the rain, bursting open the fantasies I had collected. It was what I had been waiting for. This was really happening, I told myself. I touched the collar of his jacket, his hair and his neck. It was more Paul Teagarden than I had ever had before, closer than I had gotten to him in the whole time I had known him.

He put his hands on my shoulder, and he leaned towards me. My body became flexible, bending along with his every move. "Thank you for coming to meet me at the airport," Paul murmured. I think he talked just to add our voices to the equation.

"I was glad to," I whispered back.

"Although you came dressed. You didn't do what I asked you to do."

"It's not too late."

This really set him off. It brought out something wild in me too, a little unruly, because soon I was sitting sideways in the back seat, my back against the door, pressed against the cool glass window with the door handle in my back, my legs stretched the length of the back seat while Paul pushed towards me. He melted over me with such intensity that I prayed the door didn't open because we would both pour out on the highway before the driver had a chance to put on the brakes.

His mouth pressed into my mouth. His lips and tongue spoke their own language at their own pace and I understood all of it, every soft touch and hard kiss. I wanted him to absorb me and he felt it, too, because there was a very wild energy in the back of that car. We both knew absolutely anything could happen and would have happened if we weren't sharing the little moving room with a third person.

The driver pretended not to notice us. Or maybe he didn't have to pretend, there was plenty to concentrate on just navigating the battered expressway. Construction slowed us down every mile or so. He looked straight ahead, the divider between the front and back seat half-closed. The rain made a sticky wet sound under the wheels of the taxi as we passed the old World's Fair grounds. Cars moved beside us with a deliberate slowness. It was as if the whole world were moving in slow motion.

The driver was just a distant limit. Nothing too outrageous had happened yet. We were so hungry for the basics that Paul's touch alone was plenty for me. So much had gone untouched, we were absorbed in the simplest sensations, hands on hands, his body against mine. Rain splashed against the rear window and Paul looked up, then back at me and smiled. We were sinking into something together, into the brushed velour seat, into the bouncing rhythm of the Long Island Expressway, and into sex. Paul's tongue moved into my mouth and over my lips and his grip over me tightened. A hardness was appearing in our chauffeured reunion. We would be getting into a whole new stage pretty soon if we didn't stop. Knowing this, we sat back, our arms around each other, breathing together in a damp heap.

"Grace, I'm incredibly attracted to you," Paul whispered, his voice warm and grainy like an irresistible sandy stretch of beach. He kissed my neck.

"Me, too."

"I could kick myself for not having come to New York sooner."

"Let me sit up for a second. My dress is all twisted." I almost felt like I couldn't breathe. I was warm, in spite of the air conditioning in the car. My hair was like a knot of yarn that had unraveled over my shoulders.

"Here," he said, sitting up and pulling me with him. I looked around us. We were near the city. Ahead I could see the Manhattan skyline.

"We're almost at the Midtown Tunnel, Paul," I said, still leaning into him, my arm over his back.

"Does that mean our ride is almost over?"

"I'm afraid so. Unless you want to go back to the airport and start again."

"No. I need a hotel. I'm beat," he said, kissing me. One of my legs was thrown over his. I didn't want to get too far away. "See, Grace," Paul continued, "you had nothing to be nervous about."

"At least we broke the ice."

"We'll break more ice later."

The taxi went into the tunnel, dyeing us pink for a few minutes and I felt like I was in our own private shell under the river.

As I told Natalie later, it was delicious. I didn't give her too many details. Natalie isn't convinced my affair with Paul Teagarden is the right thing for me. She likes Roger, and now that she's living with Massimo, she's become a champion of fidelity, although before him she wasn't beyond a quick fling with my guitarist while she was dating Sheldon Bagg. People adjust, I guess.

Once we were on the other side of the Midtown Tunnel it would only be a few minutes before we arrived at Paul's hotel. We talked quietly, adapting a more civil demeanor for our trip through the city streets. I brought him up to date on my preparation for the Mimi Velaci Show and my latest encounter with Hunter. The car pulled through the end of the tunnel and cut across Second, then Third Avenue.

"We're almost there," I said.

"Grace, I don't want you to leave."

"I'll see you later tonight."

"I'm half-tempted to ask you to come upstairs now."

"Why don't you?" I whispered back.

"I want to but I have too much to do. There are the people I want to call while I'm here in New York, and I have to spend a little time talking to my office in LA."

"Oh," I said, my lips near his.

"Also, I need to get a little more sleep. And if you're here I won't sleep."

"That's probably true."

"But I'll try to get done with dinner as early as I can."

Soon we were gliding up Park Avenue. At least I knew we were comfortable together now. We confirmed our plans for the evening.

Paul would call me when he was done with his meeting, which would probably include an early dinner with the client; he would call me from the restaurant at nine o'clock.

Paul was telling me about his newest project, the one that had brought him to New York. He held my hand, and with every stroke of his fingers, I thought, "later." We pulled up to the Regency and a doorman greeted us. "Madam," he said as he helped me out of the car under the big square awning of the hotel.

"Come into the lobby for a second," said Paul.

It all felt so normal, dropping Paul off at the hotel this way. I only wished things were the way they looked, that Paul and I were checking into the hotel together, that I really was "Madam." We walked through the gold and white lobby to the front desk where the clerk was occupied with another guest. Paul turned to me.

"Grace," he said, pulling me towards him. "I'm going to check in, then go upstairs."

"This was fun."

"I'll see you later?"

"Absolutely."

"Thanks again for meeting me at the airport."

"I'm glad I did. I enjoyed our ride back."

"Me, too. I'll call you as soon as I finish with dinner."

"I'll be home."

丫 丫 丫

I floated over the red carpet and out of the hotel where I entered the stream of pedestrians on Park Avenue. I was happy. I had a big night ahead, a Paul Teagarden-in-the-flesh night ahead. My body looked forward to it as much as my mind did. What a rare moment; to be absolutely sure something extremely good is about to happen. I savored the feeling.

Time provided me with a luxurious final countdown. I was in no hurry. I took the subway downtown, enjoying every stop, and when the conductor mentioned there would be a delay because there was a police action at Grand Central, I waited patiently. I was not my usual restless self. I just stood there holding my pole, thinking romantic thoughts all the way to Canal Street.

Looking back, I think I was a little delirious. I was probably experiencing some natural chemical overdose from too little sleep and too much excitement. When I got home I looked in the mirror. My face had a distinctly blurry look. It was cat-like and wanton. I straightened up. I looked back at myself and said, "Grace, remember this moment. You're not going to feel like this forever." Then I took a nap.

I fell into bed on top of the blankets, glad it was raining. My mind tumbled into a daze, twirling through the unlikely connections and odd circumstances that brought Paul and me together here in New York. Then I eased my thoughts back into the taxi ride. And reliving our ride from the airport, I fell asleep.

ך ך ך

There was plenty to do when I woke up, besides put away the clothes I had dropped all over my apartment. It was three o' clock. By the stereo in a cardboard box were the last four Death Threat disks I was supposed to review. I could do this while working on a project for Walter Wiener; he had asked me to prepare a list of record companies he could approach with our new demo.

Then I had phone calls to return. And if I still had any time left, a few hours of practice wouldn't kill me. The early start to the day had slowed me down but by four o' clock I was back on track. I had to be careful not to succumb to long bouts of daydreaming, but Death Threat's music helped keep me focused.

When eight o' clock came, I checked out of my work mode. It was almost time for Paul. It wouldn't take me more than an hour to get dressed. I knew just what I wanted to wear. A long, camel-colored and black striped rayon dress, thin and clingy. I pulled out shoes and jewelry—a few rings and a gold bracelet—and put it all together on top of my blanket. Once the raw materials were arranged, I took a shower and dried my hair, careful not to overdo it on the freezing spray.

Every time I thought about Paul, a feeling surged through my body and I would blink like someone waking up to good news. To relax, I took a deep breath from my diaphragm as my voice teacher had taught me to do. This helped. And I replaced the Death Threat disks with some Miles Davis, which helped even more.

Getting ready for a date requires emotional dressing as well as physical dressing. It's a little like going on a stage. Once the outside is in order, you have to deal with your interior outfit. When I had finished dressing, I took another deep breath and settled back in my living room chair to design my state of mind.

I wanted to be relaxed. Natural. Not in order to make any particular impression, but because it was more fun that way. I wanted this to be easy. Anxiety shouldn't interfere with a night out. Anyway, there was no reason to be anxious. Judging by my earlier meeting with Paul, all the signs were promising; he was the man I remembered.

At nine o' clock I sat perched in my armchair, legs folded under me, ready to go. All my equipment—money, lipstick, and keys—was in a black bag and my gold earrings were on, the sign of a completed act of dressing. Also on was a skillfully applied layer of make-up, thanks to years of practice before gigs. Now it remained for Paul to finish dinner and call. The phone only had to ring. Nine o' clock, that was when he said he would finish dinner. Sinking back in the chair, careful not to crush my hair, I picked up a special "Legends of Rock" issue of *Guitar World* and flipped it open. I didn't need to think anymore about the night ahead. I was ready to live it.

At ten o' clock, I was surging with energy. I felt positive as ever, even though Paul hadn't called yet. People are always overly optimistic when they're looking forward to big plans. Meetings end later than expected, never sooner. I was still sure I had a big evening in front of me. But after an hour of waiting, energy sparked through me with no place to go and it wasn't a comfortable feeling. It felt like someone was trying to start up a lighter in my stomach. I couldn't sit still anymore. Feeling worn by waiting, I stood up, grabbed a pad, and jotted down Worn by Waiting because I thought it would make a good song title. I strolled to the kitchen, poured a glass of water, then went back to my chair and finished Legends of Rock. Paul ought to call any second, if only to tell me he was running late.

After I finished *Guitar World,* I picked up recent issues of *Modern Digital Studio* and *Glamour,* and was in the middle of deciding between the two when I realized I didn't want to read anymore. I walked over to the window and looked out. The gold clock tower said it was twenty-five after ten. I was pretty sure it wouldn't be much longer. I checked my hair to see if it still had height. It still had plenty.

Time passed slower then. Still, I was cheerful. What was an hour more or less, after six months? But as the hour crawled by, every minute seemed to break down into a new unit with sixty more parts to it, which meant that 360 times an hour, the phone didn't ring. At eleven I started to renovate my feelings. I told myself Paul would probably call any second, but in case he didn't, I should remember tonight wasn't all that important. I prepared for the worst, and planted the seeds of a whole new point of view. What if he didn't call? No, that couldn't happen. I was positive. I reconsidered, detached, then re-attached and explored different theories to account for Paul's delay.

I tried to keep busy. I straightened up the apartment a little and thought about where I might put a fish tank. Stopping at my desk, I flipped through my Farms of Kentucky calendar to see what the band had booked for August and September. Then I picked up a guitar, a defensive move on my part. It meant that I was crossing a bridge, one that took me from hope on one side, to the knowledge that I had been stood up on the other.

Still, I wasn't convinced.

With an interior smile, I stretched out languidly on the couch, imagining the phone would ring any second. I pictured Paul, late and flustered, meeting me at one of the places I had picked out downtown. In my imagination, I was already at the bar with a glass of wine in front of me. Candles glowed in glass holders, warming the dark wood and brick. Paul walked in; he looked better than ever in candlelight. He apologized. I took another look; there he was again, walking in the front door, smiling, apologizing. So we would meet at midnight; no big deal. In New York, that was only the beginning of the evening for anyone who took their night life seriously. You could still get a full-course meal and a haircut if you needed one at midnight. I usually stayed up till three or four in the morning anyway. Paul would definitely call by midnight.

When you find yourself with hours that were meant to be spent doing something else, there are a lot of paths you can take. At midnight, I kicked off my shoes and reviewed the possibilities. I could change guitar strings, alphabetize CDs, look at maps, dye my hair, sew a stuffed animal that had ripped under the arm sixteen years ago, or read the manual for my four track Portastudio. I could do housework; wash the floor, wash dishes, wash underwear, defrost the refrigerator, or I could go back to working on Walter's list some more. I could meditate or light candles and stare, read a book, listen to unmarked tapes to see what they were, make someone a card for an event I had forgotten, write letters, study Chinese, call my relatives in Western Canada, clean the kitchen cabinets, look at old photos, make a collage, make biscuits, listen to the same song forty times in a row, write a song, record sounds, or practice. I could do any one of these things, and depending on how many hours I wanted to stay up, I could do all of them.

The activity I opted for was organizing my shelves of sheet music and music books. It had been a long time since I had gotten them into any manageable order and now seemed as good a time as any to accomplish this task. I pulled out piles of music from the lower shelves in the bookcase in my living room, and piled up the loose sheets, fake books and spiral bound collections. I divided them into jazz and pop, pulling out practice and theory books. I tore into this activity as if I were single-handedly organizing a library after an earthquake. I also realized I could probably change out of my outfit now. I was getting dust on my dress. I could take off my clothes and put on a tee shirt and shorts, I thought numbly, because it didn't look like I was going anywhere tonight.

I had just pulled out some Prince sheet music, which had gotten stuck in a Cole Porter songbook, when the phone rang. The ring cut through the apartment. It imposed itself on the silence everywhere at once, as if the voice of God had spoken to me, and it sounded like a telephone. It was a revolution, the first sign of the outside world that had pierced my space in hours. The desire I felt for the rhythmic ringing was almost sexual. Paul Teagarden, at last. So he was ready to call, I thought, as I ran to the phone, trying to decide on how to deal with this fiasco. Should I be furious or understanding? I picked up the receiver.

"Hi there, may I speak to the lady of the house?"

"Walter?"

"Who else?"

"Hi," I said, disoriented. I hadn't even considered someone other than Paul might call this late.

"Were you asleep?"

"Of course not. What are you doing up now?" I said. It was one o' clock in the morning.

"I just got back from a card game and I wanted to call you. I stepped into the house and what do I find in my mailbox?"

"I don't know. What?"

"Guess."

"A letter that says you just won a million dollars."

"No."

"A Chinese menu."

"Wrong. Guess again."

"A fucking bomb and god damn it, Walter, someone is supposed to call me now. I don't want to stay on the phone all night playing guessing games." How low I had sunk. I once considered myself in total control, especially around Walter Wiener. That was in the past. I stood next to the phone, strands of hair hanging over my face and a handful of sheet music clutched in my fist.

"I see we had a hard day. I'll make it quick," said Walter, not the least bit insulted. "I came home, and in my usual stack of junk mail and bills, what do I find but a postcard from your friend and mine, Gary or Hunter, as he's also known by."

"And?" I sat down on the couch.

"Let me read to you what he says." Walter made a show of clearing his throat. "By the way, there's a very nice picture of the lobby of the Gainesville Sheraton on it. It says, 'Walt, *Tomorrow Never Cares* went gold. Tomorrow cares more than I thought. Best, Hunter.' How's that for news?"

"The disk went gold?"

"Exactly. 500,000 copies of *Tomorrow Never Cares* spread across this great land of ours. What do you think about that?"

"That's great," I said. The good news put a drag on my downwards spiral. "That is really great."

"You bet it is, babe."

"A gold record. I can't believe it."

"Why not?"

"Just the sound of it. A gold record," I repeated.

"I thought you would enjoy the news. Congratulations."

"Thank you so much, Walter."

"Stick with me, there's more where this came from. Did I tell you Tina Turner is my second cousin?"

"What?"

"Just kidding!"

"Walter, I'm glad you called." I walked across the living room with the phone in my hand, stepping over the piles of music books. "Sorry I snapped at you before."

"Don't worry about it, Grace. We're all up and down sometimes."

"How come Hunter didn't just call you himself?"

"Hunter is like that. He's a very busy man. When he has something to say, he writes it on a card, hands it to Jerry, and it gets mailed."

"Amazing. I really appreciate your calling me with the news, Walter. I needed a lift." Who cared about Paul Teagarden with news like that? I told myself. Still, I felt a sadness sweeping through me.

"By the way, I took your friend, Jessica, to dinner the other night. She's a lovely girl. Very bright, very personable."

"Jessica, from the café?"

"Yes. Your waitress singer friend. You don't mind, do you?"

"Why should I mind? Did you have fun?"

"I think we had a very nice time. She seemed to enjoy herself. I know I did. I'm going to take her to dinner and a movie next week."

"Walter, that's great."

"And you? What are you up to tonight?"
"Me? Just taking care of stuff around the house."

ᛎ ᛎ ᛎ

I was asleep when the phone rang. It was ten o' clock in the morning. I reached over and picked it up.

"Hello?" It was Paul.

"Hello?" I said, not instantly letting on I knew it was him.

"Grace, it's Paul. I'm really sorry."

"What happened to you?" I said without emotion.

"My dinner. It went on and on and on. I couldn't leave. I had no idea they had a major night planned for me."

"So why didn't you call me?"

"I did. I tried. Your phone was busy. After that, I couldn't get away. I got caught up in what we were doing. It turned out to be a very intense evening."

"Intense," I repeated. It was all coming into focus. "Intense. What does that mean?"

"It means we were very involved in what we were talking about. This project is bigger than I realized, it's not just one commercial, it means shooting all over the world in each of the countries they sell in."

How classic. There's nothing more effective when you stand someone up, than finding an excuse of international scale and importance to make your date seem tiny by comparison. What's one missed evening out compared to shooting all over the world? "So you couldn't call again to let me know? Is that what intense means?"

"The meeting went on till about two in the morning. I tried to call, but your phone was busy. It was around one o' clock."

I had been on the phone with Walter at one.

"You waited till one to call?" I rolled over in bed. "Okay. Well, that's too bad."

"Grace, you're being sarcastic."

"Sorry, it's just hard to believe you couldn't make more of an effort."

"I couldn't. And believe me, I'm as disappointed as you are. But this is what I came east for."

"Right, Paul." I considered whether I should just say what I was thinking. Our connection was so tenuous to begin with that I knew I would risk ending the whole thing with a couple of harsh words. On the other hand, there was really nothing much here anyway. It was a good thing I was still groggy, because the words came out before I could think or edit too much. "You know, Paul, I've been talking to you for six months on the phone. You come to New York for one day, and you can't even stay an extra day to see me. You can't even figure out how to meet me, or even call to tell me you can't make it. I see how important this is to you."

"You don't think I wanted to see you?"

"No, not really. And what's the difference anyway, you didn't make it."

"You're being very hard, Grace. I'm calling you now."

"Yes, I know. And I'm sick of the phone. Guess what? I don't want to talk on the phone anymore, okay?"

"Fine, but you're not dealing with this. I didn't do it on purpose. I really wanted to see you."

"Bullshit. I wanted to see you. And I was here."

Paul didn't say anything. I heard him breathing. I continued. "If it were the other way around, if I were coming to California, I wouldn't come for only a day. I would leave a few extra days so I could see you. That's the difference between you and me. I would have made an effort to see you even if it was four in the morning." Suddenly, a discussion seemed futile. "Oh, what's the point?"

"There is a point, Grace. Okay, maybe there are other things going on that I'm not conscious of. Maybe I should have called. Can't we talk about it?" For some reason it seemed important to Paul that I didn't just hang up on him. His voice was gentle and focused as if he wanted to show me what he could do if he put his mind to it.

"When do you want to talk? What are you doing now?" I asked.

"I'm on my way to the airport."

"So what did you have in mind, more phone calls?" My annoyance moved up another notch.

"I'll call you when I get to California."

"What a great idea."

"Look, I see you're angry, I get the idea. I'll make this up to you. I promise, even if I have to fly back to New York."

I didn't say anything.

"Grace?"

"I'm here." I wasn't trying to make Paul feel guilty. I just didn't have anything else to say. I was sitting up in the blankets now. "Paul, I'm really disappointed. That's all I have to say about it."

"Okay, Grace. I'll talk to you later."

We hung up.

I looked around. The sun came in between the slats of the venetian blinds. It was going to be hot, I could tell already. I sat up a little and leaned forward to see the sky. My clothes from last night were on the chair. My jewelry was on the dresser. None of it had even made it out of the house.

So Paul was on his way to the airport. He was leaving New York. My big date with him boiled down to nothing more than a taxi ride. I realized I now had zero chance of seeing Paul Teagarden and I lay back down and shut my eyes. I had been blunt with him on the phone but that didn't mean I wasn't upset.

Last night had taken so much energy. When did a date ever have more preparation? It had taken six months to get ready for this one. I wanted to see him so badly. Maybe it was like he said, maybe he was too busy to call. I wanted to believe him. But my one marriage to date taught me not to hold on to illusions. Like Steve, our drummer, says, "I believe in action, man." Paul didn't show up.

Now I felt empty. I didn't want to get out of bed. I rolled over and pulled the sheet around me. The bed seemed like a completely safe place at the moment. Why wander away from that kind of comfort? I wondered if it was possible to stay in bed twenty-four hours, right to the next morning. If I got out of bed, all I had to look forward to was a lot of reminders I had blown a good dose of passion on someone who didn't even bother to call. Where there had been late night phone calls, there would now be plenty of practice time.

❜ ❜ ❜

There's only so long you can stay in bed on a hot July morning. It's not the same as lying under two or three covers in the winter when snow piles up on your fire escape and brownstones turn white. In July, the sheets get damp, especially if you're having nightmares. You get a headache.

I got out of bed. I decided it would be healthy to get Paul Teagarden out of sight as soon as possible. Walking through the apartment, I gathered all the odds and ends Paul had sent me. There were some postcards and letters, a few newspaper articles he had cut out for me, and a brochure for a film school seminar in which he had lectured. I put it all into an envelope, leaving out only a postcard of Monument Valley he had sent when he was out there shooting a car commercial. I liked the pictures of the red rock. Everything else went in the envelope, which went into the closet. It might come down again, for instance, if a ticket to California arrived in the mail. But for now, I had done something decisive.

It was a good thing Paul's no-show coincided with the week of my Mimi Velaci appearance. There was not a lot of time for moping;

I had just two days to turn from sorry loser into a television presence. It's not possible to appear devastated and perky at the same
time and I didn't want to go on the Velaci show and sit next to
Hunter and Rudy looking like I was mad at the world, although
it was a look that had worked for them for decades.

It was too bad I could not fully experience my sadness and wal-
low properly, but I had a commitment that would take total
concentration. As a first step, it seemed like a good idea to get out
of my apartment. If I were home, every second would be spent waiting for Paul to call, watching the phone. Nothing would be
accomplished. I would be writing depressing songs when I should
be studying talk show techniques. And so I took a desperate action in a time of crisis. Distraught over one man, I asked another
if I could stay at his house. And though in recent days Roger was
not particularly enchanted with me and my projects, he said yes.

The fact that nothing had happened with Paul eased my con-
science and made it easier to enjoy Roger's hospitality, I rationalized.
It was true, I needed a few days of quiet retreat. My own place was
a mess and the phone didn't stop ringing. I needed a place where
I could sort out my thoughts in quiet, and fully prepare for the
show. That's what I told Roger.

Paul Teagarden left a few messages. I did not call him back. I
was not about to call him from Roger's house, and I had nothing to
say anyway. What happened with Paul Teagarden lingered like a
shadow behind everything. But I didn't want to deal with him until
the show was over and life returned to normal. For now, my attention was elsewhere.

❦ ❦ ❦

Roger's regular visits to *Marketwatch* and other financial programs
made him a big help in preparing for the show. He had first hand
experience in what I would encounter on Mimi's set. I felt lucky
to have a boyfriend who knew what to do on talk shows.

While he was at work, I practiced appearing keen and lucid for
hours at a time in Roger's full-length mirror. On Thursday, the day
of the show, Roger left work early in order to help me get ready.
He walked into his place at one o' clock, coffee and sandwiches in
hand. "It's important to eat. You'll need energy," he said, setting up
a picnic on his coffee table. I was scheduled to leave for the studio
at three. The network was sending a car.

After we ate, I remained on the living room carpet rummag-
ing through a box of jewelry I had brought with me, while Roger

paced around me. "Just remember to talk to the host, and watch the monitors when you can."

"Will I be able to hear everyone talk? How will I be able to hear people?"

"You'll be able to hear them. It's very quiet in the studio."

"Are the lights bright? Will I be able to see?"

"Grace, don't worry. You'll be fine, I'm telling you exactly what to expect. Sit with me for a minute." He directed me to the couch.

"The car will be here soon. I have to put on make-up," I said.

"They'll do your make-up at the studio, don't worry about it." I listened to Roger.

"It's all very fast," he said in a steady voice. "Don't let that throw you. You'll be rushed on stage when it's time for your segment, and a couple of seconds later you'll see the producer counting down and then you're on."

I gasped. "I don't get to meet Mimi first?"

"I doubt it. He may come and shake your hand backstage, but it's unlikely. Don't worry, pretend you've known him all your life."

"Hunter said I should speak confidently. He said it almost doesn't matter what I say, just don't go 'uh' and 'you know.' Just talk, he said. Is that right?"

"Yes, that's good advice. People tend to pick up on hesitation and uncertainty. It almost doesn't matter what you say, but say it with confidence."

"Say it with confidence," I repeated.

"Anyway, you'll be amazed, Grace. With the adrenaline pumping, you'll make perfect sense. Just don't be self-conscious. Pretend there's no one else in the world, talk to whoever it is you're talking to and get to the point fast." Roger pushed my hair back over my shoulders. "Don't cover your face."

"Do I look all right?" I was wearing a black blazer with gold buttons, a crew neck, red and white striped shirt under the jacket, and jeans. Natalie had picked out the outfit, mainly out of her own clothes. The socks were mine. She had come over earlier and done interesting things with my hair. The rash on my neck was almost gone, thanks to Mrs. Chu's herbs.

"You look beautiful. Very tasteful."

"The producer was disappointed when I told him I wouldn't wear an orange latex dress. I said I didn't want to. He actually threatened me, can you believe it? He said I couldn't go on if I didn't wear it. You know what I told him?"

"What?" said Roger, pushing my hair back over my shoulders.

"I told him if I didn't go on, Hunter and Rudy don't go on. I bluffed. He left me alone." This was going to be a big show for Mimi, and the producer didn't want to take responsibility for screwing it up just because I wouldn't wear a rubber dress.

"So we'll meet after the show, right?" I said to Roger, as I bounced nervously on his couch. Roger wasn't allowed to come with me backstage, but he would be in the studio audience. He promised to cheer us on whenever the applause sign permitted.

I'll wait for you in the lobby afterwards," Roger said.

The buzzer rang. The car had arrived to take me to the Mimi Velaci show.

⅄ ⅄ ⅄

Wearing a black shirt that said, "Save The Chameleons" on the portion that was not shredded, a pair of red lizard-skin boots that seemed to contradict the nobler sentiments of his tee-shirt, a braided suede belt ending in loose leather strands that dangled like a cat 'o nine tails between his legs, and true to their name, an extremely snug fitting pair of tights, Hunter Burns looked like the rock 'n' roll menace he was purported to be. A black leather jacket hung low over his hips, pulling the whole outfit together.

"Hey, guess what?" he said, as he strolled through the Green Room slapping hands and giving high-fives to his boys who were there for support and now standing around the room.

"What, man?" Rudy said, lifting his sunglasses as Hunter passed. Rudy was sitting in an armchair smoking a cigarette. He looked relaxed. In fact, if he hadn't just spoken, I would have thought he was asleep. Hunter sat down on the edge of Rudy's armchair.

"Reverend Bob's people are burning me in effigy in front of the building."

"Hey, man, you always said you were on fire," said Rudy, punching Hunter in the thigh.

"I don't mind," Hunter continued, with unusual languor for a man about to appear in front of a nation. Hunter's imminent appearance had gotten a lot of press. Rock icons like Hunter and Rudy were a rarity on the talk show circuit and millions of people would be watching. "And you know why?"

"Why, man?" Rudy said, embracing his sidekick role.

"Because there's two thousand more kids out front chanting 'Burn, Bobby, Burn,'" shouted Hunter, doing his best to raise our spirits. Things were tense in the Green Room as we waited for our call.

Once more a round of high fives, nudges, and nods moved like a wave through the room. As Hunter passed me, he threw his arm around me, shouted "Yeah, Grace," and held up my hand in a sportsman-like signal of triumph. Then he wandered off to talk to his lawyer. Wisely, the producers of the show had kept our counterparts from OOFF out of our way. They knew that one obscene gesture from the Death Threat team would be enough to send OOFF walking. We were hyped up and ready for action, which meant with Death Threat, anything could happen.

I also sensed that in spite of their cavalier attitude, Hunter and Rudy were a little nervous. While we were all used to being on stage, none of us had ever had to debate. And even though Hunter and Rudy had done hundreds of interviews over the last twenty years, their political opinions had only been solicited by sympathetic rock journalists and video jocks whose most probing questions were always on the subject of torture and pollution. Tonight they were going to hold our feet to the fire.

Minutes passed as the countdown continued. Hunter killed time by making a few phone calls. He sat back in a large, squarish armchair and spoke quietly into the receiver. I think it was his way of staying calm. His tone was soft and affectionate, which meant he was talking to his girlfriend or to a record company executive.

I sat down on one of the couches and leaned back. The Green Room was the size of an ordinary living room, with two televisions, one at each end of the room, where we could watch what was happening on the network. The furnishings were plain; a few undistinguished office couches, lamps that looked like they had come from the set of an old sitcom, some tables laden with juice, soda, and sandwiches.

I felt sick inside, too terrified to eat or drink. It was as if I were about to be exposed to everyone I had ever known all at once. I closed my eyes and tried to distract myself by pretending I was someplace, any place, else. I thought of pleasant places, and in my mind, I saw sunlight coming into Natalie's big loft, and the clear water of the river outside North Gaylordsville. I pictured the garden behind Roger's sister's house, the orchestra room at college, the Gorilla House at the Bronx zoo, the Boat House in Central Park. Just then I felt someone drop on the couch next to me. Whoever it was sat much closer than the person needed to be. I opened my eyes, just as a singsong voice murmured "Hello," in my ear. It was Walter Wiener.

He stared at me like a dog that had just done something wonderful. "Surprise!" he said.

"Hey, Walter, what are you doing here?"

"I thought you could use a little support."

"The only support I need is if you go on instead of me."

"If I could, for you, I would. But as they say in Katmandu, if the queen had balls she'd be king."

"Which means what?"

"It means you're on your own. But you should know I'll be rooting for you."

"I feel better."

"Right now, though, you're too tense. I can see it," he said, squeezing my shoulder but getting mainly a shoulder pad, "Let me loosen you up a little. Turn around and let me give you a massage."

Before I could even turn around, Walter's hands were behind me kneading my shoulders.

"So, Walter," I said as his hands rocked me back and forth, "how did you get into the Green Room? They told me no one but the band and their manager could come in." It was amazing the way Walter always turned up in the heart of things. "What did you tell them, you were Death Threat's accountant?"

"No, their hairdresser. Seriously, I'm what is known as a friend of the band. Maybe I should have said I was their masseur," he said, his breath on my neck.

"Walter, stop massaging me," I ordered, peeling his hands off my shoulders. "I'm trying to relax and for some reason, you're not helping. In two minutes I have to go on in front of thirty million people. Let me relax my way."

"Grace, you'll be fine, I can tell already. The camera will flatten your face, you'll look great."

"Where's Hunter?" I said, seized by an almost childish panic. I didn't see him. Jerry was on the phone now where Hunter had been.

"He's right over there by the door," said Walter. Putting his hands back on my shoulders, he swiveled me towards Hunter. He and Rudy were talking quietly, their faces close together in conference. Marty, their lawyer, stood slightly below them in the same circle.

"Hunter is very good on television," Walter said. "I've seen him. He's very natural. You could put him in front of a room full of people without his clothes on, and he's perfectly at ease. I've seen it happen."

"Oh God, look what time it is. We're going to be on any minute," I cried. Just then the two monitors in the room began to play the familiar Mimi Velaci theme music, and everyone in the room fell silent. Hunter's voice, deep and theatrical, broke the quiet as he announced, looking at me, "It's show time, babe." I moaned.

Margo, the associate producer, waved to us. She had been our keeper for the last hour. "Let's go," she ordered, and she opened the door to the Green Room and herded us out. There was a mixture of voices, Marty and Jerry and Walter crying "Good Luck," and "Go get 'em." I felt squeezes and hands grabbing mine, and in a blur we followed Margo down the hall, past doorways and elevators to the studio where Mimi's show took place. Margo guided us past the backstage workings, not acknowledging the technicians and workers in headphones running everywhere. We stepped over cables and wires until we came to the curtain that hid us from the production taking place a few feet away.

From the side, we could see the set, and beyond it, the studio audience. Men and women shifted in their seats and talked as they waited for the show to begin. There were monitors spread across the floor where anyone on the set could watch the action from the camera's point of view. The floor of the set was a big open area, and in the center towards the back stood a carpeted platform a foot off the floor. Mimi's desk and chair were here and next to his desk, six red-orange upholstered chairs, three on each side of Mimi's desk. The rest of the set included a dark wooden bookshelf stacked with books, trophies and sports awards. I looked at the chairs, wondering on which side we would sit. Margo pointed at the set, answering my question. "You three will be sitting on Mimi's left. I want you in the middle, Hunter. Rudy, you're in the inside chair nearest Mimi. Grace, you sit in the outside chair." Very soon, I would be sitting on the carpeted platform in front of the spinning cameras and eyes of millions.

"Oh my god," I whispered.

Hunter must have heard me and seen I was panic-stricken because he grabbed my shoulders, squeezed and whispered, "Grace, relax, just be yourself. I trust you. Trust yourself. It'll be great." I heard loud clapping and then, on a big monitor at our feet, I watched as the Mimi Velaci Show went on the air.

♪ ♪ ♪

First there was a blast of sporty theme music. Then came the deep voice of the announcer: "Coming to you from New York City, the man who hits a home run every night, it's Mimi Velaci." Assistant producers swung their arms over their heads, the audience cheered, and from stage right Mimi Velaci, the stocky ex-baseball player, trotted out, smiling and waving at the world.

"Hi there, friends," he said to wild applause mingling with hoots and friendly shouts. He continued as the shouting diminished, "Welcome, and I'm glad you could be here tonight because we have a really fascinating show for you today. But let me first test your knowledge of current events." Here Mimi jogged towards the front of the stage, down a step and into the audience. "Here we go," he said. "A body in the trunk of a car. A priest having an affair with a nun. Two teenagers having sex in an empty classroom. What do all of these scenes have in common?" said Mimi in a solid, pleasant sounding voice, with an urban accent.

There was a low murmur in the audience, and Mimi continued, "They're all scenes from television shows that have been boycotted and eventually taken off the air." Mimi retreated from the audience, and now walked across the set as he spoke. "And today, we have the top members of the group that plans and organizes these media boycotts. They're a group called OOFF, the Organization of Families First, and let's bring them out here."

Clap signs flashed over the heads of the studio audience, who cheered loudly as the three-member OOFF team strode onto the set. "Let's say hello to OOFF's national spokesperson, Mary Joe Wheeler, OOFF's Deputy Director, Donny Edwards, and the Executive Director of OOFF, Reverend Bob Bailey." Holding their heads high, they took their seat on Mimi's right and looked peaceably out at the clapping audience. Mary Joe Wheeler took the center seat, Reverend Bob, tall and serious, sat next to Mimi, and Donny Edwards sat in the outside seat.

"And we're also going to meet some folks you've probably heard of. They're some big rock and roll stars from the musical group Death Threat, and today we're going to learn why they're making OOFF very, very mad," continued Mimi, in a chipper tone. "So let's meet Hunter Burns, and Rudy Rude from Death Threat, and one of their songwriters, Grace Note. C'mon out, guys," cried Mimi, and greeted by loud hoots, screams and a few boos, we stepped onto the set.

My throat tightened and I felt sick. I was shocked by the brightness of the lights. It was like daytime. But within a moment, all feeling was forced out of me by the screaming audience, the waving arms of the producer, and the focused eyes of the crew who wildly swung cameras around us. Thank god Roger had coached me to stand up straight and look up. Whatever I did, I did automatically. The assistant producer who had been handling us had to push me onto the set. Hunter and Rudy, on the other hand, strolled out as if it were their show and everyone else their guest. The moment they stepped in front of the camera, I knew I was with two pros. Hunter and Rudy projected pure rock star malevolence. They didn't hurry on the stage like I did. All I could think of was getting to my seat. They whispered to each other and laughed. They held up their heads and looked around. They oozed sexuality with every swaggering step. Hunter even took a brief detour towards the edge of the stage, where he leaned over, and languidly stretched his hand out to a girl who yelled his name from the front row. In short, they worked the room and sauntered to their chairs, waving, grinning, and throwing kisses, to the pleasure of their fans in their audience who cheered and screamed. It seemed the audience was packed with supporters of both parties, and for every whoop of support from a Death Threat fan, I spotted someone else with his lips clenched in fury, or felt an angry glare. We took our places as the producer had instructed us to.

"All right now, all right now, save me a little for later," Mimi scolded the crowd. "When we come back, we're going to learn what it is about these guys that's making OOFF so darned mad," Mimi concluded. The producer gave the cut sign, Mimi dropped into his chair and a make-up man ran out and began to touch up Mimi's face.

"You okay?" Hunter whispered to me.

"So far," I answered, tentatively.

"Don't worry. This'll be fun," Hunter said, squeezing my hand.

This wasn't the word I would have chosen. The atmosphere on the set was hysterical as electricians, cameramen, and production assistants took care of a flurry of tasks. I looked at Mimi, who talked on the telephone as the hair stylist touched up the side of his head with something in a spray can, and I could have sworn I overheard Mimi telling someone to go fuck themselves. He looked annoyed and he didn't seem interested in any of us. The audience was busy whispering. While we waited for the break to end, I tried to absorb what I could about our opposite numbers on the other side of the stage.

I recognized Reverend Bob right away. He was a big boned, healthy man, somewhere in his mid-fifties. His features were thick and a little rugged, and his face long, topped by blond hair on its way to gray. His hearty looks contrasted strangely with his pale eyes. They were piercing and unblinking like some kind of staring bird. Thick shaggy eyebrows topped his marble-like eyes. His mouth cut across his face in a straight, thin line. Perhaps the source of his healthy looks was nothing more than the layer of orange pancake make-up on his face, which gave him a nuclear glow. Reverend Bob looked relaxed, and he chatted with Mary Joe Wheeler, chuckling and nodding as if he were at a picnic instead of a talk show. He waved to followers in the audience whenever he spotted a familiar face.

I had heard the name of Reverend Bob's number two man, Donny Edwards, before but I hadn't seen any pictures of him. He was a sturdy looking fellow, but he seemed extremely ill at ease. There was something lopsided about him, as if he had been in an accident. He had a small mouth, dark hair cut very short and a little nose, set in a wide sea of a face. He wore short sleeves and a wrist-watch and looked like he might have been in the army at one time. Marty Seagal told us he was a stationery salesman. Donny sat forward in his chair, nervously kneading his hands.

At Bob's right, solid and proud in a short, peach colored suit with gold buttons, sat Mary Joe Wheeler. Instantly, I recognized her as the core of their power. Mary Joe Wheeler was the secret weapon of fanatics everywhere: a modern looking, elegant believer. This was no mousy, downtrodden victim; Mary Joe Wheeler was a knockout, with full lips, smooth skin, eyes that are a little small but look good with make up. She had a nice figure, which she was not ashamed to show. I could tell by the relaxed look on her face that OOFF's spokesperson had confidence. They didn't get any more righteous than Mary Joe Wheeler.

The OOFF contingent sat politely in their chairs, gazing at us with patient, superior stares as if they were counting down to judgment day and knew just where we all stood. The countdown began out loud when the producer, a few feet in front of us, signaled that we were about to go back on the air. He flipped his fingers in a ten-second countdown.

Applause signs flashed, assistants in the front of the audience clapped over their heads, and the audience cheered, glad to play the part of frenzied participants. Mimi welcomed everyone back. "For those of you who just joined us," he said into the camera, "we have on our stage two very different groups. They've never met before and today we're going to talk to them and watch them as they get to know each other. Meet the Organization of Family First over here, and on this side of our stage, the rock group, Death Threat," said Mimi, waving a stubby hand in our respective directions. I noticed there was always a little more enthusiasm from the audience when OOFF's name was mentioned, and I figured, in light of the fact we were meant to represent more demonic forces, the producer had stacked the audience against us.

"Now first, I'd like to know a little bit about everyone," said Mimi, "Let's start with OOFF. Hi," he said, swiveling his chair to face them. He stood up. "Hi," they answered back with neighborly good humor. Being shorter than almost everyone else on stage, I noticed Mimi generally stood up and hovered whenever possible, adding to his height.

"We told our audience a little bit about OOFF at the beginning of the show," Mimi said, "and we know your organization is all about restoring decency to family entertainment. But I'd like to know, what's driving you? Donny, let's start with you."

Hunter leaned over to me and whispered, "What kind of fifty year old guy is named Donny?" I laughed nervously.

Donny looked down for a moment, then turned to Mimi with a grin and said, "Mimi, we just want to make the world a better place, I guess." He looked embarrassed for a moment, as if overwhelmed by the simplicity of it all. There was scattered clapping. Donny continued. "You see, Mimi, we believe there's a lot of trouble in America today, I think we'd all agree on that. We, as Christians, believe it's our responsibility to make a commitment to changing things for the better any way we can. So I'd say we're driven by the desire to make life a little better for everyone."

"And you do this how," declared Mimi, picking up a little steam.

"If I may answer that, Mimi," said Reverend Bob, "We look for programs and printed material we believe stimulate the kind of violence and indecency that trouble so many families today. In particular, we look for gratuitous violence and sexual matter that portray negative acts and stereotypes we feel no child should be exposed to. And by the way, Mimi, our standard of evaluation is simple—can a family watch this material?" Mary Joe Wheeler nodded in gentle agreement. "We're fighting the commercial forces that want to profit at the expense of the well-being of the family," he added, sounding eminently practical. Could this be the same man that wanted to ban troll dolls because he claimed they encouraged friendliness towards demons?

Mimi stood up and strolled across the stage with his microphone and looked up at the lights briefly before he came to a halt. He leaned on the edge of his desk and looked at us. He looked back over at OOFF.

"Okay. We have the general picture. You've boycotted some of the biggest corporations and networks in the nation. Now tell me about these people," he said, waving his arm over us. Mimi walked around to the back of our chairs and put his hand on Hunter's shoulders, as he continued to speak. "Tell us about this man. An entertainer. A super rockstar. You're boycotting him. Tell us why."

"Mimi," began Reverend Bob, "this man produces music that epitomizes everything we object to. In particular, though, he has made a music video we find beyond all reason." Reverend Bob spoke with an educated southern accent, pronouncing every word clearly, injecting meaning into every syllable. I could see Reverend Bob was experienced at commanding attention and I only hoped the micro-phones picked up the occasional nasal squeak in his voice when he got excited. "There's only one word that describes this video, which they call 'Let Me Show You,' and I'm sorry to say it, but that word is disgusting." He didn't seem at all sorry to say it, and in fact he managed to repeat it several more times as he ran down a list of all that was immoral about "Let Me Show You." "There are women clad in costumes children should not see, exotic dancers and such things, disgusting acts going on between men and women that don't belong in a video, you name it, Mimi. This disgusting video is seen by mil-lions of children across America and frankly, we think it's wrong," he concluded.

"But why is it wrong? These children have parents, and if they let them watch it, why is it your business?" Mimi countered. There was no reproach or judgment in his voice, just a tone that came across as simple-minded curiosity. "Mary Joe Wheeler, don't these children have their own parents?"

"Mimi, of course they have parents," said Mary Joe warmly, "and we're not trying to do the work of parents. We just feel that in today's world, when so many parents are struggling just to get by, people are not paying attention sometimes. They let things go and don't notice how far they let things slip. We want to remind them of what's important. Some of the things I see on television are just shocking, and I don't think it's wrong to take a stand on this. We're all parents," she said, indicating her two associates with a wave of her hand. She gave the audience a moment to let this sink in. "We formed OOFF because we realized that together, we have the power to do something about what we view as the runaway immorality in our society. It's all about empowerment, Mimi," she declared. The audience clapped. Mary Joe spoke with a certain front-line authority, and she was not ashamed to use any language that might better package her cause.

"Empowerment," mumbled Hunter in a nearly inaudible voice, "Give me a break." Hunter was itching to dig in and I wondered when Mimi would get to us. So far OOFF was having a field day of righteousness. I could feel the will of the audience turning against

us. There was more and more applause with each new OOFF proc-
lamation. I was starting to believe we were simply here as material
evidence for Reverend Bob's case, when Mimi turned to us.

He stood next to us. "Okay, Hunter Burns. Rock star. These
people want to ruin you. What do you have to say?"

"I think they're hypocrites," Hunter announced. There were a
few boos from the audience mixed in with a comforting whoop on
our behalf.

"Why?" said Mimi, whose questions always sounded like announcements.

"Because they claim they're making all these wonderful decisions to help build up families. But they're willing to destroy people
in the process—anyone who doesn't think the way they do."

"They claim they're taking a stand."

"They're not just taking a stand, they're trying to control what
we hear and see. Who asked them to? Their values sound nice, but
they don't tell you about the people they're hurting with their boycotts."

"But what's wrong with wanting decency in entertainment?"

"Nothing. Let them watch whatever they want to. But not everyone believes the same thing they do. They don't care that maybe
someone does want to see our video. Or that maybe a record store
owner wants to carry our CDs. They don't accept that there are
different ideas about what's valuable or moral. They think their
standards are everybody's."

"Excuse me, young man," interrupted Donny Edwards, "but
our standards come from the bible. We do not make them up, this
is the word of God."

"I'm sure you know not everyone in the United States has the
same idea of God as you do."

"Surveys show most Americans do consider the bible a holy
book," said Donny.

"So where is it written in the bible that God doesn't want jiggling breasts?"

I rolled my eyes. This kind of approach, I sensed, was not going to help our cause. No matter how logical Hunter was being, the
American public doesn't like the idea of God and jiggling breasts
in the same sentence. Sure enough, there was some more booing
from the audience. Hunter flipped his hair back impatiently.

Hunter was used to having total control, but now, under fire
in front of millions of people, there was something vulnerable
about him. Both Hunter and Rudy looked extravagant, two grown

men dressed in bad-boy clothes, with pale stage-makeup covering their sullen faces. Their almost clownish appearance during such a serious discussion was not helping their cause. Still, Hunter had a certain power, which showed in his eyes. They were dark and smart, always focused on whomever was speaking.

"Hunter, if these people don't like your video, why shouldn't they boycott it?" asked Mimi, resting his arms on his knees in a pose of curiosity.

"Mimi, they can boycott it all they want," Hunter replied, slightly exasperated. "They can turn off their television. Don't buy my records. Did you hear that?" he said, glaring at Mary Joe Wheeler. "But that's not what they do. They boycott the record stores, for instance, where our albums are sold, and they put financial pressure on people to not carry any of our products. Then no one can get our disks, even people who want them. They do the same thing with magazines, movies, books, and television. They don't care that many of the things they force out of circulation are things other people enjoy or consider artistic. I would like to know what right these people have to do that," said Hunter, intensely. He was starting to get angry.

"That's a fair question," said Mimi, who never seemed to add or subtract from the discourse. He swiveled around to OOFF. "What right do you have to decide what other people watch?"

Reverend Bob gave Mary Joe the nod. "We have the same right you do to decide how we're going to spend our money, Mr. Burns." She spoke as if she were talking to an ornery pre-teen. There was some clapping from the audience.

"Hey, she's not answering the question," Rudy whined suddenly. "You can spend your own money anyway you want, but why should you decide how other people spend theirs? What if someone likes our music and wants to buy our CD, and they can't because of you?"

"We believe in a community standard, and that the higher values of the community outweigh the right of an individual to indulge in unhealthy practices," Reverend Bob said. "We stand for the rights of the family," he boomed, and there was cheering from the audience.

Things were not looking good for us. As long as they kept making declarations like "We stand for the rights of the family," we were doomed to the shadows, relegated to represent the forces of evil as if we were on Satan's own debating team. There was nowhere for us to go once OOFF claimed the higher moral ground.

Furthermore, it was clear from the way OOFF members spoke
that any point of view other than theirs was absolutely impossible.
This was all about their rights and their rights alone, and logic had
nothing to do with it. They claimed God was on their side. How
can you challenge people who are sure God is on their side and not
yours? Like Marty had said, it doesn't look good to play hardball
with fundamentalists. We needed to steer the conversation away
from grandiose claims and back to practical matters.

Suddenly, I heard my own voice. "Mimi, I'd like to say something," I began, as if someone else were speaking. My voice sounded
liquid and high-pitched. I looked down to see five different images
of me on the monitors on the floor.

"Miss Note," Mimi nodded.

"OOFF can do what they want. I just hope people see it for what
it is. It's just censorship, that's all."

"We do not advocate censorship, Miss Note, we advocate a common standard of decency," said Mary Joe Wheeler.

"You threaten people with financial punishment. You threaten
to destroy people's business if they don't get rid of the things you
don't like. What do you call it?"

"Pressure. Lots of pressure," said Rudy.

Mary Joe ignored him. "I think, Miss Note, we are representing a majority of the public when we express our point of view on
morality."

Hunter broke in, "Bull. There are polls that show most fundamentalists don't even agree with what you do. Do you think the
general public appreciates the fact they can't get perfectly legal
books and magazines, or see certain shows, because of you? Since
when is this a religious state?"

"Mimi, I would like to point out this is typical technique of
people like Death Threat," replied Bob, a slight smile on his lips.
He talked to Mimi as if we weren't even there. "They stand up for
so-called 'general public' and they talk about the rights of the minority—at least we think they're a minority—that enjoys the
kind of filth we object to. But if Miss Note and Mister Burns are
saying they enjoy shows that depict rape and child molestation,
than they're worse off than we thought."

An explosion of clapping for Reverend Bob burst from the audience. "That's the kind of stuff we're objecting to," cried Reverend
Bob, his jaw jutting out as he glared at the crowd.

"That is ridiculous," I cried over the cheering, my teeth
clenched. By my side I sensed Hunter swelling with fury.

"Come on!" Hunter shouted back, "How dare you imply that we enjoy these horrible crimes, just because you don't like the way we express ourselves. Are you out of your mind?"

"If the shoe fits, Mr. Burns," said Reverend Bob, with a contented grin. The more upset we got, the more he appeared to enjoy himself. It seemed as if nothing we said made sense.

"Mimi, this just shows how much OOFF is willing to distort the truth to advance their fanatical point of view," said Hunter, but no one was really listening. No matter how logical we were, no matter how rooted in fact, Reverend Bob would call us "indecent" and all logic was washed away in the gut reaction of the audience, in the power of the sound and the word. I could feel the spirit of the audience turning against us and I could only imagine how this looked to the millions of people watching, who saw nothing but the image of Hunter, Rudy, and I scowling in our seats, while OOFF sat genteelly poised as if the universe were on their side. I had no idea how to escape from this loop and I wished for a moment that we could start fresh.

"We'll take a break now," chirped Mimi, "but we'll be back soon with more about the people who are watching you watch TV." He pointed at the camera until the producer waved his hand and mouthed, "Cut."

I whipped around and faced Hunter. I was sweating. "How can they say that?"

"Reverend fucking Bob will say whatever he has to say to come out ahead here," whispered Hunter. "That's what he does." Hunter was upset, but he didn't seem as upset as I was. I think he understood it was all an impression that will be forgotten by tomorrow.

"Man, we're dying," moaned Rudy.

"We'll be out of here soon," said Hunter.

"This is horrible."

"Just keep doing your best. You're doing great," said Hunter, giving my hand an affectionate squeeze. Then he leaned over to his left and started whispering to Rudy.

I looked out at the audience. They pointed at us and said things I couldn't hear. A fat teenager in a blue warm-up jacket stared at me. I felt like a zoo animal, except when I caught an excited supporter waving a banner that said "Death Threat Rules." I didn't say anything for the rest of the break. It was hot under the lights and my clothes itched. Mimi once again pretended we didn't exist and occupied himself by trying to remain in an upbeat mood. He tapped

a pencil on the desk and sat back in his chair. He looked out at the
audience and stared dully toward the back of the studio.

Again I thought about what was going wrong. Why weren't
we getting our point across? It was if everything we said was getting lost in some kind of liquid medium. Our words started out
making sense, but they came through garbled. No one even heard
us. The only words getting across were charged words like "indecent," filth," "God"; the words OOFF was using. It didn't matter
whether they made sense or not.

What was going on? Listening to Reverend Bob, I remembered
a feeling I used to have when I was very small. I remember looking
around me, in school or in church, and feeling that everything was
deeply and absolutely true, whether I understood it or not. All questions had answers. Later, I realized it wasn't true. But these people
were still like that; they were sure they had the answers. Our encounter with OOFF was not about fairness or logic; it was about who
believed more.

I decided to stop trying to convince anyone of anything, and
just say what I believed. If Hunter, Rudy and I were destined to self-
destruct on national television, we might as well do it our own way.

The producer waved his arms in front of us. When the countdown concluded, Mimi sprang to life.

"Welcome back, and we're talking with Hunter Burns, Rudy
Rude and OOFF about how far is too far on television. I want to
talk to the band for a moment," he said, walking in front of us.

"Hunter, does it bother you that OOFF finds your videos rep-
rehensible?"

"No, like I said, they're free to think whatever they want."

"Do you do what you do just for shock value?"

"Some of it's for shock value. That's my job."

"Isn't that wrong, though? I mean, you have millions of kids
looking up to you."

"Hey, I'm not running for office. I'm an entertainer. I don't ask
anyone to look up to me."

"You don't care what kind of example you set for children?"

"My audience is teenagers, first of all, not children, and second of all, my purpose is to get them excited, and though it is in
bad taste sometimes, I don't take it as seriously as these people do.
And I don't think the kids do, either. There are more serious problems in the world than us."

"You know it," echoed Rudy.

"Excuse me, Mr. Burns," piped up Mary Joe Wheeler," but
we're parents and it's very serious to us."

Hunter looked at her with disdain. "If you're so serious about Death Threat, then don't let your children buy our music, Miss Wheeler. It's all the same to me. Other people enjoy it," he said in a nasty voice.

"And what about you, Grace," said Mimi, as if he were noticing me for the first time. I stared at him. "You wrote 'Let Me Show You.' Does it bother you that these people are boycotting you?"

"Of course it bothers me. These people want to destroy me and they don't even know me. It's scary. Why can't they just worry about themselves and let people alone?"

"Reverend Bob, can't you let people alone?" said Mimi.

"I guess Miss Note would like that. She could just keep on producing more videos like 'Let Me Show You,'" said Reverend Bob.

"And what if I did? It's my life."

"That's our point. You don't care how what you do affects other people." It was the same accusation I would have made to Hunter only a week before.

"I care how it affects other people," I said, "but let's keep this in perspective. We're talking about a rock video here. I'm not personally responsible for what the whole planet thinks about it. You can't please everyone."

"So that excuses smut?" said Mary Joe Wheeler.

"Maybe it does excuse smut. Maybe that's part of the price we pay to live the way we do. I don't like the video all that much myself, but unlike you, I don't think it's my job to police people. They're free to make their video and you're free not to watch it."

"So you're saying decency just isn't an issue," said Reverend Bob.

"I'm not saying that. I'm saying your idea of decent and my idea of decent are not the same thing."

"So you're saying pornography is acceptable."

"I would really appreciate it if you didn't keep putting words in my mouth," I said, my teeth clenched with anger, "I'm saying I don't need you to tell me what's decent."

"Mimi," piped up Mary Joe Wheeler, "I think Miss Note is saying anything goes, and that's just what we're objecting to."

"Will you stop telling me what I'm saying?" I burst out, frustrated. "I'm saying one simple thing. I'm saying I think you're a bunch of fanatics." I would say I completely lost it just about then. But since this was television, losing control could only help my case. Our supporters in the audience went wild when I said that. For some reason, it hit a nerve in Mary Joe Wheeler. Anger was both her strength and her weakness, for her own anger burst from her like a firecracker hidden in an expensive vase.

She glared at me, and in a strained voice hissed, "It's people like you that we're boycotting. Trash."

That was all I needed to hear. I stood up, and it was as if no one else existed, just me and Mary Joe on that little bright platform, our eyes locked. "You think I'm trash? Because I don't live like you do?"

"No, because you produce filth like these rock videos," said Mary Joe standing up too.

"I didn't produce it. It happened. I don't control everything in the universe. Things I don't like happen sometimes, that's how it goes."

"Well, we want to do something about it."

"Yes, you want to blame someone else for the problems in the world so you don't have to take any personal responsibility."

"We take plenty of responsibility, Miss Note. We've made a commitment to positive values, the kind that matter to a family."

"Whose family? Whose values? Who put you in charge of the universe?"

"I'm not in charge of the universe, God is, and He has standards." She looked at me with disgust. "We don't live in some chaotic world where everyone just does whatever they please. We all have to live together. What do you give to anyone with your beliefs? Nothing."

"At least I don't impose my standards on other people. I hate Death Threat, too, but I'm not afraid of them, like you. I make my own choices about my life."

"You think you're making a choice by tolerating every perverted behavior? That's no choice at all."

"What choice do you make? You want someone else to decide what you can read and hear. You turn people into children. You don't want to face your fears."

"Oh, please," May Joe shouted, "I live in the light, I don't have anything to be afraid of."

"You believe in this creep who uses fear to control people. You're like a child."

"Young lady, you're out of line," said Bob, irritated.

"Hey, you are a creep," said Rudy.

"You're so afraid of everything that you want to impose your fears on everyone else." The words came flying out of me, faster and faster. "You can't handle freedom so you want to take it away from everyone. Then you think you'll have power. Well, I make my own choices every single day, and I let other people make theirs, so that at the end of my life I can say I lived a rich life and made choices. Not like you."

"I enjoy my life, more than you do," Mary Joe Wheeler shouted.

"You're too afraid to enjoy life."

"You are presumptuous."

"You want everyone to be the same."

"Trash!"

"Coward!"

"Life is just a game to you!" Mary Joe shrieked.

"I'm not afraid of life!" I yelled back, "and if I had to do it again, I'd let Death Threat make the same video again," I cried. The audience went crazy. People were on their feet, screaming madly, clapping and shouting, making a deafening mixture of hissing and cheering. I don't know why, but I felt the force of the crowd was with me.

Screaming like that on national television was really very liberating. I felt so free, I didn't even notice Mimi Velaci in the background who had been shouting for some time, "Ladies, ladies, calm down." Only when the audience started to yell so loud I couldn't hear anyone else, did I feel aware enough to look around me. There was chaos. Cameras spun across the floor and the producer, knowing he had a ratings-raiser on his hands, waved his hands madly, signaling Mimi to keep going. Hunter and Rudy were on their feet, working the crowd along with the prompters. They clapped their hands high over their head, shouting, "All right," and "Yeah!"

It was an exciting moment. I stood in front of my chair and continued to stare at Mary Joe, who glared right back at me. If either one of us had been a little less decent there would have been a fistfight. But Reverend Bob, who opted for martyrdom over a crusade, guided Mary Joe back to her chair. The team from OOFF tried to maintain a look of patient detachment, though it was a little less firm than it had been just a few minutes ago.

Meanwhile, Hunter and Rudy didn't look like they needed any comforting. They successfully kept the crowd in a frenzy, in spite of Mimi's pleas, and had a look on their faces as if they were single-handedly rescuing the world for freedom. OOFF may have won the battle for righteousness, but Hunter looked like he was having a lot more fun. As if to drive the point home, with perfect timing, Hunter gave me a hug followed by a larger than life kiss, bending me over backwards in his arms, in an exact calculation of what it would take to send the crowd into a mad spin. I felt his sweaty skin, and from beneath the blackness of his long dark hair,

I heard the roar of the audience. Just then the count down to commercial began. He pulled me back up. Rudy joined us with a triumphant wave at the crowd.

"Calm down, everyone," said Mimi over the frantic crowd. We could barely hear him. He continued to talk into the camera. "We're going to take a short break now, and bring on a professional therapist who's going to talk about how we learn about morality," he said.

The producer made a cut sign, and we looked at each other. In wordless complicity, we knew we had said what we had come to say. We walked off the stage.

9

OUR DRAMATIC EXIT CAUSED an uproar. No one on Mimi Velaci's staff was prepared for disappearing guests, and the family therapist they had hidden in the wings had to come out and fill the next fifteen minutes talking about Developmental Morality Loss, something he invented, while OOFF remained on stage upholding the values of family entertainment to no one in particular.

The only immediate feedback we got on our performance came from Mimi Velaci, who stopped by to call us bastards. It was only later I learned our departure had made an impression; people who watched us on television told us we came across as clear-headed and logical. People appreciated the fact we chose to speak our minds and leave, rather than engage in debates with people who couldn't tell the difference between a rockstar and a child molester. Of course, that's what our friends said.

Still, whatever we did worked because for the first time in their career, Death Threat was called "serious" by the media and there was even an article in the New York Times that referred to Hunter's commitment to first amendment rights. It went on to note, "Mr. Burn's thoughtful comments showed both integrity and wisdom—traits that his detractors would have you believe were the property of more serious artists." Hunter's identity was overhauled. Another publication praised me for my "compelling frankness" and Hunter Burns for his politics, although standing up for the right to produce songs about sex-starved math teachers and girls named Cherry is not something I would have called an ideology. Still another article referred to Death Threat as "musicians" which was as surprising as anything else. Commentators, analysts and reviewers all had something to say about our appearance, and the fuss didn't hurt Death Threat's record sales, which in turn, didn't hurt me.

In retrospect, I understand that by walking off Mimi's show we accidentally discovered the power of the gesture. None of our words had been as powerful as the single act of exiting. I guess on television it's drama, not logic, that counts.

But at the time I wasn't thinking any of this. In fact, I barely remember leaving the stage. I recall being swept offstage in a group of assistant producers and hustled back to the Green Room. It looked as if the crowd had doubled while we were away and we were greeted by a noisy throng of Death Threat supporters who shouted and applauded as we entered the room. Dazed, I wandered around while Hunter and Rudy were swept up in a hand-grabbing, forearm-slapping crowd of fellow musicians; even Frisk and Regbert had showed up for support.

Everyone around me was wound up. I was about to throw up from nerves. I noticed there were fresh bottles of juice and soda on a table and a bucket piled high with ice cubes. Suddenly I was dying of thirst. Shaking, I lifted a quart of orange soda and poured it into the glass, then watched it splash over the edges of the cup and onto the rug.

"Damn," I cried, taking note that Rudy Rude had not even bothered with a cup and was pouring diet soda down his throat straight from the bottle. Suddenly, a pair of hands clamped themselves onto my shoulders and I jumped a foot in the air.

"Babe, you were fabulous." It was Hunter Burns. His long black hair swept over my shoulder as he kissed me on the cheek. "I can't thank you enough, Grace. You really pulled it out for us."

"Thanks," I said, wondering exactly what I had pulled out. I didn't wonder for long—I was grateful for the attention. I still wasn't sure I had even made sense.

"Was I really okay?" I asked uncertainly.

"Okay? Grace, I'm not kidding, you were fabulous." Hunter swung me around to face him. "Let me give you a hug," he declared with a kind of vivacity I had never seen in him before. I would say he was bubbly, although I would never say it to his face. He hugged me.

"You were brilliant," he continued. "When she called you 'trash' and you called her 'coward'—man, it was beautiful."

"I wasn't even thinking. It just came out."

"The simplicity of it all. It was perfect."

"Maybe we got through to them," I offered, feeling a surge of Hunter's enthusiasm.

"No way. Not one word we said made any difference. But we did a good job trying. Thanks so much, Grace," Hunter added quickly, noticing that his girlfriend, the Russian model Varina, and Jerry were about to descend on us. "Listen," he whispered, "I owe you for this."

"It was my pleasure, Hunter, I mean it. I'm glad it all happened. They were jerks," I said, caught up in the emotion of the moment. Hunter was touched by my words and he hugged me again. Just then Jerry Saltstien came over to us and, with an exaggerated look of alarm, cried, "Hey, break it up, kids, you want Varina to get jealous?" He smiled, his lips stretching across his face as if someone had put a paper clip on each side of his mouth and pulled. Varina tumbled into Hunter, giving him a kiss. Then she looked down at me—I was the short member of the group and said, "You vas so good, Grace. Congradulation."

"Thanks," I smiled back at her.

I felt alive, charged, as if I had just received a jolt of pure life. As I stood there, still in a state of television alert, my eyes met Hunter's and I knew he felt that same jolt, the same feeling of total control that hits you the moment you realize an audience belongs to you and you alone. Their power is your power and it's a thrill.

Hunter and I both laughed. It was the only thing to do with the energy rushing through us. Varina looked at us and began to laugh too, declaring, "You crazy."

Hunter was right. Not one word we said made any difference to OOFF, to anyone in the audience, to viewers at home or to anyone else in the universe who happened to be tuning in. In fact, it was only thanks to the lurid sensationalism that OOFF despised, that anyone was watching the Mimi Velaci show to begin with. Mimi's show was followed by a TV newsmagazine about a baby-sitter-husband-wife love triangle, proving that the moral decay OOFF feared was already everywhere. We would never convince OOFF to end their boycott. We could only reassure people already on our side to stay tolerant.

Now, I sensed, it was time to pick up where I had left off. It was time to return to my life of song writing, rehearsals, waitressing and club dates. I would be pretty much where I was before, only with better connections and a semi-annual royalty check. It was time to go home, I said to myself, wondering if Mrs. Chu had remembered to feed my cat today.

I looked at the faces around me. I wanted to remember the scene and I took in the sights and sounds around me like a photographer recognizing a moment that will never come again. The sounds included Rudy Rude in the background who for some reason was screaming "I wanna live!"

I had come to the end of an experience. We had met our challenger on the big stage. It was the show that everyone would be watching, the one they talked about. I might appear with Death Threat again, or I might not, but the main act was over.

"Listen," I said to Hunter, tugging on his leather jacket to get his attention. "I'm going to get going. This has been so incredible. I don't know what to say. I just wanted to tell you that I meant what I said—I would do it all again." I smiled at Hunter, and gave his arm a squeeze. I felt Hunter was a friend.

"Are you leaving?" Hunter asked.

"Hey, you can't go yet," cried Jerry, "We're having a big party at Les Deux Tartes. I've got a limousine waiting downstairs."

"Really?" I had been incapable of thinking more than two seconds ahead the entire night, and assumed I would just go home after the show. But a party made perfect sense.

"Sure, you're coming with us," said Jerry, winking at me.

"I told my boyfriend I would meet him after the show."

"Grace, forget about him. We'll take care of him," urged Jerry.

I considered the invitation. A big bash would be fun after such an extraordinary night. "How about this," I said, "I'll meet my friend then catch up with you at the restaurant."

"No, I want you to come with us now," Jerry whined. "I've got the press there and I have it planned so you all go in together. Grace, it's going to be tremendous, I need you, I really do." I could tell he was secretly annoyed that he had inherited me as part of this potential-filled event. "Please, Grace," said Jerry.

Then Hunter spoke. "Grace, I'd really like you to come with me in the limousine." I turned to him to find his dark eyes staring into mine. A humorless expression of total concentration appeared on his face. I remembered why Hunter was in charge of this whole show. He spoke in a compelling tone, eclipsing all around him with his intensity. He emphasized words in the subtlest ways to convey his seriousness. "There's some thing I have to talk to you about," he added, "something you'll find very interesting." Hunter meant business. I wondered what was on his mind.

"Okay," I sighed. "Can I just tell Roger?"

Jerry didn't want to take any chances. "We're leaving now," he blurted out. "Walter will meet your friend and take him to the party." Unnoticed, Walter had joined our little group and he stood among us in his usual waist-length zippered jacket and slacks, looking like an average Joe posing with circus performers.

"Don't worry, Grace, I'll get Roger there in one piece," Walter said with confidence.

I looked at five faces staring at me intensely. "Okay, fine. Let's go," I said. There was another convulsion of excitement, as Jerry pulled Rudy Rude off the top of the couch where he was playing some kind of balancing game with a red haired production assistant and a gingerale bottle, and we prepared to move on to our next destination. In a raucous group of musicians, producers, and hangers-on, we left the building.

Maybe it was because I was with musicians—I noticed we made a lot of noise. People shouted to each other, howling and cheering over the least little remark. They talked over, through, and around each other. The group was overcome with the bad boy spirit of Death Threat and in a final chaotic burst, we tumbled into the street where a messy metallic square dance was going on between taxis, limousines, and cameras. Word had gotten out that Death Threat was in the neighborhood, and a million kids stared at us and shouted from every free square foot of space.

The shouting grew louder as we headed into the street. Kids screamed Hunter's name, album names, and song titles as if they were on a rock and roll game show. They shouted without restraint, on the verge of riot.

"This way, Grace," said Hunter, grabbing my hand. He pulled me toward a white limousine parked in front of the building. The door to the limousine opened and Hunter pushed me inside, then climbed in afterwards. The car door shut as if closed by some invisible attendant, and instantly the noise of sirens and shouts disappeared. I was glad to be away from the mad energy and felt as if I had just been ushered into some kind of Eastern temple.

All was silent in Hunter's limousine. Soft yellow light glowed in the smooth darkness of the all-white interior, shed by the lamps near the passenger doors. They threw their gentle glow on the soft white, fleecy walls. There was an eerie peacefulness here, except for the low hum of the car's engine.

Hunter sat back on the seat next to me, his long legs stretched out in front of him. He made a perfect rock star composition; black leather on white with long black hair curling out around him. There were red stones mounted on his black jacket and they seemed to glow with a light of their own. I noticed Hunter still wore the little gold charm he had been wearing the first time we met. It sparkled in the dim light.

"Whew, what a scene out there, huh?" Hunter said, swiveling around to look though the tinted windows at the undulating crowd. "You can go now, Preston," he shouted to the driver. The car lurched forward. The acceleration pushed us back into the soft leather.

"You want anything to drink?" Hunter pointed to three crystal decanters on a small bar.

"No thanks, I'll wait for the party. I need to just sit still for a second. I feel kind of weird."

"Are you okay?"

"I'll be fine. I'm just worked up." I took a deep breath. "It was incredible being on TV like that. Do you really think we came off okay?"

"I think we did, but it doesn't really matter. We were on TV, that's what people relate to. We didn't change anyone's mind, but at least we stuck to what we believe in. I think we did our best."

"And millions of people saw it."

"You better believe it. Maybe twenty-five, thirty million."

"Isn't that mind-boggling?" I marveled.

"You get used to it," he replied. "And I want to tell you again— you had nothing to worry about. You were terrific." Hunter turned to me, leaning on his side against the soft leather. He gave me a slight smile. It left his face quickly. I could see that in the calm of the limousine, Hunter was reverting back to his more professional, detached persona. The preoccupied air that usually surrounded him returned. I didn't mind. I had gotten to know him better and recognized his cool manner as the behavior of an efficient professional. He was a little scarier now though, only because he still wore his make-up from the show. He looked like a kabuki actor. His skin had an unnatural glow that contrasted with his black eyeliner.

I stretched my legs out in front of me. You could really move around in Hunter's limousine. Lately, it seemed I was having an inordinate amount of important encounters taking place while rolling down a highway.

"I'm glad this is over, at least for now," Hunter continued, talking to himself more than me. "I'm going to do a few more interviews, and Rudy and I will make another couple of appearances. I don't know where this is all going to lead, but for now I really have a lot of other things on my mind. Which is what I wanted to talk to you about." Hunter had a deep, liquid voice that filled the car. He could have had a career on the stage if he hadn't decided to make a profession out of debauchery.

"We'll be at the restaurant soon, so let me get to what I wanted to say."

"Okay, shoot," I replied, trying to seem as busy as Hunter.

"Well, you know we came back from Japan recently. "

"I heard you talking about it."

"We have a certain schedule worked out for the coming year. We knew when we came back from Japan, we'd take a break for a couple of months, spend some time at home, and while we were here, release *Tomorrow Never Cares*."

Here Hunter nodded at me as if acknowledging that's where I came in. Before he could continue, a telephone rang. It jarred with the reality I glimpsed out the window, of cars speeding next to us on the West Side Highway.

"Get that, Preston, would you?" Hunter yelled, "Tell them I'm out."

He turned to me without a pause and said, "That's Varina or Jerry. They don't leave me alone for a second. Anyway, where was I?" He pulled a cigarette out of a gold case next to the scotch decanter.

"You were taking a break for a couple of months."

"Yes, right," said Hunter, the cigarette sticking out of the side of his mouth, "and as it turns out, this boycott thing hit at a perfect time, if you can call any time perfect, because here we are and we can deal with it and give it our full attention. I mean it's a real drag, and these people are dickheads, but it happens, and we're getting a chance to make a statement, so I can't complain."

Then Hunter pulled a small electronic notebook from the inside pocket of his jacket. Cigarette still in his mouth, he flipped open the top of the little instrument and opened the calendar.

"Okay, here we go. August 24th," he mumbled. "September 7th. September 28th. That's right. September 28th." Hunter looked up at me. "September 28th is when we go on tour to promote the record, boycott or not. I want to know if you want to come with us."

"And do what?"

"Play, babe, play. The opening act." He smiled at me, enjoying my shock.

"You're serious?"

"I don't joke about things like this. You're good. You're different. But not too different. You helped us out. I thought I could do the same for you. Jerry doesn't like the idea. He wants a band with at least an album out. But fuck him. If you can't help out your friends, what's the point?"

"This is amazing. I don't know what to say."

"Think about it. Get back to me. Get back to Jerry, actually, leave me out of it. We're talking about five months, the whole United

States." Hunter looked into my eyes, which with his mascara-laden lashes, had a singularly mad effect. "Grace, remember, no matter what you think of us, it's a break."

Hunter had no illusions, that's for sure. No wonder he wasn't a suffering artist. Here was a pro who was not afraid to help someone lower on the ladder. Hunter didn't dwell on anything that happened, not even in the last hour. He didn't care that I had told him right out how I hated his music, or that I had said so in front of the whole country. He was moving forward, on to the next project.

There was no time for sentiment. "Preston," he shouted. "Would you get Varina on the phone? She's in Jerry's car." Preston rolled down the tinted glass window that separated the front of the car from the back, and I knew our business meeting was over. Hunter called Varina, winking at me now and then as he talked to his girlfriend.

I sat back in the soft seat, taking in Hunter's extraordinary offer. It was the opportunity of a lifetime—once again. Hunter was making a habit of disrupting my life. This time, though, I knew what I was in for. Only two weeks ago, I wanted to kill him and his band. Only one week ago, I hoped I would never see them again in my life. Now here he was offering me five months on the road with Death Threat. Five months of giant venues, good money, and music every night.

Outside the car window, the Hudson River flowed, a wide swath of gray almost level with the highway. We continued up the West Side, away from the Eleventh Avenue Studio where we had spent the afternoon, and toward Les Deux Tartes. High on my right, I could see Riverside Drive, its stony wave of apartment buildings curving above us. Bright windows glowed in the night, like the windows in Roger's paintings. We pulled off the highway at 79th Street.

The summer evening was perfectly still. A man walked his dog on the grass by the sidewalk. Besides him, nothing moved except for leafy branches nudged by a breeze. The brightness and noise of the studio were distant now. There was only the dark of the Manhattan night broken by rose-colored streetlights. New Jersey glimmered across the river. Both inside the car and out, the world seemed peaceful. In spite of tonight's conflict, nothing seemed particularly right or wrong at the moment. It was clear there were a lot of different ways to live, an infinite amount of things to believe. People did things I would never dream of doing. Perfectly good people made strange choices, I thought, as I watched Hunter on the phone with Varina, his lips still bright red with lipstick. But that didn't mean you couldn't go on tour with them.

ʕ ʕ ʕ

What I thought was going to be a small party to celebrate our encounter with OOFF turned out to be a big event. Just as Jerry had promised, he had alerted the press. We pulled up in front of the red and blue awning of Les Deux Tartes where a feverish pack of photographers waited for us, their cameras flashing.

Varina, Rudy Rude and Jerry had already arrived and they stood in front of the restaurant, looking respectively willowy, depraved and obnoxious. We stepped out of the car and Jerry made a big show of greeting us. He grabbed people and whispered urgently to one person and then another as cameras flashed. Jerry aimed Hunter, Rudy and me at the various photographers and journalists but Hunter wanted to get inside. "Not now, Jerry," he snapped, and strode into the restaurant, waving over his shoulder. We followed him in, and a cheer went up as we entered the restaurant.

I realized the party at Les Deux Tartes could not have been as spontaneous as I was led to believe. This was no casual, post-event get-together. There were at least one hundred and fifty people crowded into the restaurant kissing, chatting, waving, and looking their best. The restaurant was closed to the public. After talking to a few of the guests, I realized this was actually several parties in one. Some guests, like me, thought they were at a post-Mimi Velaci party. Others believed it to be a thank-you party for the crew at the end of Death Threat's Japan tour, which accounted for why there were so many guys with gray ponytails, beer guts and tee shirts. Still others thought it was a birthday party for Rudy Rude. For most people, any excuse would do, and they were happy to see an open bar.

I walked through the throng of people, recognizing almost no one. It was so crowded I could hardly walk. People held onto plates as they squeezed through the crowd. The plates sailed past my face at eye level and I watched as endives filled with blue cheese fell onto the floor, and champagne spilled over the edges of goblets. The smell of food and sweat made me simultaneously hungry and queasy. I headed toward the back of the restaurant hoping to find food and a glass of water.

People who looked like they had invested years in picking out just the right nose ring pressed against me. There were models and good-looking press agents, enthusiastic assistants and worn out musicians. All kinds of people stood in my way as I tried to get somewhere, anywhere. I was uncomfortable and exhausted.

Still, it was exciting and many people recognized me from the Mimi Velaci Show and had a comment to make in passing, such as, "You were great," or more often, "Is Mimi as short as he looks?" I had to talk to what felt like a hundred people. Naturally everyone in the room was in Death Threat's camp and therefore likely to view tonight's performance as a triumph. I couldn't take a step without saying thanks to some well-wisher.

Through the crowd, I saw Roger. He was about twenty feet away, leaning against dark wood paneling. Alone and apparently lost in thought, he stood lodged between a gilt-framed painting and a doorway with a sign above it that said "Telephones." Walter had delivered him here, as promised.

I called to him and waved. He didn't hear me. Roger held a drink and he took a sip as he stared into the distance at nothing in particular. I squeezed between sticky bodies and overheated blazers until I was able to reach out and grab the cuff of his dark green jacket and avoid being swept away in a whirlpool of models.

"Here you are. I've been looking for you," I said.

"Hi, Grace." He looked at me for a second and then continued to stare off toward the front of the restaurant.

"Did you get here all right?"

"Sure."

"How long have you been here?"

"About half an hour. Why do they let so many people in here?" He continued to explore the room, his eyes taking in everything but me.

"I don't know. Everyone wants to be here so everyone showed up."

"I can't say I want to be here."

"Why not? What's wrong with you?" I had to shout in order for Roger to hear me.

He looked at me, his brown eyes wide. "I'm sick of tagging around after you. That's what's wrong." A weary crease lined the sides of his mouth.

"What are you talking about, I thought you like these parties?" Roger usually loved my events, and there had never been one more lively than this. Here we were in the middle of prime people watching territory, and not just as spectators; I was a guest of honor. Yet Roger just slumped against the wall, looking resolutely unhappy.

"What is wrong with you, Roger?"

He didn't answer.

"Roger, talk to me."

"Grace, it's impossible to talk here," he said, turning to me.

"Then let's go somewhere where we can talk," I said, grabbing his arm. "There are some private rooms upstairs." I had once done a party here, a trio, and I remembered the upstairs dining rooms. "Up here," I said, pushing through a doorway and we walked up the carpeted stairs. Roger followed me in silence.

At the top of the steps there was a closed door. Through a round window in the polished wood I could see it led to an empty dining room. "In here." Roger followed me into the dark room.

A row of track lights beamed dimly upwards against the ceiling. Red fleeced wallpaper covered the walls, and a mirror ran the length of the room. Beneath it were shiny leather banquettes, and tables set with gleaming plates for tomorrow's lunch.

Roger walked through the room, circling the edges of the tables. I sat down at one of the tables and watched him.

"So, did you make it to the show?"

"Yes. It was incredible," said Roger.

"Where were you sitting?"

"Near the back, on the right. Next to some heavy-duty OOFF folks. You sure got them mad."

"What were they doing?" Roger stopped in front of a drawing on the wall, an old cartoon with a French caption. He looked at it, his back to me.

"A lot of yelling. They were on their feet after you guys walked out, screaming like lunatics. It was a scene."

"You'll have to tell me what happened." I paused. "But first, what's bothering you? Are you mad because you had to come here with Walter?"

"No. I didn't mind that."

"So?"

"So." Roger paused. "So you're leaving town for five months, and you didn't bother to tell me."

"What?"

"You heard me. You're going away. Bye-bye." He turned around and faced me across the room, a sea of red carpet between us.

"Excuse me, but how do you know I'm going anywhere?"

"Apparently everyone knows but me. Walter told me."

"And exactly what did Walter tell you?"

"That you're going on tour with Death Threat for five months."

"Well, everyone may know, but I only found out about it two seconds ago on the way over here in Hunter's car. I didn't know I was going anywhere. And I didn't even say I would go."

"Fuck you, Grace, you're always playing with definitions. *I* know you're going and *you* know you're going, so don't play games with me."

"Fine, don't believe me, Roger." I felt the remaining pool of energy within me darken. "Until Hunter told me just now in the limousine, I had no idea he was going to make us this offer."

"So Walter knows you're going on tour before you do," he said, sarcasm in his voice.

"Of course. Hunter tells Walter everything."

"I find it hard to believe."

"I did, too, at first."

"It just seems like I'm always the last to know what's going on, Grace."

"What is your problem?" I exploded. "I don't care if you believe me or not. I only just found out about this tour and I can't defend myself for something I didn't even know about."

"Okay, fine," said Roger lowering his voice. He sat down on the red leather seat opposite me. He looked down at his hands. Roger seemed so drained tonight. He still appeared troubled by something. What I had said so far hadn't provided much relief.

"Is something else wrong?"

He didn't say anything for a moment. Then he spoke.

"Yes, there is something else."

"What?"

It seemed hard for Roger to find words tonight. It was as if everything he said had to be constructed thought by thought.

"Massimo came over to look at my paintings the other day.

"And...?"

"He liked them."

"That's good."

"It is. He said I should think about stripping them down even more, maybe just work with light." Roger picked up one of the napkins and started playing with it. "Anyway, we were hanging around, we had a few beers, and got onto other subjects."

"Like what other subjects?"

"Different things. He told me he's going to Paris for a month in October. He's trying to talk Natalie into going. Then he asked me how things were between you and me, and I said fine. So he said something like, 'That's interesting,' and I said, 'Why is that interesting?' And he said, because he had the impression you were seeing someone else."

"What? "

"That's what he said. He thought you were seeing someone else."

"What does Massimo know about my life?"

"I don't know, you tell me," said Roger. "What does he know about your life?"

"Nothing."

"Then why would he say that?"

"I don't know why he would say that. To be provocative."

"Grace, are you saying he just makes stuff like that up?"

"I'm saying he doesn't know anything about me."

"Oh, come on, he lives with your best friend."

"So?"

"So why would he make that up?"

"He doesn't like me, he wants to make trouble for me," I said, my voice growing louder. "I don't know why Massimo says the things he says."

"So you're saying it's not true?" Roger glared at me. His face was getting redder.

"What, that I'm seeing someone else?"

"Yes."

Here I was, the famous fork in the road; to lie or tell the truth. I could even watch myself choose in full three-quarters view, thanks to the mirrors that lined the room. I caught my reflection, eyes blazing and neck stretched forward, my hair falling behind me as if I had been electrified, challenging Roger to accuse. A lightning fast debate took place in my brain. Was I seeing someone else? Not anymore, not after the other night. And was I ever actually seeing him anyway? Paul and I had done a lot of talking, but not much seeing. Okay, it was taking things very literally. But whatever we were doing, we weren't doing it anymore.

I looked at Roger. He absorbed me with all his senses as he waited for an answer. This mattered to him.

"Roger, it's not right for Massimo to get involved in other people's business and set you against me. But because it came up, I'll answer." I looked in his eyes across the table. "No, I'm not seeing anyone else. There was another man I got to know, someone I was friendly with. Someone you don't know. But nothing happened."

I could see Roger considering this. "What are you saying?"

"I'm saying that's probably who Massimo was talking about."

"I understand that part, but I don't know what that means. What does 'kind of friendly' mean? You're friendly with lots of people. What made this different? Was it a relationship?"

"I don't know, I don't have labels for everything. It was just a friendship. I didn't know myself what to call it.

"So you were seeing someone else."

"No, it just wasn't worth mentioning. Massimo is the one who thinks it's a big deal."

"It was a big enough deal for Natalie to tell Massimo. Do you still see this guy?"

"No." At least that was the truth. "And I wouldn't call it 'seeing,' Roger. I told you, it wasn't dating, it was just a friendship."

"I don't know why, but somehow I don't believe that's the whole story."

"Well, I don't want to talk about it anymore. Not right now. Haven't I already answered enough questions today?" My voice rang through the quiet dining room. "I am really fed up. Is it important that you bring this up now?"

"You asked me what was bothering me, Grace, and I told you."

"Well, I've had enough. I don't want to talk about it anymore."

"And I don't want your friends telling me you're seeing other people. I waited till the show was over to bring this up, but I'm not waiting anymore. I'm upset."

"I'm sorry. I would be, too. But I don't want to deal with this now." I closed my eyes. "And Massimo isn't my friend." The quiet in the room rolled over me, soft and dim like a fog. Nearby, from the upstairs kitchen, I could hear a radio playing.

Roger sighed. "Okay, Grace, we don't have to talk about it now." He slid around the horseshoe seat of the banquette to my side. "You're right, this has been a long day." He picked up my hand and gave it a squeeze. I felt the familiar shape of his fingers, the warmth of his grip.

Roger put his arm around me and pulled me towards him. I let my head rest on his shoulder. "Grace, I'm tired," he said. "I'm going home."

"Should I come over after I leave here?"

"No."

"Are you sure?" I felt my throat tighten.

"Yes, I need time to think about this. It's funny. You're not as nice as I thought you were." Roger kissed my hair.

"What?"

"I have to decide what to do about it. You go back to the party. We'll talk about it some other time."

"Whatever."

"I'll see you," said Roger. He kissed me and then left.

ᛉ ᛉ ᛉ

The restaurant was as jammed as ever. I shuffled down the steps back into the main room. I faced a room full of strangers, at least as far as could see. I let myself mindlessly follow a path through the crowd, falling in behind a man with long blond hair, as if I were joining a stream of ants. The party was louder, hotter, more crowded now, and Les Deux Tartes had turned into a Manhattan piñata full of a million curiosities. The sounds of a party in full swing exploded around me and I listened to cries of surprise and high pitched laughter, as I wondered what had just happened. This encounter with Roger had consumed the last of my reason. Feeling a wave of sadness move through me, I closed my eyes for a moment, hearing Roger's words again.

All my energy must have been spent on the Mimi Velaci show, because as I stood among the crowd, I didn't know what to do or think anymore. Like my body, my mind moved aimlessly and I felt myself traveling away from the warm lights of Les Deux Tartes to a place inside myself where everything seemed to be unthreading.

So Massimo turned me in. That low life. I knew it was a bad idea, him and Roger getting together. Roger and his new pal. What did Roger mean, I'm not as nice as he thought I was? And where was everyone? I didn't recognize one face among the hundreds around me. Perhaps I could regain a foothold by once again lecturing Walter Wiener on why he should stay out of my personal life. Looking for Walter gave me something to do, and I wasn't sure whether I wanted to find Walter in order to yell at him, or to have a friend.

I didn't see Walter anywhere, but at least I found an alcove off the main part of the restaurant where I could sit down and think for a moment. It was a small, low-ceiling room where people could have their after-dinner drinks in privacy. There were red velvet couches and oversized arm chairs strewn with pillows that portrayed duck hunting scenes. Here the music was not so loud and the crowd not so dense. I sank into the pillows and put my head back. How was it possible that this day had still not come to an end?

People mingled in front of me forming a human wall of legs and chardonnay glasses. I watched it undulate as I rested on the couch, grateful for the opportunity to sit down. I must have been sitting for ten minutes when I found myself staring at a familiar, short pair of legs. I should have known the second I stopped looking for Walter, he would turn up.

"Hey, babe," he said, sinking down on the couch next to me. "Want some company?"

"Definitely, Walter. Where have you been?"

"Circulating. And you? How are you?" He gave my arm a friendly squeeze.

"God, so much has happened, I don't even know," I said.

"How's things?" Walter looked concerned and rubbed my knee.

"Things are all right," I replied, unable to lift my head up from the huge couch.

"What's up?" he said, stroking my back.

"Walter, stop asking me the same thing." I sat up and looked at him. "I can't even think straight anymore. This has been a truly incredible day."

"I know. For me, too, today has been like something I could never have imagined. And I want to tell you something. Today, in front of everyone you've ever known, you were fabulous. I am really proud of you."

"Thanks, Walter. It was pretty scary."

"And how. I could not have done what you did today. I'm impressed. You kicked the, pardon my French, shit out of those people."

"Do you really think so?"

"Hey. I saw it with my own eyes. You had passion. You believed in what you were saying. You made your point."

"I'll get a tape of it later. Jerry said he would get me one. I think Roger taped it, too. By the way, speaking of Roger, why did you tell him I was going on tour?" I glared at Walter. "How could you do that? It's none of your business."

"Excuse me for living, I thought it was good news," he squeaked.

"Don't you think I should be the one to tell my own boyfriend?"

"I was excited."

"Well, I just want you to know he was really upset." I didn't want to tell Walter the whole story.

"Grace, I didn't think. I assumed Roger would want to know."

"And how do you even know we're going to do the tour? Maybe the guys won't want to go."

"They're going, Grace, don't worry about it," Walter replied, rolling his eyes as if the idea were too absurd to consider.

"I swear, Walter, I don't know about you sometimes," I declared, falling back on the couch.

"I'm sorry I got carried away. Forgive me," he said. I didn't answer. I wanted him to think I was still fuming. Nothing seemed to discourage Walter. He just stared at me and smiled wistfully.

"What are you looking at?"

"Grace. I'm looking at you right now and I'm seeing something that reminds me of what I see when I look at a display case full of chocolates that sell for twenty-five dollars a pound, the kind made in Belgium with hazelnuts or almonds. I'm seeing something that's really special. You were special tonight. And I think you know that, personally, I find you very intriguing."

"It's hard to believe right now, Walter," I said, arranging some duck-hunting pillows behind my head. "I'm angry at you."

"Grace. Do I ever say anything I don't mean?"

"How would I know?"

"Listen, you may be surprised, but we all see the world a different way, and maybe I see a part of you that other people don't see. What can I tell you? By the way, did I ever tell you the story about the candy corn?"

"No, how does it go?" Walter's stories were perfect for moments like this when I didn't want to think or talk. He needed little encouragement.

"Pittsburgh. Imagine a warehouse the size of the entire town of Roslyn," Walter said. "It's two months before Halloween maybe fifteen years ago, when kids still went crazy with the costumes and everything on Halloween. So a distributor gives me a big order for candy for his stores, and he orders 500 gross of candy corn along with all the other usual trick or treat type candy. So I make the delivery, everything's fine until I get a call from the distributor who says, 'How much candy corn did you send me, I got enough fucking candy corn,' you'll excuse my language, 'for the next century.' So I look into it, and I find out we delivered 5,000 gross instead of 500, which if you multiply it, is a couple of hundred thousand bags of candy corn.

"And what's the point?"

"The point is I made this mistake. I said, 'Lou, I've got to be honest. I made a mistake. I'll pay for the truck, don't say anything, leave the candy corn on the skids, and it will be gone tomorrow.' And that's what I did. Gone. A forty-foot truck of candy corn. But why I'm telling you this story is so you'll understand me. Because the reason I did this—I, who am normally very efficient—is because I wasn't thinking clearly. I was involved with a woman and things weren't going all that well and I wasn't concentrating."

"And what's the point?"

"The point is—" here Walter sighed and put his hand back on my arm. "I'm getting distracted now. It's not good. But before I give up on you completely, I wanted to check back in, and see how you feel." He absentmindedly stroked my arm. "Maybe you've had time to think about things."

I felt fond of Walter at that moment. It was just like he said a thousand times—he was very sincere. Walter felt what he felt, and it hadn't changed. Walter had been a friend to me, he had never let me down. Now he was letting me know his feelings hadn't changed either. I don't think I had ever met someone as steadfast. On the other hand, you could also say Walter was out of touch with reality.

"Thank you for sharing that with me, Walter. I'm glad you checked back in. But nothing has really changed"—except that Roger thinks I'm a jerk and Paul stood me up, I thought.

He shook his head, as if he felt sorry for me. Then he smiled and looked me in the eyes. "One of these days, maybe you'll let yourself go."

"Don't count on it."

"I won't plan my life around it, don't worry. But believe me, you would enjoy yourself. And Grace, let me tell you one last thing. Don't take this the wrong way, and I won't say another word after this. But I have to tell you. You're a run-away freight train."

"Thank you."

"I look into your eyes and I see fires."

"That must be the engine room."

"You joke. But I see it inside you. You're out of control, and you would go flying off the rails if you let yourself go." Walter's voice had a kind of deep gurgly sound. He was getting too excited. I didn't like that side of him as much as his sincere side. I sat up.

"Walter, thank you for sharing this with me. Enough now."

"I understand. Would you like a soft drink?"

"I think I'll get up and walk around. I'll get it myself." We stood up.

♩ ♩ ♩

I wanted to have a drink before I left. Roger was gone, he was mad, and there was no bringing him back. Before I sulked home, I wanted to be at the party for a few minutes in spirit and not just in body. This was my night, after all. I had made it though the show, and not too badly, either, from what people told me. I inched through the thick crowd to the bar where I waited while the bartender, a good-looking guy with his hair in braids, poured me a drink. Amid the merry noise at the bar, I heard someone call my name.

"Hey, Grace Note," said a distinctive voice, cutting through the air. I recognized it right away.

"Hey, Hunter," I shouted back, between two girls in sequins. I waved. We had all turned around when we heard Hunter's voice. He stood about ten feet away from the bar in the middle of a small group of people.

"Grace. Come, come, come," he said waving me towards him like an old sage.

"Just a minute. I'm just getting a drink," I shouted back, pointing at the bar.

I grabbed the vodka tonic the bartender held out for me and squeezed towards Hunter. He was taller than the people around him at that moment and I kept his wild black hair in sight, like it was a reverse lighthouse, a dark beam in the middle of all the sparkle and light.

Hunter was enjoying being the patron of the party, and the words "Hey, babe," seemed to radiate from him in every direction. He was definitely a little drunk, and I think he was getting sentimental. It's easy to feel sentimental when you have one hundred and fifty guests at a party, and one quarter of them wish they were you, with another quarter on your payroll. As I moved towards him, he stretched out his arm and as soon as he could, he grabbed me as if he were roping me in, and pulled me into a circle of people all chatting vigorously.

As I reached his side, Hunter put his arm around me, and squashed me under the arm of his leather jacket, making me feel like a just-hatched bird. "Grace," he said looking down at me from what felt like fifty feet above, "Grace, I'm glad you're here."

"I'm glad I'm here, too."

"Are you doing okay?"

"I really am. I feel much better than I did before."

"When?"

"In the car."

"Oh, right," mumbled Hunter. "But the important thing is you're coming with us on tour," he said.

"I hope so."

"Yes, of course you are." Just then someone caught Hunter's attention because he excitedly squashed me harder with his right arm. "As a matter fact," Hunter said, "Here's someone I want you to meet. He's a very important part of the show, you must get to know him."

He waved over Varina's shoulder to someone in a leather jacket who was pressing his way through the crowd in order to join us. It was getting increasingly difficult to move and the person reached our group in pieces; first a hand with a drink appeared, then his shoulders wedged between Varina and someone's back until finally he squeezed in front of me just as Hunter was saying, "Grace, this is Paul. Paul, say hello to Grace, she's going on tour with us."

I looked up from under Hunter Burns' wing to find myself staring at Paul Teagarden.

"Oh, no," I said.

"Grace," he said, nodding at me serenely.

"What are you doing here?" I felt dizzy. This was too much.

"You know each other?" asked Hunter, in wonder. No one else was paying much attention to our conversation.

"Yes, we've met," I said.

"Fabulous, isn't this fabulous? You talk, I have to move," said Hunter. He turned around to greet a cluster of people from his record company.

♪ ♪ ♪

Paul's tranquil state weathered surprises well. He didn't look the least bit ruffled by this coincidence. He just smiled. He seemed glad to see me. I couldn't say the same.

"I can't believe you're here. This is so weird," I said.

"You don't seem too happy to see me. I said I would come back to New York."

"Why should I be happy to see you?"

"You're still mad about what happened."

"I haven't had time to even deal with it. Maybe you've noticed, but a lot has been going on around here."

"Sorry, Grace, I know it's been crazy. I saw you on the show. You were great."

"Thank you."

"I was impressed. You seemed natural and credible," he said as if he were reviewing a theater piece.

I listened to his words but I kept getting distracted by his very presence. It all seemed so bizarre. "Paul, what the hell are you doing here?" I finally sputtered. "And what did Hunter mean when he said you're an important part of the show?"

"Can you handle one more surprise?"

"What?"

"I'm going on tour with Hunter. And with you."

"What?"

"We're doing a concert film of the band and we're shooting this tour."

"No, it can't be."

"Hunter contacted me. He remembered me from a few years ago and still wanted me to shoot it. Hunter told me you were the opening act—I mean Swan Venom. He's quite excited about it, by the way. I was going to tell you the news when I was in New York. When that didn't work out, and I couldn't reach you at home, I thought I would just surprise you."

"You surprised me, all right." I'll admit, I was annoyed. Once again, his excuses made perfect sense. It's true, I hadn't been home the last few days. And I didn't return his calls. Still, how could he just show up this way? He could have at least told me sooner he was talking to Hunter about shooting Death Threat's tour. I, Grace Note, had just about reached my limit of interesting surprises. Unfortunately, there was one more interesting surprise planned for me; this one in the form of a very attractive woman with straight, dark hair pulled elegantly back in a high ponytail, dressed in a dark blue suit with a white tee shirt. This surprise walked up to Paul, put her arm around his shoulder, and then relaxing against him casually, looked at me and said, "Hi."

"Grace," said Paul, "this is my girlfriend, Roberta."

IO

"IF I WERE YOU, I WOULD TELL HUNTER that you would rather Paul didn't go on the tour with you."

"Yeah, right, Natalie. Hunter takes my advice on everything. And while I'm at it, I'll tell him Death Threat should open for Swan Venom instead of the other way around."

"You could try. Dino says 'The universe respects bold acts.'"

"That's in Dino's universe. In this universe, I'm lucky to have a job. Forget bold acts, Natalie."

"By the way, what does his girlfriend do?"

"Besides look perfect? She's some kind of film executive."

"So I guess that means she has her own car."

"Yes, Natalie. She's not a waitress. Hard to believe?"

"Nice."

"I don't really care if he has a girlfriend, it's just that he didn't *tell* me he had a girlfriend. He kept everything secret and private, and all the time he was pushing me to tell him more, more, more."

"More, more, more," Natalie repeated, like some kind of beat poet. "That really is too much." She sat back on her plush, white canvas couch with one leg bent over the other. Natalie wore an off-white sweatshirt and natural cotton pants. She looked like an ad for a hotel.

I sat on her rug with my arms folded on top of the glass coffee table. "He might have mentioned he had a girlfriend," I muttered.

"You mean in all the hours you talked to him, you never even asked?"

"No. I don't know why I didn't ask. I must have sensed something."

"So it's not that you didn't listen to him. You didn't listen to *you*."

"Whatever," I snapped. "Anyway, it's not about having a girlfriend. It's about being honest. He could have mentioned he was involved, somewhere during one of our endless phone conversations. I feel like a complete jerk."

"Maybe he was taping your conversations. Maybe he's going to use them for a screenplay."

"You have too much imagination."

"Then face facts," Natalie exclaimed, leaning towards me, "he was just enjoying himself. So were you. But the guy has a life. He lives three thousand miles away. What do you expect? So he's involved with someone. So are you."

"Not anymore."

"Oh, come on."

"Come on nothing. Roger won't even talk to me, thanks to Massimo."

"We've been through this, take it up with Massimo if you don't like him spreading the truth."

"Let him spread his own truth. Who asked him to spread mine?"

"Don't start again. I'm not getting dragged into this."

"You're in it already. I told you not to tell him anything I told you."

"Grace, Massimo is part of my life, and he knows what's going on even if I don't tell him directly. He hears us on the phone all the time."

"So he had to go tell Roger?"

"Massimo does things like that. He likes intrigue. What can I tell you?"

Natalie and I had already had this out on the phone earlier today. I didn't want to push it at the moment. I needed whatever friends I still had left. "Roger said he needs to think for a few days."

"He's hurt. He'll come around."

"Maybe."

"When you do talk to him, are you going to tell him about Paul?"

"Tell him what? That I had a telephone affair? That I was stood up when the guy finally came to New York? I don't know what I'm going to tell him. I'm glad I'm going on tour. I've got to get out of here," I said hopping to my feet. I paced across Natalie's loft. "At least with Paul, I tried to be honest, right from the start."

"Oh, that makes you superior. You were honest about lying."

I looked at Natalie exasperated. "I'm just saying Paul has a whole life he didn't tell me anything about."

"Well, you have a life too," said Natalie, finally deciding to see things my way.

294 I, GRACE NOTE

"That's right. I have a life too. I'm going on tour for five months. I'm getting paid $800 a week. I'm subletting my apartment."

"You have a great life."

"That's right," I cried, although it hardly felt true at the moment. Still, it felt good to get angry. "I'm really mad." I paced across her living room propelled by a stimulating mixture of adrenaline and fury. "That jerk. First he comes to New York and doesn't make time to see me. Then he comes to New York and doesn't tell me. He doesn't even bother to tell me he's coming on tour with Death Threat. You know what he said, Natalie? When Roberta went to the ladies room?"

"What?"

"He said..."—here I spoke in a whining voice, imitating his, although I admit he didn't sound quite so sniveling—"'I know this is awkward, but I didn't expect this to happen, Roberta being here. I want you to know I meant all the things I said to you on the phone.' Can you believe it?"

"That's easy to say."

"In that voice of his. Low and sexy, like it's going to make everything okay. Then he says, 'Hunter's people contacted me about shooting the tour about a month ago. I was going to tell you about it when I was in New York. When that didn't work out, I decided to just turn up and surprise you.' So I say, 'You wanted to surprise me? With your girlfriend?' So he says, 'No, she wasn't supposed to be here. She decided to go at the last minute and see friends in New York.'"

"Do you believe him?"

"I suppose so. So, I said to him, 'If you cared about me so much, why didn't you at least tell me you were involved with someone?' And he goes, 'It didn't seem relevant. This was about you and me and she doesn't have anything to do with it.' So I said, 'Oh, really? It's relevant to me. It's relevant because I thought we were being honest with each other and I don't appreciate the fact that you didn't let me into your life while you were busy encouraging me to tell you everything.'"

"And?"

"And he says, 'You know everything you need to know about me.'"

"Like he's some great mystery."

"The usual cryptic bullshit. So I say, 'I don't know anything about you, do I?' Natalie, I was practically screaming. Picture it, we're in the middle of the Les Deux Tartes and Hunter Burns is about ten feet away, and God knows who else is listening. He didn't say a word. So then I asked him if he lived with his girlfriend and he goes, 'Yes.' So I say, 'You're really unbelievable. I can't believe I have to spend the next five months with you.'"

"So what did he say?"

"He looks at me and says, 'Sorry, Grace, I didn't mean to hurt you.'"

"And this guy is supposed to be creative?"

"Really. When it's easy to talk, 3,000 miles away he has plenty to say. But when reality catches up with him, when he turns up with his perfect girlfriend at my big event, he thinks he can make it all just disappear with 'Sorry.'"

"'Sorry,'" pronounced Natalie with disdain. "Sorry. How many times have you heard that in your life?"

"Too many times."

Just then the door to Massimo's studio opened and he stomped out. "Sorry, ragazzi, you are going to have to stop this yelling. I am trying to work in here."

"Fuck you, Massimo."

"Oh, ciao, Grace."

"Massimo, why did you tell Roger I was seeing someone else?"

"I am showing sympathy for my friend Roger."

"Who asked you?"

"We're almost done, honey," Natalie called to him, "Grace, you better go."

"Eh, excuse me," Massimo said with a shrug. "I just asked Roger if you were seeing someone else. There is a law against that?"

"Yes, there is. You should be arrested for being obnoxious."

Massimo laughed loudly at this, an exaggerated, deep "Ho, ho, ho." Now that he had caused me trouble, he seemed in a perfectly delightful mood. "Grace, I have to stick together with my friend, Roger. You are two tough women. Roger and I have to help each other, eh?" I rolled my eyes at this. "Besides, I don't want Natalie to get any ideas from you."

Here he gave a hearty laugh again, although there didn't seem anything funny about this.

"How do you know I'm not giving Grace ideas?" said Natalie.

"Don't joke about that," said Massimo.

"Well, I want you to know Roger was very upset," I continued.

"And is that my fault?"

"Yes. Mind your own business next time."

"Grace, you're so serious," he said, pronouncing it "zo zerious."

"I'm going to work, girls. Ciao," said Massimo, and he slammed his studio door behind him.

"Natalie, I'm going home."

"I'm sorry about Massimo."

"You have to live with him."

"How about you, Grace. Are you okay?"

"About what?"

"Everything."

"I guess so. I'm a little depressed. I don't know what's going to happen on tour. Not only did everything go wrong with Paul, but now I'm going to have to see him every day for the next five months. He's going to ruin my tour, too."

"Don't think that way," said Natalie, standing up to walk me to the door.

"I can't believe the things I said to him. Oh, God, I'm going to die of embarrassment," I moaned, looking up at the ceiling.

"I have to see this guy, Grace."

"You'll see him when you visit me on tour."

"He really got to you."

"I know. Maybe I'll write a song about it."

"That's a great idea."

"That's it. I'll put the whole mess into a song."

"Great. Work that anger. Channel it into a cry from your higher self."

"I think I'll just write a song," I said, lifting the bolt and opening the door.

♪ ♪ ♪

Greene Street felt like a hundred degrees. There are no trees on Natalie's block and the sun burned into the iron loading docks and cement sidewalk, sending waves of heat upward from the ground. It felt like mid-morning on Mars. I walked downtown and turned left on Grand Street.

This was not what I had in mind when I said I wanted a career in music, I thought, as I walked despondently through the streets of Soho. If I had known this was what was in store for me, I would have called it quits with the Freshman Mandolin Club in college. But no, I wanted to be a musician. I wanted to live an existence of singular focus, practicing my craft with the concentration of a Tibetan monk practicing his gyaling each morning at dawn. I thought I would practice, create and invent, or plink and fiddle as my great-grandmother Fayette used to say, after a hard night at Bingo. That's what I wanted.

Instead, here I was with my personal life overwhelming my craft. And at that moment I wanted nothing more than to practice my craft. In case you have forgotten, my craft is song writing. I felt a powerful song inside me, demanding to be written. I even had a sense of what it would be. I wanted to write something sad and strong, with a simple melody and a powerful lyric; something with total conviction. When you have this feeling, you go with it. I hurried home.

In Chinatown, street vendors hawked their wares to summer tourists, crowding the corners and sidewalks with a hostile air. The smell of broiling souvlaki and Chinese noodles didn't make the crush at the curbs any more pleasant. I finally made it to my door. As soon as I was upstairs, I walked directly to the bedroom, picked up an acoustic guitar and sat back on the bed.

But once I was ready to go, I found it impossible to relax my mind. Thoughts flooded my brain every time I tried to direct it towards a more wordless state. That's a familiar problem for a creative person; just when you're on the borderline of creativity, the bright details of real life pull you back. For instance, just as I was about to transcend to a world of dimensionless sound, I would think about Paul Teagarden and experience the immediate frustration of knowing I would have to face him every day for five months. Then fifteen minutes would pass before I would remember music, usually when the guitar began to cut into my chest because I was leaning on it so hard. Again I would try to concentrate.

And once again, just as I lost myself in an almost meditative drone, as I strummed on a chord that seemed to represent my state at the moment—I think it was a perfect fourth—I would start thinking about the tour, about Paul and his wires and camera and his girlfriend, and bam, no music. My feelings were stronger than I wanted to admit in front of Natalie. In front of her, I was angry. Now I was just depressed.

I had been sure I would see Paul Teagarden again. I was sure he would come to New York to see me. It had just been a question of when. And I had been sure of a lot more than that. I was sure he would laugh with me in New York, dance with me, take a walk with me down West Broadway. I saw him standing in my apartment, his arms around me while I showed him the sights from my window. I saw him with me as clearly as I saw myself in the mirror. I imagined being places with Paul Teagarden—on an overgrown path in Central Park, on a small sidewalk down in a quiet part of the village, maybe on Jane Street. I wanted to show him so many places, my favorite skylines, the roofs of Soho at night, the view over the Hudson on a clear day. I wanted to be lost with him in New York. He had mattered to me. I know I had no excuse to fall in love with him, but I couldn't help it. Looking at him had been magic.

Maybe the power of the attraction was that I never actually saw him. I don't know why I developed such big plans. Even now, after all that had happened, I had that very same feeling of familiarity as when I saw him for the first time, as if I knew him much better than I possibly could. I felt as if he belonged in my life and I belonged in his. I knew that was ridiculous, but there was definitely some force at work. Now, knowing none of my plans would ever come true defied my reason and affected my concentration.

I strummed. And even if I could deal with my hurt feelings, even if I could stop and see the whole thing objectively, then I had to deal with the coincidence of it all. Why did Death Threat pick him? Why now, instead of years ago when he was supposed to shoot them? I felt like I would cry if I didn't get back to music. I tried one more time. I listened to the drone of the chord. I let it repeat without judging, and I let distractions wash through my mind, noticing them with indifference until they drifted noiselessly away. I let the music come slowly. A melody emerged as I strummed. Words followed. Right away I knew the song would be about Paul.

I heard far away ringing, then a voice so fine,
You picked up on me, when I picked up the line.

A simple chord set it all in motion. I let the chord repeat and I started again, embedding the song in my mind, and writing down the words on a sheet of notebook paper.

I heard far away ringing, and a voice so fine,
You picked up on me, when I picked up the line.
Through a thin connection, thinner than I knew,
I listened to you baby, tell me things half true.
I looked into you like you were a bed,
and I was tired, I lay down in my head.
With miles of dreams you tied me up every way,
tied me so tightly, that I had to stay.

But I'm up now, and I want to lay it flat,
Lay it flat,
Baby, baby c'mon now,
Lay it flat.

It wasn't meant to work out between us. I should have seen it. Long distance relationships never do. I won't date anyone who lives above Fourteenth Street. How could California work?

In the night I felt your electric grip,
Your coast and mine on a digital trip.
Through miles of dreams I tried to keep you in sight,
Like a diner sign in the night.
I tried to melt that snow that spread over you like lace,
and wake up touching the lines on your face.
I dreamed you were forever but you shook me hard,
and when I woke up, I only found your phone card.
Now I can't hear you, can't hear what you said,
I'm talkin' to no one, cause the line is dead.

But I'm up now, and I got to lay it flat,
Lay it flat,
Baby, baby, c'mon,
Lay it flat.

All those things I said on the phone; they were so personal.
How could I have said them? Now I felt stupid as well as depressed.
I reminded myself I had nothing to be ashamed of. Our conversations had been wonderful and full of passion. Maybe I should have talked on the phone more often with Roger.

I put all my feelings—sorrow, regret and a dash of guilt—into my song. They had to go somewhere. Even if the song was terrible, unlike Paul Teagarden, at least it was mine.

I added a bridge:

What made me believe the things you said,
when sleep is a frozen river?
What made me think I'd wake up and find you
next to me on the pillow?

I stopped to think. The song needed detail. I always have an eye on the commercial possibilities, even when I'm depressed. I thought I'd introduce some tidbit, a specific time and place to give the song a little more substance.

I pictured us together, on that walk,
Down to Madame Jackson's where we would talk.
With the window shedding light on our cups and hands,
And you'd take me back to your own land.
I talked out loud, deep in slumber,
Repeating only your phone number.

Answer me, babe, did you dream the same thing?
Dressed in colors I can't even see.
We were connected, a twisted pair,
But it was only a long distance ten-number affair.
I thought it would go on,
I thought it would start,
I thought it was real,
I thought it was in your heart.

But it's daytime now and I got to
Lay it Flat,
Baby, baby, baby
Lay it Flat,
Wake up now,
Lay It Flat,
Put it down now,
Lay it Flat,
Uh-huh,
Lay It Flat,
Hey, Hey,
Yeah, Lay it Flat.
(fade).

II

AND THAT'S HOW I WROTE IT, my best song yet. I knew the extraordinary events of recent days could only be expressed in an extraordinary song.

"Lay It Flat" has a dreamy quality, a slowness that carries the listener along in a hypnotic, middle-of-the-night current. There's a simplicity to the tune that captures perfectly a feeling of loss. Yet there is also acceptance, in the chorus, with a detour into regret at the bridge.

The chorus, "Lay It Flat," is a bedspread metaphor. It's about how things can be messy and tangled, but in the morning you get up, make the bed, smooth down the covers, and you're ready to make a fresh start.

"Lay It Flat" is a special song. It does something to people. It has a kind of "Hey Jude" effect; you don't want it to end but when it does, you feel as if something happened and you were there. Hunter loves "Lay It Flat." He says it touches him deeply. No one would believe Hunter would say anything like that, but I've gotten to know him pretty well since we've been on tour. Under his cold and arrogant exterior is a warm and arrogant guy.

Hunter thinks "Lay It Flat" is my most mature song. He says it's about what we wish and what we fear. You wouldn't think Hunter Burns saw the universe in such a complex way, but he does. He has a lot going on under his signature trench coat. For instance, that little symbol he wears, which I thought was some alchemistic sign—he told me it's a Hebrew letter called "Chai," which means "Life." So just when you think he's your typical rock and roll megalomaniac pagan, you find out he's wearing a Chai and doing other average-Joe activities like calling Varina five times a day, or making the tour bus stop at backwater rest stops so he can buy souvenir salt and pepper shakers for his sister Debbie's collection.

It goes to show people aren't always what they seem, except for Walter Wiener, who is exactly what he seems.

Paul Teagarden, on the other hand, wasn't at all what he seemed. Sure, there was chemistry between us and there still would be if I ever talked to him. I decided the best thing to do is ignore him. I plan to ignore him from Boston to Amherst, from the New Haven Coliseum to the Waterbury Bowl. I've already ignored him through most of the Midwest. It isn't easy. We see each other often and I still got a powerful feeling when our eyes meet. I try to avoid him, yet I find I'm always looking for him. It reminds me of high school. I never know when he's going to appear at breakfast or turn up in the dressing room. Sometimes I find myself watching for him at the show. I'm secretly disappointed when he's not there. Then I step into the hotel lobby or the bar, and there he is with his crew, in his tight jeans and those workshirts. He always stops and looks at me, then he says "Hi" in that short, terse way he has.

I'm courteous when he talks to me, but I keep our exchanges to a minimum. It's difficult for me not to say more. I know so much could happen between us. We have nothing but time and hotel rooms. Sometimes, late at night after everyone else has gone to sleep, after Regbert, Rudy, and Blackie, the road manager have disappeared into someone's room for a private party with fans, I think about Paul only a few rooms away, and it's as if there's a magnet in the hotel, pulling me.

Sometimes Paul is even on the same floor as I am. Maybe he's in room 421 and I'm in 425. We're that close. I know I only have to walk down the hall and knock on his door for something to happen. Maybe between here and Seattle I'll do it. But for now I'm resisting. I know anything that happens with him will lead nowhere. Worse, it will only hurt me sooner or later. What's the point? I don't think he's a nice person.

The hardest part of seeing Paul Teagarden, though, is when I know he's looking at me through the camera. It doesn't happen often because Swan Venom is strictly background material. But sometimes Paul is at a sound check and I know he's watching me watching him watching me. I look toward his lens in the dark amphitheater and perform for him. This tour can be described as a lot of flirtation going on between very long bus rides, with a show every night.

It's ironic that after months of long distance, we're together almost every day, and we don't even speak to each other. And I never even had a chance to tell Roger the whole story about Paul

Teagarden. After our encounter at Les Deux Tartes, Roger made up his mind that something serious had happened and he wouldn't talk to me anymore.

I called him to apologize. I wanted to come clean. Roger answered the phone the first time I called, and said he needed more time to think. After that, his answering machine picked up the phone. Eventually I stopped leaving messages.

It was strange not having Roger to talk to every day. Without my really noticing it, he had filled the spaces in my life, Sunday mornings and late nights after gigs. I know it doesn't sound romantic; I may not have the passion I had with Paul, but Roger was a friend. I missed his enthusiasm. It was especially strange not being able to share my excitement about the upcoming tour with him. A few days before we left, I had a goodbye dinner with all my friends and everyone was there except him. It was sad, and Zermin kept asking where Roger was.

Finally, he spoke to me. It was the night before I left for the tour. I called him one last time, thinking maybe he would pick up the phone. He did.

"Hi, it's me," I said, when he answered. "I wanted to call to say goodbye."

"I thought you might call."

"You did?"

"Yes. You're leaving tomorrow, right?"

"You remembered."

"Of course. Just because I haven't talked to you doesn't mean I haven't been thinking about you.

"That's nice."

"So where's your first stop?"

"New Jersey."

"Why there?"

"I guess they have a lot of fans there."

"Are you ready?"

"No. I'm terrified. I'm all packed, though, if that's what you mean."

There was a pause for a moment. "I was hoping you would call," Roger said.

"You could have called me. I left a lot of messages."

"I got them. I didn't want to talk to you."

"You're still mad."

"Yes. You really caught me off guard. I realized I basically have no idea what's going on in your life."

"I'm sorry."

"I don't understand you, Grace. I thought we were close. We're not close at all. You completely undermined our relationship."

"I undermined your idea of our relationship." I could tell this remark used up some of the warmth Roger had initially felt at hearing my voice.

"That's not true. Anyway, I don't want to fight. I didn't call you because I just didn't have anything to say."

"And now you do?"

"Not really. Only that I've missed you. And I hope your tour goes well."

"I've missed you too. And Roger, we are close, in a way." There was quiet for a moment. "So what do we do now?"

"I think I'm ready to at least talk to you."

"But I'm leaving."

"That's okay, I'll talk to you when you're out of town. Maybe it's better that way. We can talk on the phone."

"On the phone?"

"Sure, why not?"

♪ ♪ ♪

I faxed Roger my schedule of hotels and he called me when we were in Charlotte, North Carolina. Naturally, I had a lot of bad associations with the telephone. I did my best to overcome them. I applied a lot of what I had learned in my months of California phone calls to my conversations with Roger, which at least made our calls lively. I told him about Paul. Not in any detail, but enough to give him an idea of what had happened and what hadn't happened.

Roger listened. He accepted what I had to tell him. He said he understood, though he didn't actually forgive me. He just added this to my list of crimes against romance. He said he was still attracted to me, but he trusted me less than ever. Not at all, in fact. And while Roger won't forgive me, the fact is we missed each other. He's someone good, someone familiar, which means a lot when you're away from home for five months. So we've declared a truce while I'm away and put our problems on hold.

I even talked Roger into visiting me on tour. I told him after all the times I tagged around after him on business trips, he deserved a chance to try it himself. It took a while for him to get used to signing my name on the room tab, but he's adjusted. And he loves coming to our shows. Seeing me play in a stadium is a turn-on, he says, and he doesn't even mind being the oldest person in the audience. Roger has a great time and he's going to try and spend a few days with us around Christmas when we'll be in South Florida.

Roger says I picked a good time to leave New York. His company is under investigation by the Securities and Exchange Commission, mainly because one of Roger's friends, Victor Bemus, is making too many private offerings to other people whose last name is Bemus. Roger is weathering the storm at work by doing a lot of painting and attending jazzercise classes at his health club. Although I told him all about Paul, I kept one last secret. I didn't tell him Paul is on tour with us. That would only hurt him. Roger has no idea that the guy making a rockumentary of our tour is the one I was in love with. I admit, it makes me feel a little sleazy to hide things from Roger. But when you're on tour with Death Threat, sleazy isn't such an unusual way to feel.

ᛉ ᛉ ᛉ

In spite of all the personal complications, I haven't forgotten why I'm here. I try to concentrate on my job. The guys and I put on the best show we can every night, which is not always easy because there's a lot of activity when Swan Venom is on. Traditionally, the opening act is the time when people look for their seats, grab that last beer, eat, buy tee-shirts and check in with their friends fifty seats away. That's okay. We know people are coming to see Death Threat, not us. Even if only half an auditorium or concert hall is listening, playing music in front of such huge crowds is an incredible experience. It's the most thrilling thing I've ever done. Hunter has even let me come on stage with Death Threat twice to sing back-up during their encore. Up there with them, I feel a solid wave of human energy directed at the stage. It's magnificent. And Hunter really comes alive in front of a crowd. Performing "Disgrace Me" in front of 30,000 people, Hunter sheds twenty years before your eyes.

When we're not playing, I hang around with Ray or Geoffrey, and we practice or work on a song. Walter was right about the guys in the band—they were ready to drop everything to go on tour. When I first told Steve about the tour, he thought it was another one of my schemes until he got the contract in the mail. After his girlfriend explained it to him, he knew I had finally come through for the band. His only reservation was when he found out he couldn't take his pet gecko, Johnny, on tour with him. I told him he could always rush home on the occasional day off. And he could always call.

Geoffrey was really excited about the tour. He had never played before an audience of twenty or thirty thousand people. Not that any of us had, but it meant a whole new world of things that could go wrong for him. His relationship with his girlfriend had completely fallen apart and he was glad to have an excuse to take a break from substitute teaching, although it didn't mean he would be wearing a tie less often. He's become good friends with Regbert, Death Threat's bass player. They hang around a lot together and it shows in Geoffrey's playing. It's giving our music more of an edge. We're also sounding much tighter, mainly because we've been playing so much. So the tour has really been good for the band.

Ray is taking it all in with his usual detachment. Along with Natalie, he's still my closest friend. Whenever I feel the strain of Paul Teagarden's presence, I hang around with Ray. We lie on the bed with the television on, laughing at the local newscasters, drinking scotch from the mini-bar, and we work on songs until I got my sense of control back.

𝄞 𝄞 𝄞

Mostly on tour, I spend a lot of time waiting: waiting to get to the show, waiting for the show to start, waiting to get back to the hotel, and waiting to get on the bus again. It's often boring but I, Grace Note, am grateful for the chance to see life on the road up close. And spending ten hours at a stretch on a tour bus sometimes, you really see things up close. For instance, very few people knew that Rudy Rude likes to knit in his free time. His doctor says it's the best way to deal with the occasional hallucinations.

Things will be different when I get back to New York. My first royalty check for "Let Me Show You" will be waiting for me. I don't know how much it will be, but I'm sure it will be enough so I can put waitressing behind me, at least for a while. And when the tour is over, Hunter wants to produce Swan Venom's first album.

"Lay It Flat" is the song that did it for him. He has his record company talking to us, and they say they'll sign us if Hunter produces the album. He said he would. I'm thrilled. I accept his taste for what it is; raunchy but highly musical. He accepts the fact that I think his music is cheap and commercial. And if we ever do a video, Hunter agrees to stay away. He doesn't care if I take a critical view of him and Death Threat, as long as I promise to buy him any good salt and pepper shakers I see. It's not that he doesn't take things seriously. It's just that to Hunter, it doesn't matter all that much. He takes the long view. The other day—we were sitting in the lobby of Frenchy's Gourmet Palace in Grand Rapids—Hunter said, "Grace, in five years all the sixteen-year olds who would die for us today are not even going to remember they have our music. So don't take it all too seriously. We're not doing heart transplants." I promised him I wouldn't, which is how I got the nerve to write an autobiography that covers less than a year.

Maybe before the end of the tour, I'll even tell Hunter about Paul Teagarden. He would get a kick out of knowing what the song was really about. "Lay It Flat" might seem like a typical pop song— enigmatic words about a melancholy affair that went nowhere. But it's even better when you know who I'm singing about.

J. Schwartzman has had short stories published in Mademoiselle Magazine and the New York Press. She won the 1990 Mademoiselle Short Story Prize. Schwartzman is the author of *Graphic Design for Desktop Publishing* (DDC Publishing). She is a native New Yorker, and graduated from Yale College. Her ongoing serial novel, *I, President Grace*, is online at igracenote.com.